ZEUS IS DEAD:

A MONSTROUSLY INCONVENIENT ADVENTURE

BY

MICHAEL G. MUNZ

RED MUSE PRESS

Red Muse Press
Seattle WA 2016

Cover Design by Greg Simanson
Edited by Bethany Root

*This is a work of fiction. Names, characters, places, brands, media, and
incidents are either the product of the author's imagination or are used
fictitiously. Any resemblance to similarly named places or to persons living
or deceased is unintentional.*

Print ISBN 978-0-9977622-4-2

Library of Congress Control Number: 2014909747

I dedicate this book to my parents, who gave me my first book on mythology. Unless that was from someone else. Like Uncle Frank or something. It was a long time ago, so it's hard to remember. But my parents are pretty cool and supportive people, so let's go with them.

(No offense, Uncle Frank.)

TABLE OF CONTENTS

PART ONE:

ZEUS IS DEAD, AND THOSE WHO PROPHET

CHAPTER ONE

"The question of who killed Zeus is unimportant. Trouble neither us nor yourselves further with this. It is only for you to know that the gods of Olympus have returned."
"'Cept I'd also add that it was me. Next question?"
— Hera and Ares (live press conference, June 18, 2009)

"Though none of them ever went into details publicly, it seems clear that the Olympian gods' return was sparked by whatever happened to Zeus."
— excerpt from The Gods Are Back and How It Affects Your 401(k)

ZEUS WATCHED HIS CHILD stumble through a rain-drenched wilderness, the victim of a mudslide that had lamed an ankle and snatched a pack containing food, water, and a spectacularly nifty smartphone. The child winced with every step back to the trail, but did not stop. The king of the gods swelled with pride at his offspring's courage even as his immortal heart broke: no aid could he ever give.

Long ago, it would have been simple for him to help. He could have stopped the rain, ordered Artemis to lead the child to safety, or even dispatched a full squadron of rescue helicopters. (Okay, so helicopters weren't an option 3,000 years ago—save once, and that was a very special case—but he had used the other options a dozen times over.) Now, he could not risk even dropping a granola bar into the child's pocket as encouragement.

That Zeus could blame no one but himself for his inability to act only deepened his heartbreak. His own decree had forced the gods to withdraw from mortal affairs many centuries ago. He'd never told the others why, never shared the prophetic vision that led him to believe the Withdrawal necessary. There was no need; he was their king, and the vision contained knowledge he preferred to keep secret. They would obey his commands or suffer the consequences.

Yet standing idle while his mortal progeny suffered was one of the things Zeus hated most about the Withdrawal. There was also the greater discretion now required in siring those progeny, but that was more easily managed. The lack of mortal worship via temples and sacrificed bulls wasn't terribly wonderful either. His mouth still watered at the thought of a burger made from sacrifice-beef.

In truth, the danger that his child would fail to make it to safety was not a major concern for the king of the gods. *His* mortal children were always exceptionally capable. Perseus slew Medusa when he was younger than this one, albeit with a few gifts from Zeus to help him along. On the plus side, the forests were long cleansed of hideous, snake-haired women of Medusa's ilk, and his Withdrawal decree prohibited any Olympian from loosing any more of them upon the world. Even so, he longed to reach down and lift his child to safety.

And replace the smartphone, of course. Really, who liked losing their smartphone?

With a grumble, Zeus turned off the 200-inch plasma screen Hephaestus had built him for such viewings. As long as the danger to Zeus's own immortal life was mounting, voyeurism was an indulgence. It was ironic: the child was a *result* of indulgence (and his love of redheads), and yet that same child was his ace in the hole.

If he needed it.

If he had time to prepare.

If he was even right that a threat existed, really.

Lacking omniscience, Zeus couldn't be sure. If there was still a threat, then his attempt to prevent it with the Withdrawal had failed—which meant he'd misunderstood the original prophecy and could reach down right now, save the child, and deal with things in proper fashion. Yet if there was no threat, to lift the veil of discretion that hid the gods would surely bring doom of a different nature upon him.

Thrice-damned prophecies! They were twisty buggers. More often than not, a prophecy didn't help you escape trouble, it just stressed you out while you failed to do so. Then before you knew what happened, you'd killed your father, married your mother, or been deposed by a son you thought you'd properly eaten already.

Zeus grinned despite himself, thankful he'd been on the winning side of that last one.

For the hundredth time he considered consulting Apollo. Though Zeus would never admit it to the other gods, Apollo was far better at the prophecy thing than he. Perhaps it was no true shame. Apollo was his own divine son; would his glories not reflect upon Zeus as well? Yet consultation required trust, especially with enemies likely lurking. Zeus was unwilling to share his suspicions with anyone until he was certain about his foes.

The door chime sounded, followed by Aphrodite's tentative, "Daddy?"

"Enter, child," he called. He turned toward the door and masked his worry to appear, he hoped, stronger than he truly was of late.

The door swept aside at Zeus's will, and Aphrodite stepped in. He was unable to keep from smiling at the sight of her. In her hands she held a small, wrapped box. "A gift, Daughter?"

"Of course, Daddy."

He smirked at the lurking falsehood in her tone, eyes narrowing in amusement. "From *you*, Aphrodite?"

Her answer came only after she set the gift upon a little table. "Not . . . exactly. It was outside your door, and as it had no tag . . ."

"You sought to take the credit as your own?"

She blushed. "Oh, come now, Daddy. Is it not wonderful to see me as always? What better bow on a gift than for your favorite child to deliver it?" She flashed a dazzling smile that weakened under Zeus's scrutiny. She pitched the detached tag onto the table. "All right, so Athena left it."

Zeus's smirk turned to laughter despite his troubles. "Aphrodite, goddess of love and beauty, though it's true I love you highest of all, you must work on your honesty."

"All's fair in love, Daddy."

"Not war? That is how the saying goes, I believe."

She rolled her eyes. "Not today. Ares and I are fighting."

Zeus frowned. That she was embroiled in a millennia-long extra-marital affair with the god of war didn't mean she had to mention it so boldly to the father who'd betrothed her to another. "Ares is always fighting. And you should be faithful to your husband, Daughter."

"As you are to your wife?"

"That's different."

"Not to hear Hera tell it."

Zeus groaned. He had enough troubles without thinking of Hera. Aphrodite changed the subject.

"Besides, somebody has to pay attention to Ares. All the other gods are cranky with him for all the glory he gets from the mortals' wars."

"This again? Have you come to visit only to press your king again on an old decision?"

"At least allow the monsters back, Daddy. There are so few opportunities for mortal glory that don't involve fighting wars. Grant them a few creatures? Where's the harm in that?"

"Few opportunities? Are you not still goddess of love?"

"Yes, yes, sexual conquest, romance's triumphs and all that. But oh, it's so much *hotter* when the man has just driven his sword through some fearsome beast!"

"Such subtle imagery. And isn't that why you invented porn?"

"Daddy, that was Dionysus." She pouted. "Can't you keep that straight?"

"I only tease, Daughter."

Aphrodite flashed one of her haughtiest looks and turned with a huff toward the door. "Fine! Open your gift by yourself, then! It's probably just another stupid lightning bolt cozy anyway!"

And with that, she was gone.

One nice thing about not being able to contact your mortal children, Zeus supposed, was that they couldn't act like brats to your face.

He glanced at Athena's gift and decided to let it be until he had finished his preparations. He was nearly done making that loathsome amulet, yet there were still instructions to impart, lawyers to call, contingencies to set up. All of that was preamble before he tackled the real problem of finding out just who had stolen the god-killer.

Zeus picked up the amulet. Its central purple sapphire glinted amid its gold setting. Not for the first time, he questioned his decision to create it, this talisman that sapped his strength and wits, before taking care of the other details. Yes, it was necessary, but should he have waited? Yet what good were instructions without the amulet?

Gah! Had creating it drained him of his confidence as well? By the Styx, someone would get a lightning bolt where the sun didn't shine if crafting the amulet had actually rendered him impotent.

It occurred to him that Athena, though charged to protect him, might be duped into sending a gift that would attract his attention. Perhaps someone planned to attack from outside when he was distracted with opening it! Still holding the amulet, Zeus rushed to the window and looked out. Even searching for the telltale signs of an invisible assailant, he saw only sky.

The peculiar thing about gods—or one of many peculiar things, really—is that they're just as prone to stupidity as mortals, if not more so. Ego gets in the way of clear thought at times. In fact, only after Zeus felt the immortal-killing sting on his suddenly no-longer-immortal backside and tumbled out the window down the slopes of mighty Olympus did it occur to him that perhaps Athena hadn't sent the gift at all.

It also occurred to him that he had very little time to make an impossibly accurate throw. Three seconds later, things stopped occurring to him entirely.

Fortunately for the rest of this story, plenty of other things occurred afterward to lots of other people. Some of them involved cellular phones. Gold ones, even.

And savage man-eating kittens, but let's not get ahead of ourselves. Like Marley, Zeus was dead: to begin with.

~   ~   ~

For a reference index of the so-called "mythological" characters in this tale, please refer to the Who's Who at the back of the book. You likely won't need it, but you may find it a fun read—or an obligatory one, if you're one of those completionist types.

CHAPTER TWO

"Poseidon: New king of the gods, also god of the sea. Moody, wrathful, big on earthquakes. Creator of the horse and (later) the motorcycle."

"Hera: Queen of the gods, as well as the goddess of marriage and childbirth. Widow of Zeus, has recently married Poseidon."

"Ares: God of war, conflict, and aggression. Son of Zeus and Hera. Note: Ares should not be confused with Athena, the wise battle goddess who values tactics and defense, and doesn't spit."

—excerpts from the official Olympian press kit

"It is ironic that Apollo, with his skill at prophecy, seemed at the press conference so blissfully unaware of events to come. Foresight-hindsight is twenty-twenty, I suppose."

—personal journal of Clio, Muse of history

ZEUS'S EDICT OF WITHDRAWAL died with him, and not long after, the Olympian gods burst from hiding like the proverbial genie from the bottle. (Note that this is merely a simile; the actual existence of genies would be downright silly.) Moments later they realized it had been centuries since they last demonstrated themselves to the mortal world. They returned to Olympus to plan, each god and goddess proffering that the pantheon must reveal themselves in a truly fantastic fashion. It was a rare moment of agreement for them, which they took as a clear sign of the rightness of their decision.

It should be noted that the Olympian gods will often take anything as a sign of the rightness of their decisions. Sometimes a god takes the mere instance of losing an argument to another god as a sign of their own rightness due to the sheer "rarity" of the occurrence—akin to the birth of an albino elephant. But in this case, all (Olympians, not albino elephants) were agreeable about their being in agreement, so they could all agree to agree about the agreement being, well, agreeable.

Some may be put off by the preceding sentence. To those difficult individuals, it can be said only that Olympian language is difficult to translate at best, and do try to relax a bit.

And so the Olympians put their heads together and came up with a stunt that would both announce their return to the mortal world and demonstrate their power:

They would raise the lost city of Atlantis.

There was some debate about this, but it primarily consisted of Ares's claim that General William Tecumseh Sherman had already done such a thing during the U.S. Civil War. Others swiftly pointed out that what Sherman had actually done was *raze Atlanta*. Ares was promptly laughed at; those who had foolishly named Atlanta after a doomed sunken culture were then laughed at as well, and the plan continued unabated after that.

Natural laws being what they are, even the gods could not raise Atlantis without sinking something else to maintain the balance.

They went with Iceland.

They nearly opted to sink Atlanta instead just for the sake of symmetry, but finally decided on Iceland. This was partly due to the fact that Iceland, unlike Atlanta, was also an island, but primarily because the gods honestly didn't think anyone would miss a country located entirely above the timberline. And so one late November afternoon, the whole of Iceland was unceremoniously plunged under the sea— swallowed up in a horrible torrent of water, destruction, and sheep.

A new island simultaneously surfaced off the northwestern coast of Spain. Truth be told, it didn't surface nearly so much as hurl itself from the water like a spastic whale before crashing back down to the ocean surface in a cataclysm that instantly shattered the remaining ruins of ancient Atlantian culture. But it was above sea level, and that was the goal.

No one noticed.

Atlantis hadn't been in that spot before, of course—and that is to say, ever. This was a large part of the problem. Before it sank (due to one of the first and most wholly catastrophic experiments in flushable toilets), Atlantis lay off the coast of Crete. It's just that none of the gods were ever truly happy with the island's previous location, so they deemed it worthwhile—and altogether more divinely impressive—to move it. Yet now that Atlantis suddenly existed in a spot on which absolutely zero historical scholars had staked their careers, recognition of the island stood to invalidate numerous theories, and so none of them cared to pay it much heed.

Everyone else was busy wondering why there was now a large tract of open sea northwest of Britain and trying to determine why the price of wool had just gone up.

So the gods made other attempts to get noticed. Apollo held the sun in place in the sky for a full hour, which people mistook for another revision to Daylight Savings Time. Hades incited an entire cemetery's worth of corpses to rise, create picket signs announcing the gods' return, and march outside United Nations headquarters. All were promptly arrested for holding a sci-fi convention without a permit. Even Ares had an idea: pull to Earth some debris from Saturn's rings and create a gigantic "marquee of the gods" from the resulting meteor shower! He got only so far as yanking the rocks out of orbit before the others informed him that the debris would take a number of months to reach Earth.

It was Hermes, with his communications savvy, who finally suggested the press conference.

The conference was already in progress when local Seattle television Assistant Producer Tracy Wallace arrived in the control room. Late. For the second time in as many days. Right in front of her boss. During a major news crisis.

Without a cranberry-orange nut muffin.

The muffin wasn't really an issue, but as she was listing everything that was going wrong that day, the lack of her usual cranberry-orange nut muffin should be on there somewhere.

She shot an apologetic smile to her boss and, suppressing a yawn, limped to her usual place beside Chelsea. Her boss fired back a glare that Tracy ignored as she sat down; she did damn good work, and he knew it. Besides, they were essentially just on standby while the national feed of the conference came through. And she had enough drama in her life this week to think about already. And no one had prophetically left a cranberry-orange nut muffin at her workstation.

"Got you some coffee," Chelsea whispered as she handed it to her.

She gave a thankful grunt and shotgunned the life-giving ambrosia until she could no longer ignore its scalding temperature. Okay, so that was a poor choice.

"Thanks. I slept like a crack addict." She blamed her friend's stupid uncomfortable couch; though she'd had trouble sleeping in her own bed the nights before too, she supposed. *Okay, wake up, Tracy. There are gods on TV for crying out loud.* She rubbed her eyes behind her glasses. "What'd I miss?"

"Not too much we didn't know from the press release yesterday. The Greek gods are back, and their king Zeus is dead. Oh, and 'Posideron' or something is king now. They opened the floor for questions pretty fast."

"Poseidon?"

"Yeah, sea god."

"I know."

"Oh, and Fagles is standing by in the studio with some mythology expert in case the network doesn't preempt us for their own post."

"Like that'll happen." She slipped on her headset and focused on the press conference the entire world was watching.

Six men and six women sat at a long table, each with a nameplate and microphone in front of them. Clad in reasonably modern fashion, they looked nothing more than human—save for an intense, almost otherworldly regality and an inner radiance that seemed to light up the stage. No, she amended, that bit was from the spotlights. Well, mostly. None of the gods seemed to be under six feet tall, though it was difficult to tell while they were sitting down. At the center of the group sat a stern, white-armed woman and a stormy-eyed, bearded man holding a trident. The man she guessed to be Poseidon even before she saw his nameplate.

A trident at a table? Well, that was just trying too hard, wasn't it? Tracy realized they each carried a symbolic accessory: Apollo a lyre, Artemis a great bow, Athena a National Rifle Association jacket. It was like a photo shoot for some sort of ensemble TV show. Featuring gods.

Hera, the white-armed one beside Poseidon, was speaking.

"Hades has chosen not to attend this conference. My brother has much to attend to in the underworld—"

"And he likes being mysterious," shot Hermes, the youngest-looking god present. Tracy had only a moment to notice he had a British accent.

"—but he wishes to assure everyone that he, too, has returned, and that he shall meet all of you . . . eventually."

"Is Hades the devil?" shouted one of the reporters lucky enough to be in attendance.

Hera glared as Poseidon frowned and ordered, "Do not shout questions. My brother is the god of death, *not* the devil."

"If I may, Uncle?" Athena spoke, leaning closer to her mic to address the reporter. "In modern times, Hades endures much bad press for being god of the underworld. He is god of precious metals as well, yet mortals see only his connection to death and deem him evil."

"He's actually a decent enough chap," Hermes chimed in. "A bit inexorable. A tad strict, perhaps, but it's his job to keep the dead out of the world of the living. You don't want someone like me in charge of that. One good distraction and wham! Zombie apocalypse!"

Some of the press chuckled at this. Hera motioned to one of the many other reporters with hands up. "Speak."

"Are there—?"

Hera immediately cut off the question. "Address the gods with respect, child! 'Queen Hera' will do in this case."

The reporter—a woman Tracy knew to be in her late fifties and used to humoring such demands due to more than a decade's worth of experience in the White House Press Room—gritted her teeth and began again. "*Queen* Hera, are there other gods not in attendance?"

"Only my sister Hestia, goddess of the hearth—and as such something of a homebody. However—"

"However," Poseidon said, "there are other, lesser beings whose existence you will soon relearn: the Muses, the Erinyes, and . . ."

As Poseidon continued, Tracy leaned over to Chelsea. "Hera's queen, Poseidon's king; are they married now or something?"

"So they say."

"And he just cuts her off like that? She looked annoyed. Could you see it?"

"She looks annoyed at everything so far." Chelsea turned to her. "Still stinging over your breakup? Maybe you're projecting."

"Still? It was two days ago." Two days since Tracy walked out on Kevin. Two days she'd been crashing at the apartment of a generous friend with an uncomfortable couch. "And yeah. Now shh! Gods."

"Hey, you brought it up."

"What about the Titans?" another reporter was asking.

Poseidon pounded the butt of his trident on the floor. "Speak not of them," he ordered. "Our precursors remain safely locked away, and always shall be so."

Hera nodded. "Hear also that we are the *only* gods from your 'mythologies' who truly exist. Mortal speculation has reached our ears that others, such as Thor of the Norse stories, may also 'return'. Know this: those cannot return who never were. Thor is a god only in your mortal imagination, just like Loki, Anubis, and Elvis Presley."

"Queen Hera, what about Christ?"

Silence took the room as the Olympians exchanged glances. The assembled reporters awaited their response with bated breath. It was Hermes who finally spoke.

"He's not really what you'd call a team player. Put it this way: We don't bother Him, He doesn't bother us."

"I will allow no further questions on the subject," Poseidon warned.

"That's going to tick off a lot of people," Tracy whispered. And why did Hermes have a British accent?

"Everything ticks off a lot of people. It's a big world." Chelsea turned to her again as Poseidon began introducing each god in attendance and their major purviews. "So you heard about Patrick?"

"Getting the *Seattle Scenes* job? Yeah, I heard. Shh."

"Sorry. I was pulling for you."

She shrugged. "Other shows'll need producers."

Okay, so it probably wasn't a very convincing shrug. She'd wanted that job, damn it. Maybe what she needed was an idea for a show so good they'd have to make her the producer. Yeah, and then she needed a magical goat that vomited money.

"Yeah, but since you broke up with Kevin—"

Tracy covered her mic and cut Chelsea off with a whisper. "Would you shut it? There's frigging *gods* on TV now, and I'm trying to do my damn job!" Frustration boiled up as if she were still having the argument with Kevin; she couldn't force it back down. It wasn't that he got the Miami job while she was trying for one in Seattle; but he just expected her to go with him without even asking her!

"Okay, sorry, I didn't—"

"Forget it," Tracy told her. They weren't even married and he'd treated her like a damn accessory! *Okay, let it go . . .* She took another swig of coffee and tried to focus. "I'm sleeping like crap lately."

"Yeah, you mentioned that." Chelsea winked. "Don't worry about it. Now, shh. Gods."

At the conference, Poseidon had finished the immortal introductions.

"Understand that we have no intention of ruling over the everyday trivialities of your international affairs. You are free to govern yourselves as you see fit, to make war and peace as you see fit, and to live your lives as you see fit. We will simply require the recognition and worship that is our due. As god of the sea, those who sail the oceans would do well to respect me. Those who farm the bounty of the land should give thanks to Demeter, goddess of the harvest."

"Et cetera, et cetera," Hermes added.

"Sacrifices will be rewarded," Hera said. "Insults will be punished. You may find it difficult to adjust at first, but we will guide you. As in times of old, those who worship best and are beloved of the gods will find great rewards."

Poseidon nodded. "And for those of you who believe you have no need of gods, who point to the advances mortals have made in the last two millennia, know this: Never have we who dwell on high Olympus been gone entirely. We simply have not made ourselves known. Many of the advances you mortals claim as your own came from immortal hands."

Reporters clamored to ask further questions, but Poseidon spoke over them. "The influence of Apollo and his Muses on the creative arts is widespread. Shrewd Athena, goddess of defense, originated the idea of nuclear deterrents"—(Athena smacked an open hand on the tabletop. "And it's not 'nu-CU-lar,' damn it!")—"and prior to that, Ares, god of war and conflict, aided the development of the Manhattan Project and many of your political pundit programs."

A particularly bold reporter shouted out, "Did one of you invent the Internet?"

Poseidon scowled at the interruption as messenger-god Hermes cleared his throat. "Ah, no. That was Al Gore."

Chelsea suddenly leaned toward Tracy. "You know you're pretty enough to work in front of the camera if you want to, right? Why hide it?"

She bristled. "My looks aren't what I want people to care about."

"Oh, come on, you're sort of . . . Athena-esque!"

"You're not helping." Tracy redoubled her focus on the conference.

"Regardless," Hera announced, "now that we have returned, we shall be taking credit for our deeds from now on."

"King Poseidon, what happened to Zeus?" This question came from a younger member of the press. He paled for a moment as all twelve immortals focused on him. "Er, just curious."

"Gone," the sea god spoke.

"Killed," Ares added. "Big damn part of why we're back."

Poseidon pounded his trident anew and glowered at Ares.

"But . . . killed?" someone in the room asked. "An immortal can be killed?"

"What's the connection between Zeus's death and your return?" another called out. Others shouted questions over each other in a sudden free-for-all until no one could be heard clearly. Tracy caught Ares smirking on one of the feeds amid the din.

Then the camera began to shake. Reporters reached out for something to hold on to, with startled glances to the ceiling, the floor, and everywhere. Questions were forgotten. "Earthquake!" someone shouted. A few of the gods on stage looked about nervously as well, yet most—Poseidon in particular, his overturned palm held out before him—merely presided over the chaos.

"Are they causing that?" Chelsea asked.

"Probably a good bet at this point."

"Awesome. Maybe this *is* real."

In moments the quake retreated, taking the reporters' clamoring with it. Hera looked out over the throng. "Witness the power of Poseidon, Earth-Shaker!"

"None may slay an immortal," Poseidon announced, finally answering the question, "save for another immortal, and then only in the most extreme and unlikely of circumstances. I will say only this: the events that culminated in Zeus's death precipitated our return. That is all you need know."

A brave member of the international press raised her hand. "Queen Hera?" All seemed to hold their breath as the goddess's eyes turned to the woman and seemed to give her leave to continue. "Who—that is to say, may we ask who killed Zeus?"

Tracy caught traces of what was either uncertainty or discomfort across the immortal stage.

Hera raised her head high. "The question of who killed Zeus is unimportant. Trouble neither us nor yourselves further with this. It is only for you to know that the gods of Olympus have returned."

Ares cleared his throat. "'Cept I'd also add that it was me. Next question?"

Chaos threatened to break out amid the reporters again before Poseidon once more held out his palm. The reporters quieted instantly. "You learn well," the sea god said. "Next question, one at a time. On a different topic."

Seconds passed as the press murmured and attempted to change direction.

"King Poseidon,"—the next question came from a "correspondent" for a prominent fake-news program on a comedy cable channel—"a lot of you have names that start with *A* or *H*. Just what's that about?"

The question garnered a few snickers about the room. In the wide shot, Tracy caught sight of Apollo, Hermes, and Dionysus cracking smiles. Poseidon merely arched an eyebrow.

Hera, however, lifted her arm, raising the correspondent out of his chair with a small demonstration of power. Following a moment's study, she flicked her wrist to one side. With a yelp, the reporter ceased to exist in the room.

"Next question."

No one asked just what she had done, but the correspondent did fail to show up for work for the rest of the week.

"Neat little trick," whispered Chelsea.

Tracy nodded. "I've had job interviews like that."

CHAPTER THREE

"Of glorious Apollo, son of Zeus, twin brother to Artemis, all shall sing praise! Great things does Apollo bring us, for he is god of the sun, of healing, of music, of archery, of prophecy, and so much more! He gives us poetry, he gives us light, and he brings to us the wonder of gelatin desserts! Though there are those more powerful, no other god upon Olympus holds such broad interests."
— Your Olympian Gods: Wondrous or Fantastic? (propaganda booklet)

"Artemis: goddess of nature, goddess of the hunt, goddess of the moon. Despite being a chaste and childless Olympian, Artemis is often equated with the concept of 'Mother Nature,' though she refuses to comment on this. While close to her twin brother in temperament, she seems far more focused. Note to the media: though archery is a shared interest of both Artemis and Apollo, the question of which of them actually invented it seems to be a subject of contention and is not a recommended topic for joint interviews."
— A Mortal's Guidebook to the Olympians' Return

"SO NOW THAT MORTALS are getting more environmentally conscious, are you planning to ease back on this whole climate change thing of yours?" Apollo watched his twin sister draw back her bowstring, sight down the arrow, and hold it.

"Oh, probably. Or maybe. Well, no," Artemis answered with a shrug. "Our return has distracted them from the environment. Should I turn the heat down too soon, they'll forget all about it and learn nothing. Besides, I wish them to go green. That was the whole intent! So many buildings and cars everywhere. It's not natural."

"Shall I point out the irony of your saying so while relaxing atop a skyscraper?"

"You probably shall, yes."

Her eyes narrowed and she let the arrow fly. It sped down from the top of the skyscraper and through two open corner windows of another building before embedding itself in the skull of one of the monsters below. "Ha! Right between the eyes. Beat that."

Apollo squinted. Right between the eyes, indeed. "That means little when your target is a seven-eyed beast that's mostly head."

"Stop trash-talking and take your shot. You're terrible at it."

He pulled an arrow. "Trash-talking?"

She grinned. "That too."

"And yet I'm the one Homer called 'Archer-god.'"

"Only because you snapped it up first, Brother."

"And invented the bow."

He nocked the arrow and looked for a worthy shot. The five remaining creatures skittered over the outside of a city bus, looking like nothing more than large, boggle-eyed heads with talons sprouted behind their ears. There was good reason for that: they *were* nothing more than large, boggle-eyed heads with talons sprouted behind their ears. Funny how that worked.

"Ha! Right, 'invented' the bow. But that's what you do, you snap things up. 'Music? I'll do it!' 'Healing? I'll do it!' Exactly how full does your portfolio need to be?"

"Someone has to do it."

"Overachiever."

"Tree-hugger."

Artemis whapped the back of his head with her bow. "Darn right. My question stands."

Apollo spotted a perfect bank shot before he could answer and drew back the bowstring, concentrating. "There's . . . only . . . so many of us . . ."

Shrill beeping from the phone at his belt dashed his efforts.

Artemis snickered. "Case in point. Too busy."

He relaxed the bow and checked the incoming text message. "More worshippers. A garage band just sacrificed a keg to me in hopes of a blessing."

"They drank it on your behalf, of course."

"Of course. They've yet to get the hang of that 'sacrifice' concept. 'Twig?' What kind of horrible name for a band is Twig?"

"Sounds bluegrass."

"Country-jazz fusion. It's new. And not my fault."

He put away the phone, drew the bowstring back again, and aimed for a stop sign at just the perfect angle to skip the arrow and hit one of the creatures. Everyone loved bank shots. Well, maybe the thingama-monster he was about to hit wouldn't, but—

Another text alert jarred his concentration as he released the arrow. It skipped off the stop sign well enough but caught only a small piece of the monstrous creature.

"Styx on a stick!"

"Well, don't *wound* them! That's just unkind." Artemis quickly sent another arrow after his—without the bank shot, of course—that put the monster out of its misery as Apollo went to check the message. "You know you could try ignoring those for a bit."

"Not like I used to. There's entirely too many now." Nevertheless, he turned the phone off without checking it, knowing even as he did so that it would grate on him. He was supposed to be relaxing, yet who had time to relax? He couldn't just ignore those who had the good taste to worship him, could he? "You're really not having trouble keeping up with everything now?"

She shrugged. "I never have before. And it's your shot."

"But so many mortals know we exist now. I'm not complaining about the recognition and worship, but there's a lot more to do. I got rusty."

"That's what you get for being the multipurpose god. Are you going to shoot, or are you going to brood about it?"

He scowled at the nickname, apt though it was. Even as he sighted down his arrow and looked for a shot, he couldn't shake the thought that he really shouldn't have taken this break. Entirely too much work awaited him: worshippers to care for, musicians to inspire, Muses to manage—not to mention keeping up with Olympian politics. With Zeus's killer still unknown eight months after the fact, the tension had yet to resolve itself. Officially the gods were all outraged, but most were either too immersed in the thrill of the Return or too afraid of being slain themselves—or both—to look for a guilty party. The very topic had swiftly become taboo.

Too late, Apollo saw an opportunity and fired. His arrow flew clean through the skull of one of the creatures and out the other side, narrowly missing another creature that had been right in its path only moments before. So close! Still, he smiled, trying to pass it off as being exactly what he'd intended.

Artemis glanced at him, shaking her head after a beat. "Wow. You really are preoccupied, aren't you?"

"I go for a solid shot instead of a fancy one and that means I'm preoccupied, does it?"

"I speak of you hitting that mortal in the leg."

"Oh for the love of—!"

She was right. His arrow had ended its journey sunk in the thigh of a young man who had been snapping photos of the spectacle a moment before. Apollo considered claiming that the man was a blaspheming oil baron utterly deserving retribution, but doubted she'd buy it.

"Oh, he'll be fine. His camera's okay; look how well he held on to it when he tumbled! In agony." Apollo sighed. "Listen, do me a favor and finish off the creatures while I fix this, will you?"

She grinned and nocked two arrows at once.

Healing the mortal's wound was simple enough for the god of healing, and the man had the good sense to be gracious about it. (It helped such things that five months ago, a Hollywood starlet had sued Aphrodite over a botched facelift after she'd sacrificed a luxury convertible to the goddess. Aphrodite didn't bother to show up in court. She collapsed the hillside under the starlet's house and dared her to keep complaining.) Really, the man would now be something of a local celebrity for a few days, enough for a few free drinks at least. Apollo even posed for a photo. Stern. Dignified. Taking a moment to bask in mortal adulation while his sister quietly dispatched the monsters behind them. She didn't like city crowds anyway.

Of course when he joined her atop a nearby hill, he realized he now had even less time to relax than before.

"I really need to be going now."

"Already? I'm telling you, Brother, you must to learn to delegate more."

"Don't start."

"I'm serious. It's not as if you don't know how. The Muses are quite independent, are they not?"

"Zeus's daughters, if you recall. He forced them on me." You don't say no to Zeus, after all. Or you didn't, anyway.

"Truly, but they're good at what they do, yes?"

He gritted his teeth. "Mergh."

"I didn't catch that."

"I said 'Mergh.' And very well, maybe. Most of the time." In truth the Muses were his closest friends on Olympus and among the best things that had ever happened to him. They were up there with his automation of the sun chariots and accidentally inventing solar panels, but admitting so would lose the argument. He tried changing the subject. "Did we decide where those monsters came from?"

"Who knows? Lousy design, though. Hideous, but inept. Perhaps Aphrodite?" She grinned.

"Shh. She might hear." It was unlikely, of course, but feuding goddesses had destroyed nations, and cleanup was a bitch.

"Ha! Like I'm afraid of her. Goddess can't even take a little knife wound without crying to daddy, and now that he's . . ." She trailed off at the mention of their slain father. "Anyway, delegating. Just give it some thought before you drive yourself crazy."

Apollo's evening appointment to evaluate an apprentice prophetess for transfer to his Oracle at Delphi was canceled. This was a mixed blessing. On the one hand, it gave him a free half hour to catch up on things. On the other hand, the prophetess had cancelled because she'd been hospitalized after an encounter with one of the many swarms of "razorwings" plaguing the southwestern American countryside of late. She would recover, but really, if the apprentice prophetess had any promise whatsoever, the woman should have seen it coming.

He supposed the evaluation took care of itself at that point.

Ancient myth has long told of how the prophetess stationed at his Oracle at Delphi would seek the divine vapors hissing from the rock fissure. In doing so, went the legend, she would be possessed of Apollo so that she might have oracular visions. Modern scholars theorized that the vapors merely contained a powerful hallucinogen that caused the Oracle to experience what primitive Greek culture misinterpreted as prophecy. Neither theory was more than partially correct, and had anyone thought to ask one of the gods about it, they might've learned the truth. (Then again, they might not. Mythology is filled with contradictory versions of the same stories, stemming from various gods' attempts to spin those stories in their favor. Plus, some gods simply enjoy pulling a mortal leg or two. Ares once convinced one of the more ambitious tribes of Crete that properly grown olives would explode when thrown, a lie which led to the simultaneous destruction of a culture and invention of salad dressing.)

While it is true that the vapors do contain a hallucinogen, its single curious effect is to make the prophetess see, of all things, lithium batteries amid the rest of the prophecy. To counter this, the prophetess simply omits any mention of lithium batteries before relating an interpretation—a mostly harmless practice, save for when the prophesied future does indeed involve lithium batteries, which was blessedly rare prior to the 1970s.

Nor was there any distasteful and time-consuming possession involved in seeking visions. Apollo had merely imbued the vapors with his power so they enhanced the prophetesses' natural gifts, allowing them to seek visions for others. Clearly the apprentice didn't have enough natural gifts to enhance.

In any case, the cancellation gave Apollo a little more time to work with than he'd expected. Artemis's advice continued to weigh on him as well. Combined, the two topics forced the realization that he'd not actually sought a vision for himself in months.

He'd not done it often, of course, even when he did have time. Despite his superior skill, looking into the future was akin to performing exploratory laparoscopic surgery through a kaleidoscope. Sure, you'd see some things, but while they'd probably look cool, there was no guarantee that they'd be any more useful to you than planning ahead like a normal person.

But when in doubt . . .

On the door of his apartments on Olympus, he hung the golden sign Artemis had given him for his 2,000th birthday (*Divine genius at work. Do not disturb.*) and stole away to the roof. After seating himself on a mat of silk, Apollo looked up to the sky, spread his arms, and willed himself into the trance that would, eventually, produce a vision.

His breathing slowed. His mind opened. Images of dolphins wearing hats floated by as they always did for some reason. Apollo focused on the mellifluous music of the future made by vibrations in the strings of time (a difficult task when one is simultaneously trying to avoid being bothered by overwrought, melodramatic phrasing that tested the patience of even the god of poetry). He awaited . . . anything.

The dolphins stuck around longer than usual. One wore a green and purple reindeer sweater. Momentarily recoiling in aesthetic horror, Apollo managed to dismiss the dolphin and its eldritch sweater as mere ethereal rubbish.

There was floating. There was waiting. There was more floating. There was, perhaps unsurprisingly, more waiting.

Then with a flash, the vision came. (That is to say the flash was a part of the vision; the vision itself slipped in like a cat and was suddenly just there. Any vision that comes with a separate flash before it is of course a sign of impending brain aneurysm.)

The flash is lightning. It reflects on the eyes of a young man who clings to an iron frame high above a crowded, brightly lit cityscape. Rain begins to fall, pelting his sandy-blond hair moments before he looks up with a curse.

No, not a curse. A name. "Zeus!"

As Apollo ponders the futility of calling to a dead god, the vision widens. He recognizes two things: the structure the young man climbs and the figure perched above him at the very top. The figure gazes down on the man in both amusement and curiosity—the figure whose manifest power and life fill this vision of the future.

Zeus.

"How did you find me, mortal?"

Lightning flashes again, and the vision ends.

Apollo opened his eyes with a curse. Zeus, alive again? Or never dead? Two possibilities immediately occurred to him: either Zeus had faked his murder to test the Olympians' loyalty or his killer had been sloppy. Either way, the true king of the gods would be more incensed than a minotaur at a barbeque.

A knot in his stomach, Apollo rose to look down upon the world and realized that he now had even more problems than when he started.

Mortals were right; ignorance was bliss. Total ignorance, at least; partial ignorance was a pain in the ass. Was it really Zeus? Was it some sort of trick or a figurative vision? (He hated those.) He needed to learn more.

Temptation tugged at him to seek another vision, despite the likely futility. Seeking a second vision on the heel of a first was doomed to failure more often than not. Yet given the stakes, he had to try.

Apollo returned to the mat, hoping for further clues, for further insight . . . or at the very least for dolphins with better fashion sense.

That sweater was an abomination.

CHAPTER FOUR

"Magic? Darkness? Secrets? Any intelligent person must agree that Hecate is certainly among the worst of the false gods currently plaguing our world. Let it be known that Hecate—and her worshippers—are now and forevermore on the NCMA's Top Ten List of Number One Enemies!"
—*members' newsletter from the Neo-Christian Movement of America*

"Numerous Christian organizations have stated multiple times that the NCMA is merely a fringe group of fanatics and should not be taken to represent the viewpoint, manner, or beliefs of Christianity as a whole."
—A Mortal's Guidebook to the Olympians' Return

BRITTANY SIMONS KEPT a secret vigil in the light of a single candle. The candle, lit in secret, sat at the center of a temple. The temple? That, too, was secret. To reach it required one to know a secret exit from a secret building that led to a secret path. (The secret exit was really just the back door of a college dorm, but no one really used it except during fire drills, and the dorm itself was really only known to those on campus, so Brittany figured that was good enough.) That very secret path wound its secretive way through some secret bushes to a secret chamber tucked beneath the off-ramp of a secret, heavily used, six-lane interstate highway.

Okay, so maybe the highway itself wasn't so terribly secret either, but it was a *very* secret off-ramp; the sign alerting drivers to its very existence was partially hidden by the boughs of a tree. In the coming spring, when the tree actually had leaves that might block a letter or two, the ramp would be even more secret. Brittany looked forward to that season with secret anticipation.

Yes, Brittany liked secrets. Dark, secretive secrets wrapped in the most secret secrecy. Indeed, one could say that Brittany's affection for secrets even eclipsed her aversion to thesauruses, though Brittany would sneer at anyone who made such a suggestion.

Especially if that person referred to her by the name "Brittany," for she was Brittany no more!

Except on her driver's license.

And on the nametag they made her wear at her part-time barista job.

And on the envelopes containing the bills stamped *past due* that arrived in her mailbox on an increasingly frequent basis. And, yes, fine, on the mailbox too.

Clearly she needed a secret mailbox.

But she was no longer Brittany in her (secret) heart. No, she was Wynter Nightsorrow, Priestess of Hecate, and tonight Hecate's loyal servant would attempt her greatest ritual ever.

She sat amid the circle of power, reveling in the firelight and the darkness around her, the air thick with the scent of energy, incense, and anchovies from the pizza she'd sacrificed to begin the ritual. She could feel her senses spread throughout the goddess's temple. Her temple. Her gift to the goddess.

Yeah, it was funded with the money Wynter's parents sent for her tuition. But Wynter was the one who had (secretly) dropped out months ago, so she was pretty sure she deserved the credit for creating the temple. If you could ask the seven figures hunting for Wynter out in the darkness beyond her senses, they'd tell you she deserved the credit too. But you can't, so just ignore them and their pointy weapons for now. They'll just be our little secret.

Ah, secrets!

Wynter always had a thing for them, though she could never say why. (She liked to think that her subconscious knew; it just wasn't telling.) As a little girl, she loved writing notes to friends in code that no one but she could read, or coming up with private names for her dolls that only she knew. It made no difference that no one had ever cared to uncover such secrets; it was the secrets themselves that mattered.

Hecate, goddess of night, was queen of secrets. It was a good fit. Wynter first began the whole Hecate-worshipping thing after she graduated high school nine months ago—just prior to the Return. To those who knew her—or to those who hadn't left town for college, anyway—her transformation seemed to come out of nowhere. "It's the true dark calling of the secret mysteries of my heart," she'd explained. She'd spent a full two hours thinking of just how to phrase that.

At the time, the only secret Wynter really cared about was that the whole business was just a way to mess with people—to freak out her family and show them that yeah, she was going to college as they'd wanted, but it was *her* life. The day her friend Gail left town, Wynter had picked up a vampire book on a whim. Then she'd cloistered herself in her room and decided that, what the heck, she'd go Goth.

It seemed fitting. She was alone. No one really cared how *she* felt because graduation had stripped her of any friends her own age—and if there's one thing TV and music had taught her, it was that friends her own age were the only ones who could possibly understand her. Her family just couldn't wait for her to go to college, to start her new life.

So why not mess with them a little? Even better, why not freak them out by worshipping dark powers they wouldn't understand? The whole "queen of secrets" thing was just a bonus. The day she dyed her hair black, her anticipatory grin hung from ear to ear. They'd think she'd gone mental.

"Magic isn't real!" they'd say. "Hecate isn't real!" they'd cry! "Look what you've done to your hair!" (It would've been better if her hair weren't already dark, of course. She did consider going blonde for a day just to accentuate the contrast, but she'd been on a budget.)

Then the stupid gods had to actually show up at that press conference and ruin all her fun by being real.

It was so unfair! Before she even got the chance to disturb her parents with a crazy bedroom shrine to a made-up goddess, legitimacy thrust itself upon her, and her parents proclaimed her a visionary. Suddenly she was a young woman who'd seen an opportunity in the new world order and positioned herself to properly take advantage.

In short, they were thrilled. Robbing her of her rebellion, they even had the nerve to call her happily—happily!—by her new name.

Just her luck she'd wind up kin to a bunch of Pragmatists.

Human reaction to the Olympians' reappearance ran the gamut, with Pragmatists smack in the middle: just going with the flow to capitalize on whatever benefits they could gain with lip service. At one end of the spectrum hung the True Believers, Olympian zealots who welcomed the "new" gods with open arms and sincere worship. Balancing them out at the other end—beyond those who refused to call Olympians "gods" but still tolerated them as a testament to the complexity of God's creation—raged those who declared the Olympians false gods. Any mention of their divinity was reviled as heresy. These groups gave themselves all sorts of names, but the media wouldn't stand for that—viewers had enough to keep up with, after all. So the media collectively dubbed all of these groups Pious Reactionists, whether they liked it or not.

At first the Pious Reactionists openly showed their defiance. Groups as large as entire countries took a stand against the false gods. When the frequency of natural disasters in these countries spiked dramatically— alongside curious "coincidences" of government leaders developing a second head or a stubborn case of death—the movement gradually went underground to avoid further reprisals. Yet it was still out there.

Wynter would've caught hell if just one of her close family members had fit into such a group. Yelling, screaming, fights—maybe even random searches of her room that would force her to hide her materials of worship.

In short, it would have been awesome. Stupid supportive family.

Yet Wynter wasn't a quitter—not this time, anyway. She kept trying to evoke a reaction, dropping hints that maybe a certain closed-minded uncle might want to visit and trying to scare them with Latin chanting. She even left a few pamphlets from the ultra-extremist Neo-Christian Movement of America lying around the house with the hope they'd take the propaganda to heart, but no dice.

Perhaps, had Wynter known that the aforementioned seven figures and their pointy weapons would eventually be coming for her, she would have taken comfort in that looming confrontation. Except we're still not talking about them, so forget we mentioned it. Sorry about that. Back to Wynter.

She had spent the summer learning the ways of worshipping her new goddess, guided by the Internet and a few books provided by her dreadfully encouraging parents. It wasn't until she got to college that she realized that at some point during the past few months of fakery, she'd grown to truly enjoy it. Her devotion to Hecate blessed her with divine dreams, a sense of belonging, and the discovery that Melinda—that "redheaded" bitch—secretly dyed her hair. (It wasn't enough to break up Melinda and Chad, but it was close, darn it.) Hecate's mastery of secrets even helped Wynter get the answers to numerous midterm exams. They weren't actually for any of the classes she was taking, but they still fetched quite a good price on the black market.

Wynter mostly flunked out of her own courses.

That didn't matter. Hecate's power was all she needed, and by abandoning college, she could use her tuition money to transform the secret underpass alcove into a proper (and secret) temple. Real gold paint was expensive, after all—as was bribing art students to make a few statues and carve the devotionals into the concrete without telling anyone. (Constantly re-dying her hair was also starting to add up, frankly, but it was necessary: she hoped to eventually prevent any light from escaping it whatsoever.)

Now the evening's opening convocation to the goddess was complete. The anchovy and artichoke pizza sacrifice sat in ashes upon the ritual coals. Incense hung heavy in the air. Her laptop computer displayed the (secret) spells of Hecate that she'd found online and then improved upon with her own touches. The candle of power burned before her. Wynter focused on the tiny flame and calmed her mind, awaiting the touch of the goddess.

In the temple, Hecate was there.

Not, you know, *there*-there, but present in spirit, called by worship. The goddess's gaze turned upon her disciple in admiration and thanks. The attention glowed (secretly) within Wynter's mind. A smile crept its way onto her lips, and, ever vigilant, she forced it into an *unsmile*. Those cloaked in the secret embrace of Hecate's shadowy arms, after all, did not smile. Smiling was full of daintiness and, therefore, beneath them.

She was certain she'd seen that on TV somewhere.

Not smiling was one of Wynter's first rules when she began her worship. The problem was that when she felt the touch of the goddess's power, she felt happy. She could only surmise that the feeling itself was somehow allowed, yet the contradiction irritated her—until a fit of divine inspiration and tequila led Wynter to create the "unsmile," a completely different expression involving an upturning of the corners of the lips.

Okay, so it was exactly the same as a smile, but that just made it even more of a secret that she was, in reality, *un*smiling.

And so, with an unsmiling glance at the laptop, she began to chant the incantations. The words flowed from Wynter's lips as she traced designs with gold dust on the pristine floor. Feeling the power surround her, she repeated the words until she could no longer recall when she had begun. Each iteration added onto the last, lifting her higher and higher until, euphoric, she could no longer even see the temple around her.

Nearby, swiftly approaching figures (of whom we're still not really speaking yet) caught the scent of burned anchovies and adjusted their course. Each moved as silently as the moonlight, as graceful as a hunting cat. All right, so one of them stumbled and fell. (His name was Bob Higgins, in case you ever meet him and wish to make fun.)

In her mind, Wynter felt her goddess's presence as she floated among a sea of stars and the ritual reached its zenith. Wynter's arms spread over the sacred parchment (butcher paper purchased from the local office supply store and treated with a secret, ritualized process involving glitter). Holding a golden pen, she whispered quietly to Hecate, Outsider of Olympus, Queen of Secrets . . .

"Queen Hecate, with the deepest reverence I beg of you: entrust to your loving servant a secret, a great secret, the greatest you deem me worthy to receive. I who have created this temple for you, I who have sacrificed much in your name, I who am sorry I was late in my usual devotions because Mr. Winn made me cover a shift at the café even though I *told* him he was meddling with mystical secret powers he couldn't possibly understand . . . I am an outsider, just as you. On this moonless night, share with me a Secret of the World!"

Wynter's hand began to move. On the parchment, it scribbled words of the goddess's own volition. Wynter had no idea what she was transcribing, but the ritual was working! Hecate was smiling on her, or unsmiling on her or—heck, who cared, it was working!

Or she was having a stroke.

Wynter decided that was less likely and gave herself over to the goddess, eyes closed, furiously sketching and writing across the paper. Her heart raced. Her breath quickened until she was nearly hyperventilating from the power of the goddess's secrets pouring through her. So lost in the sensation was Wynter that she utterly failed to notice the seven figures slipping, ninja-like, into the cave.

Well, six, actually. After his failure to be graceful, they had sent Bob back to the car to think about what he did. In fairness, the six figures didn't so much as slip (ninja-like) into the cave as they did barge in and shout for Wynter to "stop in the name of the Neo-Christian Movement of America! . . . and Almighty God!" Even so, this was done as ninja-like as possible, with a great many of the flips and katana-twirls that they had seen in movies. They were, after all, ninjas themselves. Their leaders told them so.

Perhaps one of the most unpredictable changes resulting from the Olympian Return was the sudden rise of ninja training camps run by far-right Christian groups. Once the Pious Reactionist movement was forced underground, operating in secrecy grew paramount to survival. Furthermore, leaders of fanatical groups such as the NCMA swiftly realized that they had something of a public relations problem. The youth of America (and indeed the world) had been seduced by the utter coolness of actual beings purporting to be mythological "gods". Cults sprang up overnight. A person couldn't turn on the TV without seeing news such as the new Las Vegas casino Dionysus had opened or the latest lucky mortal to be seen with Aphrodite. Hermes even had a regular show on MTV.

The NCMA urgently needed to become more competitive, or it faced a coolness gap. The necessity for both coolness and secrecy led them to the inevitable and obvious concept of ninjas. Kids loved ninjas! (Kids loved dinosaurs, too, but the NCMA's efforts at cloning a few proved disastrous when they accidentally funded some Texas A&M fraternity brothers posing as scientists. The "scientists" bought a used Godzilla costume and spent the rest of the NCMA's money on the biggest keg party the Aggies had ever seen.)

And so the first Christian ninja squads were trained.

On a reduced budget.

No one was really sure just what to do with these squads at first, but the program proceeded, based on the philosophy that it was better to have ninjas and not need them than to need ninjas and not have them. Even so, the first groups completed training before the ninja squads even had a suitable name, as a few dissenters who considered the training a waste of resources and refused to dignify the effort.

It was then that the monsters began to appear: harpies off the coast of North Carolina; poisonous, winged kittens terrorizing America's heartland; there was even talk of a hydra dwelling in Lake Michigan. Such new horrors silenced the bickering over the value of ninja training. God in His wisdom had clearly chosen to demonstrate his approval of the ninja program by causing to appear something for which they would need ninjas!

This is not to say that the ninjas were then put to work, roaming the country to slay monsters. The NCMA astutely noticed that the Olympian "gods" regarded monster slaying as a good and glorious thing, and clearly the Ninjas Templar (as they eventually came to be called) could in no way support an Olympian agenda! Nor was the NCMA particularly worried about the monsters. They were, after all, a sign of God's approval of the ninja program. He would undoubtedly take the monsters away once the NCMA had trained enough ninjas to please Him, and the problem would, therefore, take care of itself.

And they would have ninjas.

In the event that they needed them.

On a reduced budget.

There were a few heretical souls in the NCMA who lay awake at night, harried by a feeling that something was not quite right about the whole thing. But for this reason, they often overslept and missed key policy meetings. This in turn led the others to vote them out of the policy committees on grounds of truancy, and so no one had to be bothered.

It wasn't long after that the NCMA decided the Ninjas Templar might possibly be used to strike against "cells" of Olympian insurgency.

And so it was with cries of "Death to false gods!" that the squad of Ninjas Templar (sans Bob) rushed into Wynter's temple. They knocked over a statue of the goddess, kicked out the sacred fire, and swept away the still entranced Wynter in a flurry of righteousness. They gathered up what treasures they could (to be repurposed or sold to fund the NCMA), set fire to the temple (or as much as they could, given its concrete construction and off-ramp location), and threw the heathen laptop and texts upon the flames to be destroyed forever (except for the ritual parchment—because the glitter was kind of neat, and Bob might enjoy it once he was done with his penance).

It was not until the Ninjas Templar returned to their black Ford Econoline of Righteousness parked a mile down the road that they noticed the words Wynter had written upon the parchment. Beneath a half-completed sketch of what appeared to be nine elaborately decorated cylindrical containers, the following words were written:

Within nine cans depicted here
Resides that which Olympians fear.

It was, Bob decided, even better than the glitter.

CHAPTER FIVE

"Looking back, I suppose it's not as if Apollo didn't give the whole thing some careful thought. The decision to act must have torn him apart long before he brought us in on the plan. I can't help but wonder how things might have turned out differently if those visions had included just a few more details."
— *personal journal of the Muse Calliope*
(written under house arrest)

SEEKING A SECOND VISION left Apollo with good news and bad news. The good news was that he now knew the first vision to be only something that *may* be rather than something that *will* be (to borrow back a phrasing he once gave Dickens). As for the bad news, well, that was the same as the good news. (So really, there was twice as much bad as good. Some days it didn't pay to get out of bed. Not that he had much use for money, but still.)

The second vision also strengthened his impression that the young blond man clinging to the Eiffel Tower would play a part in restoring Zeus. Or, he corrected, *may* play a part.

And therein lay the rub (more borrowing back).

Apollo wanted Zeus to return—or at the very least, he wanted a return to Zeus's policy of withdrawal. If this mortal played a part in that, Apollo would help. More to the point, Zeus would know that Apollo had helped and spare him the wrath that he would surely visit upon the other gods for their inaction. Nobody liked wrath, after all; it hurt, or at the very least it was itchy. The Titans' full share of it got them sealed away for eternity.

Yet there would be others who would try to stop him if they learned of his intent. As far as Apollo knew, he was the only god no longer enjoying the Return and the additional worship it entailed. Ares and Aphrodite positively reveled in it. Even Athena, Zeus's self-appointed bodyguard, held a grudging enjoyment of the situation behind her vow to find Zeus's real killer. Ares had claimed responsibility, of course, but the brute claimed responsibility for just about anything if he thought it would make him look tough. No one really believed him; he just wasn't smart enough. The real killer—or killers, Apollo figured, given the level of conspiracy killing the king of the gods likely had required—would have even greater motivation to stop him. The fact that there were zero clues to the identities of those conspirators made a minefield out of confiding in anyone.

Apollo couldn't shake the feeling that the whole endeavor was doomed to end in disaster.

The following morning Apollo strode the verdant expanse of the Olympian courtyards. It was a ritual he'd managed to cling to despite his busy schedule, yet lately his time there grew shorter with each visit. Today, the dawning sunlight and crystal blue skies failed to penetrate his thoughts. Frigging god of the sun and he couldn't enjoy it.

Good gods, he was getting whiny! He reached a hand into a stream, splashed the cold water on his face, and gave himself a mental kick in the butt. If he could kill a dragon when he (Apollo, not the dragon) was four days old, he could get through this.

May be, might be . . . but how likely? The question danced in front of him with infuriating little hops and pirouettes. He wasn't a gambling god like Dionysus. Betting on the long shot of this blond mortal, if it was indeed a long shot—

"Great Apollo."

The greeting from behind him broke his train of thought. Even had he not recognized the voice, its formal tone alone gave away its speaker's identity. Apollo froze for a fraction of a second to bundle up his worries before turning with a smile on his face. Caution required that he at least appear as pleased as everyone else until he puzzled out what to do.

"Queen Hera," he returned. "A pleasure to see you this morning."

"And you, Stepson. A fine morning we have. You are looking . . . well?"

The queen of the gods stood atop a wide block of granite beneath a pomegranate tree—the white arms that had so enthralled the poet Homer folded within her robes, nose raised high as she looked down on him from her dais. A smile perched on her face with the unmistakable pleasance that declared she wanted something from him.

"It's always a fine morning on Olympus," he answered. A compliment couldn't hurt; Hera played a part in overseeing the keeping of the grounds. Yet he could hear the distraction in his own voice as he said it.

As if sensing it herself, Hera's smile wavered; Apollo considered the possibility that she wanted something from him the way the hawk wants something from the rabbit. Was it related to Zeus's murder, or matters more mundane?

Or was he paranoid? Either way, he was no rabbit (except for that one time, but that was strictly experimentation). Apollo returned the smile and strode forward to step up onto the same rock and equalize their footing.

"What brings you to the courtyard this morning, Queen Hera?"

Hera's eyebrow arched at that approach. Too abrupt? She shrugged and looked about the courtyard. "Pomegranates." She reached up and plucked one. "And looking for you, Stepson. I have a . . .," She paused, perhaps considering the word. "Request."

Apollo considered the word himself. Hera's "requests" tended toward the compulsory end of the spectrum. He gave no response beyond his continued attention.

She went on, regarding the pomegranate. "The world needs more. By which I mean pomegranates. My sacred fruit grows poorly without ample sunlight. I therefore wish you to adjust the sun's path to shine more toward the poles during the summer. Without depriving the central regions where already they thrive, of course."

Apollo couldn't suppress a chuckle. "That may be difficult, Stepmother. Doable, perhaps, but . . . difficult. To do properly, I mean. Especially for both hemispheres. There's a delicate balance, and—"

She tossed her hand. "Well then forget about the southern hemisphere, there's less land down there anyway. Just the northern will do fine, for now."

Styx on a stick, one more problem to deal with! Apollo rubbed his temples, feeling a headache coming on. "Could you not simply reengineer the pomegranate itself to require less sun?"

Hera gaped. "I beg your pardon? I'll not reengineer that which is perfect! Shall I get Botox injections and dye my hair as well?"

Apollo cleared his throat. "I . . . meant no offense, Queen Hera."

Hera turned the full force of her regality upon him, eyes narrowed, head high. "*Look* into it," she "requested".

"As you wish. Though it may take a while. I need to do feasibility studies, plan out a new path—plus it's a change in the established order, so I'll have to run it past the Erinyes just to be thorough, and you know how busy they are these days. Plus the sun chariots are getting a bit run down."

"They are automated, are they not? Your sun chariots?"

Apollo let a slightly overwhelmed sigh get away from him. "Yes, but they do need maintenance now and again. I understand number two's clutch is slipping lately. I've been meaning to take a look at it some night, but—" He forced himself to stop before revealing too much of his stress.

Hera cocked her head. "Meaning to? While your work has nearly always been exemplary, Stepson, it won't do to neglect your duties. You grow too busy, perhaps?"

Idle courtesy, Apollo wondered, or suspicion? Hera wore a smile of indeterminate sincerity.

He smiled back and attempted to lie, knowing it wasn't his strength. "No, Stepmother. I've merely overindulged in the pleasures of our return to the mortal world. Artemis and I went target-shooting just yesterday, in fact."

"Overindulgence is hardly your nature." She paused, searching his face. "Do you feel quite all right, Apollo?"

"Yes, just fine."

"Ah." Her smile faded for a moment. Or maybe he had imagined it. "Perhaps you're taking after your father more, now that he's gone."

Apollo's spine straightened involuntarily. If that wasn't a probing statement, he decided, he was a walrus. What was she on about?

It was true that Hera vocally condemned her husband's assassination from the moment it became known. To say her marriage to Zeus could be rocky was to say that analogies can be tedious, and Hera had possessed a talent for infuriating Zeus like no other. Spats ending in lightning-struck pomegranate groves were common. Further, Zeus had spawned numerous children via affairs with mortal women; Apollo himself was born of an immortal pairing from which Hera was conspicuously absent.

Yet with all of the squabbling and extramarital affairs, she had stuck by Zeus. Some (and this would be both a real and hypothetical *some*) would say that she simply enjoyed being married to the king. But as the goddess of marriage, the very concept of divorce offended her—she once turned one of her own priestesses into a cow for even hinting at the idea. Some (a different hypothetical *some* from the previous one, for variety's sake) might consider that attitude a prime motive to kill Zeus in order to escape a rather loveless marriage. Yet Hera was not a fan of the concept of love. It was duty that drove her. As abhorrent as divorce was, the murder of one's own spouse was at least doubly so.

Or so she maintained. A poor liar himself, Apollo was also lousy at judging when someone else was lying. While he knew Hera well enough to believe her condemnation of Zeus's murder to be genuine, he also knew enough about his own instincts to hold that judgment suspect. After all, some would point out (and this increasingly opinionated *some* really ought to watch their backs given all the goddess-bashing in which they've hypothetically engaged) that it took all of twenty-four hours for her to marry Poseidon once Zeus was dead. Secret affair? Power play? Or was being single simply against her nature?

Caught up in such considerations, Apollo realized he still hadn't answered Hera's question. "Not consciously taking after him, if so," he said finally. "You must miss him yourself, to bring it up."

He'd said it as a deflection, and it was Hera's turn to hesitate, but only for a moment before her gaze caught Apollo's in a net of thorns. "Your father was a troublesome, obstinate, egotistical philanderer. What insanity could possibly possess me to miss that?"

"So you're glad he was killed, then?"

Apollo sensed the blow a fraction of a second before Hera struck him across the face. He chose not to anger her further by avoiding it. Allowing her strike to speak for her, Hera stepped off the granite and stormed away. She turned, only once, to thrust a commanding finger back at him.

"Pomegranates!" she ordered.

Unable to come up with a response to so masterful an exclamation, Apollo let her go.

Damnation, he really shouldn't have asked that. Apollo stalked out of the area himself, chagrin beating him in the back of the head like an errant woodpecker.

He was testing her! Yes, he decided, that was it. He was testing her reaction in an attempt to verify her professed innocence. Feeling better about himself, he began to whistle.

Not that the test told him anything concrete. Damnation again.

Apollo continued his journey through the courtyards, searching internally for guidance that wasn't there. Worry? Check. Stress? Check. Twenty-three recipes for sun tea? Check. Guidance?

"Reply hazy, ask again later."

He caught a glimpse through the trees of Artemis on a routine stroll of her own, brushing her hands over tall grasses, clearly at peace. Possibly high, but probably just at peace. Some gods had all the luck. His sister hadn't seen him yet, so Apollo ducked into some trees and headed back toward the Olympian halls.

The courtyards soon gave way to the towering, white marble gate that led into the vast halls and apartments where many of the gods dwelled. Though all of the gods had quarters there, not all of them chose to live there regularly. Hades spent most of his time in, well, Hades (as this was the name of both the god himself and the underworld he ruled, Hades's lack of imagination eclipsed even Donald Trump's). Yet Hades (the god, not the realm) still maintained a seldom-used bungalow on Olympus. Aphrodite had a second home in Hollywood. Dionysus lived in Las Vegas. And Zeus—obviously Zeus was gone.

Zeus had shared a part of his quarters with Hera, though one wing was his own entirely. Poseidon ordered it closed after the murder, sealed up in honor of his brother and predecessor. The sea god's own small quarters were expanded and linked with Hera's after their marriage, and a majority of his rooms were underwater—a reminder of the undersea dwelling from which his kingly duties so often kept him. If the Olympians used regular contractors, the caulk portion of that renovation bill alone would have bankrupted a small country.

How involved was Poseidon in his brother's death? Another unanswered question . . .

Apollo made his way to his own quarters, located in the eastern wing overlooking the secondary stables. (Not a day went by that he wasn't thankful for the olfactory shield Hestia had invented to contain the smell. Apollo loved the fire-breathing horses that once guided the sun chariots, but they subsisted on a steady diet of sulfur and chili.) His footsteps echoed on the polished marble floor. He was out of time for the moment. Work awaited him, again. Dreading the number of messages surely stalking his inbox, he climbed the stairs past the Muses' quarters on the way to his office.

"Are they *insane?*" The question burst from the Muses' quarters, leaving no doubt about the opinion of the one posing it. "How is that the same? No, answer me! How is that the same!"

Apollo halted his climb and turned instead toward the doorway to poke his head through the silk divider curtains. Thalia stalked back and forth in the middle of the atrium, red hair blazing behind her in the sunlight. She focused all her attention on the phone clutched in her hand.

"No, look!" Thalia caught sight of Apollo and put him off with a nod before directing her ire back into the phone. "I don't care how much of an advance he's getting. You tell those producers the character stays as is or you're backing out! . . . Who *cares* if there's a contract? This is—I'm a Muse! I inspired that whole story! I—" She squeezed her eyes shut to trap welling tears and turned her back. "Fine!" she managed. "Just—fine! You just tell Mr. Brown he'll—he'll have to write the next book without me!" She jammed a finger at the screen to end the call and took a few steps toward the window, her breath ragged, her back to Apollo.

"Thalia?" he tried. "Are—?"

She cut him off with a scream culminating in her hurling the phone against a nearby couch. It barely bounced, landing on the cushion in still-pristine condition. She turned on him.

"If you take the character of a jaded, balding, wheelchair-bound mathematician in his late fifties and turn him into a female twenty-two-year-old blonde ex-gymnast stripper who's just 'good with numbers,' how does that possibly retain the spirit of the story? Why can't so-called 'creative' executives leave well enough alone? Or hurl themselves off a cliff? Can I shove one off a cliff, Apollo? It would make me ever so happy." She smiled with one of her better doe-eyed expressions.

He smiled back, despite his troubles. "Probably not the best idea, Thalia."

She heaved a sigh and picked up her phone again to polish it. "It wouldn't have to be a big cliff." Eyelashes fluttered at him.

"Stressed?"

She wiped the remnants of a tear. "No? Me? Stressed? No, not at all. Why do you ask?"

"I—"

She hurled herself backward onto the couch. "It's not that every single mortal seems to be invoking us for inspiration for their work. It's really not. I mean it's positively risible that every single slack-jaw on the Internet begs for comedic inspiration each time they make a smart-assed crack on a forum; I can more or less keep my sanity by just ignoring them. But dear gods, it's having to sift through it all!"

"Reminds me of—"

"But hey, I'm a big girl. I can do that, right?" She thrust her fingers into her hair and mussed it, her coiffure looking like a poofed dandelion as she cut him off. "I mean sanity's overrated anyway, isn't it? Got to find the really deserving writers and such out there amid the offal, don't we? Very well, so I'll miss a few gems in the sifting, but hey, them's the breaks, that's luck, not meant to be, right?"

Thalia suddenly caught her reflection in the mirror that made up half of one wall, and her tirade of annoyance continued unabated with a, "Sakes alive, look at my hair!" In a single sweep of her hand, it was perfectly coifed again. Thalia launched a wide-eyed grin at him that all but screamed, "Ta-da!"

Apollo tried to stay on topic. "I suppose that given—"

"But it's—ugh! It's those executives!" She jumped to her feet again. "Those studios and producers and focus groups and—and just the diabolical dumbing-down that everyone seems to think is compulsory! It's driving me positively ape-shit! I mean, excuse me, I know that's not very becoming, but oh my gods, Apollo!" She unscrewed a bottle of ambrosia and began to pour out a glass without offering any to him. "You just shouldn't take a 1,000-page novel and turn it into a two-hour movie! It doesn't work! Do you know how many scripts I've inspired since we came back? I mean just scripts, not even books being made into scripts! Every single one of them altered by philistines who think they know better than a Muse! More breasts! More explosions! More fart jokes! *Fart jokes!* Jiggle-boom-fart-bounce-fart! It's the nimrod anthem!" She suddenly stopped, considering. "Nimrod." She giggled. "I like that word."

As Thalia took the opportunity to down the ambrosia, Apollo took the opportunity to get out a full sentence or two. "You've inspired scripts that were changed before. Before we came back into public awareness. It didn't seem to bother you so much then."

Thalia finished the glass and poured another. "Yes, but it's happening more now. Cumulating, drop by drop!" She sighed again, looking at the full glass before setting it down. "Anyway, I'm being boorish, aren't I? Hi there. How're you?" She forced a dazzling smile and flashed her lashes again.

He laughed. "Trust me; you don't want to know."

"Oh hmm, that certainly doesn't make me curious at all."

"I've been a bit out of touch. Do you know if your sisters are having the same cliff-shoving urges?"

She shrugged. "More or less. I mean except Urania. You know, I still don't see why I got science fiction and she didn't."

Years ago, as the modern genres came into being, the Muses each took on new duties. Thalia added sci-fi to her existing purviews of comedy and poems about farming.

"You picked it yourself. You like science fiction."

"Oh there you go, bringing facts into the argument. She muses astronomy; you should've made her take it. She's got, like, zero workload."

"You drew lots. She picked last. It's your own fault."

"She's only got to worry about astronomy texts, calendar photos, and those stupid little sayings on coffee cups!"

"And bathroom wall graffiti."

Thalia snorted and then blushed at the sound. "Oh, yeah. Maybe she's been talking to those executives."

Apollo walked to the window and gazed out over the stables. Thalia, perhaps sensing he was weighting some sort of decision, said nothing. Her uncharacteristic silence was actually more distracting.

"Thalia," he said at last, "gather your sisters. There's something we must speak about. Don't tell anyone else."

"Ooh, secretive. Sounds like fun. Give me a couple of hours to get them all here."

Apollo shook his head. "Not here. Not on Olympus."

Thalia nodded, perplexed. "Would this have anything to do with cliffs?" she asked. "I've got one all picked out."

CHAPTER SIX

"On all of Olympus, there is no better spy than Hermes, no better prankster, and no better thief."
— *"Your Olympian Gods: Wondrous or Fantastic?"*
(propaganda booklet)

"Off the record, the fact that a god like Hermes is also the god of merchants has some rather unsettling implications, if you think about it."
—U.S. Attorney General (not off the record)

IT WAS SEEING Erato and Polyhymnia leave Olympus together that first aroused Hermes's suspicion. The two sister Muses had feuded for centuries. Going somewhere together meant something interesting was surely happening, and if something interesting was happening, Hermes wanted in. In fairness, he supposed it was curiosity being aroused rather than suspicion, but suspicion was so much more interesting. He'd consider a downgrade to curiosity depending on what was going on. At least he was feeling aroused. Aroused was almost always a good state.

Besides, it was a slow morning and there was an alarming lack of mischief lately for Hermes's tastes. He loved a good eavesdrop. He'd even recently figured out a way to wire-tap the river Styx, just to listen in on any interesting oaths people made—though little had come of that, and direct spying thrilled him more anyway. Besides, who could be more fun to spy on than the Muse of erotic poetry?

Granted, Erato's updated portfolio also included crossword puzzles—a choice Hermes could not fathom—so there was a risk that his suspic-iosity would lead to mind-numbing, grid-mounted tedium. Ah well, risk was what existence was all about. Wrapping himself in a cloak of nothingness, heedless of the treacherous boredom that very possibly awaited, Hermes hummed an inspiring anthem and flew off in pursuit.

No crosswords, no crosswords, no crosswords . . .

They were headed, it seemed, for London. So far, so good. If this did turn out to be nothing, he could at least spend a little time kicking around his adopted home.

The modern world just couldn't seem to get enough of Hermes's British accent. In the first days of the Return, whenever he consented to an interview, the first question was always about the accent. "That's a curious accent you have. Why is it different?" "Are you English? I thought all the Olympians were Greek?" "Are you just messing with us or what?"

"Yes," Hermes would say, "it amuses me. I'm messing with you. That's what I do. I'm Hermes, I mess with people!"

It was true that he liked to mess with people, but not in the case of his accent. Though he was god of messengers, travelers, and merchants, Hermes was a trickster first and foremost. Any mythological scholar could tell the tale of how he (Hermes, not the scholar) had stolen Apollo's cattle by nightfall on the very day he was born. (In truth it was by midafternoon, but Hermes wasn't huffy about the distinction.) Giving him the responsibility of messenger-god was initially just a means of keeping Hermes off Olympus and out of everyone's hair. Zeus routinely sent him to the relatively far-off British Isles for that very purpose. Eventually Hermes spent so much time there that he picked up the accent and a bad case of rickets. Of the two, the accent was the one that stuck, and its cause was a sore spot.

Hermes sometimes wondered if he might be less of a scamp had Zeus been a better father. Probably not, he usually decided. When one could fly faster, hide better, and listen farther than any other immortal, the temptation for mischief was just too great. Still, one could never be sure.

The Muses landed amid the trees in Hyde Park and shifted into the guise of regular women—or regular gorgeous women, anyway. There wasn't enough secrecy in the world to cloak a Muse's ego. Hermes continued to trail them as they entered the Hyde Park Corner tube station. Subtle as always, they didn't bother buying tickets but simply waved their hands over the turnstile sensors and stepped through as they opened. Unwilling to risk invisibility in a crowd, Hermes chose the guise of an unassuming backpacker and followed them.

The Muses continued ahead of him, oblivious. The longer Hermes followed, the more he felt this had to do with something bigger than crosswords. At the limits of his senses, something dangerous tingled, the source of which he couldn't quite place.

Erato and Polyhymnia reached Platform 2 and halted in apparent anticipation of a train. Neither spoke to the other. Whatever the cause of their journey together, it wasn't reconciliation.

Ignoring each other with practiced flair, they instead fixed their attention on a street violinist in a bright blue woolen cap. Behind a case spattered with coins, the violinist had been plying his skills to produce what could only very generously be described as an uninspired jig— until Erato took an interest. After only a few moments under her stare, his tune transformed into a seductive melody of unparalleled intensity. Heated and tempting, it all but peeled the clothes from a listener's body. Heavy, needful. It rippled through the small group of Londoners. Their eyes widened. Their faces flushed. Though immune himself, Hermes could sense every chord resonating within the listeners' blood as it pumped hotter, full of desires aching for release.

Also immune was Polyhymnia, whose expression implied that the only thing of hers aching for release was a troublesome lump of bile in her throat. The Muse of sacred songs, of oratory, and of rhetoric (and more recently of legal disclaimers) rolled her eyes, cleared her throat, and nodded once toward the performer. Again his music shifted, this time reforming into a flowing processional easily at home in the grandest temple. Reverent strums of the violinist's bow dissolved the previous spell as every measure testified to the glory of all creation. Hermes saw tears forming in the eyes of the more easily inspired listeners.

Erato's own eyes merely blazed with competitive fire as she strove to regain control. The Muses' dueling influences soon tugged at the poor violinist's inspiration like two dachshunds with a towel. The music of chaos resulted: Pious sexual melodies teased at Tube-goers' ears with sensual whispers of offers void where prohibited by law. Achingly passionate appeals slithered along napes of necks with the desire to consult a doctor if listeners experienced dizziness, dry mouth, or uncontrollable yodeling. The violinist himself sidled up to a nearby woman, his instrument held whisper-close to her ear, his heated gaze fixed upon her . . . his bow clearly demonstrating the health warning of a wall-mounted whisky advertisement.

Hermes tried his best to snicker in silence. Even though his curiosity had not yet been satisfied, the god of mischief already judged his trip worth it for this spectacle alone. He edged closer, trying to keep from laughing lest he blow his cover as another immortal in disguise.

He failed. As he tried to pass the laugh off as a reaction to swallowing a bug, Polyhymnia shot a glance toward him, eyebrow cocked. Hermes avoided eye contact. He turned his back, intending to give a show of clearing his throat, when he was shocked to see Apollo himself stepping onto the platform from the tunnel. Though Apollo wore a disguise of his own, the god had a habit of reusing faces. Hermes recognized him instantly and froze.

As minor immortals, the Muses lacked the power to truly see Hermes for who he was. (The consensus among the Olympians was that he was far too skilled in deception for his—or, more accurately, for their—own good.) Yet a god of Apollo's stature might very well spot him if given cause to look closely enough. Two other women whom Hermes pegged as additional Muses flanked the sun god, and now things were starting to smell terribly clandestine. Were that the case, they'd be on their guard. Polyhymnia would likely tell Apollo of the traveler who had failed to react to the music as any mortal would. One way or another, they could easily discover his eavesdropping.

The god of mischief cursed under his breath. The Fates seemed to be conspiring to seriously ruin his fun, not to mention his reputation: Hermes did not get caught! Not unless he wished to, at any rate.

At that moment, the Piccadilly Line thrust its way into the station. While getting caught by Erato under other, more private circumstances could be interesting, Hermes took the opportunity to back off from the whole group. In the crowd of travelers beginning to swarm the platform, Hermes slipped past Apollo and back up the station tunnel. He had time. Few things were faster than he, and a Tube train wasn't one of them.

Hermes spent a few minutes pretending to study a Tube map until the train continued on its way through the tunnels, and then he rushed back to the tracks where a once-more uninspired violinist's jig filled the air. Though Hermes gave the area an extra few moments' study, there was no sign of Apollo or the Muses. Now he had only scant time to reach the next station when the train did so he could properly track them. He jogged down the length of the platform, spent precious seconds dropping a few bills into the violinist's case as thanks for the amusement, and then ducked behind a beverage machine just long enough to go invisible without attracting attention. Moments later he was streaking down the tracks after the train.

He caught up to the train a short while before it made its next stop at Green Park Station. Settling in atop the train itself, Hermes pored through the crowd on the platform for any sign of the group and came up empty. Either they were still on the train, or Apollo had shifted his guise and he'd missed them. Hermes counted the first more likely.

It was a disquieting thought. Either Hermes was still on the trail of something small, or he had lost the trail of something big. Or, he realized, Apollo had shifted disguises but remained on the train. Or Apollo just wasn't shifting no matter what was going on. Or they were all just going out to a concert or something and didn't want to be mobbed by mortals and paparazzi.

A proliferation of possibilities topped the pile of reasons that Hermes disliked over-thinking things. He went with his gut (it hadn't steered him wrong yet): they were still on the train. Even so, he fought the urge to try to peek down through a window.

Now any mortal yahoo somehow able to observe the situation would likely wonder why Hermes, being invisible, didn't just slip into the car, or why Apollo and the others wouldn't travel invisibly for the entire journey. Mortals have something of a fascination with invisibility — some secretly desire to avoid attention, others just wish to slink through a locker room of the opposite sex. Make no mistake, the immortals of Olympus go invisible for these very reasons (the latter especially). The trouble is that invisibility isn't nearly as effective when trying to hide from other gods. At best, it produces a telltale shimmer effect that only goes unnoticed by immortal eyes if not directly viewed. If the immortal is making any effort at all to see an invisible party, invisibility is akin to throwing a sheet over one's head and pretending to be an unwanted pile of linens, which is more or less useless unless one is trailing another through a laundry room. A few gods have even developed an uncanny knack of *hearing* an invisibility field. Disguise is a much more effective method, and most Olympian egos prefer their majesty to be seen in some form, anyway.

As it turned out, the group remained on the train for a number of additional stops, finally departing together and making their way to the streets above. Hermes became visible in an alcove near the exit and followed Apollo and what appeared now to be six Muses at a discreet distance. Apollo was silent. More remarkable, so were the attending Muses.

A short while later, Hermes was crawling along the sticky floor of a movie theater balcony.

The group had entered the theater ahead of him and slipped past the *Balcony Closed* sign in what even Hermes had to admit was a remarkably discreet fashion for a group of six devastatingly attractive women and their lucky male escort. After a five-minute lead time to allow Apollo to check for eavesdroppers, Hermes crept up after them, spied the three remaining Muses waiting for them in the otherwise empty balcony, and quickly changed into a turtle.

With all due respect to the Spanish Inquisition, Hermes thought, no one expects the turtle. He had always liked turtles. Adopting the guise of a creature with all the flamboyance of a dead rock was useful for remaining unnoticed. Besides, the irony of the fastest god in the bunch taking the form of a turtle was just too enticing to resist. Plus they were just darned cute.

Hermes turtled his steady, silent way through spilled beverages and dropped popcorn toward the meeting, for a meeting it was, he'd decided. The theater was showing *Fart-Boom 3: The Jiggling,* and not even Dionysus, whose hedonism had drunk his good taste under the table long ago, would see something like that in the theater. So then, what was so secret that they couldn't just meet on Olympus? The tingling sense became a buzzing, with a slight reggae beat. The last time he got a sense that powerful, Zeus wound up murdered. Nursing a growing suspicion, lucky Hermes crept in behind Calliope's foot and listened.

Apollo wasted no time once they'd reached the balcony. Within the first five minutes, he questioned the Muses about their extra workloads and frustrations in dealing with modern mortals since the Return. True to Thalia's prediction, nearly all save Urania were feeling the pressure.

Before Urania could offer to help balance things, Apollo went on to tell them of how he'd sought a vision to aid him with similar troubles. The nine of them gasped in unison at the tale.

"Much is unclear," Apollo said. "Chiefly, how likely Zeus is to truly return, and just what part this mortal does play."

As often happened when the entire group was together, Calliope spoke for them all. "Do you know who he is? Or why they were on the Tower at all?"

Apollo shook his head. "I cannot be certain the vision is a literal one. I don't yet know who he is, no. But I have a few details. For one, he's an American."

Clio (Muse of history, historical fiction, and travel writing) chuckled. "Ah, the Americans. It's always about them, isn't it? Do you know they're remaking *Gandhi* and setting it in Indiana to make it more accessible? Is that not insane?"

"Oh my gods, I know!" Thalia chimed. "Accessible: I absolutely loathe that word! Goodness forbid they should—"

"—should ever be asked to relate to something beyond their own precise experience! Exactly!" Clio finished.

"The public isn't nearly as closed-minded as Hollywood thinks," Erato purred. "They're only adding to the problem—"

Apollo cleared his throat. "If we might concentrate on the matter at hand . . ."

The Muses returned their attention to him en masse and merged their voices in a nine-toned chord to deliver a unified "Sorry, Apollo."

He loved when they did that.

"Obviously this isn't something we can tell anyone else about. Not yet, not until we know more. Whoever killed Zeus has a vested interest in stopping his resurrection. Those uninvolved still enjoy the fruits of the Return to the point where we cannot be sure of their loyalties."

"Apollo," Calliope began, "someone can kill *gods*. You don't know how certain Zeus's return is. Is it worth the risk to pursue this and possibly be slain yourself?"

"Weigh that against the risk of Zeus's wrath should he return, and a continuance of our current difficulties. I believe that to be the greater peril."

"What about Artemis?" asked Calliope. "Surely you can trust your twin sister?"

"I don't want to involve her just yet. If we're found out, the less she's involved, the less danger she'll be in, and—"

"Oh, but you're just fine endangering us."

"—and the better position she'll be in to help us if we get driven off Olympus." He fixed a stern gaze on the protesting Melpomene, Muse of tragedy, horror, and children's books. "I endanger you whether or not you're involved. You're Zeus's daughters and my own subordinates. Should anyone discover me, you nine are guilty by association. Working together, we're stronger."

Melpomene gave a wicked chuckle. "Oh, I know. I'm simply injecting a little conflict for the sake of drama."

Apollo sighed through a grudging smile. "Flex the Muse-muscles later, please."

"Use it or lose it."

"Time and place."

"But what are we to do, Apollo?" Calliope asked. "Secret meetings off Olympus are all well and good—"

"Though a movie theater is a tad clichéd," Terpsichore added.

"—but talk alone will only get us so far before it gets us hanged. So to speak."

Thalia patted her shoulder. "Nice phrasing."

"Thank you. Did you like it? I thought it could've been better."

"It was good for off the cuff! Maybe needs just a little polishing."

Apollo crossed his arms, considering just the right words to make a fine, thrusting point. "Hey!" he decided.

Again they turned toward him as one. "Sorry, Apollo."

It gave him a fantastic shiver.

"To answer your question, our next step is reconnaissance. Track down this mortal. Once you learn who he is, follow him. Try to figure out just what he's got to do with Zeus or what he could be doing to bring Zeus back."

"Might this fellow be one of Zeus's mortal children?" Calliope offered. "It seems likely if he's connected to resurrecting him. Dramatically speaking, anyway."

Apollo nodded. "It's possible. We know nothing of how Zeus was killed, nor the exact manner of his return, so for the moment it's only speculation."

"Or . . . it's foreshadowing!" Melpomene declared.

"This is reality, Melpomene," Apollo warned. "Even were it not, I'd rather the Muse of tragedy not be writing it."

"You forgot children's books."

"Yes, she's a modicum less depressing now," Erato said.

"Regardless. Find this mortal and follow him. Do not approach—not yet—and do it in shifts. All nine Muses following around a single mortal is bound to attract attention sooner or later. And I'm going to remind you all because, frankly, I worry that you're not taking this seriously enough: speak of this to no one."

Calliope nodded for all of them. "Don't mistake playful for ditzy, Apollo. You ought to know that much about us by now."

"Ooh," Melpomene snickered, "is *that* foreshadowing?"

Apollo ignored her.

Caught up in thought, Hermes belatedly realized that he was chewing on a discarded gummy worm. He spit it out and watched Apollo and the Muses file out of the theater as he pondered just what to do. It didn't take long. Really, Hermes didn't see that he had much choice. He liked Apollo, he really did.

It was a shame he'd have to tell the others.

CHAPTER SEVEN

"Forget Hephaestus's plasma screens, I don't care how enormous they are. When you're mortal-watching, they just don't offer the same video quality as a good starlit pool. And if you knew half of the secrets I do about plasma screens, you'd never want to get near the things."

—Hecate (blog entry, January 12, 2010)

"Oh, please. The only 'secret' Hecate knows about plasma screens is that she broke hers and Hephaestus refused to fix it for a decade. Don't ask how she broke it. She's . . . weird. Adopted, too, you know."

—Aphrodite (The Early Show with Danny O'Neill, January 14, 2010)

IN A CONCRETE, whitewashed chamber in the middle of a secret compound, Brittany Simons (a.k.a. Wynter Nightsorrow, a.k.a. the young woman from Chapter Four) sat tied to a chair. Her captors had tied her up with a distinct lack of mercy—the ropes binding her wrists cut and chafed until she'd abandoned trying to escape. Sweat beaded on her forehead under the blinding, hot lights. Every once in a while, her captors would come in to ask her questions or try to convince her to turn from her heathen ways, and each time she refused to answer with anything but curses. To those who observed, she was clearly miserable.

Yet inside, Wynter couldn't stop unsmiling. At last, some persecution! As a bonus, her captors had let slip that she was now held prisoner in what they described as a "secret compound". Jackpot!

Yes, Wynter hid her elation well. So well, in fact, that deep within the Olympian courtyards, Hecate gazed into a starlit pool displaying Wynter's distant image and saw nothing but suffering.

Though none were watching Hecate, the goddess's own displeasure was plainly apparent to those nonexistent observers: the insult was unimaginable! That these so-called Ninjas Templar would dare to desecrate one of her own temples was repugnant enough. That they would kidnap and attempt to "save" one of her favorite priestesses set her seething. That they had burst in on the cusp of a ritual of secrets enraged her beyond words!

Worse, not all of that rage was directed externally.

She demanded it repeatedly of herself: Why, *why* in the name of all that was shadowed did she have to pick that exact moment to share that particular secret? Hecate, goddess of night, mother of witches, queen of secrets, had a new secret: she was in deep, deep trouble.

She could have chosen some other secret with which to bless Wynter: The true name of the now-deceased Loch Ness monster (Larry), the first of the eleven secret "herbs and spices" (disturbingly, also Larry), or which of the Three Stooges was really a British agent (curiously, not Larry). Had she chosen to disclose any one of those secrets, she would have been free to exact retribution upon these Ninjas Templar and their masters. This is not to say that she was incapable of retribution as things stood, but the price was far too high. Dispensing divine wrath attracted the notice of her fellow immortals. Other gods paid attention to see if the wrath was directed at one of their own favorites, and if not, then simply for professional interest. Now that the Olympians were back, many of them anticipated the return of the annual Wrathy Awards, as well, and it paid to keep track of the competition. Any scrutiny of the situation would lead to the discovery of just what secrets Hecate had shared with Wynter:

The secrets of the Titans' prison.

Everyone knew of the Titan War in which Zeus, his siblings, and some mercenary giants barely defeated their elders in a battle that nearly shattered the world. (Scholars and poets knew it officially as the Titanomachy, but Athena decided "Titan War" had more kick.) Everyone knew that after the war, the Olympians imprisoned most of the Titans in eternal voids in Tartarus, the worst part of the underworld. Those were the broad strokes. The details were much less known and far more dangerous, and Hecate had given them out like Halloween candy.

It wouldn't matter that Wynter had been interrupted before she could write down everything; the very act of sharing such things with anyone could very likely get Hecate herself locked away in eternal nothingness.

The goddess stifled a scream. She shouldn't have shared it, but Wynter's devotion was so exuberant! The young woman began her worship before the Return, before she even had evidence that the goddess existed. She was trapped in a family that failed to understand her, her friends were long gone, and her college demanded tuition in payment for acceptance—tuition that she sacrificed to Hecate. With her adoration of the magic of night and secrets, Wynter was a kindred spirit who reminded the goddess of herself.

No one on Olympus listened to *her,* after all. No one cared. They were only her adopted family. Oh, sure, she was as powerful as they, but no one acknowledged it. When she originated the idea of hiding cheese in the crust of a pizza, none of the gods gave her credit. When she became a successful supernatural romance novelist, they didn't read her books. Heck, even after she created some of the most interesting monsters since the Return, they didn't pay her one single compliment. Hecate supported Zeus's death, supported the Return; she even knew who was responsible. The murderers met even now in a room Hermes thought was a secret. Yet did they ask her to help? Not even for a moment.

She just wanted someone to talk to, someone who understood.

Wynter understood.

So telling her about the Titans' prisons was a mistake. She'd deal with that. The pool in which she watched Wynter could only show her the room her priestess was in; she had no ties to the mortals who held her. They lurked in separate rooms, likely discussing their find and what to do about it.

It remained for Hecate to determine what she would do about them.

Elsewhere on Olympus in the secret chamber Hermes himself built long ago, five Olympians had gathered to tackle their own particular problems.

"You did it wrong," Hermes told the others.

"Did it *wrong?*" the goddess shot.

"If Zeus can still be brought back? Yes!"

"It was a trap," Ares snarled, turning his wrath on another god among them. "Ol' Zeus knew it wouldn't work! He just blurts out some bull about a god-killer, and you go and think he let it slip 'cause he's drunk! It was a loyalty test! You doomed us all!"

The smooth-voiced god whom he was addressing straightened up. "Zeus was drunk off his ass, believe me! Strongest ambrosia-liquor I've ever tasted. The poor fellow blacked out, didn't remember a word. I'd bet my life on it."

Hermes rolled his eyes. "Really, you already did, you know."

"Hey, I only passed on what I heard. It was her idea to kill him!" he blurted, pointing at the goddess.

"Okay, even if it ain't a trap," Ares went on, "point is the son of a Titan is coming back."

At that, the immortal who had been sitting silently in the corner cleared his throat, once.

Ares winced. "Didn't say bein' a son of a Titan is always a bad thing."

"*Might* be coming back," the goddess corrected.

"*Might be*'s as good as done, far as I'm concerned."

"But it's got something to do with this mortal?" the goddess asked.

Hermes nodded. "So Apollo thinks. And you know how he is with visions."

The god of war perked up. "Easy answer, then: find this poor loser, and kill him! Problem solved."

The silent god in the corner cleared his throat again.

Ares gritted his teeth. "What?"

Hades stood, moving out of the corner to stand behind Ares. His face was grim, his eyes deep. "Mortal deaths release . . . energies," came the answer.

"Hades is right," the goddess said. "We don't know enough. Killing him might very well lead to resurrecting Zeus. Somehow."

"Somehow?" Ares snarled.

"You know how these things go!"

"Yes." Hermes grinned. "You make one simple bet about who's prettiest, and suddenly the entire Trojan nation is wiped out!"

The goddess glared. "You just shut up about that, Hermes! The others were—I didn't—it wasn't my—shut up!"

He winked at her before going on. "Apollo did think the mortal might be a child of Zeus. That might even increase the chance that killing him could be what starts things in motion."

Hades gave what was, possibly, a conceding nod.

"Might. Might not." Ares shrugged. "One way to find out."

"It's a bad idea until we know more," Hermes said.

"Kill first, ask questions after!"

"Sage advice!" Hermes sniped. "Are you a god or a stereotype?"

"Yer a timid damn pussy, Hermes."

"Oh yes? Who risked himself to steal the god-killer in the first place, eh?"

"We didn't ask for your help!"

"Ah, well you did, actually. 'Don't tell our secret, Hermes! Steal the god-killer for us, Hermes!' With all 'due' respect, Ares, you're not the brains of this operation. Frankly, I don't even gather just what you bring to the table, so why don't you let the rest of us do the thinking and—"

Ares shot to his feet. "Yer all a bunch of pussies!"

Hades put a single hand on the war god's shoulder. His whisper close against Ares's ear somehow echoed through the room regardless. "We shall not kill him. Yet." A firm arm pushed Ares back to his seat before Hades returned to his corner.

"Okay," Ares tried, "so we haul out the god-killer again and off Apollo."

Protests echoed about the table from all but Hades, who merely shook his head.

"Yer worried about Poseidon's new 'no attackin' another god' rule? We're not attackin' him; we're killin' him!"

Hades stared at Ares with infinitely patient disapproval. "No."

"No one wants to investigate who killed Zeus," Hermes added. "We do it again and we might not be so lucky. Besides, Apollo's usually a decent chap."

"But—"

"We're not killing him, Ares," the goddess insisted.

"Okay, okay, it was just an idea," he said. "Damned good idea, if ya ask me . . ."

"So what, then?" asked the smooth-voiced god. "Ideas, anyone?"

"We have him followed, for starters," said the goddess suddenly. She turned to Hermes. "Any one of us can find a mortal to do a favor."

"Discreet," said Hermes. "I like it."

"Come on, following?" Ares grumbled. "That's it?"

"Yeah," the smooth-voiced god agreed, "that's not enough."

"We can't take action until we know what this mortal is destined to do. Apollo said he wasn't even sure if the vision was literal, so—"

Hermes brightened. "Oh, that's perfect! Look, we can't kill him, but we can't just let him go about his business, right? So, obviously, we find a way to distract him!"

Ares grinned. "Good solid boot to the head's always mighty distracting, I find."

The god gave a sly chuckle. "Not quite what I had in mind. But first, we've got to find the lucky fellow and get just a teensy bit of Aphrodite's help."

CHAPTER EIGHT

"Monster Slayer: *He keeps you safe! He lets you watch! Wednesday nights on the Adventure Channel!*"

—Monster Slayer *television promo*

THE LUCKY, SANDY-BLOND-HAIRED FELLOW now sought after by two separate groups of immortals resided in the college town of Bellingham, Washington, about twenty miles south of the Canadian border.

Despite Apollo's visions, Leif Karlson had never been to Paris. He did, however, spend an inordinate amount of his free time in cafés. It had little to do with coffee. Leif liked coffee just fine, but he wasn't a snob about it. What he liked more was the excuse to get out of his apartment ever since he lost his job. Though he made an effort to try a new café every once in a while, the Sacred Grounds Café topped a small list of favorites based on two factors. The first factor—free Wi-Fi—Sacred Grounds satisfied in epic proportions. The other was atmosphere.

It had occurred to Leif that anything worth thinking about was worth categorizing, and so he'd decided that atmosphere was a combination of the lighting, the attractiveness of the baristas, and the number of patrons in the place at any given time. As such, Sacred Grounds was also at the top of his list. The lighting was perfect (not too bright, not too dark, the perfect level of warmth); the baristas were top-notch (primarily female, primarily cute, and, also primarily, appearing to be just over twenty years old—so the twenty-six-year-old Leif could flirt with them without feeling creepy); and the number of patrons was usually just enough to give the place life without making it too loud.

Usually. Today was not one of those days.

He stood at the end of the bar, waiting for his drink order to make its way through a mass of people and wondering just what the heck was going on. Initially he counted himself lucky to get a table at all, though after placing his order, it was apparent that there were other empty tables as well. The sea of people hanging about, most of them women, centered mainly around a table in the corner and seemed more interested in getting a glimpse of whoever sat there than finding a spot of their own. Unfortunately, that didn't stop the stragglers from crowding the bar with drink orders to pass the time.

A celebrity of some sort? Maybe even one of the so-called "gods"? It was impossible to ignore the chatter of the women nearby.

"Can you believe he's here?"

"I know! I hear he just got back from filming a show in the mountains. He's even cuter in person."

"Ohmigod, did you see the episode where the monster just ripped his shirt right off? I nearly lost it then and there. So hot!"

"So very hot! I hear he's a son of one of the gods too. You know, like Herculor or whatever!"

"Really?"

"That's the rumor."

"Mm, Herculor. I've got to find something for him to sign!"

"Oh, I've got something he can sign, honey."

Both women exploded with laughter. Leif tried his best to get away from them before he threw up.

So apparently it was a celebrity, and likely that guy from TV who made a show out of slaying the monsters that had shown up soon after the "gods". Jason . . . Jason something. He couldn't recall. But so what if he was a celebrity? It's not like the guy would have anything to say to Leif. Maybe Jason Whatshisfinger would leave soon and give everyone else some peace. Leif was just thankful he'd managed to get a table.

The call from the barista came, finally. "Tall mocha on the bar for Leif!"

He reached for it only to be intercepted by the woman waiting beside him who snatched the cup first and glared as if he'd just stuffed a dead rabbit down her shirt. *"Excuse* me!"

"Excuse you? That's mine, sorry."

She gaped. "Is your name Lisa?"

"Leif."

"Exactly!"

The barista—a young blonde woman named Jen who reminded Leif of the cheerleader who repeatedly shot him down in high school—was focused on making the next order in an ever-growing queue and wasn't paying either of them a lick of attention.

"She said 'Leif,' actually," Leif tried again, reaching for his drink.

"Rude! Wait for your own latté!"

Annoyance clashed with amazement at the scope of the woman's mistake. All Leif could get out at first was, "That's not a—"

"Ugh!" She spat out the first sip and slammed Leif's mocha down, sloshing the contents across the counter before hurling her outburst at the barista.

"There's *chocolate* in this!"

"What the hell, lady? That's not your—"

The woman ignored him completely. "Hey! You put chocolate in my latté, you stupid—"

The barista spared her a hurried glance. "That's not your latté; that's his mocha. Please be patient." Though harried, she flashed Leif one of her customary smiles that he always assumed resulted from large tips. "I'll remake yours in a sec."

Before he could respond with more than a smile of his own, the latté princess came back with a, "No! You don't understand. That latté is for Jason Powers! Don't you know who that is? Now make it right! Now!"

Jen put some milk under the steamer. "Who's that? And if it's for him, why'd you take a drink?"

"You know damn well who he is! Now make my latté before he leaves!"

Jen grinned at him. "I thought she said it was Jason Powers's latté?"

"She did say—"

The woman smacked her hand on the bar. "Listen, you little slut—"

"Hey!" Jen and Leif both shouted at once. Jen whirled on her and kept going before Leif could find the words. "I called *his* name; you drank his damn mocha! For crying out loud, lady, you were in line behind him! Shut up, be patient, and try not to be such a virulent bitch!"

". . . Yeah!" Leif added to what he hoped was great effect.

The entire bar line was staring now, all focused on the crazed woman. It took a few moments under Jen's glare for her to regain her wits. "Fine! See if I ever come back here again!" For a second it appeared she might manage more until she turned and stormed off.

The remains of Leif's mocha went with her.

"Hey!"

Jen turned back to the espresso machine. "That felt good."

Leif pointed after her. "She—the nutbar took my mocha!"

"Go ahead and sit down." She drew a breath. "I'll have someone bring yours out to you."

"Yeah, okay. Thanks," he answered. Why was he feeling stupid now? He wasn't the one who took the wrong damn drink. "I was just about to tell her off, myself, you know." He turned to go as she nodded, then stopped. "Jason Powers is here?"

"And about five hundred more fans like her, I'd guess. Fun, huh?"

"Frigging insane." At least he could get away from the crowded bar. He returned to the table he'd staked out, sat down, and powered up his laptop. "Leif, Lisa," he grumbled to himself. "How the heck do those names sound at all the same?" It infuriated him more the longer he thought about it.

The laptop was taking its sweet time to boot up. He turned to the dark-haired woman occupying the table beside him whom he might have found attractive were he in any mood to care. "Geez, it's nuts in here today, huh?"

She looked up from the smartphone she'd been tapping on and smiled behind her glasses. "Jason Powers is here."

"Heh. You knew, then." Great, another one. He'd just wanted a nodding grunt from her that would kill a bit of time until his laptop was ready. He hadn't really intended to start a conversation. "I didn't take you for a fan, all the way over here."

"I'm not. A fan, rather."

"Oh, whew! Yeah, you look too smart for that." Thank goodness! "Bunch of fan-girls running around here, crowding up the place and acting vacant over nothing. Show's all fake anyway."

The woman's smile at his first comment melted away at his second. "What's fake about it? He makes the journey out to where the monsters live and fights them without any help. It's not staged, if that's what you think. That's why people like it."

"Oh, come on. He just goes out there and kills stuff. What's the big deal? It's a glorified fishing show, for crying out loud. Just because he's attractive and muscular—" He flung an arm toward the scene of his bar altercation. "I mean, did you see the kind of idiot it attracts? Lowest common denominator!"

The woman frowned and set down her muffin. "Jason Powers risks his life and protects his crew every time he goes out there! It's real, it's exciting, and that 'lowest common denominator' is what makes a show successful!"

"Yeah, right." Leif didn't bother hiding an eye roll. "Probably scouts the whole place by helicopter and dopes down the monsters before fighting them, just like that one wilderness-guy who they caught sleeping in hotels that were 'rainforest-adjacent.' Even if it is real, it just makes him an idiot risking his life."

She snorted. "If that makes you feel better about yourself."

"What? It's just a mindless reality show! What next, *Busy Highway Jaywalker?* How about something original, with plot and writing and—"

"Wait, *bona fide* monsters show up in the world, ravaging the countryside, and you don't think that's interesting? How jaded are you?"

"Fiction has imagination; reality's just boring. If you're not a fan, why're you defending it?"

The woman smirked then handed him a business card from her wallet. "Tracy Wallace, field producer for *Monster Slayer.*"

"Ah, so you're glad dangerous monsters are running around."

She had the nerve to roll her eyes. "No, that's why we *hunt* them. 'Terrifying' and 'interesting' aren't mutually exclusive. We provide a valuable service and entertain people at the same time."

Leif shook his head, put her card facedown on the table, and turned back to his laptop. It had finished booting. Conversation over.

"Right. Whatever. Thanks for filling my café with brainless meatbags."

"My pleasure. You have yourself a fantastic day, sir. Be sure to catch *Monster Slayer* Wednesdays at 8 p.m. on the Adventure Channel."

Leif grunted and assumed it counted as the last word. It was a good, decisive grunt, with just the right amount of contempt. The woman gave no response, focused instead on texting someone. *Good.*

Why did he talk to her, anyway?

Leif happily went on with the business of ignoring her—or tried to. He logged on to the online poker Web site, where he had recently discovered he could make a fairly decent living, and promptly lost three straight hands. So apparently he didn't play well when cranky. Or distracted. Cards floated before him, but all he could think of were things he could've said to the fan at the bar or the producer beside him. That none of the comebacks were very good—or at least not good enough to bother with—only rankled him further.

Distracted, distracted, distracted. It was like the day that weird old man at the table beside him whistled the same tuneless pattern over and over until Leif finally had to flee the café to get it out of his head. He considered changing tables away from the woman, though he wasn't sure it would help even if there were a table to change to.

He lost a fourth hand and then a fifth, which led him to flick Tracy Wallace's card off the table with a single finger thrust. That she utterly failed to react didn't help his mood.

It was then that the sound of squawking from across the café caught his attention. Jason Powers was leaving. The commotion caught Tracy's attention too. Or maybe it was that the tall, chiseled, muscular hero-type waved to her and called her name. Probably it was that. Still texting, she stood and acknowledged Powers with a wave of her hand that had the entire group of fan-girls staring daggers at her. She rushed off, heading for the exit with Powers and his harem in tow.

Leif breathed a sigh of relief and was immediately dealt three of a kind. Clearly Tracy Wallace was cursed.

She wasn't gone more than a minute before he noticed that she'd left her wallet behind. Leif glanced toward the door, expecting her to return for it, yet there was no sign of her. He grabbed the wallet, half standing to try to catch her before he stopped and sat back down. Why should he bother? If she was so damn smart and successful, let her come back for it herself. He tucked it inside his laptop case for safe-keeping.

After all, he wasn't a thief. His father had instilled "Thou shalt not steal!" pretty deeply into his head a long time ago, so he supposed he was just taking it to keep anyone else from stealing it. Or something. He was going to turn it in to the barista when he left, but five winning hands later, he completely forgot about it.

The two Muses sitting three tables away, however, did not.

CHAPTER NINE

"From what we can tell, certain Olympian gods —who may take any generic human form they wish—rarely appear as themselves in public, preferring to remain unnoticed outside of official events. Therefore, should someone looking like a god ever actually approach you in public, it is far more likely to be someone with a good mask pulling your leg. Even so, anyone claiming to be a god who does not look like one is also quite likely pulling your leg because, let's face it, who the heck are you to warrant a visit from a god?"

—How to Tell the Olympian Gods
(and What Not to Tell Them)

THE FOLLOWING DAY found Leif in the same café drinking the same drink in nearly the same seat. The place was blessedly devoid of reality TV stars, though there did seem to be one or two more women hanging about than normal. Maybe they were hoping for a return of the Big Damn Hero, or maybe it was just coincidence. This time he managed to get his drink without having it stolen, so frankly he didn't care. The extra women made for good eye candy.

Garbage-television producer Tracy Wallace's wallet was tucked in his laptop bag. He'd belatedly discovered it after he left yesterday, called the number on one of her business cards, and told her he'd be at the café again the next day if she wanted it back. Yes, he was that guy who didn't like her show. No, he didn't want a reward. No, he didn't want to bother leaving it at the front desk of her hotel (even if it was on his way, which he didn't tell her). She was lucky he was honest, though he didn't tell her that either; the sixty-second conversation was long enough. He hoped the conversation when she picked it up would be even shorter.

Leif was a quarter of the way through his mocha and considering the foolish risk of drawing on an inside straight when he sensed someone approaching. Instead of Ms. Wallace, the newcomer was a man, tall and comfortably dressed in a formal, Eddie Bauer sort of way. Leif gave him his attention without being sure why. The man put his hand on the back of the empty chair at Leif's table.

"I beg your pardon. Might I make use of this chair?"

"All yours."

The matter ended, Leif returned his attention to his poker hand and opted to keep the ace, king and discard the rest. The first card he drew would've completed the straight, and so caught up was Leif in cursing his choice that it took him a moment to notice that the man hadn't taken the chair to another table, but had actually sat down at Leif's.

"Oh, um . . . sorry. Didn't realize that's what you meant." Numerous nearby tables were conspicuously empty. Leif prepared to rebuff a sales pitch.

"You don't mind, I trust. It's just myself and my tea. I abhor standing and drinking, and there are no open tables."

"Uh, there's that one." Leif pointed. "And that one. That one too. Oh, that one has a free newspaper on it—"

"Yes, a poor lie," the man admitted. He leaned closer. "I wish to speak to you directly, Leif Karlson, and am trying to be discreet about it."

Leif blinked. "Um . . . flattered but not interested, thanks. I've got company coming in a sec anyhow." Who was this guy?

The stranger scowled. "Perhaps I should introduce myself: I am Apollo. I expect you've heard of me."

Leif laughed. "Apollo?" A few heads turned.

"Lower your voice, mortal."

"Right. Apollo. Sure. And I'm a Nigerian prince with millions of dollars for you!"

The Olympian wannabe arched an eyebrow. "Have you truly been living in a cave for the past nine months? With your hands over your eyes, perhaps, and carrots jammed in your ears?"

"Hey, just because there're 'gods' now doesn't mean I'll take some guy on his word that he's one of them. Billions of people in the world, and 'Apollo' wants to talk to me? Right."

The man's eyes narrowed. "I dislike your tone, mortal. Even a god's patience has limits."

"Mm. You know, you don't look like the guy in the photos. Shouldn't you be driving a sun chariot or something? And where's your bow, your lyre? Geez, didn't you research this at all?"

"Obviously I am in disguise," the man responded. He caught Leif's eyes with his own as he did so. Unable to look away, Leif gasped.

Each Olympian has the ability to make his or her divinity manifest, be it a wide burst to cover a crowd or narrowly focused on a single person, such as, say, a blond, skeptical poker player in a café. Power flared in Apollo's crystal blue gaze. Within it Leif witnessed the shining glory of the sun, brilliantly blazing majesty, and . . . dolphins, for some reason. The god stared into Leif as the young man's mind gaped, his soul quaked, and his stomach tried to claw its way out of his ear. It was like getting a root canal from an amorous supermodel—painful but awesome—and he couldn't look away.

And then it stopped. Leif swallowed.

"So. Apollo. Um . . . crap. Heh. Sorry, um, about that." His stomach plunged back to where it belonged, clearly unhappy about the trip. "So . . . um . . ."

Apollo smirked. "At a loss for words? A little unusual for you, from what I've been told."

"What you've been told? That's . . . Why?"

"It's all right to be nervous, Mr. Karlson. We Olympians tend to have that effect."

"Who said I was nervous? I'm just, ya know, surprised."

He swallowed again, surprised at how nervous he was. Never for one moment since the Return did Leif ever believe the Olympians were actual gods, but the fact remained that they were inarguably powerful, whatever they were. The most powerful person Leif ever spoke with was the chairman of the art department in college, which was hardly adequate preparation for this experience. On the other hand, Leif had once personally forced Alexander the Great to surrender—sure, only in a computer game, but talking to a god was bizarre enough to easily slip the tag of reality. *So hey*, he told himself, *you've done this before. No biggie.*

And to think his mom thought those games were a waste of time.

The god smiled. "Nervous, surprised. Whichever makes you feel better. But there's no need for that, you know. Gods are just like mortals, only . . . better. You have heard of Dionysus, yes? I believe *Maximum* ran an article on him recently titled 'God of Frat Boys' or some such."

Leif considered the best way to ask if Apollo was going with the standard "put someone at ease by telling them a pointless story" trick and finally decided on, "Uh-huh."

"One of the twelve gods on the Olympian council for a time, yet he was part mortal when he was born."

"That so."

"It's a long story. Born of Zeus and a mortal woman, then later Zeus elevated him to full godhood with a bit of star-stuff and some really good fudge."

Leif blinked. "Some . . . really good fudge?"

"Oh, there's more to it than that, of course. I wasn't there at the time, and Zeus had many more children to whom he granted no such boon."

Leif cleared his throat. "Came all the way out here just to tell me that, huh?"

"In a manner of speaking," Apollo answered. "Do you remember your father, Mr. Karlson?"

"What? I talked to him just last week."

"Are you sure he's your real father?"

"Well, yeah, we do weekly blood tests just to make sure. Doesn't everyone?"

Apollo scowled. "My question was a serious one."

"Oh, come on. A serious question is what do I think of gay marriage or climate change. 'Golly, Leif, didja ever think your daddy might be Zeus?' How'd you even ask that with a straight face?"

"Foolishly glib. Do consider it a moment. Do you look like your father? Act like him? Could you possibly have any reason to suspect—?"

Leif mimed typing on the laptop as he cut him off. "Dear Mom: How are you? I am fine. By the way, a god called you a slut today. Ever doink any guys with big thunderbolts? How's the weather?"

Apollo didn't laugh. "So you've never had any dreams of Zeus? Read about him? Had any interest in him you'd call unusual?"

"I read about lots of people. Doesn't mean they're my dad."

"Mr. Karlson, I have no wish to do you grievous harm, but I have very little time. Answer my question now, please."

Leif had heard more sinister death threats in his life—he gamed online, after all—though this was the first time he'd experienced it face-to-face. Somehow that made it easier to shrug it off. "Well, yeah, I read about him. I read about all you guys. I haven't for a while, though. And never particularly about any one god."

"Not for a while? Why is that?"

Leif shrugged. "Just lost interest, I guess. That why you're here? Wouldn't it be easier to hire a publicist instead of doing one-on-one interviews?"

"I dislike delegation."

"You're really bad at determining whether a question is serious or not, huh?"

"You're really bad at knowing whom not to criticize."

"Just sayin'."

"Enough of this. I shall make my point."

Without warning, every sound in the café ceased. All else continued: conversing patrons' lips moved, customers entered, drinks were made—it was as if someone pressed the mute button and no one seemed to notice but Leif. The sheer abruptness of the silence was enough to make him jump, and the jump was enough to make him feel stupid.

"What just happened?" he asked, surprised to be able to hear himself and immediately feeling even more foolish for trying to speak when he'd thought he'd been muted. At least no one knew that part but him.

Apollo motioned to the rest of the café. "We cannot hear them; they cannot hear us. I do not wish to be overheard."

"Cool. What's it called?"

"Excuse me?"

"Well, it's a power. It's got to have a name, right? Sonic Shield? Sound Bubble? Hey, why didn't you open with this?"

Apollo ignored the questions. "We've been observing you, Mr. Karlson. By all accounts you appear an average man: unemployed, sarcastic, judgmental, easily irritated, and skilled at online games of chance. What you are *not* is heroic, bold, or particularly remarkable."

"Nice of you to at least insult me in private."

"I'm not finished."

"Then you shouldn't pause like that."

"A brief while ago, Mr. Karlson, I had a vision of you. Multiple visions, in fact, that strongly suggested you will be involved with the resurrection of Zeus. This would seem at odds with everything we've observed in you—"

There was that "we" again. "Wait, we? We who? You mean to say all the gods are watching my unremarkable ass?" Great, now he was insulting himself.

"No, none of the other gods know of this. However, you may have noticed a number of lovely women keeping watch on you. In that time, you've done nothing that we can discern as being related to Zeus's return."

"I'm sorry?"

"Apology accepted. I have decided it's time for you to pursue the visions more actively."

"Well," Leif declared, "good for you, then."

"That sounded like a refusal."

"How do you know these visions are right? Those things are deceptive, you know."

Apollo raised an eyebrow. "You know of such things?"

"I watch movies, read books, play games. There's always some twist in any prophecy about a 'Chosen One,' isn't there?"

"I did not call you a Chosen One."

"Close enough, and my question stands: How do you know this isn't some horrible trick? Didn't work out so well for Anakin Skywalker, you know."

"This is not a movie."

"Not yet."

"What?"

"Look, if you want Zeus back, why're you the only god who knows about it?"

Apollo frowned deeper. "Complicated."

"Uh-huh." Leif frowned back. "So say I do as you're asking—"

"Always a wise choice for a mortal to do a god's bidding."

"Yeah, but what do you actually want me to do? Anything to do with those 'lovely women' following me around? 'Cause that couldn't hurt."

Apollo didn't answer. Leif couldn't be sure if the god was choosing his words or just pausing for effect.

"The visions," he spoke finally, "were not that detailed. Yet it stands to reason you would have a better chance of fulfilling them if you actively pursued them, researched Zeus, or made some other modicum of effort. You accomplish nothing by sitting in this café playing games of chance."

Leif pointed to his laptop. "Pays the bills," he said. "Fun too. Besides, I get the feeling the other gods don't know about this because they wouldn't like it."

Apollo gave no answer.

Leif leaned back, arms crossed. "That's it, isn't it?" Treating this whole exchange like the diplomacy segment of a computer game was working pretty well, he realized. More fun, too—computer game diplomacy was always so limited.

"They would not oppose it." Apollo took a sip of tea.

Leif had learned to write his name when he was four and immediately spent the entire afternoon practicing on the walls of his bedroom with a permanent marker. Upon seeing *Leif* scrawled over every surface below three feet high, his mother asked him if he knew who was responsible. Leif suspected the look on his face when he blamed it on the dog (who was never a good speller) was more convincing than Apollo's current expression.

"You're a lousy liar."

The god's smile was bitter as he set the cup down. "I am aware of this."

"So none of them want Zeus back, which basically means either I tick all of them off if I do what you want, or tick you off if I don't—and as far as I can tell, there's only one of you. Lousy odds on helping you."

"Have you read *The Iliad*, Mr. Karlson?

"Long time ago, yeah. Skipped the part where they list all the boats for a chapter or three."

"Do you recall the part when the Greeks insult a priest of mine who comes to ransom a kidnapped Trojan? So many plague arrows did I shoot at the Greeks that day. Consider now the important distinction that none of the other Olympians would know you were helping, while declining just now would most certainly be apparent to me. My stake in this is far beyond such minor indignities as an insult to the priesthood."

Leif bit the inside of his cheek, mulling that point a bit and finding his second in-person threat to have a little more traction than the first. On the other hand, what was he supposed to do, wander around calling out for Zeus? It sounded like an epic waste of time, to say nothing of the problems of being a pawn in some Olympian chess game. Weaseling out of it sounded a whole lot easier. Now that was something he was good at.

"So," he began, "you'll punish me for not doing what you need me to do—"

"Correct."

"—except you don't know what it is that you need me to do in the first place. Maybe my doing nothing *is* what you need me to do. You think of that?"

"You cannot resurrect a god by accident."

"Won't know until you don't try."

Apollo grimaced. "Frankly without the vision, my mind would boggle at the concept of you being capable at all, but the fact is, you have the potential. You must try!"

Leif chuckled. "A little green guy once said, 'Try not. Do, or do not.' Until you've got some strong idea of what it is I need to do, I'm choosing the latter. And maybe I'll tell the other gods what you're pulling if you keep harassing me, eh?"

Apollo fixed him with a glare like the beating desert sun—or what Leif assumed the beating desert sun would be like, anyway, having grown up in the near-perpetual showers of northwestern Washington.

"Mr. Karlson, those who threaten gods rarely have the chance to make further mistakes." The god held the gaze, and Leif couldn't look away. Sweat trickled down his back. His mouth parched. His entire body felt as limp as a dishrag. "What makes you think they would take your word against mine?"

Leif swallowed. Apollo's gaze cooled.

"You wouldn't really hurt me," Leif managed. "You need me. Just . . . let me think about it, okay?"

Even as he said it, Leif was fairly sure he wouldn't do a damn thing. Well, maybe if it were as easy as pushing a button or something, but anything more than that and he wasn't getting involved. True gods or no, getting caught up in their affairs sounded like a colossally stupid idea, especially for the weaker side. The others would find out eventually, and they'd stop him.

Plus, the latest *Complete Warfare* game was coming out tomorrow. He had plans to immerse himself in that as much as humanly possible.

Apollo took another sip of his tea, never letting go of Leif's gaze. Leif broke first and did his best to disguise his slipping nerve as confident detachment. He guessed it worked about as well as his childhood dog could spell. Then motion at the café entrance caught his eye: Tracy Wallace had returned. She scanned the café for the holder of her wallet.

He had only a moment to wonder if she'd be able to enter the god's sound bubble when it ceased, and the café ambiance flooded back into Leif's ears as abruptly as it had gone. Leif's startled-yet-manly flinch caught Tracy's attention just as he knocked his own mocha out of his hand. The cup struck the edge of the table and would have spilled to the floor had not Apollo darted down to catch it inches from impact. Tracy had the nerve to smirk.

Apollo smirked as well and set the cup back on the table. "These sorts of things were always so much easier three thousand years ago. I shall be patient with you for the moment, Mr. Karlson. We shall see what fruit that bears." He stood. Tracy began to make her way toward them. "In the meantime, we will continue to watch you. Should you pass up an obvious opportunity, I will hear of it."

Leif cleared his throat and gathered up the cup again in an attempt to recover. "Fine. My company's here, so you should probably go if you want to keep this a secret."

With a final stern look, Apollo turned to leave. His back was to Leif as he passed Tracy. Leif had only a moment to gasp at the suspiciously sharp pain that pieced his chest before it vanished and he found himself smiling excitedly and standing to meet the suddenly lovely television producer.

Outside, Thalia attempted to console an increasingly frustrated Apollo who was walking in disguise down the sidewalk. "It's just the hero's journey. This is how it's supposed to happen! He's got the call to adventure; now he's resisting. This is how it always goes."

"No, it is not how it always goes. They sometimes go right away. The brave ones do."

"Oh, very well, not always. All I'm saying is it's not the end of the world. So he's not answering the call right away—you just have to be patient. I always thought it more interesting when heroes do the resisting thing at first anyway."

"I'm not looking for interesting, Thalia. A great many things depend upon this."

The Muse slid her arm through his and leaned her head on his shoulder. "It'll turn out all right." She gave his arm a pat.

What worried Apollo, of course, was that things did not always turn out all right. Even if a hero did finally take up the call, the typical events that persuaded him to do so tended to be decidedly unpleasant things that the hero—or more importantly, those who demanded his aid in a café with patience far beyond what was deserved—might have avoided if he hadn't been so damned reluctant in the first place. This assumed Apollo could even apply the term "hero" to Leif at all.

Perhaps Apollo would have been even more worried if he or any of the Muses had spotted the mortal watching Leif Karlson. This concern would likely have inflamed further with the knowledge that the mortal's mother was an immortal conspirator responsible for Zeus's murder. Had Apollo known that the conspirators had persuaded Aphrodite to pierce Leif's heart with an invisible arrow of love designed to preoccupy him with lustful distraction, an arrow which she shot from the café's kitchen door moments after Apollo stood and walked away . . .

Well, why dwell in the hypothetical? Apollo did not know.

Neither, for that matter, did Leif.

Neither did Tracy Wallace.

Neither did the president of the United States, the Society for Archery-free Cafés, nor the director of the Red Herring Fishing Society.

Aren't lists fun?

CHAPTER TEN

TO: *All Olympians*
FROM: *King Poseidon*
RE: *Release of monstrous creatures*

Congratulations to all of us on a successful first press conference announcing our Return. Many of you have suggested the return of monstrous creatures to the world. We have all bred a number of them during the past few millennia for the creature design contests; they now swell the pocket dimension in which we've stored them nearly full to bursting. You may therefore release half of them into the mortal world—or as many as you can until I say otherwise, I have yet to decide. I know you will all agree that such measures will make the world more interesting and give the mortals something to do.

Furthermore, I see no reason you may not give occasional aid to mortals against the monsters if you wish, or sabotage the efforts of undeserving mortals to slay one of your own creations if you wish that. Whatever. Yet heed this command: do not allow the mortals to know that it is we who sent the monsters into the world! Mortal resentment toward any god in this matter will eventually spread to cost all of us worship. This is also for their own good: they may not admit it, but mortals crave heroism and things to slay.

Finally, let it be known that my octo-shark is the most fearsome beast in history! If a mortal can kill it, I'll eat my trident. Or maybe I'll just use my trident to skewer the one responsible; I'll ride that wave when it comes.

—*Inter-Olympian memo, June 19, 2009*

"USUALLY YOU LET SLIP what sort of beast you're looking to tangle with, 'time we get this far. I'm thinking either you're angling to make a surprise of it, or you don't have a damn clue yourself." Dave pulled his hot dog from the campfire, eyeballed it for some ineffable quality, and then bit off the tip before returning the rest to the heat. "Last surprise I had was the harpy," he added, his mouth still full. "Didn't much care for that."

Dave eyeballed Tracy and Jason across the fire with much the same scrutiny he'd given the hot dog. The *Monster Slayer* cameraman, Dave had a face that suggested he'd chosen the proper side of the lens on which to work. His personality wasn't much better, but he had a great eye for camerawork.

Of course, he'd had two eyes before the harpy. The shot he'd managed to get at the cost of his other eye was the same one that put *Monster Slayer* on the map. Tracy admired his dedication.

"We don't know exactly what it is," she answered. "The ranger whose horse it ate claimed it was somewhat man-shaped and about ten feet tall."

"He saw it from a distance, don't forget," Jason added.

"Whatever it is, it's about half a day's hike from here to its territory, given the reports. And it cut the horse in half with one blow. Ate the ranger's dog entirely."

Dave grunted. "Wide lens, then."

Jason flashed a grin and bit into his own hot dog with zero scrutiny. "The things you get me into."

"Hey, I've got a feeling about this one, all right? It'll be good," Tracy said.

"As good as when I saved those hikers that cyclops captured?" Jason asked. He never missed a chance to mention his favorite episode.

"Maybe. I've got a strong sense of something. Call it producer's intuition. Strong intuition." She turned to Dave with a smirk. "Like he wouldn't jump at any excuse to go to Vegas."

"Damn right," Jason said, "and like you wouldn't either. You have fun with your new friend last night, Tracy? I know you went out after him." He winked with all the discretion of a nude crossing guard.

Dave turned his eye to her. "What's this, now?"

About a ten years her senior, Dave was protective of her in a way she neither needed nor wanted, and the same went for his advances toward her when the show first began. At least she had to turn him down only once before he backed off. His protective attitude started after that, likely an attempt at keeping her available until she came around and fell for him or whatever. She supposed it was better than constantly fending off his advances, especially since he was too good at his job to replace.

"Nothing," she told him. "Just a weirdo."

Dave grunted. "Vegas has 'em in spades."

"Pun intended?"

"How's that?"

Jason laughed. "This one wasn't from Vegas. He trailed her all the way from Bellingham. Stole the poor guy's heart, then broke it! Come on. Tell the story."

"No." She fixed Jason with a warning glare. Sometimes even hearing about another man making a pass at her would foul Dave's mood. At best, he'd be even more of a crank. At worst, he'd be too distracted to do his best work. She hoped Jason would get it.

His nod assured her he did, yet Jason had a habit of thinking it more fun to pretend otherwise. "If you don't, I will."

Yup, she thought. There we go.

"Yeah, c'mon, Tracy." If Dave's smirk were any more satisfied, it'd have started clapping on its own. "Tell us all the story of the poor man whose heart you broke."

Tracy removed her glasses. She polished them with the end of her sleeve while she stalled for time and considered the long odds that Jason would let it go if she refused. "Fine. You'd just embellish it all." The largest spider she could find was going to find its way into his tent.

It is a little-known fact that the act of beginning a story sends a miniscule spark through the nether-stuff that binds together what mortals have obsessively labeled as reality. Such sparks speed near-instantaneously to the most appropriate Muse, who then decides whether or not to aid in the story's telling based on numerous criteria: the subject of the story, the worthiness of the teller, and, most important, the local "whether patterns" (i.e., whether or not the Muse is already sufficiently entertained or feels like lifting a finger at that particular moment).

By virtue of being a true story, the spark set off by the beginning of Tracy's tale burned with a weak historical flavor. It sped its way through the Earth's core to Clio, who at that very moment was in Paris attending the opening of a new exhibit at the Napoleonic Museum and who frankly—and some would say anticlimactically—couldn't be bothered.

The irony (and Muses do love irony, which either adds more or less irony in this case; authorities are undecided at the time of this writing) is that, had Tracy intended to make the story funny rather than as dull as possible so as to rapidly end the conversation, the spark would have traveled the grand total of twenty-five feet. Such was the distance to where Thalia perched in a pine tree, watching the whole affair—or had been watching, anyway, until getting drawn into a conversation of body language with a particularly belligerent owl. Though the whims of Muses are impossible to predict, it's highly likely Thalia would've taken up the cause of a story told right in front of her, were it in her area of expertise.

But it wasn't, so she didn't. On the plus side, it would leave her less distracted when what happens later happens.

Later.

On a further plus side, the preceding tangent has caused us to happily miss the entire bit where Tracy tells how she returned to the Sacred Grounds café to retrieve her wallet from the suddenly love-struck Leif—who was both less obnoxious (in the sense that he was being friendly) and more obnoxious (in the sense that he was, if you follow, being "friendly"). Moreover, we have missed the word-for-word recap of his clumsy attempt at kissing her hand, the description of how he called across the café to order an unwanted drink for "the most beautiful woman in the world," and the tedious account of his wounded denial that he had, in fact, stolen her wallet just to have an excuse to see her again. Under normal circumstances it would be possible to go back and review such things in greater detail; however, there is a horde of bloodthirsty creatures scheduled to soon descend upon the campsite, and they are, as you may imagine, particularly touchy about being kept waiting.

We now rejoin Tracy's narrative as she describes her escape from the situation.

"I don't know why I told him where our next hunt was. You know how sometimes things feel more persuasive if they're detailed, right? I should've said, 'I have to go now, I have to catch a plane,' or something. Or, 'I've an appointment,' or maybe even, 'If I don't leave now, I'm going to chew my own arm off.'"

"Last one's tougher than it sounds," Dave commented.

"But anyway, I specifically tossed out that I needed to catch a plane to Vegas, and the rest just spilled out when he asked. I was rushing, I wasn't thinking. So then I get out of there, not looking back, right? Down the street to the hotel, went up to my room, finished packing. I didn't even think of the guy again until I checked out and saw him sitting there in the lobby."

"Yeah, sure. He was on your mind all the way up that elevator, I bet," Jason teased. "Your handsome geek, stealing your heart."

"Bite me."

"Ask nicely."

"Let her tell it," Dave shot.

Jason just smirked.

"He say anything?"

"Nope, just watched me. I think he said, 'Hi,' at the door as I left, but all that got him was a nod and me walking faster. In hindsight I might have spotted him at the airport when we were checking bags. I figured I imagined it."

"See? Fantasizing."

Tracy ignored the comment. "So long story short, he followed us to Vegas. I don't know how he found out where we were staying. I guess he bribed the room service guy or something because the next thing I know, I'm opening the door and he's standing there with the cart looking giddy."

"Psycho," Dave grumbled.

"Just what I thought, but I was too stunned to say anything. He wasn't really threatening or aggressive or anything. Perfect gentleman—I mean, except for the stalking bit. Didn't even have a creepy smile on his face or anything. Just apologized and asked if he could come in and talk."

"You let him in?"

"No, I didn't let him in! I couldn't even say anything. I just slammed the door on him after I regained my wits."

"And grabbed your sundae," Jason added.

"Well, duh, I'd already paid for it. Except a few minutes later, he was still there, just hanging out in the hallway. I mean I guess I could've just ignored him, but I yanked the door back open and told him to go the hell away or I'd call security."

"He had the cutest lost puppy look on his face," Jason said.

Dave shifted. "You were there?"

"Headed back to my room with a little company."

Tracy rolled her eyes. Jason had a knack for finding fans—female ones, especially—anywhere they went. Or perhaps they just were attracted to his looks and cash and weren't fans until he informed them how fantastic he was. He was actually frighteningly subtle about that last part too. At least at first.

"So up comes Jason and asks if everything's okay—and you know you could've gone on past; I can fight my own battles."

"Yeah, but women love when men come to the rescue."

She skewered a marshmallow and plunged it into the fire. "I didn't need rescuing, and since when do you care what I think?"

"I meant the other woman. Had to keep her engine running, ya know."

Tracy's eyes rolled anew. "Uh-huh, no one cares." She pulled her immolated marshmallow from the fire, waited for the flames to blacken it completely before blowing it out, and then pulled the charred perfection off the skewer to pop it into her mouth. "Soh thehnm Jhashon—"

Jason cut her off. "I told him he'd better stop bothering the lady or I wouldn't wait for security to toss him out. That usually works. Except I think I'm less intimidating when I'm drunk, 'cause he didn't just turn and run."

Tracy swallowed quickly and nearly choked to speak before Jason could elaborate. "Well, no. But then he left."

"Ha! Just left? The guy freaks out!"

"Jason—" So much for not riling Dave with the rest.

"Accused us of trying to have a threesome! Says that's gross, that he won't stand for it unless—this was the cutest part—unless he was involved."

"Threesome, eh?" Dave grumbled. "Do that a lot?"

"Well . . ." Jason teased.

"No!" Tracy stabbed another marshmallow. "I nearly told him he was welcome to go with Jason and his lady friend. Before I could, he starts going off on Jason—"

"Getting all up in my face, yelling that I should mind my own business and calling me . . . what was it?"

Tracy grinned. "Called you a 'testosterized meatbag.'"

"Yeah, what's that even mean?"

Tracy figured he could look it up and rushed toward the topic's end. "People were opening doors, looking out. Freaking nightmare, and at that point you've got the car-wreck thing going; I should've just closed the door on him, but I couldn't look away, right? Finally Jason grabs him by the back of the shirt, hauls him to the elevator, and shoves him in."

"Told him if he came back, I wouldn't use the elevator to get him down next time."

"Door closed," she said. "End of story."

"I still say you went out after I was gone and—"

Tracy glared. She didn't mind the teasing so much as the risk of putting Dave into a mood. "Don't push the temper of a woman with a hot poker in her hand."

"Oh, is that what you went after him for? A hot—"

She put up a hand. "Did you hear that?"

"Hear what?"

"She's just trying to change the subject."

"No," Tracy insisted. "I'm not. Shh." She really wasn't but was grateful for the distraction all the same.

As everyone shut up to listen, a chorus of distant mewling became distinct. It carried toward the camp from a swarm of whitish-gray motes that glowed in the moonlight with the occasional flash of red or blue. Dave stood to peer with his one eye. Scores of tiny greenish eyes became discernable within the swarm, each gazing back at them.

With dawning recognition, Tracy abandoned her earlier welcoming attitude. "Razorwings!"

"Aw, hell!"

Jason clambered to his feet. "Are you sure?"

"Get to the SUV!"

Greek "mythology" is festooned with stories of fearsome creatures: the Erymanthian boar, the Lernaean hydra, the tickle-spider of western Achaea. All are creatures that strike fear in the hearts of listeners and posed a mortal danger to both the peoples they tormented and the heroes who fought them. These monsters' formidability sprang from their terrible weapons and unique strengths. While in ancient times, the luckier mortals possessed bronze shields to protect themselves from such foes, as well as swords or cunning to wield against them, the monsters claimed massive, razor-sharp teeth, eyes that could turn a person to stone, or fiery breath. Even should a hero manage to avoid such dangers, he or she still had to contend with the beasts' thick hides, acidic blood, or powers of flight.

While many of the monsters that had appeared following the Return possessed such classic attributes, in the modern world, with its more abundant weapons and more organized humanity, mankind had other weaknesses at which a monster could strike. And so it came to be that the creatures eventually dubbed "razorwings" were among the most fearsome of all for one particular reason.

They were impossibly cute.

In fact, they were kittens—fuzzy, adorable kittens, each the color of fresh snow and no bigger than a cantaloupe. They were also feral; spat a paralyzing poison; and flew on colorful, batlike wings capable of slicing through a human arm. Yet once you attached all that to a kitten, it became the zoological equivalent of a death threat on pink stationery with hearts dotting the *i*'s. It was difficult to take them seriously, even in the swarms in which they generally traveled. Sharp claws? Check, but attached to a kitten. Piercing teeth? Yes, but, again, in the mouth of an adorable little kitten! One in ten able to chew through metal? Oh, you'd better believe it, but wookit da kitty!

Obviously this schmoopifying effect diminished after people actually encountered the playfully savage swarms of the things. Coos of adoration would swiftly turn to shrieks of dismay, which would then escalate into screams of terror when the abhorrent act of killing one adorable creature resulted in two more of them springing alive from its corpse. On the rare occasion this failed to happen, it was only because the creature's death instead resulted in a fiery explosion and—in a characteristically laughable fashion—a shower of peppermint candy. (Some hypothesized that similar creatures in ancient times had inspired the modern piñata, but the idea fell out of favor due to lack of evidence and the fact that no one likes a piñata filled with death.) Those first few survivors who attempted to tell their tale of terror-by-kittens were ridiculed by their friends, dismissed by the mainstream news agencies, and finally laughed out of UFO conventions.

It would be inaccurate to say that the phenomenon was completely ignored, of course. The problem was that no one wished to mobilize the National Guard or allocate funds to counter a threat presented by *kittens*. The creatures' "adorability armor" (a term coined in an NPR retrospective) allowed them to flourish under the radar of public concern.

A prodigious breeding rate coupled with the aforementioned death-bifurcation soon swelled their numbers. Further sightings were documented: The creatures destroyed farms. They terrorized small towns. They reduced countless yarn outlets to mind-scarring disarray. Reports of such incidents, given further life by the award-winning television exposé "An Inconvenient Kitten," gradually moved the general populace to grasp the idea that such darling creatures actually posed a serious danger.

Even with the threat realized, campaigns to get people behind exterminating the "death-kitties" provoked only giggling. To overcome the masterful public relations coup that the creatures' own nature had created, the Powers That Be rebranded the beasts as "razorwing sky terrors." (Certain pundits suggested throwing the word *socialist* in somewhere for additional effect, but the idea was abandoned to reduce printing costs.) Even when colloquial usage swiftly shortened the name to "razorwings," it was enough to imbue the little devils with the proper gravitas. The anti-razorwing campaign had begun.

Yet by then, the damage was already done. Razorwings now roamed the American heartland in such numbers that extermination was an epic task. Their bifurcation made it nearly impossible to simply kill them with bullets. No metropolitan area wished to risk the collateral damage sure to be caused by large-scale explosives or chemical poisons. Scientists were making a concerted effort to study the creatures to find a more feasible solution, yet capturing them was difficult and containing them was complicated by the fact that the blue-winged variety could chew through metal.

As scientists struggled to find an answer, civil leaders petitioned Athena for aid. The goddess rewarded their deference by providing defensive insights that led to a strategy of deterrence. Where budgets allowed, urban areas constructed devices designed to safely redirect the razorwings' already chaotic impulses. Helicopters towing masses of dangle-balls on strings patrolled Las Vegas. Phoenix erected a network of laser pointers to fascinate any incoming razorwings and redirect them toward unpopulated areas. Kansas City simply used existing irrigation systems to spray them in the face.

Yet the razorwings' coloring held another defense: the white kittens' wings were either red or blue, and the red-white-blue combination led to a grassroots effort among some (located notably outside of razorwing territory) to declare them a manifest symbol of American strength. Some even lobbied for razorwings to replace the bald eagle as the national mascot. Their argument was clear: in light of the razorwings' patriotic color scheme, the bald eagle and its utter lack of red or blue plumage was clearly phoning it in, and why did the bald eagle hate America?

It could be argued that if these fringe groups had not hampered efforts to speedily eradicate the beasts, then Tracy, Jason, and Dave would not now be forced to abandon their campfire in a mad rush to the illusionary safety of their vehicle.

The slam of the doors after the three piled into the SUV jolted *Monster Slayer*'s Doctor Ian Aaronson out of his catnap. "Gah! What is it?"

"Start the engine!" Tracy yelled.

"Bugger all, Tracy, are we late?"

The horrible meowing cacophony that overtook the campsite preempted her response. Diabolic kittens swarmed across the windshield and into their pitched tents. Nylon was torn and stakes were yanked from the ground as the razorwing swarm flung the tents into the air with feral curiosity. Supplies and clothing spilled to the ground, only to be snatched up again by tiny paws as the creatures began their playful vivisection of the area.

Ian gave a shout of comprehension and grabbed frantically to turn the key in the ignition.

"Drive!" Tracy shouted.

"Where?" Ian came back.

"Anywhere!"

"Stop yelling at me!"

"Who left the back door open?" Jason demanded.

They all turned to see the rear cargo door hanging wide open. Numerous white flashes of fur streaked past, threatening to get inside at any moment. Jason vaulted over the rear seat, crawled over video equipment, crushed a long and apparently empty cardboard box, and yanked the door shut.

"Furry bastards got my watch," Dave grumbled, peering out.

Half a dozen razorwings perched on the hood, one of which began chewing its way through. Ian revved the engine. The razorwings leaped into the air as the SUV lurched forward, rolled up an embankment, and began to turn around.

Much of the swarm was now landed in the campsite and wreaking destruction. Sleeping bag stuffing floated like snow. Two razorwings had torn into the remaining hot dogs and were engaged in a tug-of-war that was simultaneously the cutest and most horrible thing Tracy had seen all month.

The doctor steered them right toward it all.

"Where are you going?" she demanded.

"Back to the road!"

"Not that way! Get us out of here!"

"I said stop yelling! Let me drive!" He rolled them forward over a rock that sent the SUV bouncing upward, spilling Jason forward over the backseat as he tried to climb over. The big man cursed in pain.

"Next time sit in the *back* of the truck, Doc!"

"'Drive anywhere,' that's what you told me!" He veered toward the left of the swarm. Dozens of eyes flared in the headlights, deadly interest piqued. "I'm merely attempting—"

"Watch out!"

A monumentally stupid man rushed out of the darkness ahead of them, madly waving his arms and planting himself directly in their path.

It was Leif.

Leif?

Before Tracy could pick the right profanity for the situation, Ian jerked the wheel to the right, throwing her against him. Narrowly missing Leif, the SUV plowed instead into a landed group of razorwings. Piteous cries of pain ended abruptly with a thundering bang and the sound of tearing metal. The SUV lifted up on its left wheels and nearly tipped completely before it crashed back down again.

The vehicle was righted, but the engine was dead. Tracy was too stunned to curse. Dave, always having her back, cursed enough for the both of them. Jason was the first one with anything coherent to say.

"Don't just sit there, Doctor, start it up!"

Ian obliged, fruitlessly attempting to turn the engine over as Dave turned to look outside. "Who the hell's that idiot?"

"My stalker." She looked behind them, fully expecting Leif to come pounding on the door at any moment. "Anyone see him?"

"It won't start!" Ian yelled quite needlessly from the front seat. A handful of razorwings clawed their way up the side of the damaged SUV to crawl across the windows.

"Keep trying!" Jason turned around with them, then pointed. "There, by the campfire. They spotted him."

Tracy looked, spotting Leif herself as he waved his arms in an attempt to defend against the creatures that now swarmed him. Tiny claws tore at his shirt as they swooped in, half attacking, half playing like any regular kitten clawing its owner's forehead as if to say, "Why in the world are you sleeping at 4 a.m.?" One of the beasts landed on the small backpack Leif wore and panicked him into discarding it entirely.

Stalker or not, they couldn't just leave him out there.

"Did anyone unpack the laser pointers yet?" Tracy called.

"Still in the back, I think!" It was Dave's turn to clamber over the backseat. "Stuff's all shoved around! Where's the green bag?!"

Tracy cursed. "Why'd you put them in there? I think it's on the bottom!"

"Why'd you put it on the bottom?!"

By the campfire, a burst of spit flashed in the firelight and caught Leif in the face. He staggered, stumbled, righted himself, stumbled again, staggered a second time, failed to right himself, then finally went down.

(Thalia, watching from the tree above, gave him a 9.5.)

Dave tossed bags about in a mad search as Tracy wished she'd thought of the laser pointers earlier. Glancing between Dave and Leif threatened to give her eyes whiplash.

Jason, doing the same, finally bent down to reach under the driver's seat. "You won't find them in time!"

"Best I can do with one friggin' eye!"

Outside, the razorwings settled on Leif's fallen body and backpack, growing more and more frenzied as they found new toys to play with. Six of them tore the backpack open and dived inside in a squirming mass. Nearly a dozen more seemed poised to do the same to the paralyzed Leif at any moment.

In a flash, Jason pulled the official *Monster Slayer* sword (crafted by traditional American weaponsmiths, official replicas available for just $99.95 plus shipping) from under the seat. "Stay here!"

He jumped from the SUV, tore the sword from its scabbard, and plunged into the swarm before Tracy could think of stopping him. He knocked three razorwings from Leif's back with the flat of his blade before they'd even noticed him, then batted away another two with the backswing. A chorus of enraged mewling rose from the rest as dozens of brilliant eyes all turned on the new violent man with the shiny object.

As the doctor continued his futile battle with the ignition, Tracy climbed into the backseat with Dave. "Hurry! Jason's out there!"

"Yeah? Tell him to bring back my watch!"

Jason's intervention was brilliantly heroic, but razorwings were even more vicious when defending themselves. Tracy shuddered to think of what the monsters would do to Jason if he couldn't handle them.

She shuddered again to think that they wouldn't even get it on camera. They'd have to do a clip show or something and find a new hero.

Jason whirled the blade around, not attacking the razorwings so much as trying to scare them off. They took to the air, whirling around him in a frenzy of soft fur and pointy bits. Within moments they were swooping in two or three at a time, wings wide in an effort to do some slicing of their own.

"Found 'em!" Dave gave a triumphant bellow and pulled two laser pointers from the bag so victoriously that they flew out of his hand, hit the ceiling (also victoriously), and clattered onto the floor under the passenger's seat (perhaps less victoriously). "Ah, crap."

In the moment between Tracy's dive back to the front seat and slamming into the also-diving doctor, she had just enough time to spot Jason putting Leif over his shoulder while two razorwings clawed their way up his legs. (Her peripheral vision was excellent.) Tracy seized one of the pointers as Ian grabbed the other.

"Open the door!" Jason yelled. He ran for the SUV, Leif slung in one arm, sword in the other.

Dave swung the back door wide. "Gonna put an eye out if he keeps runnin' with that thing," he muttered. "Behind you!"

While the majority of the swarm circled Jason, three razorwings went for a more direct approach. Bladed wings spread, they dived down from behind, eyes wide, teeth bared. Whether due to Dave's warning or his own instincts, Jason spun about to backpedal toward the SUV, sword raised. The swooping razorwings spit as they neared. Jason sidestepped and sliced the blade through two. Both fell to the ground wailing as the third slashed its way past and caught Jason's arm with one wing. Two more spit and hit him straight in the face. Jason had just enough time to turn, lunge through the open door with Leif, and collapse in an affectedly heroic position.

Dave pulled him in completely and yanked the door shut. It slammed on the tail of a single razorwing who'd made it inside with them. The creature's scream tore through them like nails on a chalkboard that also had just slammed a razorwing in the tail. The thing flapped about in a mad attempt to free itself as Dave tried to beat it unconscious with Leif's leg.

Now robbed of their toys, the razorwings outside turned their full fury on the SUV. They tore off windshield wipers. Three gnawed the antenna into a knot. Metal tore as the blue-winged variety began carving the SUV's roof open like a can of tuna. With a shout to Ian, Tracy switched on her pointer. She shined it out the window on the ground in the middle of the swarm and waved it about like an idiot. Ian followed suit.

Anyone who has never seen a kitten go after a laser pointer dot yet claims experience of true focused tenacity is a dirty liar who should rightly be punched in the mouth. At once the creatures dived for the two glowing dots, clambering over each other in a spastic attempt to capture the light. Tracy and Ian jumped the dots from place to place around the vehicle until every razorwing was enthralled. The ground outside became a mass of jumping, batting, and eerie feline screams. Gradually, Tracy and Ian directed the dots farther away from the campsite, each time backtracking a little to catch any stragglers before shining the lasers away again. The swarm moved farther and farther off until, finally, they were just an indistinct cloud of white in the moonlight.

Then, at Tracy's signal, they turned off both pointers. The swarm's momentum carried it away into the night.

In the back, Dave had pulled the shoe off Leif's foot and was pummeling the crazed, fuzzy beast into unconsciousness without the benefit of depth perception. One troublesomely satisfying blow later, the razorwing collapsed.

It was a moment before Ian finally asked, "Is it dead?"

The cameraman stared, catching his breath. "Ain't dead. Dead'd mean it'd split. Or explode."

"It's a miracle that thing didn't spit at you."

Suddenly the piteous monster convulsed, coughed once, and hacked something up before collapsing back down again.

Dave peered at the discharged object. "Got my watch back."

Diligent readers who recall previous statements about Thalia not being distracted when the razorwings arrived may ask themselves just why that mattered at all. Thalia, they point out, clearly did nothing but watch. Such bothersome people are plainly unaware that nearly all Muses (save Calliope, who holds a black belt in slow-motion kickboxing) are pretty much worthless in a fight. It's just not their thing. No, Thalia's lack of distraction merely allowed her the best vantage point for observing the spectacle, the lack of which would have seriously hampered her mood.

"Unimportant!" someone might say. This someone clearly is not Thalia. Nor, just as clearly, have they considered that a Muse in a bad mood (and a redheaded Muse at that) is not a Muse with which a sane person wishes to deal.

While it is regrettable if such earlier statements confuse any readers, those who insist on complaining should be advised that they are quite likely reading the wrong sort of book. If it makes them feel better, they could consider that Jason clearly received some sort of heroic inspiration to rush out amid the razorwings and save Leif in time, and that perhaps Thalia had something to do with that.

But only if it makes them feel better.

CHAPTER ELEVEN

"I'm Jason Powers. I hunt monsters, and most of the time I know what I'm doing. Please, do not try this sort of thing at home."
—Jason Powers (Monster Slayer *disclaimer*)

"You know, we do that warning at the start of every show, but I have to think that if viewers have monsters in their homes, they've got bigger problems than a bunch of ivory tower lawyers."
—Jason Powers (*interview,* Adventure Channel Magazine)

LEIF WOKE TO SEE three kneeling blobs watching what felt like an invisible elephant stepping on his head. As his awareness returned, he recognized the elephant to be a mere savage headache, and one of the blobs took the appearance of the radiant Tracy Wallace. Flanking her were two men of whom he was decidedly less enamored. The glower coming out of the man with the eye patch gave Leif the impression that the feeling was mutual.

Leif groaned a greeting that failed to coalesce into any sort of verbal form before he finally managed, "What happened?" The last thing he remembered were razorwings swarming him. The fact that he wasn't dead left two options. He picked one. "Am I a hero?"

To his disappointment, Tracy didn't return his smile—if in fact that was what he had managed to do with his face. At the moment, his muscles were a bit wrapped up in contract negotiations with his brain.

"If you were a hero," Tracy said, "wouldn't that make you an 'idiot risking your life'?"

Leif admired the way she brought back his previous words to bite him. He smiled weakly and tried to charm it up a notch or two. "Yeah, but you seem to go for the idiot type."

"You're not a hero, Mr. Karlson."

"Though y'are an idiot, I'd wager," said the one-eyed man.

Hey neat, Leif suddenly registered: *a one-eyed man!* It struck him that he had overheard the man's name once earlier, but it hadn't managed to stick. "I asked you to call me Leif?"

"And I asked you to stop following me. Hold up your end and I'll hold up mine."

He let that battle go for the moment, turning instead to a newly stitched gash on his forearm. "Er, what did happen, exactly?"

"Before or after you decided to stalk her?" the one-eyed man asked.

"I'm not stalking her, I'm—" Fine, maybe he was stalking her. Before he could ask what business it was of One-Eye's, the other man—who Leif was fairly certain was named Ian, or Rupert, or maybe Bill—spoke up.

"You got hit with razorwing spit. Do you know what razorwings are?"

Leif sincerely hoped he managed an adequately derisive stare. "Oh, gee, maybe those things in the news all the time that attacked us just a bit ago? I wonder."

"Charming fellow. Yes. You fell, hit your head, and suffered a few minor lacerations. I've stitched up some of the deeper ones for you. Nothing you won't recover from."

The one-eyed man grinned. "Hope ya got insurance."

"That was about an hour ago," Tracy added. "Jason saved you, actually."

"Oh, my hero," Leif muttered.

"He's fine, by the way."

Jealousy twisted the knife a bit. "Yeah, I figured from the way you're all not sobbing."

"We fixed you up," Tracy continued, "so now you'll return the favor: Where's your car or whatever? You're driving back and sending a tow truck."

"And not coming back with it," One-Eye added.

The other guy shook his head. "He has to come back with it so the driver knows where to find us. There's not exactly a house number hereabouts."

"What's wrong with your SUV?" Leif asked. "Or is it Jason's? It's awfully big. What's he compensating for, I wonder?"

"Some razorwings exploded under the engine. It's not going anywhere."

"Yeah, thanks for that, by the way," One-Eye added again.

"Ah," Leif said. "You want to know where my car is?" He pointed at the SUV. "I stowed away in the back."

"You stowed away in the—" Tracy glared at One-Eye.

"Heh. Wondered what that box was."

Leif rated One-Eye a little higher on the likeability scale.

"Great," Tracy went on, "it's worse than I thought. What the hell's your problem? You thought I'd suddenly swoon at the gesture, or were you just hoping to steal a pair of my—"

"You were leaving. It was the first thing I could think of!"

"What about just taking 'no' at face value?"

Leif felt flushed and hoped it was merely an after-effect of the poison. All he'd really thought about was how much he had to have her, and that if he let her leave, that'd be the end of it. Grand gestures seemed the way to go. Eventually her anger would subside and she'd realize how much he must care, right? She'd come around.

That was always how it worked in the few romantic comedies he'd had the misfortune of sitting through, anyway. It was stupid, but he couldn't stop himself.

Regardless, he didn't want to have this discussion in front of the other two.

"Look," he said, "just—I can't just walk all the way back now, can I? Not alone with those things still out there."

One-Eye smirked. "Could give him a laser pointer, send him off."

"We're not sending him off by himself." It was Jason, speaking up from where he lay on a half-shredded sleeping bag. Leif was sorry to see him sporting a few wounds of his own. It made the guy look all the more heroic. "After those things attacked? Then what, we kick a puppy?"

"I'm not a—"

"At the very least not until he's had time to rest," added the man whom Leif rather hoped was a doctor.

Jason shook his head. "Why send him back at all? Guy's got guts. Maybe we can work him into the episode."

"Oh, great, sidekick to a steroid addict. Yay me."

Jason laughed. "Watch the cracks, guy. I'm the only one on your side here."

Tracy shook her head. "Insurance would have a fit. Geez, what a night."
Something about the way the whole group waited on her next word struck Leif as very sexy. Strange that so much about her struck him that way, so much that he hadn't even noticed on their first meeting. Well, maybe not that strange, considering the fact that he had a conversation with a god right before he met her. Was this Apollo's doing? Still, why question a good feeling?

"Okay," Tracy said finally, "you can stay." She swiftly pointed a finger at Leif's sudden beaming expression. "I hear one thing about how attractive I am, how much I should give you a chance, or how damn much you admire me, I'll stake you to the ground with catnip around your neck, understand?"

"She's hot when she gets forceful, isn't she, Leif?" Jason said.

Tracy's finger shot toward Jason. "Goes for you too, Powers."

Leif smirked. Maybe she didn't like the guy that much, after all?

"Tomorrow he stays here while we film," she finished.

"Then you'll have to tie me up, 'cause I'll just follow you," Leif warned before he could stop himself.

"Wasn't kidding about the catnip, Mr. Karlson."

"Hey, no points for honesty? I'm serious. I'm not staying here."

"We could tie you up in the SUV," Tracy suggested.

Leif winked. "Kinky."

"Hey!" One-Eye burst, grabbing him by the collar. Leif's vision shuddered from the jostling. "Shut yer damn mouth and treat the woman with a bit of—"

Tracy grabbed One-Eye's arm. Her fatigued sigh alone seemed enough to stop the man mid-recrimination.

"Dave," she said (Leif at this point coincidentally recalled that One-Eye's name was Dave), "let the half-drugged, helpless idiot go."

"He was mouthin' off." He let go, nonetheless. Leif's vision continued to wobble, also nonetheless.

"My problem, not yours."

"Ah, let him come along, Tracy. He can stay behind the camera," Jason said.

Dave grunted. "Far behind it."

"Fine." Jason grinned. "He can stay back with Tracy and the doctor."

Leif smiled. "Fine by me."

Dave scowled. "Now wait a damn minute."

"Might I suggest," the doctor began, "that we all get some sleep now and leave the bickering about just where Mr. Karlson shall walk for the morning? Dangerous monsters are not to be confronted with half a night's sleep if the show's hero is to survive to season two."

"Doc's right," Jason said. "The hero needs his rest!"

Tracy sighed. "Yeah, the doctor's right. Standard watch order while the razorwings are out there. Mr. Karlson will take Jason's slot so he can rest up."

Dave slowly grinned and poked Leif in the shoulder. "I'll be sure to wake ya in plenty of time."

Leif smirked. "Do you have to keep watch twice as long because of the, ah . . . ?" He tapped his eye.

"No, I just kick twice as many skinny butts to make up for it. Get me?"

". . . Okay, g'night, then!" Leif had a better comeback, but for once his mind was quick enough to shut his mouth. He lay down, instantly comfortable and far too weakened from the poison to really care what he was lying on or why that owl was looking at him so intently.

The following day, the group of five moved with a purpose through the rocky hills and sparse trees. The purpose differed for each person, of course, save for "don't get killed". At least that's what Thalia assumed as she traveled invisibly behind them. Leif had repeatedly suggested that Jason might have a death wish, though Thalia sensed in the TV star only the supreme confidence and love of attention that befitted any halfway-decent hero. Calm, focused, and wearing a snug vest of modern body armor, he led the group into the hills as if he knew precisely where he was going.

He didn't, of course, but he was at least confident admitting so to the camera as they traveled.

Leif mostly kept quiet while the camera was out. The rest of the time, he wouldn't shut up, and the others did their best to ignore him. Jason seemed focused on the path and trials ahead; the doctor, lugging along the narrow bundle of a collapsible medical cot, was plainly preoccupied by his own nerves; and Tracy and Dave were busy getting shots or doggedly not responding to all but Leif's most direct inquiries.

It didn't really help. Thalia wondered how Leif was supposed to play a part in Zeus's resurrection. If Apollo hadn't foreseen it, she wouldn't have believed it possible. On the other hand, the young man had at least managed to crack Jason and, to a lesser extent, Tracy. (At one point Jason grabbed Leif by the arm and pulled him in front of the camera to introduce him to the viewers. Tracy protested at first, but then loudly observed that Leif could always be edited out of the footage later.) Perhaps Leif was fated to inspire Zeus to will himself back to life for the sheer purpose of telling the young man to shut up? Beyond that, Leif didn't seem up to what Apollo required of him at all.

"So you've got a gun or something hidden under that riot gear you're wearing, right?" Leif asked after a time. "You can't possibly just use the sword."

Jason glanced at him, amused. "Knives too. Crossbow now and then. But no guns on this show."

"Well, not *on* the show, but come on, you can't be going after these things without one. Sure, Rule of Cool and everything, but what happens when you run into something you can't handle? You can't just judo-chop it in a nerve cluster and ram a sword through it. No one'd think less of you for softening it up with a few bullets offscreen. Just another thing she could 'edit out,' I'd think."

"I'd think less of me."

"We run an honest show, Mr. Karlson, despite what you seem determined to see," Tracy said.

"Uh-huh. Well, just give the signal when you need to pull the gun and I'll turn away so you can stay all hero-like."

Jason turned to Leif with a smile that he proudly displayed to Dave's camera. "Haven't met the monster yet that's been able to kill me."

"Ooh, impressive. Most people who aren't dead yet can't say that."

Jason unsheathed his sword for a punctuating blade flourish. "Right you are!"

Thalia's smirk matched Leif's. Tracy just shook her head and turned away such that Leif was able to get a good ogling of her bum without anyone else noticing.

Not for the first time since Leif dashed off in a mad pursuit of Tracy, Thalia wondered at the source of his feelings. After observing him the day he first met the woman, Urania and Melpomene said nothing about any sort of attraction. Then again, attraction wasn't their area, so it was possible they just hadn't noticed. Come to think of it, as Muse of comedy and science fiction, realistic romantic attraction wasn't really Thalia's expertise either. (The closest she came to it was dealing with romantic comedies, which she'd be the first to admit had little or no basis in real romantic relationships.) So perhaps she wasn't the best one to judge.

Yet it did seem . . . strange. Odd behavior, or merely an aspect of his character previously unseen? She wondered what Calliope would have made of it, had Thalia not agreed to take her turn watching Leif today. (She hadn't felt much like flying back home anyway, and the break from musing was nice enough. Plus Calliope promised her a favor in exchange.)

They continued over rocky, scrub-covered terrain, passing in and out of what few shadows the light tree cover afforded.

"How much farther, you figure?" Leif asked after a while.

Jason kept walking. "Don't know. No sign of tracks yet. That rise up ahead might hide a cave, so that's where I'm making for." He said it again for the camera at Tracy's suggestion, with a couple manly huffs of exertion for flavor.

"What if the monster isn't there? You could be hiking around all day and not find anything."

Tracy heaved a sigh. "You're perfectly welcome to go back to base camp, Mr. Karlson. Encouraged, even."

"No, I'll stick with you. Just seems like a big hike and hassle for nothing, though. Assuming you do find it, what do you figure'll be in its lair?"

Jason clambered up a rock for a look around and then turned to help Dave up. "The beast will be there, eventually. Kind of the point here."

"No, I mean what else? It's got a lair, and the lair's your objective. This isn't some random encounter with a wandering monster like last night, so the lair has to have something of interest in it, right?" Everyone else was too busy scrambling up the rock to try to hide their disinclination to answer. "There's always some sort of reward in places like that."

Jason played to the camera as he helped Leif up. "Ridding the world of monsters is its own reward."

"Yes, that's why we're doing this all on TV!"

"Don't talk to the camera, Mr. Karlson."

It wasn't such an outrageous thought, Thalia considered. Monsters did tend to be attracted to nodes of power. Such nodes had their own special ways of luring things of value, one way or another. It was no accident, for example, that a little patch of Nevada desert had turned into one of the top destinations for vacationers to turn over their money. (Ships and planes that vanished in the Bermuda Triangle were the unfortunate example of what happened when similar phenomena were buried beneath large quantities of water.) Thalia could sense no nearby location of comparable magnitude, but smaller nodes were everywhere, and she was no expert. Most monsters were far more sensitive.

Growing bored with shadowing, Thalia flew up toward the rise herself. Indeed, it did hold a cave—of sorts. It wasn't so much a cave as a smallish canyon that wound its narrow way into the rock to a wider section in the middle, which itself connected via another narrow passage to a second wide section at the end with no further exits. Each wider section featured shallow openings barely sheltered by rocky overhangs. Animal bones lay scattered about, picked clean by nature and whatever had brought them there in the first place.

Flying a bit higher, she spotted the hero's quarry hunched atop the thirty-foot wall of the canyon's middle section. For the moment, the creature's gaze was elsewhere.

Invisible to the creature, Thalia made a close pass to study it. By the design, she judged it to be Athena's work, at least primarily, though she noted the beast's armored hide wasn't entirely without flaws, especially on the left side.

Thalia wondered if the goddess herself would show up to see one of her creations tested. Immortals sometimes did, if they were aware it was being hunted, and they were either particularly proud or had a bet riding. She saw no invisible gods lurking about, but then that wasn't her area of expertise, either. The Muse backed off and settled atop the canyon entrance to await the others.

Leif's babbling heralded their arrival. "If you do manage to kill it," he was saying, "make sure you remember to take the head off. These things are never dead until you take the head off. And maybe set it on fire."

"Quiet! . . . And I have done this before, you know."

"Just saying." Leif didn't lower his voice one bit. "And it's when things are completely quiet that it's staring down at you from above, so just remember that too."

Jason held up his hand to silence him again. Leif actually complied and then looked expectantly toward the top of the canyon. He was looking straight through Thalia, though she doubted he realized it. She toyed with springing down to startle them all but deemed it not funny enough to blow her cover and risk a slashing.

Jason took a tiny, headband-mounted camera from Dave. "Stay here."

Leif gave what Thalia suspected was the cheesiest thumbs-up he could manage. After waiting for Dave to set up for a shot of the entrance, Jason drew his sword, crept into the canyon, and disappeared behind the first bend.

"So this is where he takes the gun out, huh?" Leif whispered. Apart from him, Thalia was the only one who smiled. As it was one of her smiles, she counted it a shame that no one could see it.

Well, screw that! Enough invisibility. She was a glorious kestrel falcon a few moments later, and a few moments after that she had winged her way after Jason.

The creature, she noticed, was gone.

Jason took a few minutes to explore the full length of the canyon. Caution guided him, albeit figuratively. (Thalia had never met an actual incarnation of Caution and was disinclined to believe one existed, but she was on a first-name basis with Death—Doug—and occasionally had breakfast with Sleep, and so she felt she oughtn't rule anything out.) Nevertheless, Jason found nothing alive save for a few wildflowers.

"Creature!" he called in admirable abandonment of the advantage of surprise. "Show yourself!"

The creature, if it was still around to hear him, was unwilling to shed the same advantage so easily. Nothing answered.

He cast a suspicious glance upward at Thalia, who took a moment to show off her current plumage and give a falcon's call of encouragement. The hero studied her. His hand shifted toward a dagger at his belt and he appeared ready to throw it. If he mistook *her* for a hideous monster, support from her quarter was going right out the window.

Again, figuratively speaking.

Jason appeared to abandon the idea. He turned around and, with one last look at the end of the canyon, made his way back to the others. Thalia followed and landed on a rock behind the camera.

"No contact so far," he said. His eyes remained alert, his body tensed. "But there's a nest of some sort, plenty of bones. Just no creature. Might be out hunting."

"Maybe it's out filming a cable show of its own," Leif suggested. Jason scanned the top of the canyon. "Could be hiding. Maybe I startled it. Could be . . . stalking us."

"You want to set up here?" Tracy asked. "We could get some wide shots of you waiting. Might be a good spot to do a voice-over later talking about . . . oh, I dunno, something. We can figure that out later."

Jason nodded. "It's bound to return sometime."

"No, no, no." Leif said. "I thought you've done this before?"

Jason's only response was a grin for the camera's benefit.

Leif continued. "You're supposed to relax your guard! Tempt fate! Say something like, 'Well, guess it's not home! Break out the sandwiches!' Something like that."

Perhaps humoring him, Jason waited a few seconds. Nothing came of it, though the wind did tousle Jason's hair in what might have been a heroic fashion.

"Could check up top there," Dave suggested. "Turns out to be clear, be a great place to set up a shot for when it does show."

"Clever as always, Dave," said Jason, apparently looking for the best place to climb. "I was just thinking that myself."

Leif was undeterred. "Well you can't just—You have to *say* it's safe or something; that's always when the monster attacks. It's like Murphy's Law or irony or whatever! How can you be on TV and know so little about it?"

Jason laughed.

"Say it, Jason," Tracy suggested with a mocking smirk at Leif. "I just got an idea for that voice-over. Something about this hunt being especially challenging because you have to put up with our guest."

Jason rolled his eyes with a grin. "I guess it is not home," he intoned. "Whatever shall we do?" They all waited, but still nothing came of it. The wind ceased tousling Jason's hair to instead flutter about them with a mocking pleasantness.

"You're not doing it right." Leif took a few steps toward the camera. "Looks like he scared it off. It's gotta be miles away by now."

Everyone waited, if only to think of a suitable smart-assed remark. The wind finally gave up, blowing off elsewhere to harass some tumbleweeds.

Tracy broke the silence. "Did we *bring* sandwiches?"

Jason sheathed his sword and patted Leif's shoulder. "Thanks for trying, kid, but things don't work that way."

The creature barreled into Jason without further nonsense. Man and monster tumbled into a clump of sagebrush. Teeth snapped on armor, metal unsheathed, and the fight was on.

"The sword!" Leif smacked his forehead. "He had to put away the sword! I knew I forgot something!"

Tracy pulled at Leif's shoulders. "Get back!" The four retreated behind Thalia's rock, watching and filming as Jason took firm hold of the monster and kicked it off him with a yell. It tumbled away, regained its squat footing with its shelled back to the camera, and shrieked.

"C'mon, Jason. C'mon, get up," Tracy whispered. "We need a shot of the thing's face . . ."

"Not very big, is it?" Leif asked.

Jason hurled himself from his back to standing with a single kick of both legs, sword brandished impressively. The creature shrieked louder, and Thalia regretted choosing an animal form that lacked arms she could use to cover her ears. The monster continued, backing off a few steps, its low, flat body swaying from side to side as if daring the hero to attack or to flee.

Jason did neither. Sword held out protectively before him, he circled around and positioned himself to one side of the shot. The creature turned with him, growling low, its face coming into view.

"Huh," Tracy observed. "Well, that's . . . kind of man-sized, right?"

"Maybe you can give it bigger arms in post-production," Leif suggested.

The thing's stubby forearms were, indeed, terribly unimpressive. The creature itself appeared to be the monstrous offspring of a frog and a turtle: its back broad and armored, its hind legs long and bent under it. They were thicker than would be found on a frog of similar size, except that a frog of similar size would be roughly the size of a large washing machine. Each hind leg ended in terrible claws that squeezed into the dirt as the creature waited for Jason to make a move. Its turtle-esque head growled through teeth that, while certainly large, looked more suited to grinding flour than rending flesh.

Such distinctions make little difference to anyone who has ever had their head crushed in a flour mill, of course, and neither did they make a difference to Jason. He dodged and feinted, sword still held defensively as he tested the creature's reactions and, very likely, drew out the moment just a bit for future viewers' benefit. After about thirty seconds of this, the creature ceased growling and drew back its thick, round head to blink in what was likely either curiosity or amusement.

"Aww," Leif cooed.

"Almost rather cute, isn't it?" observed the doctor.

"Uh-huh," Tracy said. "We'll need to edit that bit out, or we'll be getting e-mails." She stood, hands cupped to her mouth. "Kill it, Jason!"

Leif turned a surprised look in her direction.

"What?" she asked. "We got the snarl shot. He'll take enough time to make it interesting."

"You're gorgeous when you're ruthless, you know."

"Didn't know, don't care."

Jason charged in, sword swinging. The creature snarled again and jumped back—but not fast enough. The blade glanced harmlessly off the side of the shell as it turned. Jason guided the rebound around into an upward slash along its underbelly.

It was Jason's turn to be too slow; before he could make contact, powerful legs launched the beast up along the outer wall of the canyon. It found purchase on the rock, scrambled madly, and then disappeared up over the top, its entire body shifting colors to match the rock, like a chameleon on speed.

Jason withdrew cautiously back to the camera, his eyes on the cliff. "It's trying to lure me into the canyon. Clearly it's a trap." Clearly he was narrating. "We have a saying on *Monster Slayer:* 'The first step in avoiding a trap is knowing of its existence.'"

Leif balked at the others. "So Frank Herbert stole that from you guys, then," he whispered. "And ah, shouldn't the second step be, ya know, not walking into the trap? Anyone tell him that part?"

No one answered. With a tilt of his head that Dave took as a signal to follow with the camera, Jason crept toward the canyon entrance.

Thalia took to the sky herself. She really shouldn't leave Leif completely, but then she was a Muse, not a fighter. If the beast chose to attack him, there wasn't much she could do aside from trying to blind it with her robes. Besides, she was starting to think it could be Jason who had something to do with Zeus's resurrection. He was the classic Herculean hero: strong, determined, and not weighed down by too much intelligence. (Clever had its place but didn't always do what it was told, after all.) She circled the area, watching everyone with falcon's eyes.

Jason entered the wide section at the middle of the canyon and paused, trailed by the one-eyed cameraman. Both were looking upward at the top of the canyon walls.

Unfortunately, Jason was looking upward in the exact wrong direction when the monster peered down over the edge and launched itself straight at him. The hero somehow reacted in time, barely, whirling to one side just before the beast would have tackled him. Sharper than it looked, the edge of the monster's shell sliced across his outer thigh, and the impact sent them both to the ground in a cloud of dust. The sword flew from its owner's grip and rang against a rock.

"I'm all right!" he called to Dave.

He didn't look particularly all right, Thalia thought. Though he got to his feet almost as fast as the creature itself, an ugly wound flowed red beneath his now torn and dirty pants. Thalia winced in sympathy; they were very nice pants.

Pressing its advantage, the monster launched itself at Jason's head. With no time to recover the sword, Jason could only throw himself to the ground. His attacker sailed over him, latched on to the rock wall, and then turned and sprang back before Jason was even halfway up. Again the hero dodged in a barely controlled rolling fall that took him farther from his weapon, narrowly avoiding the monster's strike. It landed this time near Dave, who struggled to backpedal without losing the shot.

The monster, however, in what was likely an unintended bit of professionalism, ignored the cameraman completely and focused entirely on Jason. It sprang at him again, too widely in its haste. Jason needed only to be sure he didn't collide with it as he rushed with a laugh to regain his weapon, and the fight was even once more.

For a time the two combatants regarded each other across the bone-strewn canyon floor, each sizing the other up or just waiting for the other to make a mistake. Jason's face hardened in concentration, studying the creature until he seemed to realize that such a thing looks very dull on camera. He twirled his sword in the sunlight with a flourish as impressive as it was pointless, then grabbed a knife from his belt and hurled it into the creature's neck.

The beast gave a violent cry, staggered back just a moment, and then yanked its head down into the shell to snap the blade off against its armored collar. Jason stepped forward, sword raised. Before he could close the distance, the monster reared up on its hind legs and stretched its midsection until it stood a furious eight feet high. From under its shell unfolded powerful arms. Previously hidden, they were thrice the length and thickness of the smaller pair, with serrated chitin on the outer edges. The monster spread them wide and hurled ear-splitting shrieks at Jason as if to say, "Look! I have more arms!" or perhaps simply, "Ouch." (Monster shrieks, like prophetic visions, are difficult to translate.)

"Tell me you got that!" Jason called to Dave.

"No, I had my head up my ass! Camera's on! Camera's pointed! Hell, man, why people always gotta ask that?!"

"Seemed like the thing to ask?"

"Just kill the damn thing!"

Jason charged, sword swinging in a two-handed grip that put the monster on the defensive. He struck against the chitin of its arms, knocking them away so he could slash at the thing's chest. The blade did as much damage to the thick hide as nails to a chalkboard, with twice the spine-jagging sound.

The beast roared and swung both arms for Jason's head. Jason ducked the first, whirled away from the second, and swung high and fruitlessly for the beast's head in return.

"Skin's thicker than it looks!" he shouted.

Thalia thought it looked plenty thick enough already, except for that one thin spot she noticed earlier . . .

Man and beast clashed anew, striking, slashing, blocking, dodging. Once more the monster sprang up the canyon wall, greater arms folding in before it clambered up over the top.

Thalia wondered how long it would take for Jason to see the left-side vulnerability she'd spotted on her first inspection. Maybe his eyesight wasn't as keen. She was a lesser immortal and using a falcon's vision to boot, after all. Below, Jason waited for the monster to come back down. Thalia could just make out the camouflaged beast stalking around atop the canyon wall, hiding beyond the rim. She took the moment to fly down and alight on a crag beside Jason.

"Wait! Wait!" she croaked. Ugh, falcons had lousy voices. Ah, well, couldn't be helped. "Your chance is rising! Look for the hollow of the left breast as he dives and turns above you!"

Jason blinked at the talking falcon before him and cast a surprised glance at the camera before returning his watch to the cliffs above. To his credit, he appeared otherwise unfazed.

"Talking birds," Jason muttered to himself. "New one. Thanks but no thanks, little falcon! No hero ever took advice from a bird!"

Leif, Tracy, and the doctor crept into the area in time to see a falcon rolling its eyes at Jason and taking off again. Leif opened his mouth immediately.

"Where is it?"

The only response was Jason's dismissive wave and three shushes from the others. Jason pointed up to the canyon top, drove his sword point into the ground, and rolled his sleeves up.

"Ooh, this is going to be a good ep," Tracy whispered. "But if he dies, I'll kill him."

Jason scooped up a handful of rocks and flung them one by one at various places along the top of the canyon wall. Everyone else took cover as some of the rocks bounced back down with splintering cracks.

The beast appeared atop the edge of one side and sailed down at Jason. He spotted it, dodged left as it passed, and then hurled half the remaining rocks at its head with a battle cry that was either wordless or poorly enunciated. The rocks bounced off the back of its shell moments before it turned to face him. Jason continued to throw, one at a time now, backpedaling and aiming for the head. Each bounced harmlessly off the monster's armor.

Even so, few creatures will suffer the indignity of being hit with rocks if they can help it. This one shrieked in rapid succession, unfolded its greater arms again, and knocked the thrown stones away. Jason hurled his last at the monster's feet and rushed it. Too caught up in trying to block the low throw, the creature didn't realize Jason was charging until the brave and crazy mortal latched on to the thing's left arm. Swiftly gaining a firm grip, Jason continued past the beast to wrench its arm back with all his weight and momentum. It toppled backward, taking Jason with it and half trapping him beneath. Thalia gasped as the pants sustained another terrible ripping in the struggle.

Dave rushed forward, camera pointed. (So shocked were the others that no one thought to ask him if he got that, so there was no way to tell if he had.)

Ragged squeals tore out of the creature as the two wrestled in a tangle of grasping limbs and dust. The beast thrashed its free arm about in an effort to swing back and hit Jason, who was himself yelling in exertion and pain as the thing's weight ground what it could of him against the rough earth.

Then somehow Jason managed to turn himself perpendicular to the creature's body. The jagged shell edge loomed perilously close to his legs. He did his best to distract the creature from this fact by repeatedly ramming it in the head with a thick-booted heel. Its angry cries were soon muffled by the thing's own shell as it pulled its head down as far as it could go and threw up the other arm to block.

The beast's thrashing slowed while it tried to defend itself and sought to stand again. Jason was faster; he drove the soles of his boots against the side of its body, knees bent. He clutched the thing's left arm in both of his and shoved with his feet as if trying to uproot a tree. The creature screamed and grabbed for Jason with a right arm that, while thick and strong, just didn't quite bend at the angle required to reach him. Jason yanked further, straining against muscle and credulity as the beast bucked like a bull trying to throw a rider. It finally succeeded in launching Jason on a brief airborne journey into the canyon wall, where his head cracked against the rock.

He slumped to the ground and lay still.

The monster's triumphant cries rose further in a violent crescendo upon noticing that the dislodged hero had torn off its arm as he went. The tiny arm shielded the gaping socket hole left behind by the larger one. Renewed shrieks drove higher, higher, and then slowly came back down as the beast stood there, reeling . . . or perhaps catching its breath. Everyone watched, awestruck, just waiting for the moment when it would finally lose enough blood and topple over.

For what were likely purely selfish reasons, the beast refused to cooperate.

Dave panned back and forth between the creature and Jason's body while the other three quietly backed the hell away.

"You know, traditionally, ripping the arm off something like that'll kill it, no questions asked," Leif said. "What, no one's read Beowulf?"

Tracy ignored him. Her own gaze mirrored the camera movements as the monster shrieked and turned toward Jason's body. "Doctor?"

From what Thalia could tell, save for some blind and half-hearted reaching for his collapsible cot bundle, the doctor was rather frozen in place. The beast took a few more steps toward where Jason lay defenseless.

Tracy scooped up a few stones of her own. "Doctor!" she tried again, whipping a stone right into the back of the monster's knee. With a cry of pain, it spun around to face them, head out, eyes blazing and fixed on Tracy.

"Tracy, get back!" Leif tried, but she only hurled another stone. The creature ducked it and charged at her.

"Aaaaaaugh!" Leif's scream was either cowardly or courageous. He threw himself between them, arms held up to protect himself, a statue of unwilling heroism.

"Leif, get out of the way!"

"No!" he yelled at the creature. It was Tracy to whom he'd spoken, but conversational eye contact fails to be a priority when a giant, angry turtle-frog is bearing down on you.

Perhaps the creature might have been amused enough to fall over laughing at such a display were it not filled with the pain of a torn-off limb. As it was, its hesitation was brief. For only a fraction of a second did it stop to regard Leif's fearful bravery (the way a Buick might regard a possum)before continuing forward with a wild cry, its one good arm raised to strike the defenseless mortal.

It occurred to Thalia that, were this a television program, this would make an ideal spot to go to commercial.

CHAPTER TWELVE

"Monster Slayer: You can't handle this much awesome! Wednesday nights on the Adventure Channel!"

—Monster Slayer *advertisement*

ROOTED TO THE GROUND between the monster and Tracy, Leif prayed for a miracle, for a distraction, for anything! A heartbeat later, a falcon appeared between him and the advancing creature. The bird flapped wildly in the monster's face in a way that Leif, had he been more in control of his wits, would have deemed unnaturally altruistic.

The beast assessed this new element for a fraction of a second. The brief distraction allowed Leif the exact bit of time he needed to waste the opportunity entirely.

Then the falcon was forgotten. The arm-deprived creature reared back to strike with a soul-piercing scream.

The claws rending Leif's tender flesh sounded a great deal more like a shotgun blast from behind than he would have expected. Much less painful too. A second blast followed the first. The beast's scream turned into a horrible, mangled gurgle as a third blast took the beast in the face.

Leif blinked in realization and looked over his shoulder as the monster staggered backward. There stood the doctor. He held a wicked-looking sawed-off shotgun, apparently pulled from within the collapsible cot that now lay on the ground beside him.

"Aha!" Leif spun around completely, arm flung wide and pointing at the weapon in triumph. "I *knew* it!"

"Karlson, get out of the bloody way!"

"Wha?" Leif turned back as the doctor scrambled around for another shot. The beast loomed, its eyes blazing in an eviscerated face, far more enraged than wounded by the blasts. Leif had no time to even think of defending himself before the monster knocked him aside and rushed for the doctor.

That could have been the end of the doctor, of Leif, of Dave, and of Tracy, who were perhaps saved by only the considerable number of pages remaining after this one—though if you really wanted to, you could give credit to Jason.

Recovered from a brief tango with unconsciousness, Jason lunged to his feet, scooped up his fallen sword, and drove it hilt-deep into the beast's gaping shoulder wound. He gave no battle cry or clever one-liner to punctuate the strike. Perhaps were Jason not of the "strike first, quip later" school of combat, the beast might have had a chance to avoid the three-foot lance of steel now embedded crosswise through its vital bits.

Lungs punctured and hearts pulverized, the monster gave barely a gurgle of pain before it collapsed to its knees, pitched face-first into the dirt, and moved no more.

"There now," Jason declared. "All dead-like."

The major reason Jason preferred the "strike first, quip later" method was because he so seldom could come up with something clever to say in the moment. As it was, his triumphant comments were often written by someone else after the fact and added to the footage via post-production camera tricks.

Everyone else stood, either stunned or checking themselves for injury.

"Nice timing," Dave managed.

"Thanks." Jason yanked his blade free of the creature's body and, with a nod to Leif's frantic gestures, severed its head in a single cleave.

Tracy turned to Dave. "Tell me you got all that."

Leif was too wired from fear and adrenaline to catch Dave's response. Flush with the dual triumph of being right about the gun and seeing the creature slain just after he'd thrown himself in its path like a selfless idiot, he could barely catch his breath! He was alive! Tracy was alive! . . . *He* was alive!

And the gun hardly even hurt it?

"Guy killed it, Trace," Leif whispered. "Killed it with a sword." He went to sit down and realized he hadn't gotten up yet.

Jason sank down to lie on his back with a groan. "After I get at least an aspirin, Doc, you're going to tell me how long you've been toting that gun around."

The doctor hurried over to examine his leg. "It was rather her idea," he answered.

"Tracy!"

She blinked calmly back at Jason. "What? It's for our safety, not yours. We'll edit it out later. I don't know if you noticed but the gun didn't do much to it anyway. That was all you."

"Still. It's just not right. Dishonest."

"Okay, so we blame it on the new kid," Dave offered.

Tracy nodded. "Workable."

Leif blinked. "Wait, what?"

Jason laughed and then winced at the doctor's needle. "That's probably worse. Just . . . I don't know. We've got time to figure it out, I guess."

The doctor forced them to wait before exploring the canyon lair any further. The hero needed rest, he declared, and his wounds needed patching, all of which was fine with Leif. The hike, the fear, the smack in the head by a giant turtle-frog—likely in ascending order—they'd all sucked the energy right out of him.

Jason complained at the delay but did so on his back with his eyes closed and a smile on his face. Dave happily reviewed the footage. Time drifted on for a while as they rested. Tracy gradually began to pace.

"What's wrong?" Leif finally asked.

"Nothing. Why?"

Jason opened his eyes. "Getting antsy, Trace?"

"Not antsy. Just . . . a feeling. There's something else in that canyon, I think."

"Another of . . . those?" The doctor gestured to the dead creature.

"No, just . . . Look, I don't what it'll be, or how I know. Call it gut instinct. Producer's sense. We'll find something interesting in there."

Leif grinned. "That's what I said!"

"I don't mean treasure, Mr. Karlson."

Leif scowled. He'd hoped living through the monster attack would bond them a bit, but she continued to use his last name. There'd be progress when she used his first name, he'd decided. It'd be all symbolic. That's just how it worked. "So what, then?"

"I don't really know. Just a feeling." She turned to the doctor. "We've been resting for a while now. Satisfied?"

"I suppose. Careful on that leg, though."

Jason stood. "Feels fine. Hey, let's get a shot of me saying all that stuff about something else in the canyon. Sounds dramatic."

"Good point," she said. "Dave?"

They did a few takes of Jason mimicking Tracy's intuition as his own—one solemn and weary, the other dashing and complete with broad grins to the camera.

"Cheesy," said Leif, turning to Tracy. "You ask me, you should host. He's a great fighter, don't get me wrong, but you're the brains here."

Tracy actually appeared to smile for a moment—almost. "Thanks, but no one asked you," she said finally.

"Plus, you're a lot sexier than he is."

The almost-smile vanished. "Jason? Lead on. Karlson, in the back. And shut it."

"Better do what she says or she'll bring out her producer's whip," said Jason with a grin.

"Ooh, you have a whip?"

"Figure of speech, Karlson. Now quiet."

"Yeah," Dave added. "Down, boy."

Tracy didn't realize she was walking shoulder to shoulder with Jason until Dave complained that she was getting in his shot. She slowed and forced herself to let the star take the lead. He just had to get himself a leg injury, didn't he? It was a good thing she didn't have an actual "producer's whip," she realized, or she might have used it; she wanted to be in that canyon. It further vexed her that she couldn't put her finger on just why.

Vexed? she thought. Who talks like that? She swore to not say it aloud.

The hike up the canyon was a short one, punctuated with quick stops to search within each alcove. There were those who like to say that a sought object is always in the last place you look. There were still others who, upon hearing this uttered, flashed their smug little grins and pointed out that few people continue to look once they have found something. Tracy hated the second lot so much that she once continued to look for her keys after finding them, just out of spite. As they found little until reaching the very end of the canyon, she'd have been out of luck if anyone had made that comment today. There was simply nowhere else to search. Fortunately, no one said such a thing. They were all too mesmerized by the sight of an amulet on a golden chain hanging from a small natural peg of rock at the end of the alcove.

A smallish shaft in the alcove's ceiling directly above the peg spilled daylight directly onto the amulet. Purplish glints of light scattered from the gemstone embedded in its center, which shone with the illusion of its own soft glow. Reflected light sparkled off the gold and danced upon the natural rock.

"You didn't notice that before?" Leif asked.

"Might have," answered Jason. "I was looking for a creature, not a necklace. This isn't *Jewelry Slayer,* here."

"You didn't notice it." Leif said.

Aside from the basics, Tracy had never been big on jewelry. Nonetheless . . .

"It's beautiful. . . " she whispered. Ignoring Dave's protests, she stepped into Jason's shot to reach for it.

"Looks like a trap to me," Leif said.

She barely heard him. (This was not due to any preoccupation with the amulet. Tracy had spent most of the day trying to avoid listening to Leif and was just managing to get the knack of it.)

Even so, she couldn't shake the feeling that the amulet called to her, like a cranberry-orange nut muffin. Or six-hundred-thread-count sheets. This, she knew, was for her.

She snatched it from its hanging place and slipped it over her neck before the others realized what she was doing. When the purple stone flashed a second later, they at least reacted quickly enough to catch her before her lovely unconscious skull hit the ground.

PART TWO:

MUSES AND ERINYES AND FATES, OH MY!

CHAPTER THIRTEEN

"Some things have changed since we were last seen in the world. Chastity, for one. By now most of the formerly chaste goddesses have dropped all that nonsense, and it's about time, if you ask me. We're modern now. Why let the men have all the fun? (Hestia's always at home anyway, so she's got the time.) Artemis is the only chaste goddess left. Don't ask me why. I keep telling her she's missing out, no matter how special it makes her. Obviously I'm biased ..."
—*Aphrodite* (Aphrodite! Magazine, *July 7, 2009)*

WHILE TRACY'S LOVELY unconscious skull hit the ground, copious miles away in a hotel near the center of the Las Vegas Strip, Thad Winslow sat in his suite's private Jacuzzi beside a woman who was also quite lovely, and conscious to boot. She was not, Thad lamented, as attractive as he was. Yet that was to be expected. Finding companionship to equal his own often required an exhaustive search, and he just didn't have that kind of time. Thad consoled himself with the thought that after he'd finished the favor for his mother that brought him to Vegas, he'd hang around for another week and see what he could find.

It was hardly Thad's first time in Vegas. Even had he not grown up the only child of rich parents, the modeling career he'd fallen into at age sixteen brought him here on numerous occasions. In the eight years since, he'd forgotten exactly how many occasions, or would have, if he'd ever bothered to keep track.

Thad had better things to do with his time than keep track of things. Beyond "a lot," he no longer cared how many times he'd gone to Vegas, how many photo shoots he'd done, how many other models he'd slept with, or indeed how many women he'd slept with at all. (He seldom bothered to ask what they did for a living, so their model status—or lack thereof—wasn't something he could have kept track of, anyway.) Managers and dorks kept track of things. He was there to look good.

If the excited smile of the woman in the bubbling water beside him was any indication, he did it well. Thad took a sip of champagne. He'd sipped better, but it would do. As jet-lag cures went, a bottle of Bollinger, some tail, and a Jacuzzi were all at the top of his list.

Not that he actually kept track of the list either, but it always came to mind when needed.

Thad turned to his companion. Did he not get her name, or did he just forget? "Now," he said, avoiding the dilemma altogether, "where were we?"

Thad loved saying that. It always sounded so damn smooth.

Her smile was half a whisper away from becoming a kiss when a discarded robe dropped over both of them.

"Hello, Thad," came the dropper's voice. It slid from the throat of another woman behind them like silk on fur—like *familiar* silk on fur. Thad managed to stifle a curse before pulling the robe away from his head.

His companion followed suit. "Who the hell is this?" she asked.

Thad swallowed uncomfortably. "This is . . . ah . . . my sister."

His "sister" just laughed at that. "Not quite." Clad in a bikini, she strode around the edge of the tub, dipped her toes in the water just opposite them to play with the foam, and then stepped down in to take a seat. Her sea green eyes flicked to the other woman for a heartbeat before settling back on Thad. "Usually I'd cheer such a diversion, dear Thad, but don't you have more important things to be, ah, *doing*?"

Thad's companion sat up. "Excuse me? Who the hell do you think you're talking to?"

"Hrm. I think I'm talking to Thad. You should go now." She gave a quick shooing wave. "Go on. Out! Take the champagne and find another rich man to mount in a hot tub. It'll be fun."

Thad's companion's mouth was barely open before the other woman cut her off. "Listen, missy, not another word! Out! Now! Or I'll pitch your cute little body off the balcony!"

Be it the threat, the situation, or just the look in the newcomer's eyes, it was enough to drive Thad's companion from the Jacuzzi. She gathered up her clothes and dashed for the door, stopping just short to turn around and open her mouth.

The new woman cut her off again. "Don't bother leaving your number," she called. "He won't have time."

Thad waited for the door to slam before he forced a smile.

"Hi, Mom."

Most people would be thrilled to discover that their mother was one of the goddesses of Olympus. Most people would consider it a path to fame and a fantastic boon to their modeling career, were they lucky enough to have one. Of course, by virtue of actually being the son of a goddess, Thad was not most people. That was kind of the point.

After the Return, fame-seeking mortals declaring themselves the offspring of a god came out like camera phones at a wardrobe malfunction. Most were outright lying. Such a lie risked the wrath of the Olympian in question to be sure, but most of the time, the gods seemed not to pay much attention.

Most of the time.

There was the occasional correction. One professional wrestler boasted himself the son of Ares on national television. Word got back to the god, who swiftly cursed him in the middle of a "smackdown" with the voice of an eight-year-old girl and the inability to end any spoken sentence without, "Ares wouldn't touch my mommy with a ten-foot spear." The claim was a foolish miscalculation, anyway. *Zero* gods like professional wrestling. Even Dionysus considered it juvenile and phony, and he had once nominated the inventor of the beer bong for a Nobel Prize.

Yet to some people, it was worth the risk. Many of Thad's fellow models claimed Olympian parentage, with Aphrodite, Athena, or Hermes being the usual favorites. The imposters' rising exposure and incomes tempted Thad to do the same, but he refused to be like them. The son of two mortal parents, he was gorgeous, statuesque, toned, cut, intense. As far as Thad was concerned (and as far as he knew at the time), he was so stunning he didn't even need Olympian genes, and to his reckoning that made him even better than the others. He repeatedly announced this belief whenever possible. His manager loved the idea and took out a full page ad in *Vogue* declaring Thad "mortal perfection that even gods cannot match!" Thad swiftly worked this hubris into every public appearance he could, gaining a reputation even more unique than that of those falsely claiming immortal parentage.

When his goddess mother came to him one night and told him how she'd birthed him, given him up for adoption, and that he'd better show some damned respect, he was stuck. He held a legitimate Olympian pedigree, but to claim it now meant catastrophe and scandal. He'd stood on a talk show couch and declared his pure mortal status, for crying out loud!

Thad successfully begged his mother's forgiveness with an abject (if private) apology and numerous (and ongoing) sacrifices, but she still held the secret over him, still used it to manipulate him, still blackmailed him with guilt and threat of disclosure.

It was how she'd gotten him to follow this Leif Karl-something in the first place. Another person might have called it ironic, but the definition of the word wasn't something Thad kept track of either.

"'Hi, Mom'?" she repeated. "That's all you have to say for yourself? Thad. Darling. Why are you still *here?*"

Thad shifted in the water where he sat. "Recovering. I was jet-lagged."

"*Jet-lagged?* You flew two hours across a single time zone!"

"Yeah, but there's the drive to the airport, the wait at the airport, and—Look, you don't understand, you've never taken a plane."

"Oh, believe me, dear, I've taken a plane."

"I need my rest!" he argued.

"And I need you to follow that blond fool with the arrow in his heart!"

"I did! I followed him all the way here, didn't I?"

Her features hardened, eyes becoming daggers. "You don't know where he is, do you?"

Thad was normally quite good at lying to women, but the fact that this woman was his mother blunted his skills. Or maybe it was the goddess thing. Still, worth a try. "He's . . . nearby."

"You lost him!"

"He was on a different flight! I can't make the plane go faster!"

"We told you where he was staying!"

"Yeah, well, I went there. And I found him. But there was this woman across the street, see, this absolutely gorgeous blonde with—"

"*Thaddeus Archibald Winslow!*"

"I'm sorry! . . . Are we done?"

Thad had considered telling her the second he'd realized he'd lost track of Leif, but he figured it would work out eventually. Why bother making her mad? He endured his mother's put-upon sigh without rolling his eyes and waited for her answer. It didn't take long.

"You're my son, Thad, and obviously I have to love you. But Mommy is a goddess, so show some respect. You're going after him."

"Love to, Mom, but I don't know where he is."

"Fortunately for you, we do."

"Good! Then you don't need my help anymore." He smiled, sipping the champagne.

She smacked him across the face, which was impressive considering the distance between them. "You've embarrassed me enough already! I told the others you could handle this, and I had to hear it from *them* that you'd lost him!"

"Look, Mom, I just don't see why you can't do this yourse—"

"The whole point of this is to be discreet! And don't second-guess your mother! You'll do it, and you won't screw it up this time!"

Ares listened to the boy and his immortal mother from the adjoining room. To the untrained eye (of which there were none in the otherwise empty suite), he was seething. His teeth gritted, his hands clutched at the fireplace poker he'd grabbed in the event anything should need pokering, and his pacing feet ground into the carpet in a way that would, given perhaps a decade, give the Grand Canyon a run for its money. The trained eye, however, would tell you that *seething* was the wrong word. (There were no trained eyes in the room either, but as we are also imbuing trained eyes with the power of speech, questioning their existence in a given area is unfairly pedantic.) Seething was among Ares's five resting states, along with raging, blood-lusting, hating, and missing important details. No, Ares was more than seething, more than raging, more than hateful at Thad's utter failure to do as he was told.

Ares was annoyed.

When Athena first designed the turtle-frog (official Olympian registry name: "Testudomeleon ATH-4R"), she had for whatever reason consulted Ares about its greater arms. In an uncharacteristic fit of cooperation—

perhaps brought on by either boredom or the hope that the goddess would sleep with him—he had given a small bit of help. Then the thing got killed by that *Monster Slayer* guy. Ares was the first one Athena told. The insufferable bleeding-heart-defense queen blamed the whole thing on failure of his arm design, of course. Argument ensued, and damned if it didn't come out then that the victorious hero got a little help. The pieces were easy to put together from there, especially since Ares wasn't alone when he was told and therefore had some help to figure it out.

And so Ares was annoyed. The blond mortal bugger got away from them so easily! The others were fools. Send another mortal to watch in their place? A *mortal?* Discretion be damned, that's what he should have told 'em! Who cared how much attention they'd attract? *Stupid jerk Hades!*

Okay, so they'd flick Thad back on the job and put the fear of the gods into him if he screwed it up again. Titans' armpits, that wouldn't be enough! And what the heck was taking her so long?

The goddess returned just as he'd made up his mind to yank the boy out of the water and throw him where they needed him.

"So?" Ares asked.

"Boy's as smart as his father," she sighed.

"Yeah, so?" That didn't tell him nothing, even if he'd known who the boy's father was.

"He's back on the trail. I gave him a good head start."

"A head start? That's it?"

She pouted. "Apollo's champion might have a Muse watching, or Apollo himself. Do you want them to see him just teleport in?"

Ares growled. "Then I'll go myself."

"Don't be stupid."

"I'll be what I bloody want to be! Can't matter anyhow if they see me. I said I killed Zeus all along! I got no cover to blow."

"Ares, you're a boasting, blustering brute."

"Um . . . Thanks?"

She rolled her eyes. "I mean no one believes you! They just think you stole the credit to look stronger. Please, for me, let Thad do his job."

Ares held her gaze and grunted, thinking a few moments before seizing on an alternative that would end this whole thing a small sight quicker. "You're right," he said.

She beamed. "Always am!"

"See you back on Olympus." Ares turned to go. "There's things I got to take care of."

She grabbed his arm and drew him back.

"You're planning something, aren't you?" she asked with a poke at his chest. "I mean insomuch as you plan anything."

"What? Nah." He turned again only to have her yank him back, glaring.

"Or, to put it another way, 'yes,'" she said. "It's all over your face. What is it?"

"Oh for the love of—" He shoved away her grip. "So what if I *am* planning something?"

"Hrm. We've already *got* a plan? Stick to that!"

"Your plans're what got us into this! We wait any longer for this one to work and we'll still be waiting while Zeus shoves lightning down our throats! I'll just kill the twerp! He's mortal; that's what they're for!"

"You can't!"

"Sure as Hades I can. Just one more dead mortal on a long, long list. I'll make it quick if you're so squeamish." In fairness, he supposed she didn't look squeamish. She looked angry, which frankly was quite a good look for her. Then again, it was a good look for everyone so far as Ares was concerned.

"Ares, no! Hades said you can't just—"

"You can ram a pike up what Hades said!"

"We don't know enough about what Karlson might do!"

"We don't need to know nothing!" he fired. "What if he did what he was supposed to when your little pipsqueak lost him, eh? What if he does it when Thad loses him next time?"

"Thad will not lose him again!"

"Bettin' our hides on that, are you?"

She hesitated. "Even if Thad does lose him, Karlson's distracted. He's in love! Mind-bogglingly, distractedly infatuated!"

Something slid into the war god's mind and failed to stick. Ares stopped. ". . . He's fat?"

The other blinked. "Infatu—! It means 'in love.'"

"Yeah, like that ever solved anything. This ain't a movie."

"Not yet."

"What?"

She went on. "Fine, don't listen to me. But you kill Karlson and you know, you *know* that Hades will come down on you. Hard. You know what he's like when he's angry."

"He don't scare me."

"Liar. He's older than you, Ares. You can't stand against him alone."

"So you can help me."

"I agree with him! Karlson's death might be the very trigger to bring back Zeus!"

"And . . . it might not be!" he stammered. "You don't know!"

"Exactly!"

Ares glared at her. He hated arguments that made sense. They usually meant that he couldn't do what he wanted to, if he paid them any attention. So as a matter of course, he ignored them as best he could. But she wasn't going to stop nagging him.

"Fine," he said finally. "I won't go kill him."

"And you won't go watching him either. Not yet, anyway."

He only then realized he still had the fireplace poker in his hand. He tossed it to the floor, glad for the chance at least to throw something. "Fine."

She smiled. "Thank you. You know how these things work; there are all sorts of little rules and such, especially with death."

Ares just grunted at that.

"I'll make it up to you in some, oh, creative way, I'm sure. Come on. Let's go."

"Uh-huh."

He followed, pondering. *All sorts of little rules and such, especially with death.* Another scheme was creeping into his mind in an attempt to take form. He started to hum Wagner to keep it from showing on his face this time. After all, he'd only said that *he* wouldn't kill Karlson. Didn't mean someone else couldn't. Heck, if he played it right, even Hades couldn't fault him for it.

CHAPTER FOURTEEN

"Zeus pretty much stopped siring daughters after the Trojan War, which I expect was a combination of what happened with Helen and his dislike of having attractive mortal women in the world that he couldn't sleep with. It's likely why no one suspected Tracy at first. I'm still unsure if her gender was foresight or whim on Zeus's part."
—personal journal of the Muse Thalia (written under house arrest)

IT WAS TRACY'S SECOND real vision, though she didn't know this. The first—received eight months ago, just after Zeus's death—had burrowed unnoticed into her subconscious and eventually drove her to select this particular location for a *Monster Slayer* excursion. The first vision was subtle and impressively nuanced, seeking her out to worm its way into her mind without so much as a single dose of psychotropic drugs. By contrast, this second vision walked up and smacked Tracy in the face with all the subtlety of an indoor fireworks display.

In the darkness before her the amulet spins alone, shining as if to suggest either its paramount importance to her or a jewelry commercial. The darkness soon lifts: the background illuminates from an unseen source to reveal a grandly appointed, white marble room. It holds a broad desk, lush furniture, and one of the largest plasma screens she has seen that wasn't on a billboard. There is a grand aura, a wonder that takes her breath away.

The god is there a moment later, his hand holding the amulet's chain from where it dangles. His countenance is that of a man old enough to hold wisdom and power, yet young enough to retain the wolfish attraction of his youth. Concern mars his otherwise handsome face that few women could resist, yet Tracy knows she is one of those few women. She knows not from whence this knowledge comes—nor why she suddenly uses words such as whence—*only that it comes because she knows this man to be her father. Her real father.*

Father Zeus.

"Way to go, Mom!" she whispers, and wonders if her mother ever knew. Abruptly the vision pauses, the amulet flashes, and again she somehow knows that the vision is about to speak to her.

—To reduce the risk of cerebral hemorrhaging, please remain silent during the vision.—

The vision resumes and Tracy now watches the scene as if perched within the amulet itself. Zeus rushes to a window to look out. Sunlight shines upon his face, yet her attention is drawn to the sight behind him: A wrapped gift box sits upon a table, anointed with a broad bow that slips from the top as the creature within opens the lid. Its skin a dark pewter, its eyes glowing with violent malice, the little creature skitters onto the tabletop, silent as Death during naptime. Her father is focused on the window; he does not see the threat.

"Behind you!" she calls out on instinct, knowing the warning to be useless and that she is seeing into the past.

—To reduce the risk of cerebral hemorrhaging, please remain silent during the vision.—

Damn it.

The creature brandishes a barbed tail and lunges at her father like a living bullet. From within the amulet still clutched in Zeus's grip, she watches him fall out of the window. She sees the hateful god-killer perched on the windowsill—its stinger stained with his no-longer-immortal blood. She feels her father hurling the amulet itself toward where she knows it shall eventually land, halfway around the world in Nevada in a canyon that shall within nine months become a monster's lair. Anger and desperation blaze in Zeus's eyes, in Tracy's eyes, as the amulet flies from his grip. The vision begins to fade as he whispers to the amulet, to her . . .

"You are my child, Tracy, the key to reversing my fate. Guard well this amulet. Do not let justice die with me!"

Time slows as Zeus plummets to the base of Olympus. There is no further instruction.

"But what do I do?" she yells.

—**To reduce the risk of cerebral hemorrhaging, please remain silent during the vision.**—

Why does he get to talk when I can't? *Her father crashes to the ground, his body breaking on the rocks, murdered.*

Oh, right.

The vision ends. It belatedly occurs to her that she does not like the sound of that "reduce" before the "the risk of cerebral hemorrhaging".

She slowly became aware of the voices.

"If she doesn't wake up soon, I'm taking that thing off her," said one.

"You don't know what that could do!" said another.

"I hesitate to risk it," said (perhaps predictably) a third. "She doesn't seem to be in any danger for the moment, and we can spend the night here if need be." It was the doctor, and for a time after he spoke, all were silent.

Tracy opened her eyes to the sky and bit of cave ceiling above. The sun was out of sight somewhere below the canyon walls and near the horizon. The others had yet to notice that she was awake. She lay there on the doctor's cot, processing.

"Have you guys ever run into a talking bird?" Jason asked suddenly. "A bird, falcon, I think, it talked to me when I was fighting the monster."

". . . What'd it say?"

"Oh, you know. Bird stuff. It tried to tell me how to kill the thing."

"That's 'bird stuff'?"

"Stranger things've happened today." Tracy meant to say it louder, but it came out a whisper. It was audible enough to get their attention anyway.

"Hey!" Leif practically shouted. "Er, welcome back."

He, Jason, and the doctor stared down at her. "How do you feel?" the latter asked.

The amulet lay heavy on her chest, its chain still around her neck. She sat up just a bit, cradling the thing in her palm to study it. "Overloaded." It was the second word that came to her mind, after *hemorrhaging*. She kept that one to herself. She hadn't talked *that* much.

"Maybe you should take that thing off," Jason suggested. She shook her head.

"No. I can't. I mean, I can, I think, but . . . I shouldn't." Tracy blinked, looking around suddenly. "How long was I out? Where's Dave?"

"Two hours," Jason said. "And he's fine. Doc didn't want to move you, so Dave left about an hour ago to bring some things back from the truck. Why shouldn't you take it off?"

She stood, shrugging off Leif's attempt at helping. "Just . . . just let me think a sec." It was a lot to take in. She couldn't quite believe it.

No, she amended, she could believe it. What she couldn't quite believe was how easily she was able to. She was the child of her ditzy mortal mother . . . and the king of the Olympian gods. This she knew without question (and rather suspected the amulet was to blame for that).

Someone had murdered her father! This, again, she knew. This she accepted. This she suddenly recognized as a terrible crime that demanded justice! Not that she'd ever been against justice, but—

"Tracy?" Jason snapped his fingers in her face. "You're zoning."

"I'm thinking. Maybe you've heard of it?"

"Well, think later," Jason demanded. "What's going on?"

She scowled, trying to find just the right way to put it. "I'm Zeus's daughter." No, that wasn't it.

"What?" Jason and the doctor said at once. Somewhere nearby a falcon cried out.

"What did you say?" Leif managed finally.

She waggled the amulet. "I put this thing on and . . . saw things. A vision. And I know it was a vision because there was this warning that told me—" She stopped short of adding details that wouldn't help.

"Are you certain?" the doctor asked. "You may have just been dreaming. If you struck your head on the rock, there may be some hemorrhaging that I didn't—"

"I didn't talk *that* much!" she shot at him. Okay, that probably sounded just a tad insane, didn't it? "Just listen, will you? I saw Zeus die, saw this—this metal bug thing crawl out of a gift box and jab a stinger in him. He fell out the window and . . . Well, that was mostly it, I guess."

"Mostly?" Jason tried.

"Metal bug thing?" Leif asked.

"Zeus spoke to me," she continued. "By name. Yeah, fine, maybe that's not so telling since it's—The point is he said I was his child, that I could reverse his fate. Or was 'key' to reversing it, anyway, and that this amulet was—well, that I should hold on to it. Guard it." There didn't seem to be all that much to it when she gave a recap, she realized. "I was out for *two hours?*"

"Er, not exactly," Leif answered, appearing distracted. "Hour, fifty-five minutes or so, really, but . . ."

Tracy gave him what was fast becoming the usual look. "Okay, not helping. The point is I saw this stuff. But more than that, I just . . . know it. Like I know my own phone number or that my grandparents are dead."

"One set anyway," Jason pointed out. "If Zeus is your father, then your other grandparents would be . . ." He trailed off, perhaps trying to think of names.

"I'm serious, Jason. I'm Zeus's daughter and I have to do something, probably something with this amulet, to bring him back!"

"Ah, and why is that, exactly?" asked the doctor. "The bringing him back, I mean."

"Because it's the right thing to do! Because he's my father and . . ." She shook her head. "It sounds stupid, isn't it? All this."

"No, it doesn't." Leif reached out to touch her arm for a moment before she realized it and could pull it away.

Jason was trying to suppress a laugh. "Ah, yes, it does."

She bristled. "Jason, I know what I saw!"

He held up his hands. "Fine! You're Zeus's daughter. I killed a giant, man-eating turtle-frog today, so I'll accept that. But why do you have to bring him back? You said yourself you don't even know what to do. Seems if the guy was half organized, he'd have left better instructions."

Tracy scowled. He was right, of course, at least for the moment. Zeus's daughter or not, she had no idea what she was supposed to do. She lifted the amulet again, looking through it experimentally. It was warm to the touch.

"Um, I should probably mention something . . ."

Tracy gave Leif a sidelong glance. "Since when have you hesitated to mention anything during the past twenty-four hours?"

"I met Apollo," Leif blurted. "And I think he thinks . . . I'm you."

Tracy just stared. So did Jason. So did the doctor. Hooray for solidarity.

"I don't see the resemblance," Jason said finally.

"Not that I'm—I mean he thought I was Zeus's son. That he had some vision about how I'd bring him back somehow. I said he had the wrong guy. Looks like he wasn't even looking for a guy."

"Did he say anything about this?" Tracy held up the amulet.

"Er, well no."

"I can't believe I'm going to say this, Karlson, but . . . talk!"

Thalia sat upon a rock at the top of the canyon wall, some distance back from the mortals for privacy's sake. Ankles crossed, she leaned back on one hand, sunset-kissed red hair blowing back in the wind as she tossed it to make room for her cell phone against her ear. She was visible—invisibility tended to hinder cell reception—and she was posing, though she didn't realize it. It is a habit bordering on instinct of all Muses to pose when visible, regardless of whether or not they are seen. If a tree falls in the woods and no one is around, and it hit a Muse, that Muse will be posing.

"Come on. Pick up . . ."

The call connected. "Hello, you've reached Apollo's private line. I'm sorry I can't take your call right now. If this is Hera, I'm looking into the pomegranate thing, and I will get back to you. Anyone else, leave a message and I'll be glad to get back to you too." Here there was a pause for a barely audible sigh, "Eventually."

Voice mail. Of course. She could just send him a text, but who knew when he'd get *that*?

"Apollo, it's your favorite redhead. Get out to the Nevada desert. Now. That guy I've been following? Major breakthrough." Figuring she shouldn't say more, Thalia hung up, slipped off her arm bangle, and tucked it away.

Thalia considered that she probably should have called Apollo two hours ago, right when she saw the flash of Zeus's aura as Tracy picked up the amulet. But she hadn't wanted to take action until she got some confirmation of what was going on, especially since it was Tracy, not Leif, who'd picked it up. She was supposed to be following him, after all. And what if Tracy had woken when she was away making that call?

She would've missed hearing the whole vision, then, wouldn't she? Where would they all be then?

Though she could have texted Apollo rather discretely without leaving their side . . . *Crud.* Thalia forced back a few tears of self-recrimination. She'd just leave that little detail out. So she'd hesitated. Big deal! Apollo didn't need to know. She was a Muse, not a spy!

Plus, the roaming charges out here were monstrous. Probably. Who did pay those bills, anyway?

It was then that Thalia heard the fabric of the world shudder and tear before it swiftly sealed back up. But not before something came through. There was no mistaking the sound. It was how They traveled.

Thalia went cold. *Here?*

Now?

"Did anyone else hear that?" the doctor asked.

Intent on listening to Leif's story, Tracy and the others ignored the question. Leif had just finished explaining his conversation with Apollo, the god's entreaty for his help, and his own refusal to give it. She couldn't really blame him. He'd been told even less about what he could possibly do than she had.

She yelled at him for it anyway.

"It wouldn't have mattered!" Leif argued. "Obviously I was supposed to be here and help out somehow! You didn't even want to have me along, so now who's stupid?" He blinked. "I mean, you're beautiful when you're stupid, of course."

She resisted the urge to smack him. "And Apollo didn't say anything about what—?"

The grinding scrape of stone on stone cut her off. Their attention shot upward to where a small chunk of the canyon top was rapidly sliding away. All anyone could manage was a perfunctory, "Look out!" before the refrigerator-sized piece shattered on the canyon floor not fifteen feet from them. Chips of stone flew everywhere, clattering off the canyon wall as dust billowed up from the impact.

Too late to do much good, they shot to their feet regardless. Tracy belatedly felt the pain in her shin where a piece had scraped her. It hurt but wasn't bad.

"Um, what just happened?" Leif asked.

The only answer was the crack of splitting rock in the overhang above them. At the same time, melon-sized stones began to tumble from the top of the canyon. Tracy had only a fraction of a moment to wonder if the rocks were falling of their own accord before Jason pulled them all out from underneath the overhang amid the scattered showers of rock.

"It's still happening, whatever it is!"

A cascade of small but numerous stones rained down in the passage that led to the canyon's exit. Momentarily trapped, they couldn't do anything but stand close and try to avoid the larger stones plummeting down every few seconds from all sides. At first Tracy had thought it an earthquake, but the dust devils dancing at the canyon edges and what sounded like vindictive screams from above put that idea out of her mind. It wasn't an earthquake.

Or if it was, it wasn't a natural one.

A chunk of rock the size of her head hurtled toward the doctor. She yanked him away and they both stumbled backward, landing in some sagebrush that immediately began to snake its branches around their wrists. A screaming cackle echoed through the dust from above as the others rushed to help her.

No, definitely not an earthquake.

"No, no, no, no, this isn't my area, this isn't what I do! I'm a Muse, for the sake of all that's sacred!"

Thalia rushed back to the canyon, cursing her luck and hunting for anything to say that could possibly matter to the three beings who had just arrived. She could see them up ahead, bat wings spread, hovering near the canyon edge and focused on whatever havoc they were wreaking below. They had their game faces on: monstrous, sneering, and surrounded in manes of snakelike hair (actual writhing snake heads enhanced the effect). Thalia couldn't begin to comprehend why they would go around like that when they didn't even have to, but then there was a great deal about the Erinyes that she couldn't comprehend.

Generally, Erinyes do not get along with Muses, and the "generally" part of that is redundant. More to the point, the "Muses" part is redundant as well. The Erinyes pretty much do not get along with anyone. Initially, one could hardly blame them. If you were born out of blood spilled from the castration of Zeus's grandfather, you might be a little bit cranky about it too. Yet even such traumatic beginnings can be overcome, and after so many thousands of years, it has become apparent to even the most forgiving individuals that the Erinyes are, put simply, spectacular jerks.

Make no mistake: being jerks goes well with their job of wreaking vengeful justice (or just vengeance) upon those who deserve it. It is a job that needs to be done; crimes such as matricide, patricide, double-parking, and general hubris can hardly go unpunished. Yet no one on Olympus who've had any dealings with them can deny the screamingly obvious feeling that the Erinyes are in it for the vengeance.

It's not even really the vengeance that draws them, but the violence with which they get to dispense it. Sure, justice is done, but to say the Erinyes care about that is to say that porn aficionados care about plot. The Erinyes also have an interest in safeguarding the Natural Order of Things—yet, again, this is primarily motivated by the knowledge that anyone caught violating it becomes fair game for their fury.

"I cannot even begin to tell you how much you shouldn't be doing that!" Thalia called out when she got within earshot. It wasn't a great opener, and it wouldn't stop them, but it was the best she could come up with. It might at least get their attention. Once that was done, all she really needed to do was think of something clever enough to deter the Erinyes from their vengeance! Yes! And then she could teach an elephant to dance on the head of a pin or something equally preposterous!

"Is that a Muse?" said the one spinning dust about. Her name was Megaera.

"A *Muse?*" Tisiphone, the second, laughed. She ceased lobbing boulders into the canyon for a moment to spin one atop a single talon like a basketball. "Whatever is a precious little Musey doing way out here?"

The third, known to most as Alecto the Unceasing, didn't even bother to look up from where she showered the smaller rocks into a barrier at the canyon's exit. She had an appellation to live up to.

Thalia did her best to look authoritative and imposing—a difficult task when one was outnumbered and addressing figures unperturbed by the fact that blood freely gushed from their own eyes. (Copious eye-bleeding is a side effect of the Erinyes' instantaneous mode of transport. Painful, yes, but worth it to pack more violence into a single day's time. Plus, it is really, really disturbing, and anything that makes them more disturbing—with the notable exception of wedge-heeled shoes—is fine by them.) "What right do you have to attack these mortals? Is desert videography such a heinous crime?"

"Ooh, is it?" asked Tisiphone, practically salivating at the thought of having more offenses to punish.

"Since when does a Muse have anything to say about our affairs?" Megaera asked. "This isn't some sissy *play*, Thalia. We don't have to justify anything to the likes of you!"

Alecto gleefully maintained her rock curtain at the canyon tunnel. The mortals were clustered in the open, gazing up warily.

"Maybe not to me," Thalia tried, "but to somebody!"

"To 'somebody'?" Megaera asked. "For the god-commissioned killing of a mortal or two?" She gave a practiced cackle while Tisiphone simply took aim with her boulder and chucked it at the group. Thalia winced and started, thinking she might do something really foolish and interfere, until she saw the throw go wide—likely intentionally so. Tisiphone liked to play with her quarry. The mortals scattered regardless.

Thalia ignored the "god-commissioned" bit for the moment. Let them know she was curious, and they'd never reveal who sent them.

"A mortal or two?" She pointed down, feeling a performance coming on. "One of them—one of them isn't just some mortal, you know, one of them is—an experimental nanocluster of festering, disease-causing motes!" She willed her voice to rise toward a dramatic crescendo, doing her best to enthrall the Erinyes. "Kill that one, and you set them free!" she cried. "They burst apart, infecting everyone within two hundred miles! Highly contagious, highly fatal! A mortal or two? How about an entire hemisphere? Do you really think the gods would be thrilled with losing so many worshippers?"

Yes, it was a little hokey, a little desperate, a little too sci-fi . . . but hey, in a crisis, she'd go with what she knew.

It seemed at least enough to give two of the three pause. Both Tisiphone and Megaera shifted into their more conversational forms, dropping to the ground as their wings folded up, their faces grew lovely, and their hair became . . . somewhat less objectionable. Meanwhile, Alecto sheared bits of the canyon sides away at the narrow exit point, still maintaining her curtain of falling rock. It was piled halfway up and already a major barricade the mortals would have to scramble over.

"You're making that up!" Tisiphone said finally.

"Which one is it?"

Thalia smirked. It was going better than expected. "I don't know, but there's no sense in taking the risk, is there?"

"She's making it up!" Tisiphone cried again. "She's a Musey!" Her wings folded back out. Her face turned gaunt and haggish.

Okay, Thalia thought, not going quite as well.

"What if she's not?"

"Oh for gods' names!" Tisiphone's hair writhed. "Do you even know what a nanocluster is?"

"You didn't even know what a DVD was until last month!" shot Megaera.

Across the way Alecto was apparently getting bored, starting to fling the pile of stone shards up into the air to rain them down on the mortals. Their huddled conference broke apart once more as they rushed for what cover they could.

"Sisters!" Alecto hissed. "Work ethic? Vengeance!"

Megaera growled, her bleeding eyes rolling. "Well . . . I suppose we could just grab them all, shut them up somewhere, and leave them to starve!"

"Too much trouble, not enough fun!" Tisiphone snarled and hurled a rock. It smashed above Jason's head and drew protests from Megaera and Thalia alike. "Oh, stop your bloody whining! Even if she's not lying, we've got the paperwork! Ares gets the blame!"

Megaera's face blossomed in a maw of snarling, cackling delight. "Why am I always forgetting those things?"

"'Cause you're a simpering pus-bag!"

"And a hag to boot!" Alecto added.

Megaera hissed at the insults, smiling widely nonetheless. With a raise of her arms, she gathered heaps of sand and stone into the early evening air to launch them down into the canyon with renewed vindictiveness. "Go to Tartarus, Musey! The grown-ups are working!"

Megaera's shriek as the crossbow quarrel pierced her chest a moment later completely blasted away whatever it was Thalia was about to yell in response, which was a shame because she was certain she had a really effective zinger on the tip of her tongue.

Leif gave a whoop as Jason's crossbow shot found its mark. The weapon, small and hastily unfolded once he'd fished it from his bag, was more powerful than Leif expected. The hideous bat-snake-woman-thing tumbled backward out of view. The shower of rocks blocking their exit subsided. Tracy caught the whole thing on the headband camera she'd snatched from Jason. With Dave gone, it was the only one they had left, and visions or not, she'd said, she'd be damned if she'd let this go unfilmed.

"One down, two to—"

"*Run!*" The scream came from a redheaded woman now swooping toward them in gold-gilded robes of flowing white. The sight of her surprised them enough that most of them stood rooted and blinking as two of the bat-women flew down ahead of her. Leif ducked as talons raked the air nowhere near him, although the creatures appeared more concerned with Jason, but better safe than sorry, right?

Jason managed to dodge and knock one off course with a swing of his crossbow. The other seized him as he turned, lifting him up. Tracy grabbed his ankle before he got far and the doctor sprang up afterward, fighting alongside her to free Jason from the thing's grip. They dangled there a moment like an oversized earring before the hag let Jason go and the three mortals landed in a heap. All Leif could do was blink.

The redhead landed, or more accurately stepped out of the sky. Also, she was yelling.

"Run! Run now!"

"Someone hand me another quarrel!" Jason tipped an imaginary hat to the redhead. "Ma'am."

The bat-women had disappeared somewhere over the top of the canyon. Their screams echoed down over the edge, sounding like a banshee with its hand caught in a blender. Leif hoped at least some of those were screams of pain.

"No!" the redhead cried. "You don't understand! You cannot stand against the Erinyes!"

Jason rushed to reset the crossbow. "First birds, now flying redheads. What's an Erinyes? Leif! Quarrel!"

"Oh, hell," Tracy whispered in what seemed to be recognition. "Jason, she's right, we have to run!"

"The way out is clear!" yelled the redhead. "You can get out! Go! Go! Go! Nobody listens! Why aren't you going? Are you an executive?"

Tracy tugged at Jason. The doctor was already scrambling up the rock pile. Unable to recall what the Erinyes were, exactly, Leif merely stood gripping a quarrel that Jason swiftly grabbed from him.

"Fine!" the redhead yelled at Jason, "you can stay here, be all heroic, cover their escape! The rest of you, run!"

"Jason! Tactics! You're a sitting duck in here, like Pittsburgh!"

Whatever happened in Pittsburgh, that seemed to do the trick. The big reality-TV hero turned and ran, ushering the others in front of him. Leif handed him the rest of the quarrels regardless.

"Yes!" the redhead cried. "Yes, go! Oh, you're all such bright little mortals! Hurry!"

They scrambled up the pile of stones and into the passage beyond as the Erinyes, shrieking in wordless rage, regrouped in the air behind them. The redhead turned, putting herself in the Erinyes' path and by all indications preparing to hold them at bay by sticking her tongue out, but mightily. Leif couldn't watch. Plus, there was the fleeing in manly terror to take care of. He leaped from the top of the rock pile and ran after Tracy.

"We just had to let Dave take the shotgun, didn't we?"

They dashed through the narrow passage. Leif's eyes frantically shifted from the ground in front of him to the air behind him to Tracy's spectacular backside and back to the ground (though not always in that order). The brief journey took far too long for his liking. The Erinyes' screams and the sound of talons scrambling on rock pursued them up the passage. Whatever the redhead had done, it hadn't slowed them down much.

They reached the end of the passage and passed out of the mouth of the canyon to see below them the hill they had hiked up hours ago. "Keep running!" Jason ordered.

Leif saw no reason to stop. He followed the doctor out of the canyon mouth and grabbed Tracy's hand a moment before she tugged herself free—probably just to keep her footing while running down the steep, graveled slope. (Hadn't Leif been heroically fast with those quarrels, after all?) They were halfway down the slope before they noticed Jason wasn't coming with them.

The redhead, however, was. "Keep going!" She was also missing most of her outfit for some reason that Leif regretted he didn't have more time to ponder.

"Where's Jason?" Tracy cast about.

"Being a hero! There's really no time to argue!"

Tracy stopped. "Jason!"

"Is this National Ignore Good Advice Day?!" The redhead grabbed Tracy's arm. "You cannot stay! They're Erinyes, vengeance on bat wings without mercy or fashion sense! I'm just a Muse, I can't protect you! Your only choice is to run, Zeus's daughter!"

"Tracy . . ." Leif began, thinking this Muse had probably the best idea.

The Muse misunderstood, but quickly. "Yes, yes, 'Tracy,' whatever! I'll call her 'Tracy,' I'll call her 'Zeus's daughter,' just let me call her 'running her destined little butt off'!"

Above, the Erinyes emerged from the canyon, two of them haplessly trying to untangle the Muse's robes from their heads. Jason sprang from ambush, blade out and swinging. Savage slashes cut across each of the tangled ones in two flashing strokes. Both fled back into the canyon, leaving the robe behind, howls of pain ripping the air. Leif's eyes went wide as the third Erinys sprang down the slope directly toward them.

"Okay, run!" Tracy yelled.

She didn't have to tell Leif once. He caught a glimpse of Jason following before he fled down the slope again, expecting to feel talons in his back or see Tracy snatched up.

He was vaguely concerned about the doctor. Jason, the hero, would obviously be fine.

A vindictive cry cut the air behind him, and he stumbled, staggered, and regained his balance just as a dark shape flew over him. One of the Erinyes slammed into the doctor and lifted him off his feet just as a quarrel pierced her shoulder. She dropped him immediately and tumbled away down the slope. As they stopped to help the doctor up, Leif gave Jason a thumbs-up where he stood above at the canyon mouth.

"He did it!"

The Muse shook her head. "Unless by 'it' you mean made them angrier, then no, he didn't."

Before anyone could argue, the first two Erinyes sprang at Jason from behind, hoisting him up by the arms and cackling. They lifted him high above the slope and summarily let go. He dropped, but only briefly, saved by a desperate grab at one of their ankles that left him hanging in the sky from a flapping nightmare that couldn't quite support his weight and maintain altitude.

For a moment it looked as if Jason would make it safely to the ground on that hideous flapping parachute. Perhaps he even would have, had the previous sentence not begun with *for a moment it looked as if.* Sadly it did, prophesying the moment that followed as the third Erinys, a quarrel still deep in her shoulder, rammed into Jason, knocking his grip free and sending him plummeting a good eighty feet. He crashed onto a prickled bush that was completely inadequate for breaking his fall onto the boulder around which it grew. His sword careened off the boulder and tumbled farther down the slope. His crossbow shattered instantly.

"Oh, gods," Thalia whispered. "No one survives a plummet."

Leif didn't have the heart to argue. Jason wasn't moving anyway.

Above, the Erinyes circled like caffeinated vultures.

"I love when the stupid ones try to fight back!"

"Ha! Megaera loves a mortal!"

Megaera immediately reacted to this with a snarl and flung herself toward the other two. There was an aerial tangle of blood and shrieks as the Erinyes tore at each other. They tumbled away toward the canyon and disappeared from sight.

Tracy half leaped, half clambered toward Jason. Leif followed suit.

"You're running the wrong way!" yelled the Muse. "Come back! This isn't *funny!*"

Her warnings went unheeded. In the end they had to climb down two short cliffs and jump a ravine to get to him. Leif nearly took a spill on an unsteady rock as he tried to watch for the Erinyes' impending return. So long as he kept watching for them, he figured, irony wouldn't let them show up.

Right?

When he finally caught up, Tracy was holding Jason's hand in a struggle to find a pulse. The hero's eyes stared up at the sky in vacant, unblinking surprise. "He's not breathing!" The doctor was there a moment later, pulling her aside and doing his own examination. Leif kept watching the skies. The Muse continued her litany.

"You cannot tarry! They won't be playing for long! If they come—"

"Just shut up!" Tracy yelled. "Shut up right now! You told him to stay behind! This is your fault!"

The Muse pointed back at her, eyes tearing up. "Do *not* make me play the don't-make-his-sacrifice-be-for-nothing card! Don't you dare! I can't handle the cliché right now, I'm having a very stressful evening!"

The look on the doctor's face was plain: Jason's sacrifice was officially ultimate.

Leif wasn't having such a swell time, himself. "Tracy," he started, "please, if they're coming back, we need to—"

Tracy's glare all but slapped him across the face. "Need to *what?*"

"We need to run! Find shelter, something!"

The doctor nodded rapidly. "He's right. We can come back, get his body once we're safer."

The Muse blinked. "What? He's right? I'm not just some knockout redhead! What have I been saying here?"

The screaming returned before Tracy could give an answer, and Leif cursed himself for taking his eyes off the sky. The screams came from somewhere beyond the canyon wall. Maybe they still had time, if they hurried. He fervently hoped that whatever force controlled irony couldn't hear his thoughts.

"Tracy, please."

Tracy tugged the camera headband from her forehead, stuffed it in a pocket, and then led them down the slope with a sweep of her arm. Somewhere behind them the Erinyes screamed again.

"'Please take my shift, Thalia?'" the Muse seemed to be quoting as she followed. "'I'll owe you a favor! What trouble could he possibly get into in two days?' Zut! Calliope's going to owe me a whole freaking saga before this is over! *Run!*"

CHAPTER FIFTEEN

"Some cite Ares's love of dogs as proof that the god of war is not without his positive sides. While this text has no official opinion on the matter, anyone wishing to decide for themselves would do well to also note Ares's love of dog fights."

—A Mortal's Guidebook to the Olympians' Return

THALIA'S CALL TO APOLLO had come while he was in the middle of a hurried in-flight reprogram of one of the sun chariots. Getting lax in the maintenance schedule was never a good idea, especially when replacement parts had to be special ordered from Hephaestus (whose position as senior editor of the *European Journal of Engineering* absorbed much of his free time). Apollo jury-rigged a fix he hoped would hold—at least until he could send the other chariot up to take its place. Only then did he notice Thalia's message. A few seconds after he heard her voice mail, he'd shot off to where he sensed she was.

It was just after sunset by the time he arrived. The sky was lousy with Erinyes, Thalia was shepherding Leif and two other mortals down the hillside, and Death was silently leading away the spirit of a confused and burly mortal whom Apollo didn't recognize. (He'd brought the scythe. Why did he always bring the scythe? He never actually used it anymore. He was like a college sophomore who still wore his high school letterman's jacket.) Questions in need of immediate answers numbered three in Apollo's mind: Why were the Erinyes here? Who died? And just what was the "major breakthrough" Thalia spoke of?

He was also vaguely curious why exactly Thalia was running around half naked, but that could wait. What was clear was that the Erinyes' venomous shrieks and rock-hurling put a stop to any ideas of discrete godly observation. Apollo thrust himself between the two parties and appeared with a blast of sunlight right in front of the shrieking bat-hags. They pulled up sharply and looped back around to hover, begrudging him the attention that was his due as a god.

He smiled at all three, arms crossed. "Alecto, Megaera, Tisiphone. Would you care to explain just what you're doing?"

They hissed and shrieked, spitting palpable vitriol that floated in the air before dissipating. They teleported a few yards to reappear directly in front of him and then floated back a few feet again with their eyes gushing blood, posturing. Apollo wouldn't normally put up with that kind of crap, but with the Erinyes, you had to pick your battles, especially if you were trying to speak to them mid-vengeance. Demanding manners may as well be asking for a nice vivisection-free foot rub, for all the good it would do.

"Do not interfere, Apollo!" Tisiphone yelled. "This is just vengeance you're . . . interfering with! Interferer!"

"Paperwork!" Megaera declared. "Right here!" She yanked it out to wave it in his face before stuffing it away again. Fortunately thousands of years of wading through bad poetry had made Apollo quite the speed reader. He got a pretty good look.

"Ares sent you just to avenge the death of one of his creatures? Rather extreme, that. He usually rewards bloodshed."

"Who cares?" Tisiphone shot.

"He helped create the creature! It's his right!" Megaera added.

Alecto kept quiet save for a frustrated mewling as she quaked with barely contained bloodlust. Her eyes tracked the mortals' retreat. Her talons twitched.

It *was* Ares's right, Apollo thought, but it was a right seldom exercised these days, when there were more surplus monsters stored up than anyone really knew what to do with. "Who killed the creature, exactly?"

Tisiphone pointed up the slope to the dead mortal's body. "Jason Powers!"

"Monster Slayer!" Megaera declared.

Alecto remained silent, her glare fixed. She bounced in the air like a toddler after too much Kool-Aid, provided that toddler held a wicked dagger.

"Then he's dead now. Your job is over."

"Now, see, that's what we thought just now, but then Ares came and said—"

"The job," Apollo interrupted pointedly, "is over. Now you will take your lovely faces elsewhere."

"Helped! They all helped!" Tisiphone screamed.

"No one tells us how to do our jobs, Apollo," Megaera hissed. "Not even a god."

"Yet in the past you've only gone after the party directly responsible for a slain favored creature, no? Did you change your rules, or did Ares change them for you?"

Megaera scowled. It was a moment before she admitted anything. "Ares . . . But he had a point!"

"They deserve it!" Tisiphone cried. "They saw it happen! They must suffer!"

"Yes!" Alecto burst. "Suffer! Suffer-suffer!" She quaked with giggles punctuated by stabs of her dagger.

Apollo smiled. "I thought you didn't let gods tell you what to do."

Tisiphone nodded vehemently. "We don't! Now stand aside! For the vengeance!"

"Because Ares told you so," he said.

"That's different!" Tisiphone scowled, ruminating a moment. "That is vengeance! V-E-N-J . . . and the rest! We heed not your orders!"

"You won't listen to a word I say?"

"Not a word!" Tisiphone yelled.

"And whatever I say about doing your job is wrong?"

"Dead wrong!" Tisiphone's use of the word "dead" set Alecto twitching longingly.

"Then I command you: obey Ares! Chase down the mortals! Tear them limb from limb even though they didn't kill the creature! Obey both gods!"

"No!" Tisiphone screamed. "You cannot command us! We're—we're leaving! Now! Right?"

Alecto bit her lip on a desperate mewling as if she might explode.

Megaera looked troubled. "I . . . there's something amiss about this, Sister."

Tisiphone hesitated. "Yes. Yes, there is something, isn't there?" She pointed a talon at Apollo, eyes narrowing. "And when we figure out what it is, we'll be coming back for you! Or for those mortals, anyway! *Our* choice!"

Megaera downshifted from hideous and checked a ledger. "Er, no we likely won't; there's that Cthulhu thing to deal with. We're late as it is."

Alecto spun around, eyes wide with what Apollo took to be a fearsome hope at the possibility of action.

"Cthulhu thing?" asked Tisiphone.

"Don't you remember that pack of mortals who believe some god Lovecraft made up is real, just because Olympians are? Worshipping false gods shall earn them a demonstration of *true* eldritch horror!" She cackled dramatically before pointing to the ledger. "See? I made a note. True eldritch horror."

"Ah!" Tisiphone agreed. She swooped up into Apollo's face as Alecto looked back and forth among all of them. "So maybe we won't be back. But maybe we will! You just tell those mortals *that!* Tortured, tortured they'll be in their not knowing!" She glanced back at Megaera. "What've we got after that? Can we fit them in after that?"

"It's a choice between—"

Alecto exploded into a shriek that sent animals five miles away diving for cover. "Stop it! Just stop *talking!* If we're to go, then let us be gone and be done with it! This isn't some bloody panel discussion show!" She seized Tisiphone by the neck and shook her, eyes crazed. "If I'm not torturing someone in the next thirty seconds I swear I'll rip your filthy lips off!"

Tisiphone hissed, pushing her off, and then vanished. Megaera grudgingly followed suit. Alecto laughed in triumph and stabbed at the air with giddy cries of "Eldritch! Eldritch! Eldritch!" before she vanished after her sisters in a shower of blood.

Apollo allowed himself half a moment to savor his own amusement before he dropped to the ground to dash after Thalia and the others. Thalia, at least, stopped when he asked.

"Hi, Apollo, nice timing! Hey, mortals! Stop!" If they heard her, they didn't care. "They keep doing that! I mean I suppose one can hardly blame them with the Erinyes on their tail, but they weren't listening to me when I was telling them to run either, and it's just, I mean, come *on*, do I project so little authority? Maybe it's because I'm hardly wearing half a stitch, but even before I lost the robe they were all, 'let's not pay attention to the Muse!' and so forth. You'd tell me if I was, wouldn't you? Lacking authority? I mean, not now, I guess, but hi, how'd you get rid of the Erinyes?" She beamed.

"You know that thing you came up with half a century ago with the cartoon rabbit and idiot hunter?"

"You're kidding! That worked?"

"Erinyes: not known for brains."

"Well, yeah, but—Hey, do I get royalties for that?"

"Thalia, what exactly is going on? You mentioned a breakthrough. Was that before or after that fellow died back there?"

"Oh! Golly, yes! Before. Definitely before. All right, so Leif? Not related to Zeus! At least I don't think so. Maybe he is. Could he be? I mean you so seldom know with these things, and he's got a crush on Tracy that if she gave half a whit about reciprocating would mean—eww! I mean eww for mortals, anyway."

"Thalia! In ten words or less if you can manage!"

"Ooh, word games! Um, let's see . . . Leif's in love with Tracy who's Zeus's daughter with an amulet." She paused. "Oh bother it all, that's one word too many, but the amulet's important! Now you respond in, um . . . seventeen words or less! Apollo? Hey, come back!"

Apollo had already shot ahead and landed straight in front of the three fleeing mortals. Leif and the woman he took for Tracy stopped up short. The third screamed and changed direction, dashed through a stand of cacti, and vaulted a rock before Apollo managed to grab him and plop him back down with the other two. The mortal continued to scream nonetheless.

"Silence!" Apollo demanded. It didn't work as well as he hoped.

Tracy took the panicking man by the shoulders. "Doctor, it's all right! He helped us! Doctor!" She caught the doctor's gaze long enough to apparently calm him to the point where he at least stopped hyperventilating. He nevertheless held the look of someone who'd bagged his limit of stress for the day.

"But," he managed, "who is he?"

Apollo radiated a bit of divine manifestation over the group in response. "I am the god Apollo." He just barely managed to get it out before Thalia answered for him. "I expect you've heard of me."

"See?" Leif said. "I told you." He gave Apollo a wave.

"Thank you," Tracy said. "You stopped those things?"

"Less stopped than redirected. But we can discuss that—"

Something flickered at the edge of his vision.

"Oh, now, don't be thankin' him too soon," said Ares. "I don't think he's gotten you out of this quite yet."

The god appeared out of that flicker, standing atop a collection of rocks and girded for battle. With Ares, "girded for battle" normally equated to "not naked" (and sometimes even that was untrue), but now he'd gone to special effort. The gleaming bronze armor, colored red with the blood of every war in history, was usually something he wore for only especially dangerous battles or holiday meals. Strapped to his left hand was his favorite shield, a heavy iron affair crafted in the shape of a snarling dog. His right hand held a spear he used in the Trojan War (on both sides), and a vulture-shaped helm completely covered his face save for the eye slit. Even so, there was no mistaking him.

Leif groaned before Apollo could say anything. "Why is everyone so stuck on shields and melee weapons? Haven't you guys heard of guns?"

Ares's gaze didn't waver from Apollo's for a single moment. "Heard of, invented, perfected . . . But you don't go messin' with the classics, mortal. Now shut up and think up some proper last words." At this fresh new threat, the doctor shrieked like a man crashing through his stress threshold and gleefully rocketing toward a temporary breakdown.

Apollo stopped time.

It wasn't a true stopping of time; that's just plain impossible. Yet when two or more Olympian gods stand close to each other, there exists enough malleability in the space-time continuum to create a small pocket outside of time. Such pockets are notoriously unstable and as such worthless for anything but the purpose of simple conversation, but they have their uses.

"Aww, now what'd you have to go and do that for? They were all 'bout to quake and piss 'emselves!"

"You answered your own question, Ares—which for you is amazingly astute. I assume you've been watching. What the Styx do you think you're doing, if thinking even comes into it?"

"Figured I'd kill your little pet pipsqueak there before I grab a late supper. You got a problem with that?"

"You didn't send the Erinyes for Jason Powers at all, did you?"

The god sneered. "Collateral damage. Seemed worth a shot. Damned crones can't do anything right. Some things ya just gotta do yourself."

"Why?"

"Why?" Ares laughed. "The great Apollo wants to know why? Don't play dumb, sunshine; you're bad at it."

"I'll assume that was intended as an insult."

"We know what you're doin'! You can't be bringin' Zeus back."

Apollo tried to mask the worry boiling up inside him. "We?"

"Yeah, we! Me and—Yeah, we!" Ares pointed his spear at Leif. "We know about blondie there, about your visions. He's the key to bringin' back Zeus or some such. You know what Zeus'll do if he gets back?"

Apollo considered that Ares might not really know the extent of Apollo's commitment to that very thing, and that this was a trick to get him to expose himself. Then again, Ares's tricks were usually of the "look behind you!" variety. He discarded the possibility.

"All the more reason to be the one to help him do it, I'd say. Care to join the cause?"

"You got the wrong damn pantheon, Apollo. Zeus ain't the forgivin' type."

"So you did kill him."

"Damn right, and it ain't just me. Now I'm about done talkin'. This spear? It's goin' right through your pet mortal's heart, and you got no choice in the matter."

"You think I can't stop you?"

Ares laughed. "I ain't attacking you, Apollo. You wanna stop me, you gotta make the first strike. I ain't much for laws, but you know what 'King' Poseidon decreed: god attackin' another god gets you in big damn trouble after what happened to Zeus. He ain't takin' any chances now some mysterious unknowns of us know how to kill each other."

"I can defend the mortal just as easily as you can attack him."

"Maybe. But can you stop me from attackin' again?"

He had a point, annoyingly enough. Apollo had no idea how Ares knew about the visions. He thanked the Fates that he didn't seem to know Tracy's significance, but Leif was likely still vital, and Ares was just as likely to take out the entire group once he got started.

"I can wear you out," he tried. "Defend him until you lose interest in the fight."

"Lose *interest?*" Ares laughed and flashed a smirk. "Apollo, come on. This is me here." The god of war had another point.

"Very well. What if—?"

"Nah, I'm all through talkin'." Ares raised his spear. Time took notice of them again. "Hey, towhead! Speeeeeeear's Ares!"

The god rolled to one side and thrust his spear straight at Leif. Apollo leaped between them in time to slam his boot down on the shaft, driving the weapon into the ground and snapping it in two.

"All of you, run!" Apollo ordered. The others wasted no time, dashing off again with a panicked doctor in the lead.

"Puns are lazy writing!" Thalia screamed at Ares as she went.

Ares picked up the broken spear. "Rotten Titan-whore's whelp! That's my favorite damned spear!"

"And you let it get broken by a whelp!" Apollo taunted. "That's got to be humiliating." If he could just goad Ares into attacking him first . . .

Ares's glare only turned to a sneer. "A broken shaft'll run a mortal through good as anything, Apollo, and if that don't work, I'll pound him to death with my bare hands!" Ares tried to dash past him. Apollo grabbed the broken spear with both hands and wrenched him back. Tugging and yanking, they struggled against each other for possession of the weapon. Apollo considered whether this counted as an attack, but if he laid hands on only the spear and not Ares . . .

Apollo's preoccupation with legal details allowed Ares to spin him around and away from the mortals. The war god released the spear entirely before Apollo could correct his mistake, turned back after the mortals, and sprinted away. Ares bellowed a wordless, bloodthirsty battle cry, shield arm raised to strike. He was one of the swiftest on the battlefield; there was no way Leif could outrun him. Off balance, even Apollo had next to no chance to get there in time. He hurled himself after them anyway. Thalia looked behind her and screamed, diving out of Ares's way (to land in a spectacular pose). Leif ran hard beside Tracy, not looking back. Ares closed to striking distance.

Apollo wasn't going to make it.

"Ares!" Apollo yelled and hurled the broken spear end over end at Ares's head. Ares didn't look back. The spear hit him in the back of the skull with the force of a cannonball and pitched him forward into a boulder. His helmet struck rock with a clang that reverberated into the evening sky like an alarm: Olympian had attacked Olympian. The Styx was hitting the fan.

Then again, no one particularly *liked* Ares . . .

Apollo dismissed the minor hope. It was just as useless as the non-fatal blow—Apollo didn't even possess the power to even make it a fatal blow. There would be retaliation from on high. Poseidon would be anxious to enforce his law in the face of the first real challenge to his authority.

Apollo wasn't the only one to realize it. Thalia had picked herself up and was staring in shock at Ares's unconscious form.

"What did you *do?*"

"I knocked the lights out of the god of war. Most people would cheer me."

"Oh, that's good, why do I get the feeling Poseidon isn't one of them? We're out in the open now, Apollo. You know what everyone's like! The pantheon's going to freak, and you know how Poseidon gets when someone snubs him!"

"I had no choice, Thalia."

"You've at least *heard* of *The Odyssey,* right? He's going to come down on you like a tsunami on a rowboat."

Leif spoke up before Apollo could answer. "You know, it occurs to me, this whole thing? Total *deus ex machina!* Gotta say I don't mind when I'm on this side of it."

Thalia stared. "Oh, gods! And on top of everything, now we're cliché!"

CHAPTER SIXTEEN

"Though no mortal has ever seen it, the Olympians claim to have a council of twelve gods known as the Dodekatheon, which convenes regularly to discuss various matters of Olympian importance. The council is ruled, of course, by the king of the gods, though the precise organizational hierarchy is unknown at the time of this writing."

—A Mortal's Guidebook to the Olympians' Return

"Poseidon worries more about votes and politics on the Dodek than Zeus ever did. I can't decide if it's because he's too erratic to lead well or if he just fears he'll share Zeus's fate if he makes too many unilateral decisions. Perhaps both are likely—and suddenly I'm thinking it unwise to express these sentiments in a public blog."

—(unpublished) blog entry of Athena

ONCE HE WOKE and got back to Olympus, Ares insisted on speaking to the Dodekatheon as soon as possible—so soon, in fact, that not all member gods were in attendance. Fine with him. Poseidon was the only one he cared about now, the only one with the final word on anything. The other eleven could take a flying leap for all Ares cared.

Ares belatedly realized that he was one of those remaining eleven himself, but screw that. Just details. He could take a flying leap too, if he had to. No use correcting himself. Admitting mistakes was weakness.

Standing at the center of the circular Dodekatheon chambers, he looked over those gods seated around him who were able to respond to the immediate summons: Poseidon, Hera, Artemis, Athena, the spinelessly nurturing Demeter (she was knitting), and Hermes. Speedy bastard was everywhere, only this time Ares was glad for it. Now he could show the little trickster the value of action. Still, he'd gladly trade Hermes's presence to get rid of Artemis. It didn't take a genius to guess whose side Apollo's twin sister would take.

At the moment, all waited on Poseidon. The Olympians' new king sat on a throne of coral and jade, twin to the one he'd sat on beneath the sea. His eyes were two blazing emeralds staring into the distance as he concentrated on feeling the ether of the world, searched along the Earth's lines of mystical power, and scanned down from atop Olympus for something only Apollo's elders had the power to sense.

Ares cracked his shoulders and wished the salty old fart would get the heck on with it already. It wasn't like he was trying to take Stalingrad in winter or do long division or anything. Locating Apollo shouldn't be that damn hard.

Poseidon's eyes cleared.

"Well?" Ares asked.

"Apollo is not within my sight."

"What? Now that don't make no damn sense! Get him here now! I want to do this to his face!"

"Ares!" Hera's rebuke matched the glare with which Poseidon slapped him. "Calm yourself!"

"What precisely has Apollo done?" Poseidon asked. "Then we shall see."

"What, if anything?" Artemis quipped.

Ares ignored her and yanked off his helmet. "What's he done? Only broke your highest damn law—that's what he's done! Look at this! Hit me in the back of my head with my own spear!" He pointed to the gigantic dent. "Knocked me right out! My skull's still ringing!"

Anger flashed over Poseidon. Ares could feel the god scrutinizing him. Unlike his predecessor, truth-sensing wasn't the sea god's strength, yet so strong was the god's decree that he would be able to tell just by looking if another had violated it. Ares held his ground with a righteous sneer. "Unprovoked," Ares boasted. "I didn't lay a finger on 'im."

Poseidon begrudged a nod. "Why?" he asked.

"Why? Why's it matter why? He broke the law! Your law! Punish him!"

"Apollo is no impulsive savage," said Artemis, "unlike some I could mention. I move that we wait for his side of the story. I'm certain it would be more coherent."

"And what makes you so damn sure?" Ares shot. "If he's in the right, why's he hiding, huh? For all we know, he killed Zeus!"

Artemis chuckled grimly. "I thought you had claimed that deed for yourself, Ares."

"Ah, no one believes that hogwash anyway. I'm a blustering boasting brute, ya know."

"And if he was trying to kill you, why aren't you dead? You were knocked out, unconscious . . ."

Ares inwardly cursed the stupid virgin goddess and her stupid smart questions while trying to come up with an answer.

It was Hermes, as it turned out, who had one. "Even so, he raises a good point. What does Apollo have to hide? And how is he even hiding at all? Ever since . . . what happened to Zeus, we have wondered just what power exists that allows an immortal to be killed."

"You are suggesting," Poseidon said, "that the source of this same power might allow a god to escape his elders' attention?"

Hermes shrugged. "Oh, wondering more than suggesting. We don't know for sure either way."

"Exactly! Hiding makes him guilty, can't ya see? Strip him of his duties, track him down, get him here, and lock him away!" Ares declared. "Stick him in Tartarus for a century, then see if he wants to talk."

Demeter looked up from her knitting. "But Apollo's such a nice boy. Why not just send out word that we'd like to speak with him, and ask if he could please stop by and let us know his side of things?"

"Yeah, and when he gets here we can all have ambrosia and butter cookies and dance a little jig!" Ares sneered.

Demeter clapped. "That's the spirit! Oh, I'm giving these mittens to you when I finish them, Ares. Isn't it nice to get along?"

Ares stared. Were a lump of coal between his teeth, he'd be chewing a diamond in short order.

"King Poseidon," Athena spoke for the first time, "with apologies to Artemis, is it possible that the reason you cannot locate Apollo is that he's now dead as well?"

Artemis immediately shot her a stricken look and then turned away.

"No," Poseidon answered. "Were he killed in the same manner as Zeus, I would sense it."

A bit of motion in the balcony caught Ares's eye. It was Hecate, who stepped from the shadows to lean forward and scrutinize Artemis. Not actually a member of the Dodekatheon herself, she nevertheless often lurked in the balcony, listening in and—so far as Ares felt—being weird for the heck of it.

Hera noticed her too. "Hecate, is there something you care to share with the Dodekatheon?"

The dark-haired goddess shook her head. "Answers I do not have are not mine to give. Yet sunlight shines upon the cypress."

Ares rolled his eyes. "Speak plain! This is why we don't invite you to parties!" They did invite her to parties, actually, or at least most of them, but Ares wasn't one to let facts stop a good offensive.

Hecate gave the slightest nod toward Artemis. "She knows."

All eyes turned toward Artemis, who shifted in her seat. "Something's different with my brother. I don't know what it is, but something has changed."

"Explain," Hera demanded.

"I cannot. Just recently, before we were all summoned here, something felt . . . off. I'm unable to quantify it any more than that. Please, great Poseidon, allow him time to return of his own accord."

"No!" Ares roared. "You can't just—he's not just going to show up! We have to find him!"

"And where do you propose we look, Ares?" Hera scolded.

"Ah, this is ox crap! If he'd attacked anyone else, you'd all be out in force, trackin' him down!" A stray thought struck his skull. "There was a Muse there too! Why don't ya go find one of 'em and make 'em say where Apollo is?"

"Which one?"

"Eh?"

"Which Muse?" Hera repeated.

"Oh. Umm . . . the redhead. What's-her-face."

"Thalia!" Demeter declared, beaming. "She's got such cute little dimples."

"Yeah, so's my puckered butt," Ares muttered.

Demeter gasped. "Manners! No mittens for you now!"

"If the Muses are involved," said Artemis, plainly ignoring the vitally important winter-wear issue, "it can hardly be something to do with Zeus's death! They loved him!"

Hermes chuckled. "Or appeared to, anyway."

"Ares," Hera started, "perhaps you should tell us the entirety of what transpired, and omit no *further* detail."

"I ain't leavin' out . . ." He set his jaw as a dozen acerbic comments jammed up against each other, trying to get out. The delay gave just enough time for him to register Hera's warning glare and, against all odds, pick the least offensive of the bunch. "Fine, if you wanna waste time . . ."

Ares went on to explain the truth of what happened, the partial truth, and little beyond the truth, describing his rage at the mortal's slaying of the creature he and Athena designed together. He told of his fully understandable request that the Erinyes avenge the destruction of such a rare collaboration when they could, and of his warning to the dead hero's companions regarding further attacks on his favored beasts.

"Jason Powers is dead?" Athena jumped to her feet in shock. "You killed him for *that*? I watched the fight; he fought well and nobly!"

Ah, hell. Leave it to the goddess of defense to get squeamish. "He killed our creature! I had the right!"

"Oh, for our sake, Ares, it was just a stupid turtle-frog! That you *consulted* on!"

"Athena!" Hera warned, wresting them back on track.

Athena threw herself back to her seat. "Rage-tripping jackass. I liked that show."

"And for this," Hera continued, "Apollo attacked you?"

"I dunno why he did it! But yeah, that was when. Maybe he liked the show too, I dunno!"

"If Thalia was there, perhaps he thought you were threatening her?" Artemis asked.

Ares whirled on her. "I didn't threaten her!"

"Ares, you're violent, loud, and destructive," she said with a smirk. "You threaten the air with your very presence."

"Flatterin' me ain't gonna shut me up."

"I meant that it would be very easy to misconstrue your usual demeanor for a heightened threat."

Hermes cleared his throat. "That would make sense, were Apollo not as used to Ares's temperament as the rest of us. And . . ." The god scowled and shook his head into silence.

"Speak your mind, Hermes."

He glanced at Poseidon. "I can't help but wonder if Thalia—or all of the Muses, for that matter—are in on whatever Apollo must be up to."

Artemis scoffed. "What he '*must* be up to'?"

"Might be, then," Hermes amended. "But we all know how close the Muses are to—"

"Oh, yes!" Artemis cried. "They work with him, so they're all in on some conspiracy! Why not round up anyone who's ever had anything to do with Apollo? We're most all of us related to him in some way! I'm his twin sister! Lock me up!"

Demeter leaned over. "Quiet, dearie. No one's locking anyone up, are we, Poseidon?"

Poseidon considered this for a moment. "I—"

"Now you be nice!"

The problem the Olympians faced in dealing with Demeter was her sheer sunny disposition. She'd been more like the rest of them in the early days, but centuries of playing the nurturing harvest goddess had softened her. Some viewed her as downright senile. Thinking she would be easily influenced, the others gave her Zeus's open spot on the Dodekatheon, yet she cared not a whit for political machinations, instead lending what could only be described as grandmotherly support to whichever party she perceived as playing the nicest. To appear too abrasive was to lose her vote.

Poseidon gave only a resigned glance in Demeter's direction before addressing the rest of them. "The Muses shall not be under suspicion yet but will be called before the Dodekatheon and questioned regarding Apollo's whereabouts. Apollo himself shall be placed on probation pending investigation. Hera will summon him personally. If he does not appear in three days' time—"

"Three days? Who knows what he could—"

"*Be silent!*" Poseidon was on his feet, trident slammed into the ground. It was enough to shut up Ares. Poseidon calmed, slightly, after that. "If Apollo does not appear in three days, then he shall know his uncle's wrath."

Ares stifled the impulse to ask what Poseidon's punishment might consist of, as he was pretty sure Poseidon himself didn't quite know. With Zeus—as much of a pain in the ass that he'd been for the past two millennia—you could at least count on the fact that he had a penalty in mind when he threatened you with one. Poseidon wasn't nearly so organized. There was something to be said for fear of the unknown, but it was a heck of a lot less satisfying when you were rooting for the retribution.

On the other hand, Poseidon, god of the sea, monsoons, and hurricanes—who once had spent two decades kicking Odysseus in the metaphorical crotch—had a fine track record for wrath. Even so, the three-day delay was outrageous and blunted what should have been a clear victory against Apollo. Artemis and her bloody arguments! Maybe if the virgin goddess got laid once in a while, she wouldn't be such a bitch! He and Hermes could've gotten Apollo tossed in Tartarus immediately if not for her, and now the rest of the conspiracy would give him crap for going against their damn "plan," perhaps Hades most of all.

Yeah, well, bring it on. At least he was doing something.

But why couldn't Poseidon find Apollo?

CHAPTER SEVENTEEN

"Thank the Fates for loopholes."
—*Apollo (Zeus Is Dead: A Monstrously Inconvenient Adventure,*
Chapter Thirty-five)

THE FIRELIGHT GAVE THALIA'S red hair a glow that seemed to brighten further as she ranted. "I mean, you can't just yank three iconic sci-fi characters off a starship like that, plunk them around a campfire singing 'Row, Row, Row Your Boat,' and just expect it's going to work! The fourth movie with the whales was funny, but then they got cocky. I mean, come on. 'Marshmelons?' Ugh! I take absolutely zero responsibility for that whole thing!"

"But you said you mused it," Leif pointed out.

Thalia heaved a put-upon sigh across their own campfire. "Yes, fine, but I didn't write the thing, I only inspired! There's a centuries-old Muse saying: 'You can gas up the car, but you can't make 'em drive it well.'"

"Centuries old?"

"Mm, we were all a little puzzled about that before the invention of the internal combustion engine, I can tell you. But that's why I usually try to keep comedy and sci-fi separate, even if I do them both. It's like chocolate cake and lasagna. A chef can know how to make both; he can even make them in the same meal, but if he tries to mix them up in the same bowl it's an atrocity against the palate. Same thing with handling both genres, except not really because sometimes it turns out really well. Like Douglas Adams? Oh, now there's a man that got it! But the genres don't combine nearly so well all the time, not always, which is the point I'm trying to make, and how did we get on this, anyway?"

Leif started to answer.

"Oh, yes, you asked your silly question," she finished. "You see, this is what happens when I'm stressed and people take exception to my job description, I—I—I come up with inelegant analogies!" She clenched her eyes shut as if holding back tears. "Life is so unfair!"

Tracy shot her an icy glare that Thalia missed. Apollo, lost as he was in thought beside her, didn't appear to spot it either. Only Leif noticed, but the whole-heartedly sympathetic smile he'd let fly in Tracy's direction merely drifted on past her. Tracy instead turned her attention back to her plate of beans that Apollo had somehow whipped up from thin air along with new robes for Thalia and the rest of their current camping gear. Leif had wondered at the choice of cuisine but figured it was at least setting-appropriate. Thalia wiped her eyes.

It was suddenly too quiet for Leif's liking. "So along the lines of comedy and sci-fi *not* mixing well," he tried, "did you have anything to do with Jar Jar B—"

"Oh!" Thalia shrieked. "Oh, don't you dare! I am so frelling tired of taking abuse for that! That was not my fault! How many times do I have to say it?"

"Would you two shut up already?" Tracy snapped.

Thalia nodded, going on. "Yes, yes, exactly, shut up about it! One little annoying comic character and people just—Look, for every *word* that combined comedy and sci-fi well, there's another entire work that just fails to do the same thing—"

"Hyperbole," Apollo muttered before returning to his thoughts.

"Yes, of course it's hyperbole, Apollo. Hello? Muse? But I am *not* going to sit here and be called to task for every single thing that exists—"

Tracy dropped her plate to the dust. "For crying out loud, do we have to listen to—"

"—for *every single thing* that failed to live up to some geek's expectations, the majority of which I didn't have anything to do with *any*way, because— my gods!" A tiny sob burst from Thalia's throat. "I mean, you don't know what it's like! Have you *been* on the Internet? And all I can do is work with what talent the writer—" She gasped for a breath, tears glazing her eyes. She wiped them, staring at the moisture on her fingers. "Now look what you've done! I'm crying! I can't do this, I can't have this conversation when I'm stressed!"

"*You're* stressed?" Tracy yelled. "I don't know about you, but I've had a hell of a day! I find out that not only is my father a god, but that he's a murdered god and I'm part of some inter-Olympian strife that I wasn't even aware of yesterday, plus I've got this raging urge for justice that I can't explain—though it's possibly because of this amulet that I can't seem to throw away—and on top of *that*, a good friend—or colleague, anyway, even if he was a bit of a jackass—is dead because of it all!" She was on her feet now, pointing at Apollo. "And on top of that, he won't give us any answers about anything because he says he has to think!"

"Well, thank you for the recap!" Thalia yelled back. "You're not also going to mention how Apollo used his power to help us travel faster on foot so that we're closer to Vegas than the spot you camped at last night? What about how the doctor had enough of this whole business and decided to wait back with Jason's body for your cameraman? Or that maybe we're all a little on edge and you need to lighten up, especially because Jason died a hero and is at this moment very likely to be happily cavorting in the Elysian Fields of the afterlife, and how isn't that bloody fantastic?!"

"Thalia," Apollo muttered. It didn't stop her.

"There now! Everyone's all caught up! You'd think this was the second half of a two-part TV episode or something! Why not just trot out the ol' standby 'As you know' phrase just to round it out?" She thrust her hands onto her hips. "As you *know*, Tracy Wallace, I'm Thalia the Muse, and we're arguing over the campfire because we're both a little consternated!"

Everybody got that?

"Thalia," Apollo repeated. It still didn't register.

"And I don't like being consternated! I'm the Muse of comedy! I'm supposed to be laughing and happy and light-hearted!" She flung her fingers through her hair with a scream. "Does this look light-hearted to you?!"

"Thalia!"

The Muse turned a radiant smile on Apollo. "What? I'm fine, I'm just fine. Done thinking yet? Who wants more beans? Isn't *legumes* a funny word?" She sat back down, fixed her hair in a single motion, and batted her eyelashes.

Leif just blinked. Tracy clutched at the amulet, as if ready to snipe back. Apollo cut her off with a raised hand and a single, "Please." Tracy turned her glare on him a moment before forcing it back.

"It would be so helpful to me," she managed, "if we could talk about this. I've had all the running and confusion I can take. I know you're a god, and that's all really great, but . . ."

Apollo nodded. "I've not yet said much because I'm not sure I know much more than you do."

"And he's been thinking," added Thalia.

"And I've been thinking. But to correct you on a minor point, I am not a god."

Tracy scowled. "What's that, some sort of semantics thing?"

"I knew it!" Leif said. "What is it? You guys are some sort of super-advanced other-dimensional beings or something?"

". . . Apollo?" Thalia whispered.

The not-god put a hand on the muse's shoulder. Probably he meant it to be reassuring but it didn't seem to succeed. "I *was* a god. I'm not anymore. I . . . diminished."

Thalia gaped wider. "You *what?* Apollo, are you insane? I mean, I thought I sensed something, but I figured it was just some kind of power shift or some nonsense to do with Ares or a sort of gastrointestinal thing or—"

"It was necessary."

Tracy's frown deepened. "Someone's going to explain to me what that means."

"I voluntarily renounced my godhood," Apollo told her. "My power, my standing, all are now less than they were."

"So, like, you were a general and now you're a private?" Leif asked.

"More like a major. I still retain some of my former power. But yes, your analogy is fairly apt."

Tracy's frown remained entrenched. "Voluntarily?"

"As I said, it was necessary."

"Yes, listen up," Thalia whispered, still in stunned awe. "And, um . . . well let's just start with question number one here, which I think would be something like, oh golly, let's just see . . . *Why?*"

"It is forbidden for one god to attack another."

"Well, I never heard of that."

"Neither are you a god, Leif Karlson."

"Look who's talking."

Tracy whacked him in the arm. "Don't interrupt."

Leif rubbed the spot. That was going to bruise. It wasn't his fault he couldn't resist a good dig.

Apollo went on. "After Zeus's murder, Poseidon made it law to comfort the pantheon. And likely himself. Breaking that law made me a fugitive or at the very least wanted back on Olympus to explain. Then, the moment I explain why I did it—to protect you—our secret would be out, and those who killed Zeus or simply don't want him back would have me in their grasp."

"Couldn't you just make up some story?" Tracy asked.

Thalia laughed.

"He's a bad liar," Leif explained.

Apollo nodded. "And no matter what Poseidon's ruling, Ares—whom I now believe to be one of those responsible for the murder—knows at least some of what we're up to. He and any coconspirators could try to corner me on Olympus and keep me away from you."

"What's any of this got to do with diminishing?"

"Be patient," Thalia scolded. "Exposition. This sort of thing has to unfold with gravitas!"

"No patience," Tracy said. "Answers."

Leif whacked her, but gently, and grinned. "Then stop interrupting."

"That glare she's giving you, Leif?" Thalia said. "That's how you know she doesn't think it's funny."

Apollo cleared his throat, snapping their attention back. "With a little concentration, a god can locate any god of a younger generation. Poseidon, Hera, Hades, any of them could find me no matter my location. Even if I hadn't broken a law, odds are at least one of them is in league with Ares. In fact, I'm certain that's the case."

"So . . ."

"So the rules are very explicit," Apollo said. "They can locate any *god* of a younger generation. If I am no longer a god, then I can no longer be located."

"You're kidding me."

"No, Ms. Wallace, I am not."

"I told you," Leif whispered. "It's easy to tell."

"The rules really are that screwy sometimes," Thalia said.

"They can no longer automatically locate me, and what power I have left helps me to cloak myself from the ways they might find a lesser being. Assuming they're looking for me, I'm hopeful it will take them a while to figure out what I've done. We Olympians are often ruled by a fear of losing power, some more than others. It may not even occur to them that I've diminished voluntarily. Such a thing would be exceedingly unpalatable to them. Not that I'm exactly thrilled about it myself."

"Oh, Apollo." Thalia sighed with a hug at his arm. "What if they strip your portfolio from you entirely? What will you do then? For that matter, what will I do then? I mean, they'll have to get someone to replace you, and on top of everything else, I do not want to be breaking in a new boss! What if it's Ares? Or, gods, what if it's *Hades?* He's got no imagination at all and I am *not* going down to the underworld every single time I have to—" She squeaked and clapped a hand over her mouth in alarm.

"I don't know," Apollo told her. "That's somewhere toward the bottom of our current list of problems. I still have power beyond any mortal, and I've gained us some breathing room."

Leif wondered just what that remaining power entailed and how easily Ares might beat him—or even kill him—if he showed up again. Was Apollo even immortal anymore? Though Zeus had been immortal, and that hadn't helped him much, had it? Or so went the story. It occurred to Leif that all he had to go on at this point was anyone's word. Tracy he trusted, but the others? Well, how could he be sure?

Then again, if Apollo and Thalia were lying to him, all of this would have to be one heck of an elaborate snow job, all for Leif's benefit. Leif couldn't think of why he would warrant the trouble. Then again (again), didn't things like this always have a twist at the end, even if the twist made no sense?

Hey, he'd gone a while without saying anything, hadn't he?

Tracy beat him to it. "So you've bought us some time—and I suppose I should thank you for that, as dubious as this loophole sounds—but what now?"

"Tell me again about the vision," Apollo said.

She sighed. "Fine. For the third time . . ." Tracy related it once more, as she'd done when she first woke up, and as she'd done as they'd fled from Ares's unconscious body. Leif hadn't noticed it being so clipped and snarky the first two times.

"A living weapon," Apollo said.

"I figured that was obvious the first time," said Leif.

"I may be without godhood, but I am not without pride. Show some respect." Apollo went silent, presumably thinking. Again. Leif wondered if the not-god would be doing that for the rest of the night, but he didn't make them wait nearly so long this time. "At the very least, it's useful to know that Zeus's death was not attributable to an ability that one of the pantheon has gained, nor a martial weapon easily wielded."

"Not useful enough for my father," Tracy said. "You haven't heard of anything like it before?"

"*Our* father," Apollo said. "And no. If any of the Olympians knew of such a thing, the fear it would cause with its very existence . . ."

"Fear?" Leif asked. "Seriously?"

"As I said, we are often ruled by a fear of losing power. Had we known that a weapon existed that could destroy one of us . . . It would be destabilizing at best. I doubt anyone knew."

"Zeus knew," Leif said. "He had to or he wouldn't have done that . . . amulet thingy."

"Perhaps. He may have simply been aware of a threat without knowing its source."

Thalia shrugged. "It's a moot point anyway, isn't it? We can't exactly go into the underworld as if he were a mortal and ask his shade."

"Wait, you can do that?" Leif asked.

"No, I said we *can't* do that. I swear on a screaming box of bunnies, nobody listens to me!"

"I meant with mortals."

"I know what you meant."

"So why act like you didn't?"

"Because it was a potentially funny misunderstanding!" Thalia beamed. Leif blinked. "Not very."

"Critics! I told you I'm stressed!"

Tracy cut off the exchange with a hand over Leif's mouth before he could volley back. "That weapon didn't just pop into existence in that box in Zeus's office," she said. "So where did it come from? Who could make it?"

Apollo frowned, apparently thinking once more. For a moment they all waited, and Tracy removed her hand. Leif smiled. "You know you've—"

"Compliment my skin and I'll claw your eyes out, Karlson."

"The Moirae," Apollo said suddenly as if that explained it all. Plainly no one else thought so. "More commonly: the Fates. They spin, measure, and cut the very threads of reality. Life and death, existence and oblivion, all they may bend and shape at their will. If there exists a weapon that can kill a god, surely they must know of it."

Thalia patted him on the shoulder. "Poetically said, Apollo, but that's not exactly helpful. I mean, they're not the most forthcoming beings, are they? And even if they did know something and were of a mind to tell it, wouldn't Poseidon already have asked them about it, learned about it, and told the rest of us about it before he hunted down the . . ." The Muse trailed off, somehow managing to provide her own echo for what Leif presumed was dramatic effect.

"Unless Poseidon was the one responsible in the first place!" Tracy finished.

"Perhaps," Apollo told them. "Perhaps not. As Thalia said, they may know and simply not be of any mind to share."

"Or something else less obvious," Leif suggested.

Apollo nodded. "In any case, I will pay them a visit."

Thalia gaped. "That means going back to Olympus, Apollo! You just diminished to avoid that very thing! Are you trying for some sort of dramatic irony, because there's a time and place for that and neither is here or now! Or now and Olympus for gods' sake! (Oh, I got those backwards the first time, didn't I?) How in the name of Cerberus's chew toys do you think you're going to sneak all of us up there to see them when you're not even at full strength? Things weren't already challenging enough for you or something?"

"I don't plan to sneak all of you up there. The Fates dislike mortal visits. I must go alone."

"Alone?" Thalia cried. "That's not better! Is that better? How is that better? What are we supposed to do until then, just sit around and—? I can come with you, right? I mean I need a good bath, get some of this sand out of my hair, maybe have a few dozen glasses of ambrosia and— Hey, is this some sort of 'abandon the younger protagonists to stand on their own for dramatic tension' thing because again, time and place . . . not now! . . . Or here! And I'm not much younger than you anyway!"

"Stop going back to the trope well, Thalia."

"If the shoe fits, buy twenty."

"You have to stay with the mortals, Thalia."

"Why?"

Apollo pointed at the silver bangle entwined about her bicep. "You know why. And if I know Ares, your sisters are likely being watched. None can come here to take your place."

Thalia began to protest, stopped, teared up, converted sadness to anger, geared up for an outburst, then bit her lip to shut it all down under Apollo's gaze, finally nodding. Even those readers imagining her response as quite a production are likely to have imaginations guilty of understatement.

"What're you to talking about?" Leif pressed, hating to be left out.

"Each Muse wears a bangle that makes her completely untraceable. By anyone," Apollo said. "It's one of the main reasons writers hate the question, 'Where do you get your ideas?' They can't figure it out themselves. And the bangle's power has an aura; if Thalia stays near you, none may divine your location."

"Oh yeah? So how'd the Erinyes know where to show up?" Leif asked.

"They knew where the monster died," Thalia said with a sniff.

Apollo nodded. "You can still be spotted by sight, but you're off the radar. Metaphysically speaking."

"So what do we do in the meantime?" Tracy demanded. "Leif said you were having visions about all this yourself. Any guidance there?"

Apollo shook his head. "They were about Leif only, I regret to say. While following him led us to you, I knew nothing of you specifically." Apollo pointed at Leif. "He was climbing the Eiffel Tower and talking to Zeus. There was little of practical—"

"Wait, the Eiffel Tower?" Leif burst. "Climbing? As in outside? At the *top?*"

"In a rainstorm."

"Ha!"

"That was the vision."

"Ha! No way. There's not—I can't—Do you have any idea how tall that thing is?"

"Three hundred twenty-four meters. I visited soon after having the vision, looking for further clues to Zeus's return."

"That answers my next question," Tracy said. "I take it you didn't find anything."

"No."

Tracy sighed. "Well, I can't just sit here waiting, can I? Zeus clearly wanted me to do something."

"I believe it would be wisest for you to remain with Leif and Thalia for the moment," Apollo said. "Until I learn more."

Leif didn't quite catch Tracy's protest at that. A previously minor fear of heights was swiftly ballooning in his mind. "That's not a literal vision, right?" he tried. "It's a metaphor for something, isn't it?"

"It may be, but I do not believe—"

Tracy ignored the entire exchange. "How do we even know the Fates are going to be on your side?"

"We do not, but I count it unlikely they would be against us either. They hold themselves aloof from the rest of Olympus. Even Zeus himself was reluctant to challenge them."

"Okay," Tracy tried, "so take me with you. They might need to see the amulet."

Leif remained elsewhere. "What's the Eiffel Tower?" he whispered. "There's a radio antenna at the top! A big radio antenna!"

Thalia touched a finger to her lips. "Leif. Shush, honey."

"And I'm climbing it, talking to a god . . ."

Apollo continued to Tracy. "I cannot risk your presence on Olympus, Ms. Wallace. At least not until we know more. Though it may be wise to take the amulet with me . . ."

"Nope. Zeus wanted me to have it, right? Something tells me I really shouldn't let it go."

"A radio antenna . . ." Leif jolted, thinking of something. "A radio! For talking to a god! *A radio for talking to God!* That's a line from *Raiders of the Lost Ark!*"

Tracy scowled, apparently surrendering the battle to ignore him. "And he's lost his marbles."

"Prescient visions do not reference movies, Mr. Karlson."

Leif didn't let that stop him. "No, but there's no way I'd climb the actual Eiffel Tower! It's a reference to the movie obviously! He said that in a Cairo café in the movie! We need to go to Cairo, that's it!"

Apollo shook his head again. "That was not my impression."

"So? You didn't know a thing about Tracy, why can't you be missing this too! Cairo! Or wherever Harrison Ford lives. Or—or maybe that French actor who played the archeologist in the movie! The one who said the line. Hey, he's *French*, just like the Eiffel Tower!" Leif was on his feet. "It's so obvious. Don't you see?"

"His name is Paul Freeman," Thalia told him, "and he's British."

"Oh." Leif sat, crestfallen.

Tracy turned back to Apollo. "How long will your Fates visit take? If I just sit around this campfire for too long, I'm going to go crazy."

"I understand your urgency, Ms. Wallace—"

"Zeus is dead. Jason's dead. Someone has to pay for that!"

"I said I understand," Apollo repeated. "But I must be cautious. Perhaps as much as a day, though I hope for less."

"For someone who can see the future, that's not a terribly precise estimate."

"Hey! Of course!" Leif slapped his own thigh, flush with a sudden epiphany. All eyes were on him again. He beamed back at them, explaining. "Maybe it's Paul Freeman's *character* that's—"

Apollo's glare was almost audible. His voice certainly was. "No, Mr. Karlson! That is not! It! Know that in my time I've interpreted more visions than you've had foolish thoughts in your head, and I choose such an insanely high number to impress upon you the incredible mind-boggling vastness of my experience! You will let this go! The vision is literal! Take my word for it or don't, but either way you will stop babbling and we will all be much, much happier!"

"Or at least seventy-five percent of us," Thalia cracked.

Leif cast about the group for any sort of support at all. Obviously there was none from Apollo. Thalia just seemed amused. Tracy . . . damn, she had gorgeous eyes. He lingered there a moment.

"Fine," Leif managed finally. He turned to stare into the campfire. "Know-it-all god-posers."

"I didn't quite catch that?"

"I said 'sorry,'" Leif grumbled.

"Yes, that's what I thought you said. As for the topic at hand, while I'm gone, it might be prudent for the three of you to return to Las Vegas. It's not a perfect option, but the city isn't far off, and you'll be less exposed than you are out here, provided you keep a low profile."

As the others worked out just where they would meet back up with Apollo—and how long of a hotel bath Thalia might be able to take in the meantime—Leif's mind drifted. Okay, he consoled himself, all right, so maybe it wasn't that bad. Zeus wasn't back yet, was he? Zeus had to be back for the vision to be true, so at the very least he had a little time. If the vision was literal, that meant that Zeus would be right there, and if Leif had helped bring him back somehow, surely the god wouldn't let him fall off the tower, right? *Maybe.* He supposed he would find out when—Leif gasped, seizing upon a hope: If it was a vision of the future, well, that would mean he'd survive until then, wouldn't it? Whatever trouble there was coming up the pike—angry gods; divine conspiracies; stolen mochas; vindictive, bleeding-eyed bat-women—he'd have to survive it in order to fulfill the vision! Leif was suddenly conscious of grinning like an idiot, but as it was the grin of an idiot who'd been granted a prophetic guarantee of safety, he didn't really care.

Of course, if Tracy herself wasn't in the vision, did that mean something had happened to her? The thought froze him solid. Geez, what if that was it? What if she was fated to die? He instinctively reached out to give her hand a protective squeeze before he could stop himself. So genuine was his alarm that Tracy didn't even yank it free.

"What? What is it?" she started.

Leif held on. His appreciation for the sensation of physical contact stunned him into hesitation. Just as stunning was the novelty that she hadn't pulled away. Dear gods, he loved this woman. Again, he wondered why, and again he didn't care. He suddenly noticed that her eyes were fixed on his, searching for the reason for his alarm. He couldn't bear to tell her.

"Karlson?"

"I—it's nothing."

The tolerated physical contact ended there, followed shortly thereafter by Tracy's fist driving its way into his solar plexus. Then for a little while, nothing of interest happened, so we'll just skip ahead to when something does.

It may or may not have to do with sex.

CHAPTER EIGHTEEN

"Nearly everyone likes sex. Mentioning sex at the end of a chapter is certain to get at least 80 percent of book readers to continue reading, even if no sex actually occurs. The remaining 20 percent will see through this ruse and put the book down out of disgust at being manipulated."

"Of course, you can use reverse psychology to keep most of those types interested. The smart ones hate being predictable."

—*Muses Erato and Calliope, 2010 Topeka Writers' Conference*

THERE WERE ONLY THREE of them now: the redhead, the brunette, and the blond guy. Thad supposed he should have listed the blond guy first since Thad's mother had sent him out here to track him, but it was the redhead who drew his eye. She was gorgeous and possessed such an exquisite figure that she clearly worked out at least as much as Thad did to attain his own gorgeous physique.

The brunette was passable, Thad supposed. She could probably look pretty darned hot if she tried. Except she wasn't trying, which meant he was out of her league. Also, the glasses were a turnoff.

Lousy luck catching sight of the redhead out here in the middle of nowhere. A woman like that called for restaurants and hotel rooms luxuriant enough for Thad to flaunt his wealth, but out here in East Bugsquat, Nevada, he'd have to rely on his looks alone. That still meant there was a formidable arsenal of seduction at his disposal, but chasing people through the sticks could dull even someone of his caliber. His skin was dusty, his shoes were dirty, and sweat offended his clothes after his pursuit of the group that had moved so impossibly fast on foot across the wilderness. He supposed it gave him a rugged, heroic look that all the advertisers wanted lately, but a real "rugged look" came from at least an hour in makeup. This was just sweaty crap.

Damn, but his feet ached! Thad looked forward to charming his way into the redhead's tent and the foot massage she'd surely be happy to give him. For starters. What better vantage point was there from which to keep an eye on Karl Leifferwhatsit? He would spend just a few more minutes crouched behind the bushes to watch their camp, plan his approach, and fix his hair. Then he would make his presence known.

Leifferwhatsit was already dozing. His head rested at the edge of his own tent. The brunette sat on a rock by the fire, examining some bit of jewelry. The redhead was on another rock, one hand back behind her, legs crossed, and posing in a way Thad had to admire out of sheer professionalism.

Definitely a model. Excellent. Easy icebreaker.

The dark-haired man Thad had spotted with them earlier seemed to have split the scene without taking the redhead along. Thad couldn't imagine why. Maybe he was gay. Good for him.

"Can I see that?" the redhead asked with a gesture toward the amulet. "I'll give it right back." The brunette glanced back, hesitant. Her expression was similar, Thad thought, to the look most women gave him when they had to leave his company: so very reluctant. The redhead continued, "I'm not going anywhere. I just wonder if it might show me something it didn't show you since I'm . . ."

She didn't finish the sentence. She didn't have to. Clearly the redhead didn't want to say just how much more beautiful she was than the brunette. It was sensitive of her, trying to spare the other's feelings. Thad smiled. Sensitive women were a godsend; they were that much easier to beguile.

"I . . . I don't know," the other answered. "I just have this feeling that I can't let it go, not even for a moment. It's important." Thad wondered if the amulet was important. "It's very, very important." Thad supposed it might be. "I wasn't even comfortable giving it to Apollo, so . . ."

Hold on. Apollo?

"Please? It might help."

The brunette made a reluctant move to sit beside her and held the amulet's pendant out without taking it off her neck. Thad inched (pointlessly) closer himself, suddenly torn between possible redheaded conquest and having an excuse to get himself back to Vegas. Apollo was a god; Thad was sure of that one. God of . . . he didn't know, amulets? *Whatever*. If another god was interested in the trinket and the brunette wouldn't part with it, his mother would want to get her hands on it. Yet charming it away from the brunette would possibly forfeit his chance at the redhead. Maybe if the brunette took it off and gave it to the redhead, he could time his entrance to stun them both into forgetting about who had it and he could focus on . . .

The redhead peered through the center of the gemstone and let out a gasp.

"What, what do you see?"

"Everything's all purpley!" said the redhead. "What? It's pretty! . . . Oh lighten up, Mopey Longstockings—it's a joke."

The brunette muttered something he couldn't hear, tugged the amulet away, and returned to her seat. The brief hope that she would indeed give it to the redhead dropped like a towel in a sauna. He'd have to keep his sights on the brunette if he wanted it. Maybe that was even for the best. It might be just the trick to make the redhead jealous enough to compete for his attention. If he played things properly he could take care of her too, before stealing away with the amulet in the middle of the night. He loved those sorts of challenges.

Except for the "middle of the night" bit, really. So scratch that; it was already pretty late anyway, and he'd want to take his time. Early morning, then. Though sleeping in sounded pretty good, and he didn't have either the tents or the sleeping bags that they did . . .

So. He'd seduce the brunette, make the redhead jealous, have some fun and a good long rest, and then steal off sometime after breakfast with the amulet. Before anyone was the wiser, he'd be back to a place where he could get a good mojito. Thad ran his fingers through his hair and put on his sexiest disinterested face. It was entirely possible they'd be so happy to see him that they'd eat him up immediately.

When he finally stepped from the shadows, the redhead was staring. It immediately threw his concentration. People normally stared when he made an entrance—what perplexed him was the fact that she wasn't staring at him, but rather at some vague place off in the distance. He turned, he looked, but not only did he see no other competitively attractive men, he didn't see anything worth looking at whatsoever.

This woman had some nerve.

"Who are you?" the brunette asked.

At least *she* had the good taste to notice him. Her taste in clothes, and those glasses, were another matter. He recalled his immediate objective and unleashed a slow smile.

"I'm Thad. I saw your fire." He took a few steps forward.

"And?" she said.

And? And what?

"And I thought you might like some company." He glanced at the redhead. Her stare continued as he waited for the brunette to say something stammering but inviting.

She stared, agape. "You're just . . . wandering by. Out here." Clearly she wasn't good at talking to men. He bestowed his attention upon her again and strolled closer.

"Of course. It doesn't have quite the charm of my luxury suite in Vegas, but I love an evening stroll; feeling the excitement of possibilities undiscovered, watching the way the moonlight caresses the night, the way the stars reflect in the eyes of—"

"What the hell is your problem?"

Thad scowled. "Ah, problem?"

"You've obviously got one, right? Either you're all the way out here at night without any sort of appropriate gear—which makes you an idiot—or you're pretending to be something you're not and hoping to casually ease your way into our confidence—which, frankly, also makes you an idiot."

Thad bristled a moment before his ego kicked in. The poor thing was clearly stammering. He gave her the smoldering gaze that once launched Calvin Klein's Neurosis line, and then made his way toward an open spot next to her on the rock. "Or maybe I'm simply lonely and in need of the company of a beautiful, charming woman such as yourself."

And suddenly she was off the rock and on her feet. "Charming? Right. Thalia?" She glanced at the redhead.

"Thalia? Is that her name?" He smiled, sitting down anyway. "What's yours?" Thalia, he considered. *Nice.* He could actually be sincere when he told her later what a lovely name it was. Faking genuine sincerity was always more productive. Now why the heck was she still zoning out like that? "Is she okay?" he asked. Maybe she was drunk. Good for her. Good for both of them, really.

"She's fine, I'm sure."

The reality of the situation was that Thalia was busy musing. A particularly intriguing fiction idea had surfaced in the mind of a writer in Boston as he struggled with an unrelated work of nonfiction, and she wanted to at least give it a good nudge out of the gate before he lost interest and resumed work on an e-mail to his insurance company that detailed just how the alligator had not only gotten into his kitchen, but had done so wearing his bathrobe and his neighbor's golf bag. (While it was an interesting story, Thalia didn't truck in that flavor of nonfiction and considered his idle ponderings about an invasion of extra-dimensional alligator people to have more camp potential anyway. More to the point, the creation of such a story might have helped Thalia win a particular bet with Calliope, the specifics of which are tangential to this tale at best and will not be further remarked upon here.)

Tracy, for her own part, just assumed zoning out might possibly be how Muses slept.

Thad decided to simply ignore the redhead for now and focus on the brunette until Thalia came down enough to admire his presence. "Of course," he went on. "Now where were we?" He really loved saying that. It always sounded so damn smooth.

"You were being an idiot, and I was wondering what kind." She stood there, hands on her hips, refusing to sit beside him.

"Don't be intimidated. We're much alike, you and I."

"Alike, huh? And how's that?"

She'd picked up a long stick from somewhere, though he couldn't imagine why. If he'd known she had some sort of stick fascination, he'd have brought one into the camp with him, but most women didn't particularly like sticks—none that he knew of anyway. Most women preferred jewelry. In fact, jewelry (though he hadn't thought to bring any of that either) was one of his favorite ways of getting a woman to take off her clothes. Thad suddenly noticed the symmetry and wondered if the brunette might take off the amulet if he gave her some clothes. It was worth a shot, he decided, and was nearly off with his shirt before it registered that she'd said something else.

"Come again?" He smiled.

"I said what the hell are you doing?"

He folded his stylish, white Havana shirt and offered it to her. She caught it with the end of her stick and flipped it back in his face. At first he thought it was just because of the dust and sweat that clung to it—and he supposed he couldn't blame her there. But something about her glare and the way she continued to wield the stick managed to sow in his mind a seed of the idea that, just maybe, he wasn't actually getting through to her. It stunned him so badly that he completely missed whatever it was that she said next.

Was she insane? Or was it really the shirt? Just to be sure, he tossed the offending garment into the fire, where it smoldered and caught fire. The air filled with smoke and the scent of roasting sweat and melting buttons. It failed to appease her.

"Make even one move to burn your pants and I'll put this stick where the sun doesn't shine, right?" she warned. "Now I'll ask you this one more time, and then you're going to get the hell out of here: Who are you? Who sent you?"

This really was not going well at all. "The . . . shirt was dirty," he explained.

"Don't care. Answer the question."

His mother—with a glare that still burned in his memory—had forbidden him to tell anyone what he was really up to. A glance at the redhead gave no hope of help from that quarter. Thad couldn't conceive just how it had happened, but he'd screwed things up. The wilderness obviously sabotaged his looks, and the brunette was off her rocker. There was one avenue left to him.

"I don't suppose you've got anything to drink?" he tried.

She just stared. Thickening smoke from the burning shirt drifted between them.

"Scotch and tonic? Wine? Beer? Even a little tequila, maybe?" He gave a wide, seductive grin. "Surely you must have brought something out here? You know, that smoke really brings out the passion in your eyes when—"

"Go away."

"But—"

"I said go away! Now!"

"Oh, come on, woman!" he exploded. "Are you gay? Sterile? Frigid? What is it?"

Before he realized it, he'd stepped through the smoke and grabbed the stick with both hands. She tried to jerk it away, failed, and he pulled her closer with it as frustration boiled over. Screw this, all this garbage of running through the damn desert chasing after men and damn stupid women who didn't know a good thing when it walked into their lap! He didn't need this; he was Thad Freaking Winslow! He kept hold of the stick with one hand and lunged for the amulet with the other. The brunette yelled in protest, trying to shove him away and shouting for the others. He let go of the stick entirely, instead trying to force the amulet over her head with both hands. Her knee drove up hard into his thigh, but he yanked the amulet off in terribly unimaginative fashion and spun away with a shove that sent her flying into an empty tent.

The redhead continued to zone out. Thad started to run and then paused. He turned back to steal a kiss from Thalia's lips before giving the brunette a smiling wave and then dashing off, shirtless, into the night.

Damn, but his feet ached.

Leif woke to Tracy's touch and the sight of her gazing down at him. The touch was a kick to the shoulder and the gaze was decidedly agitated, but at least it was something.

"Get up! Hurry! Follow me!"

Leif didn't bother asking why. She practically dragged him out of the tent, and why was it so smoky out there?

"Look for a shirtless jackass with an amulet!"

"A shirtless—Wait, what? Someone stole the—"

"No repeating!" She tossed him a flashlight. "With me! Run!" She gave him no chance to argue. There was hardly time to shove his feet into his shoes before he was off after her and, apparently, some guy without a shirt.

"Why's Thalia just sitting there? Who took the amulet?"

"Oh, yeah," Tracy shot. "Because I just know everything, right?"

"Hey! Why's he got his shirt off?"

Leif couldn't quite make out Tracy's answer, but he was pretty sure it was 67% profanity.

They sped over the dust and sagebrush. Leif's flashlight showed him only what to dodge. Just ahead, Tracy's wasn't doing much more, yet she set a rapid pace. After a short bout of dodging cacti and leaping rocks, he spotted what she was making for: bouncing and flickering farther ahead was the faint purple glow of what was either the amulet or the nose of Rudolph's flamboyant cousin.

"Slow down!" he called. "Pace yourself!"

"Just keep running!"

"I'm not a sprinter!"

If Tracy gave a response, he didn't catch it. She piled on the speed and closed some of the distance to the bouncing purple light and its presumed shirtless carrier. Leif did his best to catch up. He'd run cross-country track when he was younger, but that was never about getting anywhere in a hurry. It suddenly occurred to him that he had already lost track of how to get back to the camp.

Anyone running at top speed across rough terrain in the dark ought to know never to look back. Some might call it common sense, but Leif learned the hard way. A fraction of a second after spotting the campfire, his foot struck a rock and he tumbled into the dirt. The flashlight (also, the skin of his palms and forearms) broke his fall and gave its last in the effort. Tracy's light continued on ahead. The amulet bounced beyond it.

It was the distant, dancing glow of dozens of pairs of little green lights that got him back on his feet so quickly.

"Tracy! Turn it off! Turn off your light!" Her response was lost in the distance between them, but her light stayed on. Either she couldn't quite hear him or she didn't understand. He cupped his hands to his mouth and conveyed it all with one word. "Razorwings!"

Her light stopped. It went out. It belatedly occurred to Leif that now he had no way to find her in the dark. After that it occurred to him that he had no real way to protect her from razorwings. After that it occurred to him that if he kept letting things occur to him, he'd likely be falling on his face again, and so he just plain ran and watched the swarm get closer and closer to whomever had stolen the amulet.

Shirtless bastard.

The amulet's glow vanished with a shout presumably issued from the lungs of the bastard in question. Leif hurried on as fast as he dared in the darkness, a collection of bodily impulses: feet making for the amulet's last location, eyes watching in the dim light for anything that might trip him up again, mind trying to figure out why he was hurrying in the general direction of a swarm of razorwings, while also realizing that he still had no idea where Tracy was. Taking cover if she was smart, he decided, which left just him to get the amulet back, save the day, and get the girl.

And that, said his heart, *is why we're running toward a swarm of razorwings*! His mind wasn't entirely convinced, pointing out his heart's rather questionable behavior lately, but his adrenal gland swiftly tackled his mind with the help of a few lower bits of anatomy and forced it into a game of Stop-Hitting-Yourself that kept it too occupied to do much else.

The swarm dived down ahead of him. It seemed to pass into the ground and rise back up a short distance away. A ravine of some sort, he decided, unless they could teleport short distances, and damn but wouldn't that be cool?

Leif was getting close now. The swarm swiftly turned to make another pass over the area. His mind prevailed over his other parts and finally yelled at his feet to stop before he got too close. It was indeed a sort of ravine, maybe a dry riverbed. He was still too far off to tell its depth, but close enough now to realize he had no idea what to do next besides wait for them to go away. Yet they likely wouldn't go away. If he knew anything about razorwings, the swarm would land and play and grab the amulet from the shirtless guy before—

The swarm launched into the sky in a spastic tumble of fur and wings that held no glowing purple object whatsoever. Leif recalled that he did not, in fact, know much about razorwings.

Before he could react further, a shadowed, Tracy-shaped figure to his left dashed to the ravine and plunged in with a vindictive shout. Leif followed, stopping short on the ravine's edge. It was indeed a dry riverbed, maybe ten feet deep at most. In the moonlight he could see Tracy struggling with Mr. Shirtless as he attempted to climb up the rough dirt slope on the other side. He was halfway up, trying to kick Tracy's grip off his ankle.

Leif hesitated, knowing even as he did so that he needed to do something. The shirtless thief yelled something to Tracy about having had her chance to get his pants off already. He might break free and away at any moment. Leif helplessly wondered why was he just standing there like—

Oh, hey.

"He who hesitates is lost" is repeated so often that it has passed from saying to cliché. It is not a truism so much as it is simply broader and catchier than "He who hesitates sometimes spots a more fordable spot in a dry riverbed because he has taken the time to look." (It's also likely that those who hesitate just haven't gotten around to putting that saying into more common use, but one cannot be certain without extensive laboratory testing.) Leif discovered the truth of the latter saying at that particular moment. As such, the dash he made across the aforementioned fordable area to the others' place of struggle was particularly surprising to the shirtless thief.

Leif skidded to a stop in front of him, kicking dirt in his eyes in a way Leif decided he should later claim to be intentional. The thief cursed and stumbled, too late shielding his eyes with the hand that also clutched the stolen amulet. Tracy, dislodged from his ankle moments before, leaped up and caught hold of him again. Leif made a grab for the amulet and got a handful of forearm and hair instead.

The shirtless man tried to shove him away. "Don't touch the hair!"

"Drop the amulet!" Leif shot back.

"Ow! Let go, Leifferson!"

"Leiffer*what?*"

"Leif!" came Tracy's yell from below. God, he loved her voice.

"I'm here, Tracy!" he called back. "I got it! I got the amulet!" In fact he did not, but he was hoping to confuse the thief. Leif made another grab. The thief made another shove. The editor cut the details of another brief struggle. Leif slammed to his butt in the dirt, shocked to find that the amulet was suddenly his.

"Hey, I got it!" he cried. "Er, still!"

Unhappily, there was no instantly resounding cheer from Tracy. Leif struggled to his feet and consoled himself that she would indeed show appreciation once they got away from the thief still struggling with her to get out of the ravine.

Once they got away? How were they supposed to do that? The guy was bigger and probably stronger than both of them, and a faster runner unless any ravines got in his way. That realization—along with the question of exactly how he'd gotten himself into this situation in the first place—shot through Leif's mind in the fraction of a second between standing back up and getting pounced on by the razorwings.

Were Leif more calm about things at that moment, he'd probably have: (a) sedately registered the fact that two razorwings had alighted on his back while another balanced on his forearm (and goodness, weren't those claws sharp?); (b) pondered the irony that he apparently *did* know as much as he'd previously thought about razorwings; and (c) begun serenely concocting an appropriate response to the situation. As it was, he mostly just shrieked like a psychotic monkey on fire while dropping the amulet and throwing himself to the ground in a surprisingly well-executed stop-drop-and-roll maneuver that sent him straight into the shirtless thief and knocked them both back into the ravine at Tracy's feet. Leif was shocked, scared, battered, and humiliated, but at least the other guy broke his fall.

Also, it got the razorwings off him.

The amulet fell to the riverbed a few yards away and surprised the heck out of him, as amid the chaos he'd already forgotten about dropping it. At least a dozen razorwings sprang after it, crashing into each other like tiny, fuzzy linemen piling on a fumble.

Leif crouched, frozen. No way was he going to dive in after it, nor could he bear to let it go. The thief scrambled away into a narrow alcove in the side of the ravine wall while Leif brainstormed ways to get the amulet back. All of them unfortunately involved things that were impractical to carry around outside of a video game—what he wouldn't give for a simple crowbar or some manner of physics gun! As if sensing his gaze, one of the beasts leaped out from the pack and *yowled* at him in challenge.

"Leif!" Tracy yelled. She yanked him back by the shoulder and practically dragged him to cover inside the thief's alcove. Leif could only scramble in and press between her and the shirtless man before the rest of the swarm dived down from above to join the others in a wild free-for-all for possession of the amulet.

None of the three people hunkered down in the alcove dared to move. Tracy spoke up pretty quickly, though.

"I think I know what kind of idiot you are!" she hissed.

"There's different kinds?" asked Leif.

"Hey!" the other man shot, pointing across Leif to Tracy. "This wouldn't've happened if you knew what's good for you! We could be having fun right now!"

"Who *is* he, anyway?" Leif demanded.

Tracy pounded the top of the thief's hand with her fist. Leif would've been happier about it if she hadn't knocked the guy's hand down into

Leif's stomach. "What kind of vacuous women do you hang around with who just mount any man that walks out of the dark, anyway?" she shot back.

"Why are you always trying to figure out what kind of something someone is, lady, huh?"

"Are you for real? I should throw you out there with the razorwings!" she growled.

"Hey, why don't we?" Leif asked. "Did he do something to Thalia?"

"No, Leif. Thalia's just useless."

The thief laughed. "At least Thalia knows when to shut up!"

Leif blinked. *Thalia knows when to shut up?* Okay, so the guy hadn't been around them very long at all.

"Who *are* you?" Tracy shot.

At that moment the amulet flipped up out of the pack. Tracy shot forward as if to snatch it. It was already too far out of reach; she'd never make it. Leif grabbed her arm on instinct as the razorwings sprang into the air after it, their tiny, grasping paws knocking it higher and higher. Buffeted about like a plastic bag in a windstorm, the amulet flew farther upward and tumbled out of sight in a swarm of fur and glowing eyes.

The thief shot from the alcove with Tracy and Leif at his heels. They dashed along the riverbed and up onto higher ground, stopping there to watch fruitlessly as the creatures drifted off. Leif turned to Tracy, unsure what to do as she screamed out a curse.

The shirtless man reeled on them, his face contorted as if struggling for words until he finally burst out with, "I don't deserve this!" A second later he was sprinting off after the swarm, yelling a parting message as he went.

To Leif's surprise, Tracy wasn't moving. "What'd he say?" she asked.

"He said he's Thad Freaking Winslow, and his feet hurt."

"Who the hell is Thad Freaking Winslow?"

"I don't know, but shouldn't we be chasing after him?" He really didn't want to. *Please say no, please say no . . .*

"No."

Bonus. "Why not?"

"I don't know who he is—"

"He's Thad Freaking Winslow, he said."

"I don't know who he is," she repeated, "but he's at least as mortal as we are, or he'd be able to do something more than just chase after those things, right? So let's press our advantage and get the Muse on our side."

"I thought she was useless?"

"She is. But she can fly, so if we can snap her out of wherever she's blissed off to . . ." She left the sentence unfinished and turned to jog back the other way. Distracted by a sudden realization, Leif just watched her go. She stopped a moment later to turn her flashlight back on him. "Well? C'mon!"

"You called me 'Leif' back there."

"Excuse me?"

"You called me 'Leif,' not 'Karlson.' First-name basis! That's symbolic! Means you're starting to like me!"

She stared a moment, shook her head, and then continued. "Move your skinny ass, Karlson, or I'm leaving it out here."

"Move your skinny ass, *Leif*," he corrected.

CHAPTER NINETEEN

"Welcome to Mount Olympus. Trespassers will be tribulated."
—*sign, Mount Olympus*

TRANSITING TO OLYMPUS without the benefit of godhood was a greater hassle than Apollo had expected.

Though few who don't live there are aware, the gods' abode on Olympus isn't really in Greece so much as it is in a quasi-alternate space, tucked away in what's best described as a glove compartment of reality. It is no more possible for a mortal to climb the slopes of Mount Olympus and reach the home of the Olympians than it is for someone to reach the moon using a trampoline, a snorkeling mask, and a very tall ladder— unless, that is, one of the gods willed it to be so or that mortal got very, very lucky. While it is true that more than one ancient myth records the tale of a mortal who climbed to the gods' abode, not recorded are the tales of hundreds if not thousands of mortals who failed.

In other words, never was something such as this written: "Stavros climbed the slopes of Olympus intent on petitioning Zeus for vengeance on the neighbor who hit one of his cattle with a two-by-four. He slipped and impaled his skull on a rock because he's a loser and Zeus was off boning some king's daughter anyway." Such tales held little appeal to myth recorders of the time. They were short, they were dull (despite use of the word *boning*), and no one much enjoyed hearing stories about failure, as the Germans had not yet invented the concept of *schadenfreude*[1], perhaps owing to the fact that no one had yet invented the concept of Germans.

---

[1] look it up

Apollo was not entirely without means of discreetly accessing Olympus, but the usual option of shifting over directly to the front gate was no longer open to him. Not only did he have to hitchhike across the astral plane disguised as an unfinished thought, he missed his exit and had to backtrack (slowly) through the elemental plane of nougat.

Sneaking through the Olympian servants' quarters disguised as an owl was a fair bit easier. The quasi-immortals who boarded there used trained owls for all sorts of things after becoming enamored with a certain mind-bogglingly successful book series about teenaged wizardry. Athena, fanatical of owls to the point of choosing them as her symbol long ago, especially loved it. It gave the place a definite whimsy, but cleaning up the owl pellets hacked all over every conceivable surface added more work than the birds saved. Apollo was just grateful for a way to slip into the gardens without attracting attention. He only hoped he had timed this right.

Getting in to see the Fates would be even more difficult than getting into Olympus. That the Fates didn't much care for mortal visits was mostly a guess, extrapolated from the fact that there was absolutely no way for anyone but a full god to actually get through the gate to their abode. No lesser immortal crazy enough to try had ever managed it, to say nothing of a mortal doing so. If he couldn't beg a bit of help in that regard, he was Styx out of luck.

He shifted from an owl to a wolf—he felt a little dirty borrowing one of Athena's favorite forms anyway—and dashed through the garden, searching. To his relief, it didn't take long before he spotted his sister sitting in cross-legged meditation by one of her favorite pools. She took no notice of the wolf coming up to sit beside her. Animals tended to flock toward any manifestation of Artemis, so quite a few had already taken up a nearby position. He never did understand why animals were so comfortable around the goddess of hunting, but he'd long ago stopped trying to figure that out.

For discretion's sake, he remained in a wolf's shape and voice as he spoke. "I need your help."

Artemis opened her eyes to glance at him before returning to her meditation. "I'm sorry, Wolf, but it seems my brother's gotten himself into a profusion of trouble. No one can find him, and if Poseidon hears not from him in three days, the new king's wrath will be unleashed. So you'll forgive me if I seem a little preoccupied."

"Sister, it's me," he whispered. She opened her eyes again and glared.

"Oh, gosh, no kidding! You think me unable to tell my own twin brother from a wolf? Are you trying to be discreet, or shall I simply yell out your name for all to hear so you can be certain I recognize you? Give me some credit, Brother."

"Sorry."

"You're in a fair bit of trouble, I daresay."

"So I was right to sneak in."

"Does a bear crap in the woods?"

"You're the expert," he answered. "How bad is it?"

"It really depends on the bear's diet. They're omnivores, you know. They eat an assortment of things."

"I meant here, Artemis."

She sighed. "I know what you meant, Brother, but you made me wait this long to find out what's going on with you. I shall respond at least a little in kind."

Apollo sighed. It came out as more of a growl, but then so did nearly everything else with a wolf's vocal cords. "I don't have very much time, Sister. Please."

She sighed back. (Hers worked better.) "It's bad, Apollo. Ares demands punishment for the attack, screaming for vengeance. I persuaded Poseidon and Hera to wait to hear your side of things, but they want answers. You're making things worse by not coming forward, and the fact that they can't find you has more than a few of the others suspicious that you may have some extra power they don't know about. Gods are beginning to talk."

Apollo connected the dots. "I found some power to avoid Poseidon's gaze, ergo I found the power to kill Zeus?"

Artemis stared into the water. "Did you?" she asked finally.

"Absolutely not! You know how insane my schedule's been since we came back! And do you think I'm the type to *murder* any of us?"

"No. Nevertheless, I had to ask."

"So 'maybe,' in other words."

"Let it go, Brother. I believe you. Yet you see how this all makes everyone wonder about you!"

"Even Demeter?"

"Oh, no, of course not Demeter. She's all mittens and giggles as usual. She's on your side, to be sure, but not everyone is. I took some abuse for defending you."

Apollo gave a growl that was intended to be a grumble. Close enough. "Why aren't they wondering about Ares? I haven't enough credibility to attack the god of war and be given the benefit of the doubt?"

"I believe if you'd attacked anyone but Ares, you wouldn't even have this much time to come forward. Demeter's withholding mittens from him, by the way."

"Good. His hands are too bloody to be toasty-warm."

Artemis ignored the chance to commemorate what may have been the first ever instance of the term *toasty-warm* coming out of a wolf's mouth. "So why did you attack him?"

"There's too much to explain right now. The short of it's that he really did kill Zeus, and I'm pretty sure he had help."

"Can you prove it?"

"You think I'd be hiding if I could? I don't even know who worked with him at this point, or exactly how they did it. That's why I need your help. I need to see the Moirae."

"The Fates? Why?"

"They're outside of it all. They may have some insight that could help."

"Yes, well, I figured that much. Why do you need my help? You snuck in this far, didn't you?"

"I diminished, Artemis."

Her wide-eyed gaze hit him as if shot from her bow. "Shut up! Don't you even joke—"

"I'm not joking! How do you think I stayed hidden?"

"I sensed some sort of difference, Apollo, but I thought you'd found a way to cloak yourself or—Just because of Ares?"

"As I've repeated more times than I care to relate, I had no choice! Even now there are those who need protecting that are made vulnerable by my absence. I can't get to the Fates without your aid. Will you lend it or not?"

He waited for his sister's shock to fade enough for her to answer him. A trout leaped out of the pool in sheer pointless punctuation of the moment, as trout are wont to do.

"Why do you think the Fates will tell you anything?" she asked finally.

"Blind hope, mostly."

She turned back to him. "So you're desperate."

"Don't be insulting." *Not that she isn't right,* he thought. "I don't know who to trust."

"You're not telling me the whole truth either."

"There's no time for the whole truth. And I'm trying to protect you."

"Brother, I'm the freaking goddess of chastity. I can protect myself."

"That's exactly what Father thought, I'm sure. Are they or are they not casting suspicious glances at the Muses just for working with me?"

She scowled. "Hermes did bring that up."

Hermes? Apollo wondered if he was connected to the plot at all or just making his usual mischief. No time, he decided. Fates first, wonder later. "I need your answer now."

She actually made him wait a little longer, but the nice thing about the temporal concept of "the present" is that, when something happens (regardless of when it happens), at the moment in which it does happen, it happens "now".

Federal judges rarely agree with this, but nobody likes them anyway.

"What part of 'Muse' makes you think 'tracker,' anyhow?" Thalia demanded. "I mean besides the 'e' the words don't even share any of the same letters in your language! 'Wake up, Thalia! Help us find the razorwings, Thalia! Oh, they're somewhere off on the horizon in the dark, but surely you can find them!' I mean, I appreciate the vote of confidence and it's really nice to know you think I'm so talented and capable, but I really don't think I ought to be held responsible for your disappointment if I can't instantly help, do you? Silly question—of course you do, that's why you're frowning like that. You shouldn't do that by the way, it makes your face all morose and scrunchy."

The group had paused amid another trek through the dark, their campsite packed and slung over their shoulders. Thalia had just returned from a scouting flight to report that she had no idea whatsoever where the razorwings had taken the amulet.

"Maybe if you hadn't zoned out in the first place!" Tracy shot.

"All right, first of all no more sentence fragments around me, they're like nails on a chalkboard, *understand?*"

"But wasn't that just a sen—"

"And maybe *what*, huh? Maybe I'd have been able to help you? Maybe I'd have pulled out the gigantic sword that I don't have and wrestled the guy to the ground? I'm an artist, not a fighter; I was attending to some very important musing business! The whole world doesn't stop just because you want it to, you know! I mean, not without bribes to the right people, but they're really taxing to find, even harder to please, and sometimes they try to eat you so it's really not even worth it unless you're into that sort of thing."

Tracy threw up her arms, at a loss for words. She wanted to tell Thalia to shut up. She wanted to tell her to fly her butt back up there and at least try to help. All that came out was, "Hell on wheels! Could everything just stop being so damn difficult for two seconds?"

The words faded to a distant echo in the darkness. The others just looked at her, blinking.

Thalia cracked a smile a moment later and giggled. "How long was that?"

"No!" yelled Tracy at Leif before he could answer. She pushed forward into the Muse's personal space. The weight of the night's trials, momentarily lifted when she thought Thalia would help her recover the amulet, had crushed down on her again. Her world had gone to hell in the past day, and all she had for help were a flighty Muse and a devoted stalker, neither of whom seemed to be able to stop talking! She wouldn't give up. She could deal with it, but . . . "Just—just everyone shut up unless it's going to help, okay? Geez!"

Thalia cocked her head pensively, then pecked Tracy right on the nose. "*You* need to lighten up."

It was a moment before Tracy could react to that. "Lighten up?" she burst finally. "The amulet's gone, Jason's *dead*, there's God-knows-what going on—"

"*Gods* know what," Leif corrected.

"—sending Erinyes and razorwings and idiot stalkers at me left and right and you want me to—"

"Lighten up, yes," Thalia finished for her. "I mean, ever since I've met you, you've been bringing the whole mood down, and frankly it's grown tiresome. No longer funny. I need funny. I work well with funny! So—" She crossed her eyes and waggled her fingers at Tracy, somehow managing to speak with her tongue sticking out. "—lighten up."

It occurred to Tracy that she had absolutely zero idea how to deal with this woman—this Muse—who stood in front of her. Just one more of dozens of problems, and they all made her so irritated that she couldn't seem to suppress a giggle. That *really* made no sense at all, and she wondered how much it had to do with the nighthawk that just landed in Thalia's hair.

The Muse's blue eyes flicked up at it. They rolled even as she grinned. "Off the hair, please, thank you." Obedient, it instead hopped to her shoulder and warbled a series of peets in her ear. Thalia's grin grew wider. "Fantastic timing, truly. Thank you! I don't suppose you'd be willing to—"

The bird flew off with a cry before Thalia could finish.

"Oh. I suppose not, then." Thalia began to walk, flashing a giddy smile over her shoulder. "Follow me to the amulet! The little monsters dropped it."

The corners of Tracy's lips were quivering upward. "What just happened?" she asked.

Thalia stopped to heave a sigh. "I asked the bird to help me look while I was up there."

"Why didn't you say that before?" Tracy demanded.

"Say what before? 'See this bird that isn't here? I asked him to help me and he hasn't come back yet because there's apparently nothing to report?' Don't be silly!" Thalia giggled. "Well—do be silly, but sheesh, roll with the punches, sweethearts! Are you coming or would you prefer to stand there until I can find a horse to give you so you can look it in the mouth?"

Leif and Tracy both jogged to catch up as the Muse giggled again. Tracy found her mood improving and giggled a little with her, which was, again, rather irritating.

It was also somehow heartening.

"So wait," Leif started up as they trotted along. "You can talk to birds now?"

"And I could talk to them before too, see, because that's how I asked it in the first place." She winked.

"I just mean, what's being a Muse got to do with being able to talk to birds? How's that connect to writing? Or wait. Is it a music thing?"

"Stop saying 'wait'; we're trying to hurry here. And no, it's not a music thing. It's got nothing to do with writing. It's just that things got a little prosaic during the Dark Ages and I took a few extracurriculars. Is there a judgment about that you'd care to express? Does that offend your worldview or something? A Muse isn't allowed to have outside interests?"

"No, I just didn't expect it is all."

"Hrmph. I also enjoy macramé and Ping-Pong."

"*Ping-Pong*'s a funny word," Tracy observed. "Ping-Pong! Ping-Pong!" She giggled again.

Leif was looking at her strangely. She supposed that wasn't much of a change. "What'd you do to her?"

"Just lightened her up a bit," Thalia said. "It's a Muse thing."

That stopped Tracy in her tracks. A second afterward she realized stopping wasn't helpful and hurried to catch up. "You did this to me?" The tone of her voice didn't have nearly enough outrage as she'd have liked. "What did you *do*?" There. Better.

"Oh, don't fret about it, it'll wear off soon enough. Just enjoy it. It's better for everyone; trust me."

Tracy laughed. "I don't appreciate you messing with my brain!"

"This has nothing to do with your brain. It's your mood, it's more of an . . . aura . . . thingy. (Watch out for that rabbit hole, by the way. I said watch out for—Zut! No one listens!) It's hard to explain."

"Mood's controlled by brain chemicals, actually," Leif pointed out.

Thalia laughed. "Oh, right!" she mocked. "Braaaaaaain chemicals! You mortals are always so cute. Except when you're not. Which actually is probably more of the time than otherwise, but . . ." She shrugged and continued jogging.

Tracy struggled to cling to her outrage, but the anger rapidly slipped through her fingers. She let it go for the moment, recalling something else. "I have a question," she tried before bursting into a giggle. "Hehe. Braaaainss!"

No, stop it!

Thalia giggled with her. "Don't mess with a Muse."

She forced the curious image of rampaging clown-zombies from her mind's eye and focused. *Hehe. Braaaainss* . . . She cleared her throat. "Okay, so this Thad guy's mortal, right? So is it possible that he's just some idiot jewel thief? I mean, if there are other gods and such trying to stop what I'm doing, they wouldn't be sending a mortal after me, would they?"

"Sorting algorithm of evil," Leif explained. "Can't send the big-bad at us right off the bat."

"What do you call Ares?"

"Exception that proves the rule?"

"Or more likely—whoever it is doesn't want to reveal themselves to us or the other gods on Olympus," Thalia offered.

"Why not? I thought they were happy to be back? Zeus dying made that possible."

"Zeus made the edict that forced us to withdraw in the first place, yes. Once he was gone, the edict was gone too. But they're also outraged—in principle, anyway—that someone would kill him. It's all politics really, at least in the sense that some of it's politics and some of it isn't, but it's easier to just say 'It's all politics' and save a bit of pedantry."

"Yeah, you're real good at that, by the way."

"You be quiet, Leiffy-dear."

Tracy scowled. "So they like a good steak, but they don't want to know how it got on their plate."

Thalia nodded. "That old saying fits the situation pretty well I'd say. Plus, I would also like a good steak, come to think of it."

"Why'd Zeus make you go away in the first place?" Leif asked.

"He never said. Which I always sort of wondered at, really, but I figured he had his reasons. It bothered me a little too, but you don't argue with Zeus—or didn't, anyway. He was king for a reason, you know. He was the only one of his generation whom his father didn't eat, which made him more powerful than the rest of them put together, and that, if you haven't figured it out by now, is just another reason why even the gods who didn't kill Zeus might not want him back."

Well, Tracy thought, *sucks to be them.* She hurried on, following Thalia and giggling occasionally.

Before long the Muse guided them to a halt at the base of a short hill. "What is it?" Leif asked.

Thalia cast a vexed look about the area. "It should be here . . ."

"Should be?"

"This is where the nighthawk said it was! It was very specific! It said—well I don't need to go into what it said exactly, it said it was here!"

"What *did* it say?" Tracy pressed.

"It said it was here! Pay attention! I've been talking to birds for centuries, and they're always very specific and exact about locations, especially the predators. They're very good at marking—uh-oh."

Leif and Tracy exchanged glances, both returning the requisite, "Uh-oh?".

Thalia squatted in the dirt. "I . . . think that Thad guy might've gotten here first."

She pointed to a set of footprints in the dirt that stopped right next to an impression that looked vaguely amulet-shaped. As far as Tracy could tell, the indentation might've been caused by something else, but she felt compelled to give Thalia the benefit of the doubt. Tracy cursed.

"We've got footprints, at least," Leif offered, pointing to where they led. "They can't be too old."

Tracy nodded. "And his feet hurt. Follow me!"

They dashed off, yet again. Thad wasn't the only one whose feet were hurting. Once they caught up with him, they'd—actually Tracy didn't really have any idea just yet what they'd do, but once they did it, there would be resting.

The good news was that the tracks remained obvious and didn't go far. The bad news was that they ended right next to a dirt road and a pair of clear impressions likely caused by the spinning tires of some sort of vehicle.

Tracy cursed again. "He had a car."

"He might've hitched," Thalia offered.

"It doesn't really matter now, does it?" Again, Tracy didn't put nearly enough frustration into her tone as she intended. She tried to focus. "Why didn't you tell the bird to bring the amulet back when it found it?" It came out in a yell, yet not quite as loudly as she'd have liked.

"Ha!" Thalia cried. "If it's not one thing, it's another! Exactly how many animals did *you* get to aid us, hmm? Got a clan of badgers scouring the hills that you haven't told me about?"

"Don't talk to her like that!" Leif came back.

Tracy let Leif's unasked-for defense go and focused on Thalia. "You're the one who can talk to them!"

"Exactly!" Thalia cried. "I'm not Artemis here, you know! I can only *talk* to animals, I don't have some special stupid slavery-power over them! You think training a cat is bad, try getting a bird to do what you want it to do—there's a reason *flighty* means what it means! And for that matter, we're dealing with jewelry here! Birds do not like carrying jewelry for anyone! Tolkien understood that; why can't you? Stay here!"

"Where are you going?"

"Up! We've got a whole Blair Witch wander-about-the-wilderness-yelling thing going here and I'm putting a stop to that bothersome garbage right now! Plus, I'm going to look for headlights, so sit tight. Go have a fig bar or something." With that, she was gone.

Tracy turned to Leif with a smirk that she couldn't help. "I'm starting to think that yelling at the Muse doesn't help matters much."

"Got her to look, at least."

She nodded, chuckling despite herself and trying to think. The fact that Thad got into a car rather than being whisked off somewhere by a god at least gave a cause for hope. Either he really was just a wandering wilderness jewel thief (okay, not too likely) or Thalia was right that whoever sent him wanted to keep their distance. A possibility began to bloom in her tired, giddy mind, a minor epiphany that Thalia unhelpfully interrupted with her return.

"The good news is that I can see headlights in the distance. The bad news is there're more than a few pairs of them in assorted spots."

"I think that's pretty much just bad news, strictly speaking."

"Leif honey, more good news is that I'm the Muse of comedy, so I won't be kicking your ass for that."

Tracy resisted reminding them that slapstick was considered comedy, clinging instead to her previous epiphany. "He mentioned having a suite in Vegas," she said. "A luxury suite. He's probably going back there if we're lucky. If we're not lucky, we're screwed anyway."

"There's a lot of luxury suites in Vegas," Leif pointed out.

"Yes, but it's a start."

Thalia clapped. "See? See what you can think of when you're not focused on being all cranky and acrimonious? And we have to go back there anyway to meet Apollo, so this works out great!"

"Yes, great, right? Except for the fact that once we get to Vegas, we're out of clues. I suppose we could ask around and try to find out where he's staying, but I don't know how—"

"Oh!" Thalia cried. "Oh, oh, oh! No, this is good, this is—well, I guess it's a little risky, but hey, you're a woman, you can probably manage to—hrm."

Tracy turned to Leif. "That make sense to you?"

"Trust me; I'm aware you're a woman already."

"No, it's—look," the Muse went on. "I'm not sure if you know this, but Vegas is pretty much run by Dionysus! Eew, passive voice, strike that: Dionysus pretty much runs Vegas! Better?"

"I've never really—"

"Better," Thalia said. "Anyway, so mostly he just lets other people run it for him and spends his time in a hedonistic stupor, but he knows practically everything that goes on in that town, or he can find out!"

"Apollo didn't know who to trust. Is it really a good idea for you to bring another god into this?"

"You got a better idea, Miss Fussy-Britches? And I'm not going to bring him into this; you are. Don't give me that look! It's simple! Look, you probably won't even have to tell him why you want to find this Thad person. You've got breasts and you're pretty. He's not going to care about the rest. Just get him to help you track Thad down and discover what he's up to. At the very least you can probably find out if he's left town or not."

"What's this about me asking him? You're the immortal. Where are you going to be?"

"It's better if you do it," Thalia answered. "He's drunk more than half the time, anyway, so he might just think you're some mortal who wants to offer sacrifice in exchange for some help. If I'm there, it gets all political. Plus, I've thought of something else that might help us, and it'll take me a bit to go, um, get it."

"What sort of something?"

"It's a surprise—and I probably shouldn't tell you anyway unless we need it. Don't worry, it'll be a piece of cake—talking to Dionysus, I mean, not the thing I'm—anyway, I'll tell you exactly how to find him and get an audience. I'll even let you borrow the bangle. He loves women. I'm sure he'll listen to you!"

Lightened up or not, Tracy didn't like the sound of that and said so.

"You know, you're pretty uptight for someone whose mom scored with Zeus," Thalia teased. "But whatever. I'm sure you won't have to do anything scandalous. Just flash your lashes, show some leg, wear something low cut, and—don't glower at me like that, I'm not the one who lost the amulet. Look, do whatever you want. Bring him some wine as an offering. Or a wine truck. I don't know, it's up to you. We can talk about it on the way. For now, I say we hitch a ride back to

Vegas ourselves, rest up in a nice hotel, and then do our separate tasks. Before you know it, we'll be reamuletified, meeting Apollo, bringing Zeus back, and living happily ever after. Or something to that effect. Now come on, here's a car right now. Show some leg!"

Tracy shook her head. "Even if I wasn't wearing pants . . ." She stuck out her thumb instead.

"Oh, for crying out loud."

"I'm capable of getting what I want without objectifying myself, thanks very much." The car drew closer without slowing. It threatened to pass entirely until suddenly the driver hit the brakes and the car skidded to a stop right in front of them. Tracy beamed, satisfied and not above turning around to gloat at Thalia.

The sight of the Muse standing stark naked behind her nicely torpedoed the victory.

"Sorry," Thalia grinned and pulled her outfit back on. "It does that sometimes. So then, Vegas?"

CHAPTER TWENTY

"It is true that anonymous sources within the European Organization for Nuclear Research (CERN) claim to have spoken to Zeus once or twice in 2008. However, such claims may be dismissed as the fabrication of scientists who'd developed a god complex while playing with the building blocks of the universe in their Large Hadron Collider and, now that actual gods were back on the scene, were desperately concocting stories to regain attention. No credible agency of any kind—public or private—has officially claimed knowledge of the existence of the Olympian gods prior to their official return on June 17, 2009. This includes (among others) the European Space Administration, the Vatican, and—despite rumors to the contrary—the U.S. Federal Bureau of Investigation. The FBI does acknowledge, however, that there is no way to tell if any pre-Return anonymous tips were made by Olympian entities."
—A Mortal's Guidebook to the Olympians' Return

WHILE TRACY AND THE OTHERS went chasing after a male-model jewelry pirate, and while Apollo was talking his sister into opening the gates to a place usually best left alone, and while the Zeus-murdering conspirators were busy yelling at Ares for both acting openly and failing to be effective in doing so, a small task force of the Federal Bureau of Investigation was acting on divine inspiration.

Neither the group that stormed the small Neo-Christian Movement of America compound nor their superiors who sent them were conscious of being divinely inspired, of course. So far as they knew, they were acting on actual evidence that one Brittany Simons (a.k.a. Wynter Nightsorrow, a.k.a. the young woman from Chapters Four and Seven) was being held hostage in the compound by a cult that jeopardized the national security of the United States. An anonymous source had delivered to them video footage of Wynter's abduction from Hecate's temple and her subsequent incarceration and attempted brainwashing within the NCMA compound. The address of the compound accompanied the footage, along with the secret keypad access code to the back door and a box of chocolate chip macadamia nut cookies—the regional bureau chief's favorite, though he'd never told anyone about it.

Though it pained her to act so mundanely, it was the best Hecate could do for her disciple. There could be no divine wrath for Wynter's captors, no creeping avengers of shadow terrorizing them alone in the darkness, no journey into catatonia astride cosmological mysteries the mortal mind was never meant to know. She could not even simply steal into the compound herself to rescue Wynter, for fear that her fellow Olympians would learn of it and realize which secrets Hecate had entrusted to her. No other gods could know that those secrets had fallen, however temporarily, into other hands. If mortals could go through channels, she'd decided, then so could she. Her problems would be solved by the U.S. government. What could possibly go wrong?

It further pained her that the (far more apropos) Secret Service kept putting her on hold and forwarding her calls to the FBI, but those were the breaks.

The Secret Service itself was only her second choice. A particularly clandestine group within the U.S. government made generous sycophantic sacrifices to her on a weekly basis and would jump at the chance to help, but it was impossible to use them anonymously. The Circle Order Society of League Shadow Trust Syndicates was such a closely guarded secret that the knowledge of merely the group's name was divided into equal and unique parts among its highest-ranking members—the director of West Coast Operations merely knew "The"—and the group's lower echelon labored under the belief that they were actually unemployed. Simply dialing the group's primary phone number would likely cause more problems than it would solve.

And so it fell to the FBI. They stormed the compound late at night and burst into the NCMA's midst in much the same way as the Ninjas Templar had earlier violated Hecate's temple—albeit with fewer backflips. It pleased the goddess greatly. They rescued Wynter, arrested her captors, and confiscated the parchment containing the forbidden secrets as evidence. It would soon be placed into an evidence holding facility, which Hecate could later set on fire. If any of the other gods asked, she would claim that her target was the facility's entire contents, purely for the sake of creating uncertainty in numerous criminal cases. She trusted that they wouldn't dig any deeper than that.

It never occurred to her that the NCMA might have already made a copy of the parchment. *Secrets* were her specialty. A copy of something made it that much less secret.

The NCMA had copied the parchment, of course, shortly after getting it back to the compound and realizing their luck at stumbling onto something of such value. The NCMA's copy wasn't lovingly decorated with glitter, but it did accurately replicate the original's drawings, words, and strange symbols. And so it was that during the first moments of the FBI's rescue operation, the copy was being carried in a cardboard tube out of Philadelphia International Airport under the arm of one Richard Kindgood.

The call from his fellows at Compound 14—where the heathen girl was being held—came through moments before the FBI took the place. Though the call was not a long one, it was enough to give a clear picture of the situation: the compound was about to fall.

It was a blessing, really, Kindgood believed. He never much liked it there, and it was merely a small enclave of righteousness. Those who fell in the FBI's raid that night would be martyrs to the cause. He doubted anyone would be killed, of course. It wasn't their job to give armed resistance to the misguided forces of the U.S. government. It's just that they always over-waxed the compound floors, and there would be much slipping and sliding in the mad dash to escape arrest— especially on the part of that clumsy Higgins fellow.

"Oh, certainly," Kindgood once grumbled to anyone who would listen, "there's money in the budget for floor wax, but none for balance training in the ninja camps?"

The heathen girl would be rescued, of course. It was too late to worry about that now, but the failure tasted bitter nonetheless. He sighed, taking solace in one of his favorite personal prayers: "God grant me the strength to accept the things I cannot change, the courage to change the things I can, and the wisdom to justify which is which depending on how I'm feeling."

It mattered not. In truth, getting her to renounce her love of the false gods took up valuable time anyway. Even with the starving and constant berating, her resistance was almost exuberant. Such defiance was not to be permitted. Before he'd left, Kindgood gave orders for her to be water-boarded, hoping that would put her in a more receptive mood. Even with the promising captured parchment in his possession, the girl's recalcitrance occupied his mind for the entire plane ride. Now she was no longer his problem. Yes, he'd failed to fix her, but it wasn't his fault the FBI stormed the place and rescued the witch, was it? It was out of his hands now. His cup runneth over, or the Lord giveth and He taketh away, or . . . whatever.

It occurred to Kindgood that those at the compound who'd seen fit to question his methods with respect to the girl were now about to be thrown into a prison of their own.

"She's just a girl!" they'd said.

A girl who worshipped the false ones they were sworn to oppose, Kindgood had answered. Clearly that was why they'd fallen while he and Stout had escaped. In hindsight the others' devotion was no greater than those "tolerant" Christians who'd turned the other cheek and failed to take up arms against the false gods. "Love thine enemy"? Where did they get that fool idea?

So good riddance to them, really.

Of course, now he had no one but Stout to command, but the NCMA would fix that soon. The glory of his discovery could not be denied. (He was also pretty sure he could pin the compound's fall on the others who'd remained there. Or Stout, if it came to that. Gabriel Stout would certainly jump at the chance to suffer penance for the cause. It was part of why Kindgood liked him so much.) He patted the parchment tube happily, recalling the writing.

Within nine cans depicted here
Resides that which Olympians fear.

It chilled him to think that they'd nearly destroyed it before realizing what they'd found! From the clues scrawled in the margins in the girl's hasty handwriting, plus the half-finished drawings of what appeared to be nine cans—or cylinders, at the very least—they adopted the theory that the cans somehow contained the Titans, supposedly banished by the false gods many millennia ago. It was half an educated guess, half faith, but the pieces fit.

Kindgood and Stout certainly didn't believe the cans contained actual "Titans," of course. That the false gods of Olympus actually existed was insulting enough, Stout pointed out. The existence of even *more* false gods whom the Olympian gods had defeated—that was simply more ludicrous than any thinking person could contemplate. The tale was merely propaganda to further the Olympian agenda. Whatever the cans truly held was still a terror to the Olympians, certainly, but the enemy of my enemy is my friend. If the NCMA could gain control of the cans' secrets, use them for their own advantage . . .

In truth, Kindgood did wonder a little if the cans somehow held the Titans (though if that was the case, such cans surely must be of impressive size). Yet even if they did, it was plain that, if the Titans were released, the two groups would annihilate each other. Two birds with one stone, problem solved, and once again the meek would inherit the Earth.

"Kill 'em all and let God sort 'em out" was also a fully viable position.

If they were released. That was the problem. The parchment made mention of a "great and powerful secret ritual" that would do the trick, the details of which were imprinted on the cans themselves. So really all they needed to do was find the cans, and the parchment held a hint or two toward that end, as well. The words *Sidgwick's* and *Swindon were* both listed on the parchment and were presumably location names. Perhaps. The experts would tell them.

Then they would see. Everyone across the globe would see the glory of the Neo-Christian Movement of America and their triumph over the false gods, and it would be he, Richard Kindgood, who brought the truth to their eyes!

At the very least he'd get some sort of promotion out of it. After all, tithe revenues would shoot through the roof.

CHAPTER TWENTY-ONE

"The names of the three Fates are as follows: Clotho, who spins the threads of mortal lives; Lachesis, who measures their allotted lifetimes; and Atropos, who cuts them off. These facts alone have been confirmed since the Olympians' Return. Unlike the majority of the beings recently returned to our world, the Fates have made no public appearances, sought no worship, and arranged no book deals. We have, in effect, only a single laconic press release and the other Olympians' word that they even exist."

—A Mortal's Guidebook to the Olympians' Return

"The Fates are not Zeus's daughters. The ancient Greeks just made that up because they couldn't stomach the idea of women in charge. The Fates are . . . beyond."

—Athena's Little Book of Wisdom, *p. 872*

"WE MUST ENTERTAIN THEM," Clotho whispered.

"Briefly," Lachesis agreed.

"It will end, soon enough." Atropos answered.

They nodded, together, to the sound of shears.

The Fates had always been. The Fates will always be. It was clearly printed on their pamphlets and on the gateway to their abode, and anyone wishing to argue the point did so at his or her peril.

No one could disprove it, after all. None (who were talking) could recall a time when they did not exist, and none had any conclusive evidence that they would cease to be in the foreseeable future. The Fates were as old as memory, as omnipresent as time, as unceasing as—well, you get the point. Lather with awe, rinse with amazement, repeat. Show some respect is the concept we're trying to get across here.

The Fates toiled, currently, in a serviceable room above a convenience store at the intersection of the two parallel streets of Sparkwood and 23rd on the eastern side of Moose Jaw, Saskatchewan. No doors led into the Room. No doors led out. No one in the area could look at the space above that convenience store and tell you what was inside, what caused the strange lights to shine out of the shaded windows at precisely 9:53 p.m. every Thursday, or why no one even remembered a second story being built. These were not the sorts of things people near the Room wondered if they knew what was good for them. These were not the sorts of things people wondered even if (as was more often the case) they did not know what was good for them, either—for the simple reason that no one was fated to do so.

Or at least not yet. There would eventually come a time when someone would wonder. Someone would care. Someone would have a spare moment in the middle of a Tuesday evening when there was nothing much else to do and the good shows didn't come on for another hour, and someone would try to investigate. In that moment, the Room would be gone. There would be little fanfare. The Room would simply move itself elsewhere in a way that would please Heisenberg, were it possible to simultaneously find him and ask his opinion.

"He is coming, then," spoke Clotho.

"We all know this," Lachesis remarked. "Why do you announce it?"

"Because it is too quiet." Clotho's eyes did not rise from her spindle. "And because you told me I would."

Lachesis measured the length of the life of a man, into which Clotho had already spun the inability to properly use an apostrophe. He would be born in New York, spend most of his time in London, and get beaten to death by a drunken horde at a proofreaders' convention. "Ah. Yes. I knew this."

"You offer humor." Atropos cocked her head to one side, considering.

"I express my amusement."

The others fixed her with a stare. "Exuberant," one observed. "Calm yourself," said another. "He comes by the moment." The Fates resumed their work, anticipating.
Lachesis halted. "Where is Poppy?"
"In the back."
"Vexing."
"Easy now. He arrives."

Apollo stepped from the portal into the Fates' abode. The transition was utterly unremarkable. He wasn't dizzy. There was no amazing light show or tumbling through any twisting conduits of swirling mists. In fact, there was no feeling of movement at all. It just worked, transparently, akin to the way that all software is supposed to work but never does. It was completely non-disorienting. In fact, it was so non-disorienting that it actually could be said to be orienting, were it not for the fact that its unexpected unremarkability was, in itself, so darned disorienting—which might possibly explain why this narrative goes to such lengths to describe something so unremarkable.

Apollo took a moment to blink as his eyes adjusted. The light was dimmer than the distant chamber on Olympus from whence he'd come, yet more florid. He stood amid a haze of color that shined through—or was emitted from—a wall of stained glass behind him. There was no portal there, no evidence of anything he'd actually stepped *through,* just glass and the distinctly bothersome thought that he might not be able to return under his own power. As he'd asked of her, Artemis had opened the door for him without following. If the Fates decided they didn't want him to leave, he might be stuck.

So that was swell.

The Room was perfectly cubical. The really mind-boggling thing—and this was when the legitimate disorientation set in—was that the walls contained a space much larger than geometrically possible. A regulation soccer game could be played within the space between them, provided one removed the spiral staircase and table after table covered in carefully wrapped strings. Yet, somehow, the walls themselves appeared to measure no more than twenty feet long. It gave the distinct impression that if M. C. Escher attempted to walk a tape measure across one wall, he would throw up.

The less said about the Möbius balcony that encircled the place, the better.

While a god could gaze at the Room without going mad, Apollo in his diminished state figured he should stop gaping and get down to business before his eyeballs needed a Dramamine.

In the center of the room sat the Fates, beautiful crones of youthful maturity who paid him no heed as they spun, measured, and cut threads at a hummingbird's pace. Figuring he couldn't go wrong with proper etiquette, Apollo approached a few steps, bowed low, and addressed them.

"Honored Moirae, to whom wise Zeus gave greatest honor, weavers of destiny, ladies of Fate, I seek an audience. May I approach?"

The three turned their attention to him, continuing their work even so. Their eyes were clear black orbs, sharklike and deep.

"You have come," spoke Clotho.

"You may approach," spoke Lachesis.

"You will be disappointed," spoke Atropos.

Apollo nodded, doing his best to hide his discouragement. "Then I thank you, for without disappointment, how can we know joy?"

The Fates were unimpressed with his dime-store philosophizing. He focused on why he came. "Ladies of Fate, I have come regarding Father Zeus's murder, though I expect you may already know that. I must ask: Do you know how he was killed?"

Lachesis cocked her head. "Do you speak of the means or those responsible?"

"I refer to the means, but if you know the responsible party . . ."

The answer, when it came, was simultaneous. "No."

Atropos was right; that was disappointing. "To the former," he asked, "or the latter?"

"The latter," spoke Atropos.

"As to the former," Clotho began, "we suspect."

"But we do not have confirmation," Lachesis continued.

"Yet," Atropos finished.

"Do you know of a living weapon that might end an immortal?" Apollo tried. "Pewter skin, perhaps this big, with glowing red eyes and a stinger?"

The three Fates quickly glanced at each other before Clotho and Lachesis turned back to their work. Only Atropos regarded him now. "You believe this to be the weapon that slew Zeus?"

Apollo hesitated. So far they'd answered his questions without a price, but he didn't know how long that would last. Best to hold on to any answers he could trade for as long as possible. "I suspect."

"But you do not have confirmation."

"No."

Atropos turned her attention completely to her work. Any minute now, Apollo expected, she would ask the source of his suspicion. In the meantime he pondered the wisdom of using that particular piece of knowledge as a bargaining chip. He was still pondering when he realized that she wasn't going to ask at all.

"You would know more," Atropos spoke finally.

"I would," he answered, summoning up a few persuasive talking points. "Zeus was the king of all of us, more powerful than the rest of the Dodekatheon put together. An artifact that may slay a god represents a grave danger to all, to say nothing of the justice required for the murder of a king."

Atropos regarded him with the boundless compassion of a stone wall. "Passionate entreaties hold no meaning in this place, godling. There is only what has been, is, and will be. You will ask each of us three more questions. No more. Then your time in this place will be ended."

Ended?

He only barely managed not to speak it, lest he waste a question like some half-wit fairy-tale lummox. Apollo paused to consider the best use of the unexpectedly generous offer. Atropos had asked no price for their answers; he'd come expecting that much at least.

Of course, there was that ominously ambiguous "ended" bit. *Don't count your chimeras before they hatch, Apollo.* Did chimeras hatch? He couldn't recall. That was unsettling.

"Time is limited, godling," Atropos warned. "You will ask your questions now."

Apollo wished she wouldn't call him "godling," but he'd have to worry about his self-esteem later. (Styx! Even having to worry about that at all was humiliating.) Not without effort, he pushed his ego aside and seized on his first question.

"The living weapon I described: What is it?"

"The UnMaking Nexus," Atropos said. "It was created long ago, commissioned in the last days of the Titan War, carved from a meteorite drawn of Saturn's rings and imbued with the power to destroy an immortal. It was not completed until after the war and, as such, never used." She gave the slightest scowl. "Disappointing."

"Until now," Apollo suggested.

"Perhaps."

"Er, that was not a question."

She nodded. "Nor was that. You will now ask your second question of Atropos."

Great. Third-person. Atropos had some sort of slightly more lively Miss Manners thing going on. "Very well, then. Second question: Who created it?"

Shears ended more than fifty threads in rapid succession before the answer came. "It was our work, commissioned by Zeus."

Again, he hesitated, absorbing that. If the Fates created the UnMaking Nexus, they might very well still have possession of it. It was even possible they were at the heart of the entire assassination. It hadn't occurred to him until then. He cursed his exuberance in coming to the Fates so heedlessly.

Except, he thought, they claimed to only suspect that it was the weapon that killed Zeus, and the Fates did not lie . . . as far as he knew. Then again, he wasn't exactly the right person to judge that for sure, and there was still that "ended" bit. Time for another question.

"What happened to the Nexus after you created it?"

"We presented the weapon to Zeus. Having no more use for it, he kept it secret. We know neither where nor how. You will ask no more questions of Atropos." With that, she gathered up a corded group of threads, cutting through them all in one snip.

"Clown-car pileup," she explained.

Apollo wondered whom he was to ask next. He then pondered *what* he was to ask next before catching Clotho's stare from across the flying shuttle on her spinning wheel. Beginnings were her specialty. Zeus, he recalled, would begin again—if returning from death could be termed as such. Time to focus on that for the moment. After all, if the Fates were participants in Zeus's death, Apollo wasn't likely to get out of the Room himself anyway. He may as well assume the Fates were at least still neutral.

He'd deal with the philosophical topic of optimism in the face of fatalism some other time.

"Is the effect of the Nexus permanent?" he asked of Clotho.

"To the unprepared, the UnMaking Nexus is utterly fatal."

Now that sounded promising. "To the unprepared?" he asked. "What does that mean?"

"Yes, to the unprepared. There is a loophole, for those who are aware of it and prepare to use it. Immortality is the steel beam to the fragile mortal straw; it is not so easily and utterly broken. A resourceful immortal may yet return, should events play themselves out in time."

"I assume you told Zeus of this loophole when you gave him the weapon."

Clotho watched him as she worked, the corners of her lips turning into a faint smile. "You may assume what you wish, but assumption has little effect on reality outside of the stock market."

"I actually meant that as a question."

"Then you must ask it of Lachesis. You have asked three of me already."

Apollo opened his mouth to protest as he made a quick mental tally and realized . . . *Damnation.*

"If my expressing contrition will aid your acceptance of this," Clotho told him, "then I shall do so."

Apollo frowned, deciding he was a half-witted lummox after all. At least he was still smarter than Ares. It was petty but comforting. "No, that's all right. Thank you, Clotho."

She nodded and turned away. Lachesis raised an expectant gaze from amid a tangle of threads, looking like nothing more than a kitten at play amid the lives of mankind. Apollo filed the metaphor in a mental drawer for later poetical expression. Or was it a simile? By the Styx, being diminished in this room was affecting his wits.

It occurred to him that the question of whether or not the Fates told Zeus of the loophole was moot. If Tracy's vision was to be believed, Zeus was aware of it and even took steps to use it to protect himself. All well and good for Zeus, thought Apollo, but what if Ares and the others came after *him* with it?

"Hello, Lachesis."

Lachesis merely met his gaze as she worked. All right, then.

"The loophole that keeps the Nexus's strike from being fatal: How can I use it to protect myself?"

"You cannot, godling. You are diminished and no longer possess sufficient power to protect yourself. You will enjoy the irony."

Ah, yes. Enjoy. Right. Prediction or demand? "If I'll enjoy the irony, it will be at a far future date, I am sure."

He sighed. So he was vulnerable, with no way to keep himself safe from a strike. On the other hand, an ounce of prevention is worth a pound of cure. "How is the god-killer used, exactly?" If he knew how to keep them from using it on him in the first place . . .

"With malice."

"I was rather hoping for something a little more specific."

"I am measuring life-threads for 255 mortals per minute, estimated. You will allow that I am somewhat preoccupied and will wait for the rest of the answer to your question in due time, godling."

"Right. Sorry. You do it well, Lachesis."

"Compliments are irrelevant." Her lithe fingers rapidly drew out a number of threads along a measuring stick, knotted each at the ends, and set them aside for Atropos. "As the UnMaking Nexus is a living weapon, it must be fed before it may strike. It must be placed in a saucer of immortal blood and left alone. The blood must be of equal or greater generation to the intended target to ensure success. Once it has absorbed the blood, it will strike at the nearest immortal it can find. No further targeting can be effected."

"That sounds a bit imprecise, like more of a grenade than a sword or an arrow." He made sure it wasn't a question, but if it coaxed a little more information from her, so much the better.

The eyes of Lachesis narrowed. "As we informed Zeus, when *you* craft a living weapon capable of slaying a god, you may criticize. Until then, you must accept what is."

"On the contrary, it was no criticism. I might be at risk from this weapon, so it's good to know that it can't be easily aimed."

"On the contrary?" she repeated. "So now you are arguing with the Fates. None argue with Fate and win, godling."

"I wasn't—that was not my intent at all, Lachesis."

She turned her attention back to her work. "And now you correct me. You learn nothing."

Apollo had to fight off the urge to waste his last question by asking if she was screwing with him. If she was trying to get him to do that, then she was screwing with him indeed. "I am but a youth compared to you, Lachesis. My wisdom is not nearly so grand."

"So now you call me old? A crone, perhaps, unworthy of your respect?"

"You are old, Lachesis. As old as time, some say. None are more worthy of respect than you and your sisters."

He smiled.

She stared.

"You are about to ask your final question of me," she said at last. "Continue."

Yes, now that you've gone and ruined my train of thought . . . He suddenly recalled something Thalia said back at the camp. "Which of the other Olympians have learned what knowledge from you about the Nexus?"

"You try to combine many questions into one."

"I combine many inquiries into one question," he said. "A subtle difference."

"Argumentative."

"Only slightly."

"Impudent."

"I wouldn't go that far."

Lachesis simply stared at him. Apollo stood his ground and said finally, "I would ask your forgiveness for any perceived impudence, but I am told that passionate entreaties hold no meaning in this place. Regardless, if my expressing contrition will aid your acceptance of this, then I will do so." He fought the urge to wink. She turned her gaze back to the threads, measuring, measuring, measuring.

He waited.

"Upon taking his brother's throne, Poseidon came before us with questions of his own." Apollo simply waited this time, hoping for more, appreciating the rhyme. "He learned nothing."

"Nothing," he repeated. "So then either he knows nothing of the Nexus at all . . . or else he already knew about it and you didn't tell him anything he didn't already know."

"Statements," Lachesis said.

"Statements I would be deeply grateful for responses to, in truth," he said, nodding. It was worth a shot.

She stared, perhaps predictably. "You used *already* twice in the same sentence," she added finally.

". . . Yes. Thank you."

He looked around, trying to think of how he might glean any further information—if indeed the three held any that might be of use to him. He swiftly realized that looking around was exactly the wrong thing to do if he didn't want the visuals to bend his mind to distraction.

"Marble floors," he stalled. "Nice." A bit cliché too, though he supposed the Fates probably did start using marble before the Olympians were even born, so he'd have to cut them some slack. In any case insulting their decor wasn't likely to help his situation.

Or maybe it would. The Fates were tough to predict.

"You have asked your three questions. That is all you will ask of me. Now you will move on."

Apollo nodded, frustrated that no grand ideas were coming to him. "Right, so I guess my time here is ended."

"Incorrect."

"Atropos said I would ask three questions of each of you, and then my time would be ended." He had to stop a moment to reform the question he wished to ask into a statement. "I have asked three questions of you, Clotho, and Atropos." He supposed he could have risked a fourth question, but as prickly as Lachesis was being, he thought it unwise. The Fates were under no obligation to let him go, after all.

"You do not understand." With that, Lachesis turned from him, putting on a pair of earphones and listening to some unknown music. The conversation appeared to be over.

Yet, Apollo realized, he was still there and still un-"ended". Immediately another question leaped to mind: *What now?*

The question of what sort of music the Fates liked to listen to leaped up immediately after that but got smacked down as pointless color.

CHAPTER TWENTY-TWO

"Everything comes in threes."
"Except when it doesn't."
          —*First and Second Laws of Cosmological Organization*

THEY WEREN'T MAKING HIM LEAVE. That much was clear.

Except, Apollo realized, it wasn't clear at all. Were they not offering to summon an exit for him because they wanted to trap him there? Did they expect him to find the exit on his own? Did they even realize that he couldn't leave without the help of a full god? The Fates were sometimes fuzzy on the details, after all, or simply content to let the details attend to themselves in time. Then there was that whole "ended" thing, which rather ruled out the trapping bit, but he had already tried leaving the same way he came and found no door.

Apollo descended the staircase up to the second level, perturbed at the way the Room's topography caressed the brain like a belt sander. Thought itself was difficult here, and the fact that he'd only just realized the trouble he'd had formulating his questions troubled him further.

His feet gained the second level, which turned out to consist of the back of the Room. He tried not to think about that, and aiding him in his effort was the sight of a comely young woman blinking at him from behind a luminescent curtain of blackness.

You will ask each of us three more questions.

The possibility that he wasn't out of Fates of whom to ask questions slowly crept into his consciousness. Yet the Fates—there were only three. Had Zeus known of another? For that matter, had Apollo himself known only to forget after diminishing? If that was the case, what else had he forgotten? He didn't think diminishing worked that way, but it was his first time.

It was a moot point, anyway, since he couldn't remember what he couldn't remember.

Irritated by this train of thought, Apollo canned the ontological masturbation and focused on the woman instead. Fate or not, she might be able to help, and in any case she was unnaturally cute. He followed her through the curtain, blatantly ignoring those wary readers who suspect a trap. (He can't hear you anyway. He's diminished.)

The curtained area into which he passed was small with a blessedly consistent geometry. Filling it were little more than a bed and a few small tables, atop which sat some spools of thread and assorted types of mending tape. The woman stood in the center of the room, smiling at him.

She hid the smile instantly the moment he saw it, replacing it with a bland stare that somehow managed to seem self-conscious. "Apollo, welcome. Er, you have come."

"That I have, mysterious one. I would ask your name, save for the fact that I'm only allowed three questions. If you are, in fact, another of the Fates, that is."

She straightened, taller and prouder, though at her full height she was still a head shorter than Apollo. Her left foot fidgeted as her blank expression quivered. "I am. You may address me as Poppy."

"Poppy," he repeated, sure to not make it a question. "I was unaware the Fates numbered four. I regret that I've never heard of nor met you before. Your loveliness is truly a sight."

Her smile returned for a moment, only to vanish again. There was a trace of a blush on her cheeks. Apollo moved closer, curious. The Fates were not moved by flattery, at least not as far as he knew.

But he wasn't about to use any questions to confirm that just yet either.

"I'm new," she explained. "And . . . all right, actually I'm not so much of a Fate as I am a . . . I guess you could say I'm an intern."

Apollo tried to coax more information out of her with just a curious look.

She cast about suddenly. "Oh, would you like something to drink? I've only water, but . . . it's good water. I'm sorry there's not more to offer; I don't really have many guests as you can imagine."

"I would be a poor guest to decline. I'm sure it's marvelous water." He smiled and sat down on the edge of the bed, radiating what charm he still held post-diminishment. It was, he expected, still considerable. "I didn't know the Fates hired interns."

"Intern, singular. Due to increased birth rate and life expectancy, I think is what they said." She handed Apollo the water and sat down beside him. "Plus, I get to handle the special cases when someone gets brought back to life. It used to only happen once in a while, but these days it's getting a little more common. I probably owe my position to the invention of the defibrillator."

"Ah, you're welcome, then."

"Oh, that's right, isn't it? Regardless, I'm still getting the hang of things." She blushed again, spine straightening up from the more relaxed position she'd slipped into. "And according to my last evaluation, I'm really unpracticed at the mysterious detachment shtick. But I'm working on it." She swallowed, eyes hardening. "You will ask your questions now."

He waited, just watching her. Her jaw trembled slightly.

"That's . . . not really a prediction." She sighed finally. "I don't have that kind of power yet."

"That must get frustrating at times." He reached out to put a hand over hers.

"It's not bad. Except when we watch TV. Do you know what it's like to watch TV with those three? Between them all, they know exactly how everything is going to start, end, and how it's going to get there. Nor are they shy about sharing it—they're always talking about how predictable something is and ruining any surprise at all."

"One wonders why they watch at all if they find it so boring."

"I suspect they like talking about it on the Internet, and they at least need to see a show in order to discuss it. It's a weird . . . Fate . . . thing. Hard to explain. Not that I've ever caught them going online." She pulled her hand away. "Not that I'm supposed to explain things like that at all, even."

"It's all right to share things that aren't related to why I came, surely. I don't even know how you got the job or your parentage yet. You seem to be somewhat more than mortal, though I can't be sure of the source."

"I'm not really sure myself . . . which is to say, ah." She paused, standing straight and facing him. "My origins lie shrouded in mystery. They are unknowable. Enigma."

"Ineffable," Apollo offered.

"That might be a good word, but I think it's taken." She cleared her throat and took a breath, apparently doing her best to appear aloof once more. "Now. You really must ask your questions. Before Atropos decides your time is up."

"She does that a lot."

Poppy nodded. "It is her thing. Er, 'such is her nature,' I should say. Now, please, ask. Don't get me in trouble, Apollo."

"I like you," he told her. "You don't call me 'godling.'"

Poppy's countenance faltered just for a moment. "Behave yourself." She crossed her arms, waiting.

"As you wish," he said finally, adding with a wink, "Intern-lady of Fate. I know the Fates created the UnMaking Nexus. I know Zeus was aware of a loophole that prevented its strike from being completely fatal. It occurs to me that I haven't actually asked how the loophole works or how Zeus might return."

Poppy began to speak, then stopped and collected herself. "You have not." She flashed a proud grin then shut it away, still waiting.

"You're getting the hang of this," he said. "Much to my dismay. Very well: What can be done to aid Zeus's return via this loophole?"

Poppy paused, pondering. "If Father Zeus did truly suspect foul play—"

"We're pretty sure he did."

She cleared her throat. "*If* he did, the loophole requires that he first create a magical talisman into which he then siphons a piece of his immortal essence."

"A talisman not unlike an amulet."

Poppy opened her mouth to respond, pausing first to flash a little smile. "A *magical* talisman, which could be created only by him so as to be properly attuned to him. Only by his hand could it be made ready to accept and hold the required fragment of his power."

"Purple stone," Apollo fished. "Hangs on a gold chain about the neck. About yay big." He held up his hands questioningly.

"The magical talisman—"

"Amulet. We already found it."

"Hush." Poppy glared at him. It was sweet. "The magical talisman must then be delivered unto the hands of a chosen champion of Zeus's offspring."

"Look, just say 'amulet.' It'll be faster."

She frowned. "*Amulet* isn't anywhere near as mysterious as *magical talisman,* and I've got another evaluation coming in a month."

"I won't tell anyone."

"The *amulet,*" and here she imbued the word with a mysterious wave of her arms, "must be taken by the chosen champion among Zeus's offspring—"

"She's got a much shorter name too."

"You know, this would be over and done by now if you would just let me speak."

"Yes, but I do so enjoy the sight of you talking."

"So why shorten everything I'm trying to say?"

He simply smiled, leaning back and listening, trying to make her blush with his gaze under the theory that she might tell him more than she was supposed to if she became flustered again. He also just enjoyed doing it, but two birds with one arrow and so forth.

She turned her back to him instead, continuing to speak. Apollo listened intently, making a concerted effort to note every detail, every option, and commit them all to memory with special care so the process of exiting the Fates' abode—or even walking out into the main room again—didn't knock them out of his mind.

Poppy's answer was indeed detailed, yet so great were Apollo's efforts at absorbing every mote of information that absolutely none of it managed to make its way past his ears and into this retelling. Such things may only be transcribed from echoes within the cosmos, as anyone with an advanced degree in quantum fictional mechanics knows. Some narratives may claim to hide such details purely out of dramatic license, keeping them unknown so as to create tension and mystery, but that's all really a bunch of bull. Not that many would admit it.

Any contradiction between the above statements and statements elsewhere in this narrative is, of course, completely intended. Probably.

"That doesn't sound so bad," Apollo said when she was done. "Though finding the place might be a little problematic. Which brings me to my next question: Just how can I get out of here if I'm diminished? I had to have someone else open the door for me to get in."

"You'll have to ask Atropos's help with that unfortunately."

"Ask her help," he repeated, just managing to turn the inflection away from being interrogative. "That might be a problem . . . Will you ask her on my behalf?"

Poppy paused, cocking her head to one side, considering. Her eyes shut. She slowly drew a breath as her arms raised up, spreading out, fingers splayed wide as if searching the air for something. Her eyes worked back and forth under closed lids, body beginning to sway. Apollo waited, curious about what was happening, uncertain if this was some means of telecommunication with the other Fates or if she was simply trying to answer the question. Her daze lasted long enough for Apollo to worry that he might have wasted the last of his questions—and begin to hope that maybe the Fates had also hired a concierge or personal masseuse who might allow him three further questions.

And then Poppy opened her eyes to reveal darkly glazed orbs that seemed to stare at him across a vast distance. "I . . ." she began, "will ask."

Apollo blinked.

She smirked and blinked away the glaze. "How was that? Pretty mysterious, eh?"

Poppy was correct; she did indeed ask. A response was given. A bargain was struck. The cost of a doorway was a steep one, yet not so steep as to outweigh the cost of remaining in the Room indefinitely. Apollo consoled himself with the thought that he was better off without the thing he'd had to give up anyway. (As this narrative has previously stated, gods can have their stupid moments too, and they're even more practiced at kidding themselves with specious justifications. They're also better at shuffleboard, but that is neither here nor there.)

In the Room, the Fates continued their work. As they always had. As they always would.

So far as anyone knows at least.

"It is ended," Atropos announced.

"Unnecessarily announced," Lachesis said.

"Nevertheless."

"We gave up far too much," Lachesis continued.

Clotho nodded. Atropos sighed.

Poppy looked up from where she was trying to decide what to do with a box containing no spoons that someone had mistakenly delivered. "If it bothers you so much, why did you tell him anything?"

"Predestination is a bitch," Lachesis explained.

"We foresaw our own compliance." Clotho nodded.

"There was no other choice," Atropos said.

"I really don't get why you'd see yourselves doing something that you didn't want to do and not even have a reason for it after you did it."

"There was a reason."

"Because it happened."

"There was no other choice."

"For us."

Poppy frowned. "That's terribly circular reasoning."

"Yes. It works best."

"This is not to be mistaken for philosophy."

"We have neither the leather nor sunglasses for it."

"Nor the love of bullet time."

Poppy frowned. "This is like what you told me when I first arrived: that there is never choice, only the illusion of choice. Isn't it?"

"No," Lachesis answered. "That was a lie."

"We were screwing with you," Atropos explained.

"But you believed us. Such is the value of inscrutability. A lesson for you," Clotho offered.

"So you did have a choice about telling Apollo, then?"

"No."

"There is no choice, for us. We are the Fates. We are but characters in a novel."

"And not a very good one."

"Now fetch us some coffee, Poppy," Atropos ordered. Poppy left the room to do so, wondering if her confusion would hurt her next evaluation. The three paused once she was gone.

"We have entertained them," Clotho surmised.

"After a fashion," Lachesis commented.

"Irrelevant. We return to our tasks," Atropos finished.

"I shall miss the others when he sends them away," added Clotho.

The other two stopped to stare as they had known they would.

"To which 'he' do you refer?" Atropos asked.

"Yes."

"Ah."

"You knew she would say that," Lachesis said.

"Yet I was bound to ask," Atropos stated.

"Yes," remarked Lachesis. "I knew that."

"The humor grows old, Lachesis."

"It always was."

"Such is our fate," Clotho remarked.

"Please stop saying that."

The Fates continued their work.

Part Three:
(Insert Quest Here)

CHAPTER TWENTY-THREE

"O, resplendently convivial Dionysus, lord of wine and revelry! Deprive us not of your bombastic glory, lest we all wither and die of boredom upon the vine of life!"

—first daily convocation of Dionysus (typically given midafternoon)

"Free beer! (No fat chicks.)"

—inscription upon a Dionysian temple frieze

LAS VEGAS, whenever he'd seen it on TV or in movies, always struck Leif as a tremendous waste of light. Only when he was actually standing in the middle of The Las Vegas Strip did he realize how much of an understatement that was. Even in the late-morning daylight, everything was lit up—from the exteriors of the monster hotel-casinos to the thirty-foot billboard above the drug store and the lights of the myriad people who stood on the street corners and handed out card-sized fliers picturing scantily clad "dancers". It was simultaneously amazing and irritating. The question of what else might be done with the electricity used to power this single street was, when he thought about it, a rather depressing one. Maybe that was why so many people there seemed to be drunk?

On the other hand, he did like to gamble. He'd have to come back here some time when the love of his life wasn't busy being a pawn in an immortal game of Battle Chess. All right, so she was technically a daughter of the king, so that made her . . . what . . . a rook? Did it matter? What was he babbling about anyway?

Yet another man attempting to hand him another of what Tracy charmingly called "prostitute trading cards" jarred him out of his thoughts. Leif stopped and pointed down The Strip to where they'd purchased Dionysus's obscenely expensive champagne offering.

"Look!" he told the man. "You see all the way down there? That's where we just walked from! You're, like, the eighty-ninth guy out here who's tried to give me one of these, and look at me! I'm carrying nothing! If I wanted them at all, could I possibly have gotten this far down the road without having an entire armful?"

The man glanced at him, blinked, and promptly flapped the stack he held and offered a card again with a smirk that was as unhelpful as it was disinterested.

"Fine!" Leif snatched it and hurried after Tracy, trying to use the card like a badge to clear him past seventeen other card-pushers along the sidewalk. He caught up to her on the escalator to the pedestrian overpass after less than perfect success.

Tracy spared a glance at the now two dozen cards of vamping women he clutched in his hands and shook her head. "You know you don't have to go with me, Karlson. I can handle this myself."

Leif dumped the cards over the side. Drunken cries of "It's rainin' babes!" came from below, moments before the squeal of tires and the crash of a fender-bender.

"It's no bother," he assured her. "And I'm not leaving you alone. What if you need me? What if we split up and can't find each other again?"

And what if Dionysus made a pass at her? Jealousy faltered his steps at the very thought.

"Just . . . let me do the talking when we're there, at least."

"Right. Talking. Talking is good. What if talking's not enough?"

"That's what this is for." She tapped the Dom Pérignon vintage 1995 she carried in the box tucked under her arm. "It'll be enough."

"But what if it's not? What if you have to flash your—"

He stopped and stared as they gained the top of the escalator, just long enough for the person behind him to give a snarky "out-of-the-way" cough. Leif sidestepped, stared just a little more at the tall, iron structure holding his attention, and then caught up to Tracy.

"I just figured something out!" He beamed at her. "Look!"

She glanced down the Strip to where he pointed. "That's . . . oh!" She actually laughed. It was a good laugh. Leif beamed wider as she continued. "Now why didn't I think of that?"

"You're not the one destined to climb it," he said. "We might not need to go to Paris at all!"

Still gazing at the one-fourth-scale Eiffel Tower that rose out of the Paris Las Vegas Hotel and Casino, Tracy snickered. "Oh, yeah, how terrible a fate that would be, huh? Nobody likes going to *Paris!*" She turned, smirking. "You know that's still pretty damn tall, don't you?"

"Er, well . . . yeah, but . . . It's *less* of a climb. And I wouldn't have to deal with the security team of a national landmark."

"Uh-huh. What's got less security than a Vegas casino, right? Come on. And keep your eyes open for Thad."

"How come you call *him* Thad but you call me Karlson?"

"For one thing his name's not Karlson, is it?"

One of Dionysus's first acts after the Return was to openly declare himself the true founder of Las Vegas. (His *very* first act was to make it rain beer over every in-progress Major League Baseball game, which swiftly resulted in the games being called on account of loss of concession revenue.) Very soon thereafter, he raised up his own hotel and casino, the Dionysian, and declared it his official off-Olympus abode.

Dionysus built it on the site of Caesar's Palace, which he had demolished. In a press conference given moments before the old structure's implosion, the god explained that not only was it the perfect spot for the Dionysian, but he wouldn't stand for a similarly classically-themed major casino so close to his own. Furthermore, he'd never thought a place so fabulous should bear the name "Caesar" anyway, as, quote, "Augustus was a prude, and Julius got his dumb ass stabbed."

Caesar's descendants could not be reached for comment.

Getting into the hotel's grand penthouse was no problem for Tracy and Leif. There was a semi-hidden elevator to find and a keypad lock to contend with, but Thalia had left them a note with both the location and code before disappearing on her early-morning mystery errand. The elevator was so large, it had its own full-service bar and a security guard whose biceps were the size of a small child. He stared at Leif in a way that made him feel anything but welcome. Tracy didn't even get a second glance.

"I think he likes you," she whispered.

"Shouldn't you take your glasses off?"

"Why?"

"Well . . . I mean . . . I think you look even cuter with them on, myself, but I'm thinking Dionysus might have more typically male tastes. First impression and such."

She frowned, though not as deeply as Leif suspected she might have wanted to. Thalia's mood-booster was still in effect. "I have to be able to see, Karlson."

"Hey, if you're you-know-who's daughter, why are your eyes bad?"

She glared at him.

"Just trying to help."

"Well, don't." She glanced up at the elevator numbers. "You really think I look even cuter with them on, huh?"

"Oh, definitely."

"Fine, then." She slipped them off.

"See?" he said. "I knew you'd do that, that's why I—"

"No, it's not." She grinned as the doors opened. "Let me do the talking."

"You already said that."

The penthouse was vast. Couches sat everywhere—some ratty, some opulent, yet all looking very, very comfortable and most strewn with men and women (more of the latter) who were relaxing, drinking, and generally enjoying themselves in whatever ways you could imagine, provided you're not too uptight. Amid the couches were pool tables, tables cluttered with snacks, and large high-definition TVs displaying sporting events and video games. Self-service kegs were stacked high along one wall (when they arrived, Leif spotted two being newly tapped and an empty being changed out). Beside the kegs was a long bar stocked with bottles upon bottles. In one corner, a curved balcony jutted out above it all, its thick, transparent railing festooned with colorful pennants. Leif could make out the back of a huge TV poised on the balcony's edge and reflecting light off the walls behind it. A spiral staircase wound the thirty-foot distance up to the balcony's left side. Descent via fire pole was possible on the right side. Plastered across both the balcony's bottom and the back of the TV was the ecstatically mirthful visage of Dionysus himself, circled by grapes and gazing at everything below.

"Reminds me of a frat party!" Leif had to shout to be heard above the music gushing from unseen speakers. "With better decor!"

"I'm sure I wouldn't know." She pointed to the balcony. "I figure he's up there!"

"Safe assumption!

"C'mon!"

They made their way to the base of the staircase, where they were stopped by a stern-looking man at a podium who appeared to serve as a maître d' and bouncer. The immediate area around the podium was somehow quieter, as if shielded from the sound pouring through the rest of the penthouse. Leif made a mental note to brag about Apollo doing something similar with him a few days ago.

"I'm here to see the mighty, godly, and resplendently convivial Dionysus," Tracy announced. Thalia had advised them to use that exact phrasing to signal that they were connected with the god's temple rather than just regular party-goers.

"*We* are," Leif added.

The maître d' raised an eyebrow. He seemed to be the only one in the room who was not having a good time, and doing his best to be a sufficient counterweight.

Indeed, Luthor Stackpole was most certainly not having a good time. Before the Return, he was the winner of *Hanging OUT! Magazine*'s "Best Maître d' in Las Vegas" award three years running. Once Dionysus took direct control of the town, he insisted that Luthor serve him personally. Luthor had been on the verge of going back to school to pursue his dream of becoming a hydroelectric engineer, despite the obvious pay cut. To change Luthor's mind, Dionysus dropped a dump truck full of money on his house (it crashed through the dining room ceiling—Luthor preferred not to ponder if the god knew he wasn't home at the time). The god also promised him a free lifetime pass for the Hoover Dam tour. It seemed a fair compromise at the time, but that was before he knew he'd be working closely with the greatest man-child seen in the world since Nero. Getting out of his contract turned out to be impossible without trading his liver to some entities known as the "Stygian witches" for some reason, so he did the best he could to tolerate the noise, the immaturity, and the constant flow of groupies he was expected to regulate.

The obscene amount of money that made up his salary also helped. Luthor just wished it would stop arriving via dump truck so he could release the team of roofing contractors he kept on retainer in the guesthouse. The weekly dam tours helped too. During the difficult times, he took solace in counting the days until the next tour. On really taxing days, the longing would radiate off him in waves.

Leif, wondering at his own inexplicable hankering for six million tons of concrete, awaited the maître d's response. "Well, we are," Leif said finally.

"Are you now?" said the maître d' (also finally).

Tracy nodded and slipped him a $50 bill in what seemed to Leif to be a rather practiced fashion. "It's important."

"I'm sure it is," he plainly lied, "but I'm afraid His Greatness is indisposed at the moment."

Tracy smiled. "I'm sure he is, but we come bearing gifts too. Do you know if he'll be available soon?"

"I am sure I do not know," Luthor sighed. (Leif managed to resist pointing out that there was an awful lot of being sure going around.) "He is a god, and of the unpredictable sort, as you must know. And in any case, once he *is* free, he has a number of appointments waiting ahead of you, so you'd best find something else to occupy you in the meantime. I will call your name in the event he—"

The maître d' stopped, touched a finger to an earpiece and turned aside to listen. "I— . . . Yes, bombastic one. . . . Yes. . . . But, my lord, there are— . . . Well, yes, she— . . . About a thirty-six, I believe. . . . B cup. . . . Yes, your awesomeness, the cameras are most certainly high definition. . . . I will. . . . I won't. . . . Lord, I feel it only necessary to point out that the gentleman who came in earlier is still— . . . Yes, great one, I can understand how you would find her much more . . ." — the maître d' frowned as if swallowing an underdone rat kebab — "'spank-tacular' than the other gentleman, yes. . . . Very well. Rock on, my lord."

He lowered his fingertip to press something on the podium. A little gate to the stairs swung open to the sound of a guitar riff that Leif couldn't quite place. "You may ascend," he told Tracy. "And . . . your companion as well, I suppose."

After a brief word of thanks, they hurried on up the stairs with Tracy in the lead and Leif admiring the view once again. Tracy, oddly, refused to respond to his question about how often she got called "spank-tacular." There was the moment where her boot kicked back to narrowly miss his chest, but he figured that was surely just an accident.

CHAPTER TWENTY-FOUR

"I've never been entirely certain if the intoxicating effect of being close to Dionysus is an actual divine power or simply the result of thousands of years' worth of consumed alcohol seeping out of his pores. Regardless, it is a . . . unique sort of defense, isn't it?"
— Athena *(interview,* Self-Defense Quarterly*)*

TRACY ASCENDED THE STAIRS with a plan—or at least the semblance of one: Be respectful but not fawning. Keep her fascination at meeting another god under control. Treat this like any other business negotiation she'd had in the course of her career. And do *not* resort to Thalia's suggested forms of persuasion. Tracy long ago decided that was her mother's way, not her own—even if that way was likely responsible for her own conception. Tracy was dressed smartly, not seductively, despite Thalia's suggestion she grab a dress of some sort from the hotel boutique. She would do this her way, no matter her physical gifts or Dionysus's frat-boy reputation. Given that they'd had to wait until after 11 a.m. just to get the champagne and be sure the god would be awake, she'd have to do it her way and *quickly.*

Dionysus sat on what Tracy had to admit was the most magnificent reclining chair she'd ever seen. Thickly padded and extra wide without seeming oversized, it sat on a dais of intricately sculpted green glass. The sheen of the leather upholstery was remarkably luxurious, while at the same time appearing just worn enough to radiate perfect comfort. Built into one side was an open cooler holding numerous beer cans. One arm held fittings for remote controls; the other contained some sort of video game controller, a cup holder, and what appeared to be nacho cheese. The footrest was slung high, and the back of the chair was gently vibrating.

At least Tracy hoped that's where the vibrating was coming from.

The dais sat in the exact center of the balcony, facing the gigantic plasma screen TV. Behind the dais were a few couches, a wet bar, and a Jacuzzi. A mirrored elevator door that led Dionysus-knew-where was built into the balcony's corner.

The god was not alone on the balcony. Three women accompanied him, two of whom were dressed as—*good grief*—cheerleaders. The third wore one of the tightest, shortest little black dresses that Tracy had ever seen. She stood attentively beside the god, holding a laptop with the keyboard and screen facing him, presumably ready for the moment he might wish to use it. The other two women cheered as he furiously worked another game controller and concentrated on the gigantic plasma screen.

A man stood nearby, as well, built even more solidly than the maître d' and wearing slacks with a tuxedo T-shirt. He kept one eye on Leif and Tracy as they stepped from the stairs, and the other eye flashed between the game screen and the three women.

Tracy wondered if that gave him a headache.

As for Dionysus himself, he looked about how he appeared in magazines: muscularly pudgy with a boyishly handsome face, light brown hair, and—at the moment—wearing only a garland of ivy, sandals, and a pair of bright blue boxer shorts with the words *Resplendently convivial!* emblazoned on them in gold lettering.

"Kind of reminds me of Jason," Leif whispered.

Tracy shushed him. The pang of grief at the mention of Jason's name was smaller than expected, as she found herself unable to keep from focusing just a little longer on the god's chest.

Thalia's little mind trick was still working, then, right?

Leif ignored her shushing. "So are you planning to just stand here or . . . ?"

A shout from Dionysus cut off her response. "Oh for the love of—! Pass interference! Did you see that? Flag! *Flag! Ref!* Oh, come *on!*"

He chucked the controller away in disgust. It sailed out over the crowd of people below and disappeared as the two cheerleaders rushed in with fawning consolation that the god barely acknowledged. "Cheaters! I ask you, what kind of crap is that? Geez! Call the game's developer, Electronic . . . something," he told the woman in the dress. "Tell them if they don't make a better version by Friday, I'll drop a whiskey truck on their server farm. And it'll be *empty!*"

It was then that Dionysus noticed Leif and Tracy—or at least Tracy. Immediately his face brightened, game problems forgotten. He spread his arms wide while somehow simultaneously snatching a can of beer from the chair's fridge.

"Hel-lo! What have we here? Two new supplicants come to worship and party at the feet of the most awesome god in the entire bunch?" He didn't wait for an answer. "My goodness, aren't you a gorgeous sight! You may approach—which is to say c'mere. No-no, just the girl, of course. You stay back by the stairs, that's a good man. Come, tell me a name to go with those startling blue eyes. And have a beer!"

Tracy caught the can he tossed and opened it but didn't drink—she was too focused on finding the right words and hiding her irritation with the "girl" appellation. *Respect, ego stroke, put him at ease . . .*

"Most awesome Dionysus, first let me thank you for—"

"Oh, come on. One sip won't kill you! Everyone drinks in the presence of Dionysus! You there, towhead! You too! Catch!" He pulled out another beer and chucked it at Leif like a quarterback heaving a pass.

Leif just managed to catch it. He cracked it open and, with a shrug, took a quick chug.

Worried about what might be in it, Tracy would have told him to stop, but she supposed it was pointless worrying about things like that when already in the domain of a god.

"It's good," he assured Tracy.

"Of *course* it's good! Am I not a god? One cannot live by wine alone! Now shut up, man. Let the girl speak!"

Dionysus grinned and sat back in his chair to either listen to Tracy intently or undress her with his eyes. She had to grit her molars and clench her beer a little tighter to keep from protesting. She sipped—a gesture that triggered a waggling of the god's eyebrows—before clearing her throat and speaking again.

"I'm Tracy Wallace, producer of the hit show *Monster Slayer,*" she announced, presenting a business card.

"Oh, really? You'll be pleased to know I've heard of that! (Go ahead, be pleased! Ah, there you go.) Wonderful work. Would you perhaps be trying to imply that you're more than just a pretty face?"

"You're as perceptive as you are powerful, great Dionysus; I'm definitely trying to imply that. I come bearing gifts, and to beg of you a favor."

"Oh, no-no-no, you needn't get down to business so fast! Have a seat. Have another beer. Bask in the hedonistic glory of the Dionysian Casino and its god!" He beamed. Insufferably so, by her estimation. "C'mere, there's room on the chair! Think of me as a sexy Santa Claus!"

Tracy gave no ground beyond another drink of her beer, hoping that might keep her refusal from being insulting. "It's only out of respect for your glory—which is everything I imagined and more, I can assure you—that I brought it up so fast. I'm sure you've got so many demands on your time, I don't want to waste it."

"No-no. C'mere, sit. I insist!" He patted the chair. "You don't wanna be a poor guest, do you?"

Tracy hesitated, poised on the edge of shutting down his pick-up attempt and reminding herself that there was no other means to track down Thad. She needed that necklace back. She would give, just a little. Bend but not break and all that garbage. She moved to sit, eschewing the cushion for one of the chair's armrests and slipping on her glasses as she did so. The veneer of a smile accompanied it all. "Better?"

"Better!" Dionysus whipped the TV remote out to flip channels before Tracy could say anything. "Oh, you don't need to put glasses on. It's a special TV; you can see it just fine no matter how bad your eyes are!"

"That's impressive," she said, "but I—"

"Quite impressive! Designed it myself! I mean, the idea was mine, someone else did the grunt work. I forget who. So off with the glasses! And that outfit, it's far too ordinary to be wasted on you. You should try something more flattering." He pointed at the other women. "Two of my favorites. I should think . . . cheerleader for you. I'm sure I've got something in your size."

Oh, no God damn way. If it showed on Tracy's face, Dionysus didn't notice. He was too busy watching an actual minotaur rampage through the streets of the Spanish town of Pamplona. "No," she answered, "that's quite all right. But, thank you for the offer. We really should—"

The god clapped as the minotaur rammed a runner ahead of him, launching the unfortunate man into the air to crash through a third-story window. "Ha! See that? That's the fun of being a god. You can just toss a minotaur into the Running of the Bulls and create all sorts of fun. Shame that was plate glass, but he knew what he was getting into." He turned to Tracy, scolding smoothly, "No cheerleader outfit? How do you know you won't like it unless you try it?"

"I have tried it," she admitted. "So I'm pretty sure. But thank—"

"Really? Oh, I'm sorry I couldn't have seen that. Care for a repeat?"

"I sabotaged my own tryouts, so, no. My mom was a cheerleader," she found herself saying. "She pushed me into it, and as a matter of fact, you're starting to sound a bit like her in that regard, got it?"

"I am? Well that's a turnoff."

Good! She wondered what Dionysus would think if she told him they were half-siblings. Like a lot of bad ideas, it was tempting.

"We, ah, brought gifts," Leif offered.

"You still here?"

"Yes, gifts!" Tracy presented the champagne. "Our gift to you, with the humble hope you might consider granting our small request."

"Oh yes?" Dionysus accepted the bottle with relish. "Does the request involve body shots? Because it depends on if it's him or you we're talking about." He chortled at his own joke and continued before Tracy could comment. "Ah, Dom Pérignon. Excellent year. The French do know their wines, don't they?"

"I—"

"Arrogant bunch, though. I had to flood the entire Loire Valley because they had the gall to disagree with me—me!—on the way to make wine! Can you believe the hubris?"

"That's quite—"

"And very well, so I didn't *have* to, but they got far too cocky while we were gone, thinking they could come up with good ideas without a god's help! Sometimes you've got to flex a little muscle now and again, am I right?" Dionysus flexed practically every muscle from the waist up, adding, "No one will blame you for swooning." He grinned with a wink most men saved for afterglow. "What, that doesn't impress you? You're American, you're supposed to hate the French for some reason, aren't you? Loosen up, baby!"

She smiled sweetly. "You know, you remind me of someone I met last night, only more so." It was only then that she noticed herself looking him over a bit more than she intended.

"Do I? And who might that charming fellow be?"

"That's part of the favor, really. We're hoping you can help us track down where he's staying in Vegas. Or if he's left. And maybe," she added, deciding to bargain above what she expected to get, "send a goon or two to hold him there until we can speak to him."

"Oh-ho, interesting." He leaned closer, chin resting on his palm. "And what, pray tell, is the lucky fellow's name?"

"Thad Winslow. And I wouldn't call him lucky; we don't want him for anything pleasant."

"I *have* heard the name, though remembering where and how is another matter, of course. What *do* you want him for?"

The god put his hand on her knee. She lifted it off.

"He took something of mine. A family heirloom. It's not worth much, but the sentimental value's incredible. I want it back."

"Did he now?" His hand was on her knee again. His gaze caught hers before she could remove it a second time, and the need to do so slipped away in a confusing haze. She felt warm, watching those eyes, those deep, wine-rich eyes. Wasn't she going to say something? Or do something? She wobbled, suddenly tipsy, unable to concentrate, vaguely conscious of leaning in closer . . .

"And he kicked me," Leif added.

His voice shook Tracy out of the fog. She sat back up, rod straight, and shoved the god's hand off her knee before she could even think to be gentle about it.

"Good!" shot Dionysus, annoyed. "I can hardly blame him! Were you hanging around being a third wheel with him too?"

Leif didn't answer. Tracy stood up, arms crossed and unsure of what to say either. Dionysus sat back in his chair, half sizing her up, half ogling. She waited him out, hoping the whole idea wasn't a bust and starting to think about how to get away cleanly if it was.

Dionysus slowly beamed. "You know, I think I *do* know this Thad Winslow, come to think of it. I will bring him here before us both, and you, in exchange for this, will don a cheerleader outfit and spend a few hours with me. You might even like it."

"Or," she offered, "there's a *Monster Slayer* game coming out next month—multiple platform release, console and PC—and I will get *you* an advanced copy. I hear it's good. Downloadable content galore and everything." Actually she understood that most of it was downloadable content. Purchasing the game got you only a character creator and a credit card interface. It wasn't her area, but they'd said that was the direction the industry was going.

"Counteroffer: you get me the advanced copy and . . . *consider* donning a cheerleader outfit. And spending a few hours with me. An enviable opportunity if I do say so myself. And oh, didn't I just?"

Tracy chewed the inside of her lip. "I'll consider it."

"You mean you accept my offer of considering the outfit, or you'll consider considering?"

"The first. Bring Thad Winslow here, and I'll agree to consider it. But could you bring him to a room downstairs somewhere? I don't want to have to deal with him in front of so many people." *You, especially.*

"Well now, I don't even know if I have the right Thad Winslow, you know. I have to be sure at first, don't I? No-no, don't try to change my mind, you've already accepted, and he's here already for some reason if I'm not mistaken." He motioned to the woman in the black dress and touched a key on the laptop when she brought it close. "Luthor, that fellow with the urgent appointment you keep telling me about: His name was Thad Winslow, wasn't it?"

"It is, my lord," came the maître d's voice. *"He's been waiting for quite some time. Shall I send him up?"* Tracy began to have a very bad feeling. She moved back toward the stairs a bit, exchanging glances with Leif.

"Yes, send him up. And . . . tell him there's someone else who— never mind, just send him up. Quickly now." He waved the laptop away, grinning drunkenly at Tracy. "We'll surprise him."

"We'll meet him on the stairs," Tracy tried, quickly dragging Leif that way. At a look from the god, the tuxedo-shirted man blocked their path.

"Oh, come on. It'll be fun!" Dionysus said. "Also it occurs to me that I should probably find out what he wants to see me about first. All play and no work make a god . . . ah, pretty happy, truthfully, but like it or not, I do have my responsibilities. Oh! I know! Here, get behind the screen, both of you!" The god actually giggled. "This'll be good!"

Unable to come up with a better option, Tracy tugged Leif behind the TV as requested. There they crouched on the balcony edge above the rest of the party.

"We're screwed," he whispered.

"Not necessarily."

"No, we're screwed. You know those parts in movies where something bad's about to happen and someone invariably says, 'I have a bad feeling about this,' whether it's appropriate to the conversation or not? Well, I have a bad feeling about this! Why else would Thad be here if he wasn't going to see one of the gods involved in the whole thing?"

"It's a party," she offered. "He's a party kind of guy. Maybe he's just here for the drinks?" She didn't really buy that herself, but the hope was sincere.

"Tracy, you're a smart woman, and I love you, but I'm starting to think that thing Thalia did affected your judgment."

"It's not Thalia; it's *him*," she insisted, nodding toward Dionysus. "Get close to him, and I swear you'll start feeling tipsy. And knock off the love stuff. We've got enough problems already, especially if you're right."

"*If* I'm right?"

She leaned out over the edge, looking down. "Maybe we can jump. It's not too far. Think you can make it to that big trampoline?"

"Who am I, Mario?"

"There's a big couch down there. It's closer; we might make it."

"I'm *not* jumping!"

"It's just plan C, okay? Which means we need a plan B first . . ."

She could hear Thad greeting Dionysus as he gained the balcony, praising him for the party before the two exchanged pleasantries. Her mind raced as she briefly considered trying to get Leif to temporarily sacrifice himself for the cause, but she couldn't quite bring herself to do that.

"Okay," she whispered, "if he's got the amulet out, we . . . grab it and run like hell!"

"That's it? Run like hell? That's worse than 'Get 'er!'"

"It's a *work in progress*." Leif was right, though. Plan B sucked. And they were out of time.

". . . which actually brings me to why I'm here," Thad was saying.

"Why you're here? Already? Everyone's all so serious so fast around here today!" cried Dionysus. "Am I losing my touch or something? Fun first! You like fun, don't you, Thad? Guess who I've got behind the TV! Go on, guess!"

"I—"

"Wrong! Out! Come on out, you two! You're gonna love this, Thad, really. I'm working on getting her properly dressed, of course, but she's one of those 'modern' girls. Stubborn, hard to get. You know the type."

Tracy glanced at Leif, each clearly hoping that the other had come up with a plan, each disappointed. Neither budged. As long as they could stay hidden, it was that much longer they had to think.

"Hey!" The god called. "Out! That's your cue! I—oh for pilsner's sake!"

The TV abruptly rose up into the ceiling, leaving the two of them completely exposed on the center edge of the balcony. Dionysus sat in his chair, holding a remote and grinning like an idiot. Thad stood closer, not grinning, but still quite like an idiot as far as Tracy was concerned. "Forgot I had a button to do that for a sec!" Dionysus shouted. "Great inventions, buttons." He gestured to the laptop holder. "Make a note: send Hephaestus a wine basket with my compliments on the whole button idea!"

Tracy stood, hands on her hips. Thad didn't have the amulet anywhere in sight, so plan B was out. A pity too, since he still seemed pretty stunned to see her. Maybe she should tackle him anyway before he could say anything incrimina—

"They're them!" Thad yelled.

Tracy made a mental note to think less and act more. A moment later she realized the contradiction but was still too tipsy to figure out how to fix it.

The god laughed. "Yes, yes, they are! They're looking for you, did you know that?"

"No, Dionysus—"

"*Lord* Dionysus to you, bud, no matter whose son you are."

Tracy pounced at Thad, grappling him about the waist and throwing her entire weight into it. The model stumbled but didn't go down. Leif sprang into the brawl a moment later. Thad yelled for them to stop, to watch the hair, to get the hell off of him, but Tracy didn't bother listening. She did her best to rifle through his pockets for the amulet, but the struggle made it difficult. At last she seized upon something that felt right and gripped it tightly just as Dionysus grabbed her by the back of her belt and hauled her off of the man. She dangled in the air as he held her, clutching in her hands what turned out to be Thad's keys.

Dionysus was laughing. "You either told me the truth about not liking him, Tracy, or your method of getting his pants off needs practice."

The man in the tuxedo shirt kept Leif handily restrained. Thad himself was busy brushing down his outfit and re-ruffling his hair. Tracy chucked the model's keys straight at his stomach. They made a satisfying—albeit pointless—impact.

Thad pointed at Leif once he'd recovered. "Do you know who he is?"

"The towhead? I'm sure someone does, but . . ."

"He's the guy you all wanted me to follow! Or at least that's what my mother *told* me you wanted. You don't recognize him at all?"

"Well he's not much to look at, is he? Besides, I prefer this one." The god lifted Tracy up higher and then glanced at Leif. "Though he does look a little familiar in an annoying sort of way now that you mention it . . ."

So their cover, such as it was, was definitely blown. Using force to escape was right out, and Tracy was loath to make any bargains Dionysus might come up with. She wracked her brain for a story that might get them out of the situation, some sort of lie that might fool a god and render Thad mute, but nothing sprang to mind. *Don't just hang there like an idiot, Tracy. Think of something! Anything!*

Dionysus was a party god, so she needed more than a lie; she needed an *entertaining* lie. Something funny . . . No, she corrected, seizing upon a better idea. Not just something funny, something funny . . . with *cyborgs.*

She failed to think of a complete story, but she figured it was the thought that counted. It remained to be seen if her idea would work and how quickly.

"I found them last night," Thad was saying. He tugged the amulet out of a pocket. "She had this! Said it was something important, something Apollo gave her, or something, so I grabbed it and brought it back here. I don't quite know what it is, but it's so valuable she didn't want to take it off, not even for me! And obviously it was my plan all along to use it as bait so they'd follow and you could catch them."

He tossed the amulet to Dionysus. Tracy's grab wasn't fast enough—
or mounted on long enough arms.

The god peered at it, growing more serious. "Hrm . . . Now that
you bring it up, I could have sworn your mother said you'd follow this
guy to keep an eye on him. And do nothing else!"

"That was before she knew about that!" Thad pointed at the amulet.
"And come on, they were out in the middle of nowhere where it's
boring and hot! You're one of the *cool* gods, Dion—Lord Dionysus.
You understand, right?"

Tracy thought the entire argument was far too clever to come out
of Thad, but she was hardly one to judge while hanging by her belt
as she was. The belt snapped a second later, and suddenly she was
hardly one to judge while lying on the floor at a god's feet as she was.
She preferred the former. Better view.

The god looked down on her. She looked up, crawling slowly
backward while he seemed to be pondering what to do.

"So you're one of the conspirators?" Leif spoke up. "One of the
gods who killed Zeus?"

Dionysus laughed smoothly, much to Tracy's surprise. "Only an
idiot would answer that question with a yes! And haven't you heard?
Ares did it!" He turned his attention back to Tracy, seizing her by the
arm and lifting her back to her feet, but didn't let go. "But why concern
yourself with all of that, pretty one? What's the towhead said to you
to get you involved?"

"He hasn't said anything," she answered. "Not to get me involved,
anyway. In other matters he hardly shuts up."

"Ah, he sounds bothersome. I can do you the favor of locking him
away, then, if you tell me more about this amulet. It isn't just some
family heirloom, is it?"

"That thing? I've never seen it before in my life."

Thad laughed. "She's definitely lying about that."

"Shut up, model-boy, I'm talking to the girl." Dionysus smiled
broadly at her. Again she began to feel tipsy. "Tell me what I want to
know. Why did Apollo give it to *you?*"

Tracy shook her head through the fog, managing to speak a "no"
that sundered the god's smile.

"You've an irritating stubborn streak in you. Not my favorite, as streaks go. But as you like, I suppose. I'm in no hurry." He looked to the woman in the dress. "Cages!"

Cages?

Before she could voice the question, two narrow silver cages lowered from the ceiling on either side of Dionysus's throne dais. "In you go!" he declared, tossing her into one.

She landed safely; it was a remarkably gentle throw. More jarring was the discovery that, despite her protests, she was suddenly wearing a cheerleader's outfit.

CHAPTER TWENTY-FIVE

"No, the so-called 'Idiot Ball' doesn't actually exist, silly. Can you imagine how dangerous a thing like that could be were it real? It's just a concept, isn't it, Polyhymnia?"

"An abstract concept!"

"It's merely a metaphor. Muses or not, it's not as if we can toss it around and play with it."

"Even if we could, we wouldn't."

"Certainly not, because that would get us in the worst kind of trouble."

"Dreadful trouble!"

"Grievous trouble! If we could."

"But we cannot."

"Right! Because it doesn't actually exist! As we said."

"Except as an abstraction."

"Yes, precisely. Just an abstraction."

"Um, would anyone like some tea?"

—Muses Calliope and Polyhymnia, Jet City ComiCon

TO SAY SHE LOOKED GOOD in the dress was inaccurate. Though the dress was itself spectacular (low-cut green silk with a diagonally asymmetrical hem, it wrapped her body like a seduced lover), it was more apt to say that *it* looked good on *her*. The dress was mere garnish, and she moved like she knew it. Given the stare from the security guard who was clearly picturing her without it as she approached, he had the same idea.

It was also possible he stared because she'd appeared from invisibility after flying up to the rooftop helipad of the Dionysian, but surely that was only a small part of it.

The click of high heels played Thalia across the rooftop platform toward the guard, who stood in front of the elevator that led directly down to Dionysus's private quarters. She flashed her best grin to keep him focused on her rather than any thoughts of reporting her presence to anyone. It seemed to work. She did clean up well, not that she ever really got dirty. If he noticed her taking the small, heavy box out of her purse, he gave no indication.

The guard opened his mouth to speak, an action Thalia cut short with a finger to her lips before she unsealed the box. He hesitated, and she pitched the box's contents at him with a playful cry of, "Catch!"

He caught the glowing object in one hand.

"Nice reflexes!" Thalia smiled and counted her blessings that of the two great groups of humankind—those who caught strange glowing things tossed at them and those who just got the hell out of the way—this man belonged to the former. The guard glanced between her and the object, and then reached down for his radio. She stopped him with one gentle hand on his wrist. "I'd like to go down and see the god. Discreetly."

His hand relaxed, though the rest of him straightened. "I'm sorry, miss, but—Dionysus's orders. Everyone has to enter from below unless he says otherwise."

She pouted with a glance at his nametag. "I'm an Olympian . . . Leo. Can't you tell? That rule can't possibly apply in my case. I mean, look at me! Who wouldn't love for me to stop by?"

He grinned and took the offered opportunity to ogle. "I . . . I ought to call down and ask, but . . . I suppose he does like surprises."

"Right, surprises! It's so much more fun that way, isn't it, sweetheart?" She slipped the radio off his belt and waggled it at him. "Oh, and I need to borrow this. I'll return it, I promise. Now be a dear and open the elevator?"

Leo grinned with a shrug before turning to swipe a keycard in the lock. "I can't see the harm. Say, which Olympian are you?"

"That's right," she answered, stepping into the elevator. "Oh, and could I have that back now, please? Thanks so much for holding it for me, but you really shouldn't hang on to it too long. It makes you sterile, you know."

"Sterile!" He deposited the object back into the box with a start. "Just—just what is that, anyway?"

"Uh-huh!" Thalia answered. She dazzled him with a pixie grin and a wave as the doors closed.

Poor Leo. She hoped he wouldn't get into too much trouble.

Thalia sealed the box and confirmed that its internal magnetic containment field remained active before slipping it back into her purse. (Great things, magnetic fields. So very sci-fi and grandiose.) So far, so good. She gave her hair a quick brushing and smoothed her dress, preparing herself. At least she was more suited to this sort of thing than running around the desert confronting Erinyes and hunting for jewelry in the dark. Finally a crisis she could deal with. Probably. At least this was fun.

Only a short while earlier, she'd returned to her hotel suite—back from a nice deserted hilltop outside the city, where she'd spent a few hours' concentration in summoning the object from her sisters on Olympus and hoping they all wouldn't get into a desperate mess of trouble for sending it to her. She'd been about to call down to the front desk to schedule a massage for a bit of relaxation when she suddenly got the sense that Tracy was trying to spin a funny story for Dionysus. Featuring cyborgs. It was a clever attempt—in terms of alerting Thalia, anyway; the story itself was sheer offal, and cyborgs were passé these days anyhow. Yet it was enough to tell Thalia they were in trouble and compel her to fly onto the Dionysian rooftop minutes later.

Did they somehow offend the playboy god about an unrelated matter (Tracy really wasn't his type, she supposed), or had Thalia actually sent them directly into the clutches of an enemy?

She giggled at her own melodrama. *Clutches.* Not that Dionysus couldn't get pretty grabby after he had a few drinks in him (a state that had begun around five thousand years ago and continued unabated). But she hoped he wasn't involved in this. If he was actively aligned against Zeus's return . . . Well, that's why she'd run her errand in the first place, wasn't it?

As the elevator bell announced her arrival, she patted the box through the side of her purse and hoped she knew what she was doing.

Well that was silly, she amended. Of course she knew what she was doing. She switched to simply hoping it would work. At least it was an excuse to wear the dress. How often did she get out to Vegas, after all?

The elevator doors slid open with little fanfare. Before her was the god's balcony with its colossal plasma screen and other accoutrements.

The leather back of his recliner throne stared at her in that blank way leather often stares when it thinks a person isn't looking. Also staring at her were Tracy and Leif, each locked in narrow silver dance cages on either side of the throne dais.

The cheer outfit wasn't really Tracy's color, which was likely why she'd looked so unhappy before spotting Thalia.

None of the other five people on the balcony—Dionysus included—even noticed her arrival. All were focused on the screen, paying no attention to any private elevators that had no good reason to be opening. She slipped out before the doors closed.

"I can wait just as long as you two," the god was saying. "Longer, in fact. I doubt you can accomplish whatever it is Apollo wants you to do while you're locked up here, after all."

Dionysus spoke without turning his attention from the screen. *So far, so good*, Thalia thought. She could still be sneaky. She adored being sneaky. She didn't get to do it nearly as often as she liked, and obviously it wasn't as enjoyable as being funny, but it tickled her when she got the chance. A finger to her lips and a glance at the two captives later, she slipped off her heels and crept forward on delicate footsteps.

"I may," Dionysus continued, "even let you go without telling anyone about it, if you're nice enough—though you'll have to go without the amulet, of course."

"What about Thad?" Tracy asked with the slightest of glances in Thalia's direction. "He'll be reporting back to—who's his mother, again?"

The god laughed. "I'm not drunk enough to fall for *that*, girl. And I'm sure he will be reporting to his mother. That's incentive to tell me everything before she shows up. She's got quite the mean streak when she's riled."

Thalia reached the back of the dais without being noticed and then drew the box from her purse once more. What would come next would take finesse. After a moment's wait to avoid being too obvious, she began making her way toward Tracy, staying low. Skillful, quiet, a stealthy vision in a green dress, she deftly closed the distance, nearly making it completely undetected until she struck her toe on a half step in the floor and pitched forward onto her face with a comical yelp. The box tumbled from her hand.

Not quite enough finesse, she noticed; Tracy didn't even have the courtesy to laugh.

Thalia shifted invisible a moment later, but Dionysus had heard enough to think to look for her. "Hel-lo, what have we here?"

Thalia turned toward the god and his entourage, all of whom were looking at where she lay sprawled. She shifted back to visible, casting about nervously with a giggle. "I meant to do that."

Dionysus's laugh swiftly gave way to a leering stare as he turned his throne toward her. Wearing either Tracy's amulet or a remarkable forgery, the god spread his arms wide in a delighted greeting. "Polyhymnia!"

"Thalia," she corrected, and blew a strand of hair out of her face. Save for Erato, he never got the Muses' names right. "Greetings, Dionysus."

"Greetings, yes! Greetings to all of us on this fine Tuesday—"

"Thursday," corrected the woman in the black dress at his side.

"What? Already? I suppose time does fly when you're stupendous. And speaking of which, *nice* dress, Thalia. And what, pray tell, brings you to the Dionysian? No one here is spinning any tales of history, I'm sure. Is this a social call?" He beamed again, looking her over.

She ignored his portfolio mistake and concentrated on standing without looking at the box that now lay near Tracy's cage. "Quite social, definitely! I had a skosh of free time and thought, 'There's little to do this morning, why not visit Dionysus? He's always a good time!'"

"Sneaking around behind me to do so, mm?"

"It's much more fun that way, don't you think?"

"Oh, maybe, maybe. Care for some champagne? Dom Pérignon 1995, courtesy of that lovely girl in the cage over there. The outfit was my idea; stubborn one, that."

"She doesn't look very happy," Thalia observed with a step or two toward Tracy's cage. So far no one but Tracy had noticed the box, but it was out of the caged woman's reach. Thalia bumped the box with her heel, trying her best not to be too obvious. "Why a cage?"

"Why a cage?" Dionysus dismissed the question with a wave. "Why this music? Why all the booze? Why anything?" He took a newly filled champagne flute from another cheerleadered woman beside him. (*Hey, cheerleadered; I made a new word!*) He waggled the flute at her with a lascivious grin. "How's Apollo these days? I'm afraid I haven't seen him."

"Apollo? Apollo who?" She pushed the box just a little closer to the cage.

"What's that by your foot, Thalia?"

"My other foot! See?" She lifted it, toes wiggling.

He chuckled. "Ah, so you missed the box you're nudging toward my new friend there."

She feigned disappointment. "Now, Dionysus. Do you mean to tell me I squeezed this spectacular body of mine into this almost-as-spectacular dress and all you can look at is the floor? You're not getting shy on me, are you?"

He winked and held out his hand. "Bring it here."

"Bring what there?"

"That box you're so subtly pushing."

"I'm not pushing a box. Are you seeing a box? Maybe you're drunk!"

"Plastered. Rex?"

At the god's motion, the large man in the tuxedo T-shirt moved forward to grab Thalia by the forearms. He lifted her off her feet, carried her kicking to Dionysus, and set her down on the god's lap. Thalia stuck her tongue out at the man and got only a smirk in return.

"Now," Dionysus went on. "You see that little box there on the ground? What do you suppose that is?"

"I didn't have to let him pick me up, you know."

"What's the box, Thalia?" It flew into his outstretched hand just as Tracy made a try for it herself.

"That thing? I've never seen it before so I really don't know, but whatever it is, you really shouldn't open it."

"Oh, I shouldn't, should I?"

"Uh-huh. You know how boxes are; it's always a bad idea to open them! Why would you put something in a box if it shouldn't be in a box in the first place? Name me one thing that's in a box that ought to be let out! Go ahead, try. Bet you can't do it! Better just to throw it away, really. Do you want to be another Pandora, is that it? I mean, you can *have* what's in the box, or you can go for what's behind this door!" She pointed flamboyantly, humming a game show theme.

He chuckled. "I know what's behind that door: a completely kick-ass private bedroom, and it's already mine. Now if *you* were behind the door . . ." He pulled the box away from Thalia's grab. "You really don't want me to open this, do you? Just what are you trying to sneak to my captives?"

"Sneak to them? I've never seen them before. And since when do you care about captives? Isn't this a party?" She beamed and wished he'd just open the darned box. This reverse psychology was growing tiresome.

Dionysus stood suddenly, gathering her up in both arms to deposit her in Tracy's cage. The door slammed shut at his whim just as swiftly as it opened. "I know you were with them last night, Thalia. I know you're involved in all this."

"All this what?"

Dionysus sighed. "I'm a drunk, not a fool. At the very least you could have tried seducing me first. Next time, I guess. Let's have a look-see at what you're trying to smuggle in." He flipped open the lid with the same hand that held the box. "Now what have we here?"

Finally. Thalia kept silent as Dionysus turned the box over to dump the object into his palm. It very much resembled a golf ball, save for the fact that it was without dimples. Also it was golden, glowing, and much less likely to put a non-insane person to sleep when viewed on television at two o'clock on a Saturday afternoon.

"Ooh, it's a little golden ball!" Dionysus stared at it and turned his back on the cage, returning to his chair.

Thalia grinned at Tracy, who didn't return the favor.

"You sent us into a trap!" Tracy whispered. "He's in on it! Now he's got the amulet and the whatever-that-is too!"

"Oh, fret, fret, fret! Which is to say don't. Fret, I mean; he's supposed to have it. I just had to trick him into thinking he wasn't or he'd never have opened it—not if he's actively opposing us. Which is to say that's how it seems. Which is to say my bad about sending you into his clutches." She giggled. "'Clutches.' It sounds even sillier when said aloud, doesn't it?"

"Okay, so what is that thing?"

"Just a little Muse tool that I'll get into deep trouble for letting loose, but it's not my fault and these are extreme circumstances. I'm sure Apollo won't mind. And hi there, how're you? You should say 'hi' more when you see someone, it's friendly. Though not as friendly as that outfit!" Thalia continued to beam, waving to Leif. "Hi, Leif!"

Leif waved back, confused.

"So much for pretending you don't know us," Tracy muttered.

"I'm pretty sure he already figured that out. How 'in on it' is he, anyway?"

"Not quite sure, but he knew Thad was sent to spy on us. There's at least one more of them too. When he mentioned Thad's mother to him, I got the feeling she was a goddess."

"Which one?"

"He was smart enough not to say."

Dionysus rolled the ball from one hand to the other and back, enthralled. "Round things are awesome!"

Thalia giggled. "Oh, I think we've fixed that for the moment. Do you know if anyone else knows you're captured yet?"

"Ah, that's *'we're* captured,' I might point out. And no, when you showed up he'd just finished talking to Thad, who I think is getting his ego polished downstairs just now. At the risk of repeating myself, what *is* that thing?"

"Oh, nothing." She continued to beam, just to be annoying. "I just, well . . . Dionysus is now carrying the Idiot Ball."

The Idiot Ball, for those who are unaware, is the bane of good fiction. In any television show, movie, neighborhood play, or, yes, novel, whenever a previously intelligent character does something that anyone with more than badger feculence for brains would consider gut-wrenchingly foolish—or fails to grasp a solution to a problem so obvious it may as well be dressed in a neon green pantsuit, jumping up and down while playing the cymbals—that character may be said to be "carrying the Idiot Ball."

Though legions of geeks on the Internet refer to the Idiot Ball in strictly tropological terms, the actual Idiot Ball does exist in the Muses' Hall of Creative Abstract Concepts on Olympus. There it has sat since its accidental (so the Muses claim) creation, safely contained in metaphoric form where it can have no effect on anything outside the realm of fiction. While the ball is not without its uses for the Muses, they rarely speak of it and are, in fact, forbidden to remove it from the hall at all, as Apollo, in his wisdom, foresaw the dangers of loosing a ball of pure concentrated stupidity into the world.

As anyone will tell you, rules are meant to be broken.

Thalia explained much of this to Tracy who, to her credit, actually looked amused.

"So what do we do now that he has it?"

"I don't know. I'm just a Muse, silly, not some sort of idea generator." She paused just long enough to appear expectant. "Laugh! That's a joke, see, because a Muse is—oh, never mind, I'm not going to explain it, and stop looking at me like that. Though truthfully I haven't thought that far ahead. You're Zeus's daughter; it's your turn to be clever! So go on. Be clever! I can't do everything, you know!"

Tracy cleared her throat. "Dionysus! Thanks for letting us stay in the cages and all, but I think we'd like to be getting our amulet and leaving now, okay?"

The god glanced over at her and shrugged. "Nah. I prefer you there."

"But it's not very interesting in here, is it? If you let us out, we can, um, play your games with you!" Tracy appeared to think of something. "Leif plays poker, you know."

"Leif who? Oh, the towhead! He plays poker?"

Leif blinked. "Um, yeah, I do, but—"

"But he's not very good," Tracy finished. "Still, this is Las Vegas. We haven't even had a chance to gamble, so how about you let us have a little fun? Leif'll play you. If he wins, we get the amulet. If he loses, we . . . have to take the amulet to be cleaned and appraised for you."

"I really ought to tell the others I have you, but a game would be rather awesome." Dionysus considered for a moment. "I can't see the harm. Texas Hold 'Em! Both of us start with ten thousand dollars. Whoever runs out first is the loser."

"Perfect!" Tracy agreed.

Leif blinked again. "I don't—I don't really have ten thousand—"

"I'll spot you," Thalia assured him.

"Then it's settled!" Dionysus declared. "We'll play downstairs in one of the private casino rooms."

"One near an exit?" Tracy asked.

"Oh, now you're trying to get tricky."

"I'm not. Honest! Sometimes I just like to smoke; it'd be a shorter walk to get outside."

"Smoking is allowed in the casino."

"Um, I can only smoke in the fresh air. Doctor's orders."

"Then we shall play outside by the pool!" the god declared. "Cages open! Down we go!"

CHAPTER TWENTY-SIX

"Everything's better with tachyons."
— *Thalia the Muse (blog entry, December 16, 2009)*

LEIF'S EGO GOT IN THE WAY at first. Even though he knew that losing the game meant he and Tracy got to leave the place with the amulet to "get it cleaned," the thought of intentionally losing just didn't sit right. For one thing it was unsportsmanlike and cheap, and for another he just preferred winning. He couldn't help but try his damnedest. Sure it meant trying to win at poker against a god who reveled in such things (or even, as Leif continued to think of the Olympians, a "god" who reveled in such things)—but he couldn't resist a challenge.

At least not at first. He started off conservatively, trying to learn the god's playing style. Yet Tracy was right there, whispering near-constant demands in his ear to lose the game as quickly as possible so they could get the heck out of there. Having her lips so close was just darned distracting (not that he was about to tell her to stop), and, well, he just couldn't resist trying to make her happy. So as smoothly as he could, he began trying to lose.

He had to be careful about it, though. There was no telling if the god might get suspicious (or worse, outright angry) if he thought Leif was letting him win. The problem was that it didn't take long at all for Leif to learn something about Dionysus's playing style. It wasn't very subtle; he played like an idiot.

In fact, the god seemed far more interested in toying with the little golden ball Thalia had brought. He rolled it across the table (careful never to let it get near the pot). He bounced it on the poolside walkway. He even played an entire hand balancing it on his nose and trying to make up a song about it to the tune of the *Goldfinger* theme. During two nonconsecutive hands, he seemed to forget he had it, rediscovering it each time with a cry of, "Ooh, it's a little golden ball!" in such a way that caused a few of his cards to slip into view. When he wasn't ogling the ball, he was ogling Tracy, or Thalia, or any of the women poolside who'd gathered around to watch the game. (Leif had a bit of trouble not doing so himself, so he tried to focus on how pleased Tracy would be with him when he got them out of there.) Dionysus seemed to spend little if any effort on the actual game.

Leif wondered if the god's lack of focus had to do with the ball he held, or if he was just generally terrible at the game. Regardless, figuring out how to lose the game became far more difficult than anticipated.

Finally, with a kissed apology to Tracy (he got only her cheek, and she elbowed him mercilessly after, but it was still fun), he flipped back to his original goal of beating the pants off the guy—figuratively speaking. Besides, if he could say he'd beaten the founder of Vegas at poker . . . well, he didn't know just how that would translate into great things, but it made enough sense to make him want to win more with every hand.

Leif won the final pot with a remarkable bluff, worrying only in the final seconds of the hand that Dionysus's entire ploy might be to feign idiocy until Leif went all in with a lousy hand. The god called his bluff, grinning broadly and showing his cards to reveal . . .

"All black." Leif's heart stopped for a moment until he spotted the mix of clubs and spades that amounted to absolutely nothing.

Leif smiled back. "Pair of twos."

"Minos's golden balls!" cursed Dionysus before noticing the ball anew. "Ooh, it's a little golden ball!"

Leif gathered the chips in front of him and wondered if they'd have time to cash out as they left.

"So that's it, then!" Tracy declared. "We win the amulet back. That's what you agreed to."

"Hmm? I suppose it was, yes." Dionysus set the ball down, removed the amulet, and set it into Tracy's outstretched hand. She put it on immediately. "And now let's get you back to your cages."

Tracy shook her head. "No, I thought we'd—"

Dionysus finished a swig of beer in time to cut her off with a chuckle. "I don't recall that letting you *leave* was a condition of your winning." He drained his glass.

"Well, yes, but we have to take the amulet and—"

"Nope, that was if you lost." He grinned. "I'm cleverer than you look, you know. Than I look, rather. Cleverer than I look. Rex!"

Rex advanced around the table toward them, bringing his muscular torso with him. Tracy threw a glance at Leif and Thalia. The Muse shrugged helplessly.

It was then that Leif had his epiphany. It would work! It had to work! At once he knew just how to get them out of this, just what to say to—

Tracy scooped up his chips in one motion and hurled them into the air with a scream of "Run!" that shattered Leif's concentration to pieces. Startled onlookers dived inward to grab the myriad of chips. Amid the confusion, Tracy kneed the approaching Rex in the crotch and grabbed Leif's arm to drag him away through the chaos.

"Wait!" Leif shouted. "Not the money! I had an idea!"

"Too late!" Tracy shouted back.

"Go with the flow, sweetheart!" cried the muse in delight.

"Stop them!" Dionysus called behind them. "Security! Seal off the— ooh, a little golden ball!"

The two mortals ran hand in hand, leaping over poolside sunbathers as Thalia flew after them. Leif wasn't sure how far behind Rex might be or what Dionysus might do with all his power to stop them. He was a "god." Surely he'd do something, right?

Thalia kept them appraised, directing their flight with shouted instructions. "Run for the wall at the back of the property! It's low; you can climb it!"

"They'll grab us before we can get all the way up!"

"They're not following! All the guards are sealing off the regular exits!"

That seemed pretty stupid to Leif, but then that was par for the course at the moment. He didn't bother to argue but then realized how incredibly unlike him that was. "I could've got us out of there *without* throwing away the money! That was twenty thousand dollars!"

"Ten once you pay me back," Thalia corrected, "and let it go! What's done is done!"

"Let it go? I'm unemployed!"

"Why do we always have these conversations while running?" Tracy demanded.

No one answered. A moment later they were having the conversation while climbing, and shortly after that, they were over the wall and into the casino's parking area, following Thalia toward the Vegas monorail.

Those diligent and attentive readers who recall mention of the Dionysian being built upon the spot where Caesar's Palace once stood and who have been to Vegas (or those who have not been to Vegas but decided to look things up just to be obsessive—and you lot in particular really ought to seek help) may here be protesting that the Vegas monorail is, in reality, on the other side of the Las Vegas Strip and so runs nowhere near the Dionysian. Please note a particular two-word phrase there: *in reality.* Why people wish to take exception to an urban geographical error in a book telling a tale where "gods" run rampant is a question not answered in this text, and we can only suggest that such people may not have been hugged enough as children.

Such readers may also wish to consider the fact that Dionysus could very easily have used his godhood and mob connections to move the monorail to the other side of the Strip in order to better serve *his* personal casino.

It's all moot in any case. The three did not actually board the monorail at all, nor does it come into this story but for that passing mention. (Who boards an elevated track train in an attempt to escape from the very being who runs the city said train serves?) Why mention it, then? Why risk damaging reader immersion at all? Sometimes it is simply fun to tweak the sensibilities of certain neurotic types who declare that something cannot be done merely because they are familiar with the reality of the desert city in which it is set. Now that this has been accomplished, we may move on.

The three dashed beneath the monorail, taking refuge in a dense grove of Douglas fir trees across the street beyond it.

Thalia stopped them mid grove. She posed against a tree and pretended to catch her breath just for the sheer hell of it. "There! That went swimmingly, more or less. Isn't it fantastic when a plan works? Not that the plan really worked, per se, I mean, not without a hitch, but consider this an unrelated discussion on the positivity of plans working. When they do."

Tracy shook her head. "I don't think we've got time for unrelated discussions."

"It might be fun."

"First matter of business: getting back to our hotel to meet Apollo and out of this city without being caught."

Thalia giggled. "She's so in charge! Are you compensating for the cheerleader outfit, sweetie, because it *is* rather flattering. Where'd your glasses go?"

Tracy ignored the comment. Leif had the good sense to keep his mouth shut, at least about the outfit. "We're still checked in under false names," he said. "Maybe we can make it back to the hotel room and wait for him. But wait, won't Dionysus be able to track us on the streets?"

"If he thinks of it, sure," Thalia agreed. "But he's got the Idiot Ball now, so there's a fairly good chance he won't."

As out of character as it was, the Muse paused as both she and Tracy turned expectantly to Leif.

"What?" he asked.

"Don't you want to ask—?"

"I've got enough geek points to know what the Idiot Ball is. Though it explains a few things, now that I know that's what it was."

"Fooey," said Thalia. "Here I was all set to explain it again."

"Are you sure it's working completely on him?" Tracy asked. "He was smart enough to use the letter of the bet against us."

"You noticed that too, eh? It's obviously working at least a little, and powerful entities are usually especially vulnerable to it. The only explanation I can think of is that, well, I mean, he's generally drunk a lot already; maybe he's used to thinking with half a brain? In any case I don't think we should risk being seen in front of a security camera, even outside of his hotel—which definitely makes for a problem."

Leif pointed. "That Muses' armband you've got hides you from being seen from afar, right? Any way you can tweak it so it works on cameras? Or use some sort of other magic you can hand-wave or pull out of your ass?"

Thalia grimaced. "I hate that term, and I resent the implication!"

"You shouldn't do that," Tracy said, indicating the grimace. "I hear it makes your face all scrunchy and morose."

"Oh, ha ha ha," Thalia quipped before releasing a giggle. "Okay, actually that was kinda funny and cute, so points for you, I suppose, but I can't 'tweak' the armband, no. At least not without Vulcan's help, and unless you've got the god of the forge tucked away in your back pocket, that's out. But there are a few things we might be able to do. We'll need materials, which I can probably get if I fly off to another city, track down a priest of Apollo, and then have him do some shopping and blessing and—oh, no, except if Apollo's diminished—I mean, I tried him on his cell phone this morning and they'd already deactivated it, so maybe his priests wouldn't have as much power as they ought to? Except I shouldn't be asking you two since there's no reason for you to know these sorts of things, and augh! It's vexing dealing with all these unknowns, isn't it? All right. Here's what we do." She pointed to Tracy. "You gather all the fallen wood you can,"—she pointed to Leif—"and you find some rocks that look kind of sharp and maybe some bird droppings. We're going to have to construct a tachyon field generator out of natural—"

Tracy cleared her throat. "Or we pop into that clothing store over there, buy some hoodies with cash, put them on with the hoods up, and walk into our hotel."

Thalia remained paused in mid-sentence, mouth hanging open. "I suppose we could do that, yes, but my plan has tachyons, so it's better."

"I'm sorry for your loss, right? On a time crunch we go with the inferior but simpler non-tachyon plan."

"Hrmph. Fine, have it your way. But 'tachyons' is more fun to say and it's especially better than 'hoodies.'" Thalia shuddered. "'Hoodies.' Vile! I loathe that word. We can go with your silly plan, but you have to call them hooded sweatshirts or something."

Tracy nodded. "Hooded sweatshirts, then. Let's get going."

"Yes, much better! There's entirely too many things being renamed to end in 'ie' these days. Oh, and you *don't* have Vulcan in your back pocket, do you? I suppose we may as well make sure."

"Sorry." Leif answered. "I thought you guys went by your Greek names? Vulcan's Roman."

Thalia nodded. "He's also god of Trekkers now, so he prefers 'Vulcan.' I know, I know, don't ask me how he got that in his portfolio; it's a legal thing."

Tracy grabbed them both by the arms, distracting Leif with her touch before he could think of anything to say. She led them toward the store at a pace that clearly indicated her enthusiasm for getting on with things. Or maybe she just wanted out of the cheerleader outfit.

"Does anyone have any cash?" she asked on the way. "I'm not entirely sure what's happened to my wallet."

CHAPTER TWENTY-SEVEN

"Without quests, heroes would just be insufferably competent mortals laying around in equally insufferable fashion making for insufferably boring stories. Put those vainglorious folks to work!"
—Hera (inter-Olympian memo, circa 4250 BC)

"Hera should send Hercules on a quest to bring her another word for 'insufferable.'"
—Athena (off-hand utterance, moments after circa 4250 BC)

THE HOODIE PLAN WORKED, despite the odds of finding thick, hooded sweatshirts in a desert town during springtime. No security guards swooped down on them as they entered their own hotel. No divine power locked down the elevator as they rode up to their floor. No rampaging stampedes of frisky pandas trampled them in the hallway on the way to their rooms. (This is not to say that there's ever an increased danger of frisky pandas after angering Dionysus, but government-funded studies show that large segments of the population consider hormonal panda stampedes unwanted, so as we're listing things that thankfully did not occur, the pandas may as well be included.)

Tracy couldn't replace her lost glasses but didn't bother trying, as they were only prescription-free lenses she wore in order to be taken more seriously. (No god's daughter would have imperfect vision, after all.) Not that she planned to admit as much, but so far no one had brought it up.

They found Apollo waiting for them when they reached Thalia's suite.

Thalia clapped and raced forward to tackle him in a hug, adding numerous pecks on the cheek for good measure. "You made it!" she cried. "I mean sure, Obvious Statement Theater, but such fantastic timing! Couldn't be better! Unless you've been waiting here long? How long were you waiting? How are the Fates? How's Poppy?" Thalia beamed in perfectly Thalia-esque fashion.

Apollo returned the hug. "It took both more and less time than I tho—You know about Poppy?"

"Oh, of *course* I know about Poppy, don't you read the newsletter? We e-mail back and forth now and again, when there's time. Nice girl. A bit quiet."

"You might have mentioned that before I went there."

Thalia shrugged. "I figured you knew! It's not as if I could've emailed her about all *this*. For one thing she's not online very much, and for another they've got a firewall or something that filters out the kinds of questions you wanted to ask anyway, and besides, what if someone hacked their email? So she's well? How'd it go?"

"Dionysus is with Ares," Tracy announced before he could answer.

Thalia nodded to that. "Oh, that too, yes, but one thing at a time."

Apollo blinked. "I wouldn't have pegged him for having the initiative. You're certain of this?"

"Fooey, now you've distracted him," pouted Thalia.

Tracy nodded. "Pretty certain. He caged us up, the guy who stole the amulet was reporting to him, and—"

"Guy who *stole* the amulet? I see you've already solved that problem, but I think you ought to catch me up on just what's gone on down here. And why are you all wearing hoodies?"

As Thalia removed hers and tossed it onto the couch with a glare that puzzled Apollo, Tracy related all that happened since his departure from the campsite. Leif provided color commentary.

"We need to get out of Las Vegas as soon as divinely possible," Apollo said when they finished.

"I'm hoping we get to find out what you discovered from the Fates," Tracy answered. "And I'm changing clothes before we leave. Talk loudly." She hurried through the adjoining door to her own suite for a purpose that visibly showered Leif with disappointment.

Apollo sat in a plush chair before he began. "It was not a wasted trip. The Fates created the weapon that killed Zeus, but I don't think they're involved with his death. He commissioned them to create it toward the end of the Titan War, but they finished it too late, so he hid it away. I think some of the others found out about it and used it on him."

"That's awful!" Thalia cried. "And fascinating. And how's Poppy?" She gave Apollo's shin a tiny kick. It bothered him more than it should have.

"She's fine. And quite helpful, even." He went on, telling them how the UnMaking Nexus required a bit of immortal blood to prime it and how it attacked the first immortal it could find when it awakened.

Tracy returned through the door wearing belted jeans tucked into low-heeled boots; a long-sleeved, button-down shirt under a light vest; and a hat that Apollo figured qualified as jaunty. "We already know it works, right? Does that help us undoing what it does?"

"Probably not as such, but there's a loophole that Zeus knew about. Your amulet—his amulet—he's right, it's the key. As are you, Tracy Wallace."

"Right, and I do what about that, exactly? One of them told you, yes? Please?"

"You must journey to one of Zeus's temples—"

"That's something of a problem, isn't it?" Leif asked. "If all you guys built temples *after* coming—and after he died—I've got to think he doesn't have any new ones. Or can we make a temple here out of couch cushions and blankets?"

"A problem, but not insurmountable," Apollo told them. "Some still exist in hidden places."

"Though they could use a bit of paint," Thalia added.

"Does Tracy have to go there alone?" Leif asked.

"We shall make the journey with her."

"Good." Tracy smiled before glancing at Leif. "I guess."

"There's more. Once Tracy brings the amulet to Zeus's temple, she must say some words of power and make a sacrifice of her lifeblood while wearing the amulet. That will complete the ritual and reconstitute Father Zeus from the essence that he placed within it."

Tracy swallowed the macadamia nuts she'd been munching. "Excuse me?"

Leif looked stricken, likely unrelated to macadamia nuts. "*What?* How much 'lifeblood' are we talking here? Fatal?"

"Do you know another meaning of *life*blood?" asked Apollo.

"It's not exactly a word I banty about daily."

"It's 'bandy,' sweetheart," Thalia corrected.

"That too."

"Yes, the amount of blood needed for the sacrifice would be enough to kill any mortal, regardless of any immortal parentage. However—"

Leif perked up and interrupted. "However? Aha! However! There's always a however. Good. Lay it on us."

"There are two things she can do to increase her power enough to complete the ritual without making such a sacrifice: either seduce someone of sufficient heroism and absorb their power sexually, or—"

At this, Leif interrupted again. (It was one of his strengths.) "Oh, hey, done! I'm heroic. She can seduce me! It won't be that hard. Er, I mean—"

"No," Tracy said.

Thalia patted Leif's shoulder. "I think he means more traditionally heroic, honey."

Apollo nodded.

"Hey! I just beat a *god* in a game of cards! How much more heroic can I—?"

"*No,*" Tracy repeated.

"Beat him with help," Thalia pointed out.

"Hey, I'm in that vision for a reason, you know. Maybe this is my connection. Maybe I'm more heroic than you—"

"No!" Tracy insisted. "Seduction's right out, involving you or anyone else! Now what's the 'or' part?"

"You know," Apollo considered, "he may be right."

Thalia raised an eyebrow.

"Exactly! See? Apollo knows what he's talking about."

"I said you *may* be right, Karlson. I did not say—"

"I'm heroic, damn it!"

Tracy, meanwhile, buried her face in her hands in a likely effort to hide what looked to be growing frustration. Apollo spoke to her gently, ignoring Leif.

"Don't worry. We can find a better candidate easily enough. In any case, don't discount it too quickly. You're a beautiful woman. It wouldn't be that hard."

"I said no and I meant it!" Tracy growled. "Why does every problem have to be solved with sex around here?"

"I'm with her," Thalia said. "I mean, I know what I counseled before with Dionysus and so forth, but the fact is the whole mystical-power-through-sex thing is incredibly overdone these days, no matter what conventions' worth of supernatural romance authors say."

"Even if it wasn't, I wouldn't be doing it. You've got no right to say otherwise, god or not."

Apollo begrudged a nod, still wrestling with her unexpected refusal at the idea. "Are you *certain* you're Zeus's daughter?" he asked finally.

Tracy just crossed her arms and glared. Thalia put a supportive hand on her shoulder.

"Artemis is Zeus's daughter too," said the Muse, "and you know how she is."

"Thank you," Tracy told her. "Now are you going to tell us that other option? Please?"

"The other option is more involved."

Tracy laughed. "That's a matter of perspective."

"You must complete a quest, and in so doing, you shall become properly heroic yourself."

"I like that a lot better."

"Well, I don't!" Leif declared. "Now it's an MMO? She has to XP grind first? Like a 'Go gather a hundred jars of woodchuck polish and return to me,' kind of thing? What a pain in the ass."

Apollo stood in an attempt to regain a bit of superiority in the room. Why did he feel like he was losing it? Two mortals and a Muse against his own godhood—he should be just fine! Well, former godhood. Blasted diminishing! He still had power, did he not?

He walked to the window and gazed out, taking a moment to smack his sense of potency back into place before it slipped away. With any luck, the pause would add some situational gravitas for the others too.

"I am uncertain of the exact nature of the quest," he said finally, "but it must be a traditional quest, which means only a mortal regent, a true oracle, or a god may assign it to you. Are you on familiar terms with your nation's president? Or even the ruler of a small island nation?"

"Not this week, no. And I suppose it's too much to hope for that you'd be able to give me a quest directly, what with the diminishing, yes?"

Apollo nodded, wincing inwardly. "Nor do I believe we can bring your request to any other gods for fear they may be secretly against us."

"Not even Artemis?" Thalia offered.

Apollo hesitated at that. He'd still not told his sister the whole story about bringing Zeus back. He'd pondered that decision since seeing her last but remained uncertain about the nature of his reluctance. Perhaps it was intuition. Perhaps he was just paranoid, or overcautious. In any case . . .

"She helped me to see the Fates, and the others are likely watching her even more closely than I originally thought; I'm not willing to risk her involvement again when I may need her later. Fortunately—"

"Oh!" Thalia batted his shoulder excitedly. "Oh, what about Demeter? Surely we can trust her; she wouldn't be against you!"

"She wouldn't be against anybody, which is rather the problem. Besides, you know what she's like. The second we were gone, she'd be rambling to someone else about how that nice Apollo stopped by for a visit."

"You're not *that* nice," Leif offered.

Apollo focused a glare at him. "No. I'm not." He let that sink in, trying to regain a bit more respect. It didn't seem to work. He went on.

"On the plus side, we've no need to deal with a god; we *do* have an oracle. The greatest oracle in the world: *My* oracle!" He smiled broadly and waited for *that* to sink in—good news, a ray of hope, a beam of light streaming from his power and influence: "The Oracle at Delphi!"

The announcement didn't garner as much awe as he'd hoped. In hindsight, it was a miracle no one had interrupted.

Leif scoffed. "Delphi? That's a hell of a long way away, isn't it?"

"Shut it, Karlson, I'm not sleeping with you. Though if there's an oracle that's closer, maybe that'd be better?"

Apollo exchanged a knowing glance with Thalia. "Why do mortals always think us so behind the times?" he asked. "I should like to borrow your phone, Thalia. Mine's, ah, suspended. For the moment."

Thalia grinned and tossed it to him. He dialed the number by memory. It picked up after the first ring.

"Ah, hello, Elene? It's me." He sighed. "*Apollo.* That's quite all right; I realize it's late. Yes, yes, it's an honor and a pleasure, I know. I know. Now—Elene, please, I'm always happy to receive your praise, but I've no time to chat at the moment. Would you please put Verity on the phone? Thank you."

He covered the mic and turned to Thalia. "Has my voice changed at all since I diminished?"

"Oh, um . . . not that I've noticed?" She grinned happily.

"Must be your phone." He uncovered the mic as the Delphic Oracle Verity (who was originally from Canada but had lived on Delphi since the 1980s after some trouble with the law) came on the line, sounding tired. "Verity, how are you?" He sighed. "It's *Apollo!* Yes, of course you've been expecting my call. Listen, I need a basic quest assignment from you, for a mortal: Tracy—" He covered the mic again, looking to Tracy. "What's your middle name?"

"Daphne."

"Daphne? Really? Huh." Talk about opening old wounds. He uncovered the mic. "Tracy Daphne Wallace. Yes. No, nothing complex, just a standard J-stroke-fourteen. Fastest quest option you have if there's a choice, but it needs to be at least a level four. Yes. Yes, your god is pleased. Thank you. All right, text Thalia when you have it. I'm using her phone. Long story, and shouldn't you already know that? No, it's all right. Blessings of light upon you and all that."

He hung up the phone and handed it back to Thalia. "It will be about fifteen minutes, and then we should have our quest. You two should pack."

Tracy nodded and headed back to her room. Leif followed suit, heading for the other adjoining door where he stopped with a grin. "Think the quest'll be 'seduce someone?'"

"I wouldn't hold your breath."

Leif's grin crumbled, and he vanished into his room. Thalia closed the door after him. She closed Tracy's in turn and looked to Apollo.

"Does Leif's infatuation with Tracy seem normal to you? I know we weren't following him for very long before he met her so I can't be entirely sure, but it does seem unusually strong. Not that sometimes things aren't like that, and maybe knowing he's a part of things anyway because of your vision is making him feel obligated to go along with her—but, well, you know how reluctant he was to help when you first talked to him. I can't help but wonder if it's entirely natural."

"I'm pretty certain it's not, but as you said, he was reluctant when I first talked to him, and now he's helping. Like it or not, he is involved in Zeus's return somehow. For the moment it's helpful if he's devoted to the person who is the key to that return, so why meddle?"

Thalia grinned. "You devious little sun god! You did this somehow, didn't you? I didn't think you had it in you."

"On the contrary, I did not. And I do not. And watch who you're calling little."

"Oh. Well if you didn't then obviously someone else did, so that means who? Aphrodite? Eros? How are they involved?"

"Hard to be sure. We don't know which one did it, nor can we be sure why. Those two toss arrows around like business cards, after all."

Going strictly by the numbers, it was more likely Eros. (Most in the West knew him as Cupid, but he'd renounced that name some fifty years ago when the whole naked-archer-baby image got far too out of hand for the youth's liking. "Sure, everyone loves babies," the perpetual teenager had complained to Apollo during an archery lesson, "but there's no way diapers are sexy." There was also a dispute with a greeting card company that he'd been unable to resolve to his liking while the Withdrawal edict was in place, but Apollo was unfamiliar with the details.) As Aphrodite's son, he'd long ago been delegated the task of shooting random love-arrows. The goddess herself still did it too, of course, but less often.

"And even if someone shot Leif on the conspiracy's behalf," he went on, "we've no idea if the person who did it is involved in Zeus's murder."

"So there's no way to be sure if the archer is a conspirator, or if the real conspirators just dared him or her to shoot an arrow at Leif without offering a reason."

Apollo frowned. "Isn't that what I just said?"

"Yes, but sometimes it's good to be clear so people understand."

"People? It's just you and me here, Thalia."

She patronized him with a pat on the hand that didn't help his diminishment issues.

"Further on the subject of undermining my authority, exactly *who* gave you permission to loose the Idiot Ball into the real world?"

Thalia gulped and fluttered her lashes. "It was necessary? Well, it was! We don't know who to trust, like you said, so tossing the Idiot Ball at someone who's cornered us could get us out of a very tight spot, especially with the mortals running around without your protection! And it did, I might add! In fact I am adding it, see? It's added. How about a game of Scrabble?"

"And where were the mortals when you were off calling forth the Idiot Ball? Running around alone like that without the protection I told you to provide them?"

"Oh, yes, but they were headed to see Dionysus and I thought it best if I stayed out of that!" She fixed him with a defiant stare that swiftly crumpled. "I gave her my bangle; they weren't in *that* much danger! And—well, it seemed like a good idea at the time. And it all turned out just fine!"

Apollo punctuated his nod with a sigh. She was probably right. "Even so, the Idiot Ball is out there now, and that's *not* what it's for. Getting it back to its place in the Hall of Creative Abstract Concepts will be a chore."

"Hmm, well that's really not our biggest priority right now, is it? Dionysus has it and he's against us, so really, for the moment, it's fine where it is, I should say."

"When this is all over, it's your responsibility to put it back," he told her. "Do your sisters know?"

"Of course they know. Who do you think helped me get it? And so we can't use it for a while, so what? We only kept it around to use when lousy writers asked us for help and we didn't want to deal with them. We can just ignore them in the meantime." She blinked. "And what do you mean it's my responsibility to put it back?"

Apollo ignored the question. "I shudder to think how this will crash the production schedules of all those sitcoms, but we'll worry about damage control another time."

"Calliope's the one who coalesced it for me," Thalia grumbled. "Make her put it back."

The Delphic Oracle's quest for Tracy came via text message a few moments later. Tracy was busy finishing her final bit of packing, marveling at the sudden changes in her life and wondering if the slight weakness she'd been feeling since getting the amulet back was due to stress or something else. She figured that with her luck, it was something else—and anyone who disagrees with her can answer the question of just why we'd bother to mention it at all if that were not the case.

Not that it isn't sometimes fun to mention things for no reason. The platypus, for example, is not actually a terrestrial animal but a bioengineered probe designed to blend in amongst the planet's other creatures, sent to Earth by aliens who did not do enough research. There's no reason at all to mention that right now, but wasn't it fun?

Don't make that face; it's rude.

CHAPTER TWENTY-EIGHT

"Despite the obvious potential, gods never demand that other gods swear loyalty oaths by the binding power of the river Styx. It is simply not done. Such a demand both insults the honor of the one asked to swear allegiance and undermines the power of the one demanding it. Is the oath-maker an untrustworthy liar because their word alone is not good enough? No god would brook such an insult easily. Is the god making the demand so weak that he must lean on the crutch of the Styx rather than inspiring obedience on his or her own merit? Such oaths may be offered freely, but never demanded. This may perhaps be difficult for some mortals to understand, but then perhaps that is why we are gods."

—Athena's Little Book of Wisdom, *p. 1066*

"WHAT IS IT?"

"It's a little golden ball!"

"And you took it from the Muse?"

"That is what I said, isn't it? Whatever it is, she was going to give it to the blond mortal."

"And now it's ours."

"Watch it, Ares. I didn't say you could have it. Get your own little golden ball."

"I got the most balls of this whole damn group! Don't see how I shouldn't get this one too."

The Idiot Ball sat in the center of the table, which itself sat in the center of the secret room on Olympus, which itself sat not quite in the center of the Olympian halls. Four of the five conspirators clustered around the table, peering at the ball, mesmerized. None had seen it before. None beyond Apollo and the Muses were even aware of its existence, for the same reason Apollo had never heard of Dionysus's Hangover Hammer or Ares's Flamin' Racism Tongs; it was out of their purview.

"If anyone gets it," Hermes said, "it should be neither of you. All present who've not fouled things up by trying to kill the blond or letting him escape, raise your hand." He raised his. So did the goddess. Hades merely brooded against the wall and studied the ball from a distance. Hermes turned to the goddess. "Oh, and anyone whose son didn't disobey orders—"

"My son stole the amulet! He brought it to Dionysus, who then proceeded to lose it! If anyone gets the blame—"

"And maybe if your son hadn't sat around in a hot tub while those mortals were off finding this amulet, they wouldn't have gotten it in the first place, hmm?" Dionysus fired back.

Hermes smirked. "Since when have you taken offense to lounging around in a hot tub?"

"When it's me? Never! But mortals ought to do as they're told, wouldn't you say? And it's my ball! Get your own!"

The four gods at the table suddenly broke out in a squabble of accusations. Within moments they all stood, leaning over the table, shouting across the glow of the ball, none willing to make the first grab for it.

"*Silence,*" Hades spoke finally. Though only a whisper, the word snaked through the room with a power that slithered around each of the four arguing necks and squeezed until it had their attention. Hades never shouted. He never had to.

"Focus," he continued. "What is the significance of the amulet? Apollo only mentioned the Karlson mortal in his vision. Why, then, did he give this amulet to the woman, rather than to Karlson himself? Is Apollo using the mortal's infatuation to his advantage? Where have they gone? Answer these first."

"Not to mention, how we can pressure Poseidon to declare Apollo permanently suspended?" Hermes added.

"And who gets which parts of his portfolio when he does?" the goddess appended.

"And who gets the ruttin' ball!" Ares shouted.

Dionysus nodded and crouched down to peer at it lovingly. "It's a little golden ball!"

Hades strode inexorably toward the ball and scooped it up for himself. "I am the eldest. It is mine. The argument is settled."

The other four stared.

"He took the little golden ball!"

"Ah, big deal," Ares sneered. "I got two big brass ones already!"

"Hades is right," Hermes agreed. Already the need to argue over the ball's ownership was fading with its absence. "Do you have any clue what this amulet is?"

Dionysus shook his head.

"It was purple, right?" Ares tried. "Maybe that means somethin'."

"It matters not," Hades declared, peering at the ball more closely. "We must find and stop Apollo. All else will fall into place after."

"But you just said—"

"It matters *not*."

Ares grumbled at that. "I still can't figure why Poseidon can't find 'im the regular way."

"Ares, you can't even figure where the bread's gone when the toast pops up," Hermes quipped.

"You give it back, you thievin' bastard!"

"And why's Ares still allowed in these meetings, anyway?" Hermes asked of Hades. "Didn't he try to kill Karlson, despite what we all agreed?"

Any response was preempted by a clarion horn that resonated throughout the gods' domain. The others stood in response before the echo faded. "The Dodekatheon," Hades spoke. "Poseidon summons us. If there is speaking to do, I shall do it."

Ares growled as they made for the door. "Speakin's a waste of time, anyway."

Hermes smirked. "Well spoken."

Hades pointed to both of them. "Incur not my wrath."

Poseidon's glare stormed over the gathered Dodekatheon. Save for Apollo, all were in attendance. The new king of the gods began the proceedings immediately.

"Apollo's time to return to us on his own and explain himself is now gone. Until such time as I declare otherwise, all gods are tasked with actively seeking him. We will track Apollo, capture Apollo, and return him to Olympus to answer for his crimes."

Ares and Artemis both surged to their feet, with Ares stopping just short of shooting his mouth off and instead merely giving a few triumphant fist pumps. Artemis was less thrilled.

"King Poseidon, it has been only one of your three granted days. Why is this so?"

"Because I am king, and I say it is so."

"Oh, tish-tosh, Brother!" Demeter declared. She held in her arms a bowl of gingerbread dough that she was industriously stirring. "I'm sure the little dear means it would help us all to be the best little Apollo-searchers we can be if we understood what moved you to this decision. Isn't that right, sweetheart?"

Artemis nodded to this.

Poseidon tossed a scowl at Demeter that the goddess utterly failed to register. "Between our last meeting and now, Apollo visited the Fates. Therefore, he has been on Olympus without so much as a word of explanation to myself or Hera. As he could not have been here and left without subterfuge, his motives are suspect. He must be found. He must be stopped."

Artemis swallowed. "How do we know he's visited the Fates? Yet another of Ares's accusations?"

Athena chuckled. "I'm not sure Ares is smart enough for that."

"I myself spoke with the Fates within the hour," spoke Poseidon. "They reported his presence to me."

"Did they give you any indication of his whereabouts?" Athena asked.

Poseidon bristled. "Beyond mentioning his recent presence, they were tight lipped as usual."

The storm in his eyes made it clear to all present that further questioning along those lines was unwelcome. All Olympians knew that the Fates could not be coerced into revealing anything they did not wish to. Even Zeus could not bend the Fates' will to his. Nevertheless, it had remained a sore spot for Zeus right up until his death, and Poseidon had possessed far less time to grow accustomed to this shortcoming in his authority. Only a fool would dare call attention to it by asking why he hadn't learned more.

"That's it?" cried Ares. "They didn't tell you more? Where're we supposed to look?"

Poseidon's vengeful gaze cut across the silence. Ares merely shrugged it off with a glance at Hades, who was busy attempting to roll the Idiot Ball in a full orbit around his palm and the back of his hand.

"The longer Apollo hides, the clearer it becomes in my mind that he must have had something to do with Zeus's murder," Athena declared. "I salute and support you, Poseidon, in this wise decree."

Artemis turned to Athena. "Clear in your mind? And how does that follow? He strikes Ares, and thus he is guilty of killing Zeus? Is wisdom not one of your purviews, Athena?"

Athena would not condescend to acknowledge Artemis's gaze, continuing to address the group as a whole. "Apollo has the power to hide himself from his elder gods. He has slinked about Olympus and ignored Queen Hera's summons. He has attacked one of us. I see a great many things of which to be suspicious. We cannot allow a likely murderer to run free!"

"Oh, dear. " Demeter clucked her tongue. "*Murderer* is such an ugly word. Why not call him, oh, 'harvester of immortal life'? Come to think of it, what proof do we really have that Zeus was murdered at all? Perhaps he merely slipped in the shower?"

Artemis sighed. "Athena, your failure to protect Zeus is no reason to throw about foolish accusations like a cottonwood loosing seeds."

Athena met Artemis's gaze for the first time and bit off each word as she spoke it. "I cannot help but wonder, huntress, just how involved you really are in your twin's transgressions."

"I am involved in nothing!"

Athena smirked. "Such protestation. One would think she knows more than she is telling."

"Screw-up!"

"Hippie!"

"Silence!" Poseidon demanded. The word echoed throughout the broad chamber and took a few moments to fade away into nothingness. The two goddesses returned to the seats from which they'd sprung. Hades spun the Idiot Ball atop a grim fingertip.

"Has anyone *checked* the shower?" Demeter asked.

"Artemis," Poseidon spoke, "have you had any contact with your brother since his assault on Ares?"

"I have not, King Poseidon."

"Do not answer so quickly," Hera advised. "When this council adjourns, I will check the logs of the Olympian grounds for traces of Apollo. Will I find any of his movements to have crossed with your own?"

Hephaestus spoke before Artemis could. "Even if you do, Queen Hera, that would only prove that they moved through the same area within, what, five minutes of each other? If Apollo has some means of concealing himself, what would be the proof that Artemis spoke with him or even knew he was there at all?"

The god of war sneered. "Since when do we need proof for somethin'? We already know Artemis pals around with Apollo!"

"I simply appeal to the Dodekatheon for sanity and caution," Hephaestus answered. The god of fire reached toward Aphrodite and gently squeezed his wife's hand, as if trying to hold the entire group together with that strong, supportive clasp. "This whole business is a sad one."

"Indeed," Poseidon nodded, momentarily distracted at the sight of Hades bouncing the Idiot Ball between his palm and the bend of his arm. The coolly attentive gaze that the god of the underworld gave Poseidon as he did so unsettled him a touch.

"And yet," Poseidon continued finally, "the regret of it changes nothing. Does your own answer change, Artemis?"

"It does not, King Poseidon. And if Hera's check of the logs does indicate Apollo's presence near my own, I assure you I saw not his visage nor heard his voice. I pledge my efforts toward locating him."

Not a noise sounded in the chamber as Poseidon regarded her, save for the slow grinding of Ares's teeth.

"Very well," Poseidon declared finally. "You shall help. As for the Muses, I hereby recall them to Olympus and confine them to quarters for the duration of this crisis."

"About damned time!" Ares declared. He returned to his seat under the weight of numerous dirty looks. "Just sayin'."

One of those dirty looks belonged to Hades. The ruler of the underworld waited until he judged the brute well and truly silenced before standing to face Poseidon. "King-brother, I would add the Orthlaelapsian wraith to this search."

A few gasps traveled through the room. Seldom did Hades speak in the Dodekatheon unless the topic of the underworld itself came up, and his suggestion itself was worthy enough of trepidation.

"The Orthlaelapsian wraith?" Hephaestus asked. "Is that truly necessary?"

A brief aside for the curious: The Orthlaelapsian wraith represented one of Hades's first triumphs in the field of shade recombinatorics. Combining the spirits of two slain mythological creatures, the wraith possessed the best traits of each with nary the trouble of free will that always made a living being so darned tricky to deal with.

Half of the beast was formed from the spirit of the two-headed hound Orthrus, brother to the three-headed Cerberus (who to this day guards the entrance to Hades and makes a monthly appearance at the meetings of the Westminster Kennel Club). A magnificently ferocious creature possessed of terrible strength, power, and the fearsome ability to simultaneously chew up a pair of new shoes and lick itself, Orthrus nonetheless fell to the blade of Hercules during one of the first cattle rustling episodes in history.

Hades created the wraith's other half from the shade of another hound known as Laelaps. While (amazingly) possessed of only one head, Laelaps was so skilled a tracker that it was invariably bound to catch whatever it chased. Passed down to various owners from Zeus himself, Laelaps was finally set against the Teumessian fox, an animal so deviously clever that, also invariably, it could never be caught. News of the matchup ran like lightning throughout the world. Who would win in a contest between a hound that unfailingly caught its prey and a fox that would always get away? It promised to become one of the world's greatest existential conundrums, a contest of immensely philosophical proportions up there with the Irresistible Force versus the Immovable Object. Indeed, it may even have eclipsed that timeless and irritating smug philosopher's favorite "Can God create a rock so heavy he himself cannot lift it?"—were it not for the fact that Zeus got wind of it. So greatly did the matter perplex him that he decided he wouldn't put up with that sort of crap, turned both the fox and hound to stone, and spent the rest of the evening taking the form of a pole at an early Athenian strip club.

Laelaps, of course, died instantly, his shade consigned to the underworld, where Hades wove it together with that of Orthrus to create the Orthlaelapsian wraith. Empowered with the bloodthirsty strength of Orthrus and the unfailing tracking of Laelaps—wrapped together in a delicious wraith-like shell that was invisible when standing still—it would guard whatever the god wished. None could surprise the two-headed wraith. If by some miracle a thief did manage to make off with what it was guarding, it could track the thief to the ends of the earth to recover what was stolen. Unburdened of the troubles of being alive, the wraith was allowed the patience of the grave as it performed its duty with single-minded devotion. Re-tasking it was something of a pain, but as it had guarded the same thing for more than two millennia, Hades didn't particularly care.

Back in the main narrative, Hades held the Idiot Ball atop his palm and then began to levitate it from one hand to the other. So focused was he that his response, when it came, came slowly.

"I . . . believe so. There is . . . no better . . . tracker." The ball flew up into the air with a flick of his wrist before he caught it again.

Poseidon frowned at the foolish spectacle. "Brother Hades, King of the Underworld, God of Death and Precious Metals . . . What in the sacred name of Olympus are you doing?"

Hades rolled the ball in his palm, growing more and more focused on it. "Proposing . . . a course of action, King-Brother." He flipped the ball up again, this time catching it above his head. Poseidon's frown turned on Hera.

The queen cleared her throat. "*Lord* Hades, you know better than to bring toys to the Dodekatheon. Pass it here. You'll get it back after the meeting."

"This is not a toy."

"It's a little golden ball!" cried Dionysus from the balcony above. Though not currently a member of the Dodekatheon, he decided he may as well listen in while he was in the area. Were the god of the underworld not being scolded for playing with a ball, Dionysus's presence would likely have garnered more attention. (The playboy god almost never showed up to the Dodekatheon even when he'd been a member, which was why he'd lost his council seat to Hestia in the first place. Goddess of home and hearth, she could always be counted on to be around—and far less inebriated.)

"I care not what it is," Hera insisted. "I will have decorum in this chamber. Relinquish it."

"If such a little thing so disturbs you."

Hades tossed the ball to Hera, who in turn handed it to Poseidon. The king of the gods studied it a moment before dropping it into a compartment in his throne. Hades, for his part, experienced only a moment of uncertainty as the ball left his possession before he stubbornly resumed his argument. "The wraith can be set after Apollo. It will track him, unseen, wherever he may be. One head shall hold him while the other howls his presence to all who sit here. This course of action cannot fail."

"We all know what the wraith guards," spoke Athena. "Is it wise to pull it from such duties?"

Ares snorted. "Yer always frettin' so damn much about defenses."

"Says the god recently clocked in the back of the head."

"Aw, give it a rest, already. Hades is right! I say we use the shade!"

Arguments erupted throughout the chamber. Some declared it too risky. Others insisted the risk was minimal for the brief time it would take to find Apollo. Certain Artemis-shaped others asserted they'd be damned to Tartarus if they supported anything Ares thought was a good idea. Others beyond those others (being different from previous others) accused the Artemis-shaped group of being on Apollo's side and, therefore, deserving of such a fate.

Hestia had just thrown in her support for the wraith, suggesting they let it do the tracking while they all stayed home and played backgammon, when Poseidon pounded his trident to the floor. The continued shouting forced a second and third pounding.

"Enough!" he boomed when they all clammed up. It was entirely louder than necessary, but the need to lead by committee hacked him off, and gauging magnitudes never suited him anyway. "We will use the Orthlaelapsian wraith!"

"I—"

"*Silence,* Artemis, lest you be confined with the Muses!" He turned to Hades. "How swiftly can you re-task it from guard duty to seeking Apollo and . . . whatnot?"

"With utmost speed." Consternation flickered across Hades's stoicism. "Once I find the manual."

"Proceed quickly," ordered Poseidon. "The rest of you—and that means all of you, Hestia—shall commence searching on your own. Except you, Artemis. You shall search with Ares."

"What?" the two protested at once.

"Your loyalties are suspect, Artemis, sister of our quarry."

"You cannot pair me with him!"

"Do not tell me what I may or may not do! I am your king!"

Artemis gaped, perhaps realizing the need to tread carefully in light of Poseidon's tone. "King Poseidon, I assure you, my loyalties—"

"Lie with me?" he finished.

Artemis nodded.

As swiftly as he had angered, Poseidon calmed again—in much the same way as the sea does before a storm. Familiar with the sea god's dangerously unpredictable moods, none in attendance considered it anything but an ominous sign. "You will swear an oath to that effect?"

"Lord?"

"By the Styx?"

The collective gasp in the chamber at the taboo question ruled the next few moments before Artemis straightened, swallowing.

"You would dare to ask this of me?" she tried.

"You are Apollo's twin!" Poseidon boomed. "His authority is void! His portfolio shall be redistributed! His space in the communal fridge is forfeit! Shall I confine you to chambers and make your fate the same? Swear loyalty to me in totality, or face the consequences!"

Artemis shivered. Perhaps she believed Apollo already doomed. Perhaps she considered some loophole Poseidon had missed. Perhaps, goddess of nature that she was, she simply believed in a bit of unpredictability herself. Whatever the cause, after a few moments' consideration, she whispered, "By the Styx do I so swear loyalty to you in totality, King Poseidon—"

Poseidon smirked proudly. "Very well, then."

"—if that is how you must secure it." It was a jab at his fitness to rule, and all knew it. Zeus himself never demanded such an oath.

"You will still partner with Ares," Poseidon ordered.

"Aw, come on!" Ares cried over Artemis's own objection. "She swore your damn oath. Why I gotta be saddled with her fruity butt now?"

The insult turned the goddess's ire on Ares and drew both into a yelling match that necessitated another pounding of the trident—plus two more because the sound was particularly pleasing to Poseidon. It shut them up, at least long enough for him to dismiss the council and avoid hearing more on the matter. To the depths with what opinion polls said! He didn't care. He would do what he thought was wrong. Or right, rather. Right?

Whatever.

Poseidon forgot to return Hades's little golden ball after the meeting, and Hades didn't remind him. It was one more thing he could brood over.

CHAPTER TWENTY-NINE

"Despite the common misconception, the river Styx is not the river the newly dead must cross to reach the underworld. As any mythological scholar worth his salt will tell you (or any one of the gods themselves, were they in the mood to give a straight answer), one of the Styx's qualities is that any mortal bathed in its waters becomes invulnerable—provided they survive (the lawyers seem to think this important; see Chapter 14: Achilles and the Importance of Good Footwear). You simply can't leave a river like that just lying around, readily accessible to any mortal who happens to find one of the numerous passages to underworld borders. The Styx is therefore located deeper in Hades beyond the river that does border the edge of the underworld: the Acheron.

"The Acheron's ferry crossing is but one checkpoint designed to allow only the deceased to pass, thus keeping crowds of invulnerability-seeking mortals out from underfoot. This is why there is a ferry and not a bridge; it keeps away the riffraff.

"This is not to say a bridge was not tried. According to an interview with Charon, ferryman of the Acheron, it failed. Merely touching the Acheron causes extreme pain, a phenomenon that doomed any efforts of the construction crew. The best protective gear did little, and the worker turnover rate was ruinous. According to Charon, Hades did consider the possibility of using some of the mortal souls damned to Tartarus as a source of slave labor, under the theory that the damned workers would have no choice but to endure the pain. The lack of a bridge today shows us that Hades finally eschewed this option. This is likely for the best. One need only look so far as horror cinema (House of the Damned, Highway of the Damned, and Wetlands Preservation Culvert of the Damned, among others) to know that projects built by the damned seldom turn out well."

—A Mortal's Guidebook to the Olympians' Return

TRACY SLUNG THE HALF-FILLED backpack over her other shoulder and knocked on the rickety door of the wooden dwelling. A real estate agent with generous optimism would call it quaint. To anyone with a greater duty to the truth, it was a shack, and a cramped shack at that. The wood siding, perhaps once stained in times long ago, was faded and warped from exposure to the river it overlooked. Its walls had begun to lean under the weight of the roof, which seemed to have yet failed to collapse due only to the sheer will of the cosmos. The aforementioned real estate agent (whom for no reason we shall call Warren) would cheerfully point out that the walls—clearly still parallel to each other despite leaning—ably supported what would soon be a marvelous built-in skylight. Warren would likely make some excuse to dash from the room before anyone could point out that a skylight would afford only a dull view of the ceiling of the subterranean cavern in which the whole affair hunched.

Tracy gazed up at that same cavern ceiling as she waited outside the door. While not what she would call pretty, the eerie, rust-colored light that bathed the cavern at least provided a measure of atmosphere. It was no starry sky, but it did have a certain character.

Warren would have liked Tracy, if he existed. (He does not, however, and as such is possessed of more immediate problems.)

The door opened after Tracy's second knock, and she blinked at the face that presented itself.

"Oh, hello," she said with a smile. "Charon, I presume?"

It wasn't an unfair presumption. Who else would one find squatting in a shack at the ferry mooring for the river Acheron but the mythical Charon, ferryman to the land of the dead? He was the logical thing to expect to find, right ahead of a small Starbucks. And yet somehow she had always pictured him to be an old man. While the faded black robes he wore fit the part, within them stood a man who looked hardly older than she, with rich brown eyes and a full head of hair. On the other hand, the scowl that bitterly gripped his face after she asked her question fit her expectations perfectly.

"Nope," he said. "Trust me; I'm very sorry to say Charon's not here right now."

"Okay. Can you help me, then? I'm—"

The man held up a hand. "Are you dead?"

"Er, no. I was told that wouldn't be a problem."

"Told by who? Actually, you know what? I probably don't want to know." The man tested her with a poke in the shoulder. The result appeared to pleasantly surprise him. "Hey, look at that. You're not dead. Are you lost?"

"No, I'm—"

"Oh, crap, you're not with Amway, are you?" He leveled a suspicious gaze at her slung backpack.

"No?"

"Hot damn, that's a relief. The deceased ones are bad enough; even when they're dead they don't stop selling." He crossed his arms and leaned against the door frame, quickly standing straight up again when the shack creaked in protest. "So what're you doing down here, anyway?"

"Trying to get across to Hades. This is the ferry, isn't it?"

"This is a rickety old crap-shack," he said. "*That's* the ferry. But I have the singular joy of running it for the moment, yes."

"Well, then—"

"But you can't go. Sorry. Only the dead, that's the rule."

Tracy peered over the man's shoulder into the dim quarters beyond. "Is Charon in there? Could I speak to him, maybe?"

"Lady, if he was, do you think *I'd* be here?" He stepped aside, allowing a better view of the shack's interior. There was little more than a small bed, a wooden desk, and a few odds, ends, and pieces of laundry lying about.

The talk-to-the-manager trick wasn't going to work, it seemed.

"Okay, but you can't just outright refuse, can you? I've read mythology and I know for a fact that live mortals have crossed the river before."

"Mythology, and you know for a fact?" He grinned. "Want to think about that one a sec?"

"You know what I mean."

"Yeah, I know what you mean, but I was a devout atheist until a little over a year ago. Still a little bitter. And maybe there're new rules, you ever think of that?"

"Look . . . What's your name?"

"Marcus."

"Look, Marcus, the only reason I'm here at all is because some god's oracle gave me a quest. If the rules weren't bendable, I wouldn't have gotten the quest, so—"

"Yeah, because the 'gods' and their pals aren't devious pricks at all." (He did the air quotes and everything.)

She straightened her spine, summoning up every ounce of authority she could. "The point is, I need to get over there, and I'm not leaving this spot until you take me."

Marcus smirked. "I only run the ferry. I don't do the 'taking'. That's Death's job. How'd Charon put it? 'He hangs around here sometimes, and he gets uptight when someone takes the living across before he gets to 'em. Says it messes up the order, and order's his thing, you see. He's a control freak. If you ask me, he has a bit of a stick up his ass, but he does outrank me.'"

"I meant take me across the river. I've no intention of dying in the process."

"Important distinction, that." He picked a bit of lint off of his robe. "Fine, maybe I can bend the rules if you want it badly enough to do something for me in return."

Tracy bit down on demanding why everyone was suggesting sexual currency lately. "And what sort of something are we talking about?" came out after a moment of temper wrangling. Judging by the look on Marcus's face, she contained her disgust poorly.

"What? Oh, no, nothing like that. Geez, I don't even know you."

She released her frustration with a relieved sigh. "Thank you. You wouldn't believe the week I've had."

"I'm believing a lot more things than I used to, lately."

Well, that fit, she supposed. "So what do you want me to do, then? I don't really have a lot of time." Tracy braced herself for the onslaught of impending zaniness.

"I need you to go back up to the surface and get me a whole bunch of batteries. All sizes, from D on down to the tiny ones."

"Batteries?" Tracy asked. Apollo's oracle mentioned nothing of batteries. "What's the catch? Are they some special batteries I have to talk to a sphinx to get or something?"

"No catch. I just need batteries. I spaced it when I came down here. Now I've got a shack full of electronics I can't use. Things are all rigged up to *use* batteries, but that doesn't do me much good without a single one around."

"Er, okay. How many?"

"Fifty of each ought to do, just to be safe."

"You'll pay for them, of course?"

Marcus shrugged. "You look like you can afford it. If you want a rule-bending ride across, it's on you."

"My employment situation's a little up in the air at the moment."

"Want a steady job as a Hades ferryman?"

"Thanks, no."

"Well, then. Batteries. Use a credit card or something. Oh, and none of those cheapo store brands either."

It occurred to Tracy that she could stand there arguing details about one of the simplest things anyone had asked her to do in a while, or . . .

"Fine, I'll pay for the damn batteries."

Marcus laughed. "Damn batteries. That's a good one."

"Your sense of humor really takes a hit down here, doesn't it?"

He shrugged and turned to go back inside. "Good luck. Oh, and I wouldn't recommend trying to swim across instead, if you're considering that. It's, ah, bad. A hundredfold worse than labor pains."

"How would you know?"

"Just . . . don't ask."

Tracy bought the batteries with surprisingly little trouble from a twenty-four-hour Battery Bunker just a few blocks from the manhole in downtown Reno that concealed this particular entrance to Hades. The Battery Bunker wasn't crowded. She paid with a credit card. There was even a volume discount. Stepping on a blob of sidewalk gum was about the worst thing that happened to her. The night was looking up, and soon afterward she made her way back down the tunnel, bribe in hand, to knock on the door of the little shack again.

There was no answer.

She knocked once more, muttering a few profanities that she belatedly hoped might serve as magic words. Again, there was no answer.

The door wouldn't budge when she tried it, and a few glances around the shore gave no sign of Marcus anywhere. Nor, she realized, did they give any sign of the ferry she'd seen before. She muttered a little more and walked the length of the dock to fruitlessly peer out through the mist that drifted above the Acheron's obsidian current.

All she could make out of the far shore were some indistinct shapes. With little else to do but hope the ferry would be back soon, she sat down on the edge of the dock to wait.

A hand-painted sign on the edge of the dock caught her eye, but her brief hope that it might provide some clue to when the ferry would be back was dashed once she read the age-worn lettering, written in at least twenty different languages:

No swimming: Lifeguard never on duty. Do not taunt the river.

Save for a few nervous glances behind her at the shore and several half-imagined sounds, Tracy's wait was brief and unremarkable. Each time she looked behind her, she expected to be staring straight into the dead eyes of a corpse or spirit or what-have-you, but not once did she catch sight of anything. Were her mind not valiantly occupied defending itself against the heebie-jeebies, Tracy might have taken a moment to ponder something that the more annoyingly detail-oriented reader may have already wondered (or voiced, or made some snarky comment about on the Internet): It was a big world. People were dying every second. Where were all the spirits who ought to be piling up on shore by the minute?

She did not wonder this, of course—not yet, anyway—and so such readers should simply rest assured that there was a good reason for it. A very good reason. A most excellent and clever reason. In fact, many clues have already been left in previous chapters regarding this matter, and only the most intelligent and diligent of you shall be able to puzzle it out.

. . .And now that those people have all gone off on a literary snipe hunt, we can ditch them and move on.

After a time not nearly short enough for Tracy's liking, the outline of a ferry and lone boatman appeared out of the mist. She stood, half expecting that it would be piloted by someone other than Marcus just so that she'd have to negotiate all over again, but the fear was baseless. Soon the ferry was tied up, and Marcus stood with her on the dock. He gave no explanation for his absence, and Tracy wasn't all that interested in asking about it.

"Got your batteries." She opened up the bag to show him.

"Looks good. Ooh, lithium. You splurged."

"So we have a deal, then?"

"That we do. Hand them over and I'll take you across, no questions asked."

He reached for the bag. Tracy pulled it away. "Just so we're clear: You're agreeing to take me across *and* bring me back, correct?"

His anticipatory grin faded in an instant. He glanced between her and the batteries like a child told to finish his vegetables before dessert.

"Fine," he grumbled finally. "Deal. Both ways." He took the bag and carried it to the shack. "Just . . . get in the boat. And congratulations, you're officially smarter than me now."

Tracy picked up her backpack and stepped gingerly into the little ferry as instructed. Marcus soon joined her, still scowling, and untied the mooring line.

"I didn't think of that part when I first came here," he explained after they'd pulled away from the dock. "Came right on down like I knew everything."

Tracy nodded, barely listening, instead trying to concentrate on the task that awaited her on the other side of the river. Her head was beginning to buzz a bit too. Marcus either didn't notice her attempts to tune him out, or he didn't care.

"Found a path through a hole in my basement," he continued. "I lived in that house for two years and hadn't seen it, but then Miranda's cat—Miranda, she's my girlfriend—ran down into the basement when I tried to give the thing its ear medicine and—"

"I'm sorry, do you mind not talking? I'm just a little preoccupied and not really up to it. Plus I think this water's giving me a headache or something. No offense."

Marcus rolled his eyes. "I do mind, actually. I'm going bonkers from not having anyone to talk to down here, so you're gonna listen to my story. The batteries bought you passage, not silence."

She drummed her fingers on the rim of the ferry. "You ferry the dead, right? You don't talk to them?"

"Ugh, no. I gave that up after the first week. Too many questions, always the same. 'Where am I?' 'Am I dead?' 'What happened?' and my personal favorite, 'No, really: Am I dead?' It got old fast, and I realized that if I don't say much, that tends to shut most of them up. Besides, I think there's some sort of orientation seminar once they get to the other side."

"Ah."

"So anyway, there I am, chasing my girlfriend's cat down a dark tunnel, thinking how much that sounds like the start of a dirty joke, when I come out on the shores of the Acheron and spot this old guy taking money from people who, from my perspective, have somehow come down through my basement! I didn't know about the multiple-overworld-entrances-to-Hades thing; back then I didn't even know about the Hades thing. Thought it was all mythological crap and Charon was just some guy pulling a confidence scheme from people who thought they were dead."

Tracy continued to nod, still not paying much attention. Her headache remained steady yet manageable as long as she didn't lean too close to the water. They were somewhere in the middle of the wide river now, drifting through the mist as vague shadows moved beneath the water. She double-checked the contents of her pack as Marcus continued.

"So long story short, I get him to agree to take me across—he said the cat rode across already—get off on the other side, go through this tunnel and run smack into the dog."

That perked her ears up. "Cerberus?"

"Yup. Not that I knew the name at the time. I didn't know much about this stuff back then." He leaned forward to speak confidentially. "And I *hate* dogs. Absolutely hate 'em. Stupid barking stink factories. He chased me back out of the tunnel to the riverbank where Charon waited a few yards offshore, and that's when he springs on me the whole bit that, oh yeah, he never actually agreed to ferry me *back*."

Tracy stifled a self-satisfied grin, just to be polite.

"So there I am, Cerberus growling at my heels with all three heads, trapped there until I starve to death unless I get a ride back. Then Charon goes off on some rant about how he never gets a break, stuck at the ass-end of the underworld for all eternity with all that coin he gets for tolls and no chance to spend it. He tells me he'll only take me back if I swear to return in six months and spend half of every year until I *die* taking his place so that he can go up and have a vacation. So bam, here I am, and that's why the 'gods' and all of their little friends are manipulative pricks!"

"That's rough. Did you ever get the cat back?"

"Yeah, got the cat back. Tried to tell Miranda the whole story, but of course she just laughed at me. That was before the Olympians all came back, so on the plus side, I had a nice long apology message on my voice mail when I got back after my first shift. I think she's only with me now for the status, but I decided I can live with that."

"Uh-huh."

"Yeah, I know; you didn't ask. Tough."

The ferry neared the other side. A narrow stretch of rocky beach sat before a dark cave in the face of a cliff that loomed high and sheer. There was no sign of Cerberus, though from what she understood, the dog was farther up the tunnel.

"And you know what else?" Marcus snapped. "I don't even get to keep any of the toll funds! After Hades takes his cut, Charon gets everything that's left! I'm doing this for free! Do you know how hard it is to get a job for only six months out of the year that doesn't involve shipping out on a fishing trawler?"

The ferry slid ashore with an unceremonious scrape, and Tracy took the earliest opportunity to step out. Her head cleared almost immediately. "So you'll be here when I get back?"

"Depends on when you get back, but I make the trip pretty regularly. Shouldn't have to wait more than half an hour, I guess. I'd ask what you're doing, but I've got a schedule, and frankly I don't much care."

"Thanks for the ride, then." She triple-checked the contents of her pack, slung it back on her shoulder, and turned to go. "Wish me luck."

"Nah. Quite frankly I'm not above a little *schadenfreude*[2], so I'm kinda hoping you fail. No offense."

"Gee, thanks."

"Don't mention it." He pushed the ferry away from shore. "Don't let the dog bite ya in the ass on the way out. Or do. What do I care?"

When he at last disappeared into the haze, she screwed up her courage and turned toward the cave entrance. If Apollo was to be believed, the cave was actually a tunnel that stretched the final distance to the gates of Hades's domain. There would stand Cerberus, the object of her assignment. (Apollo and the oracle had called it a quest, but she'd mentally swapped out the term in an effort to create an illusion of normalcy.)

---

[2] you *were* told to look it up

Even though she knew what she had to do and she believed it was necessary, she still didn't want to do it. Hercules, whom she now supposed actually existed at one point, had once dragged Cerberus from his post into the world above—and from what she recalled of the tale, the three-headed dog wasn't all that pleased about it. While the task on her plate was a different one, it wasn't without its own challenges, not the least of which was that Cerberus would probably like it even less.

The beam of a lone flashlight guided her way through the darkness. (Historians and record keepers may be interested to know that she was the first person to think of bringing such a device through that particular tunnel, and that includes Marcus. Feel free to lower your estimations of him down just a tick. There you go.) The tunnel floor was rough and completely unworn by eons of spiritual passage, and while vines of purplish ivy covered the walls in intermittent patches, she saw no sign of animals or insects.

"What did you expect in the land of the dead, Tracy?" she muttered to fill the unsettling quiet. Each step she took was soundless. Not even her own breathing registered to her ears, and the utter lack of distraction allowed her to concentrate on worrying that she was getting involved in things far too deeply. Not exactly a helpful train of thought for a person on an assignme-quest, but there was little she could do about it besides increase her pace and get to Cerberus before her confidence had eroded completely.

Her flashlight beam illuminated a bit of graffiti carved into the tunnel wall: *Where am I? Am I dead? Who will feed my fish?* She quickened her pace and then noticed another note in a different hand: *What would Samuel L. Jackson do?* She passed it by. *Orpheus was here, bitches!* She paused at that one just long enough to feel unspoken skepticism about its authenticity and then left it, too, behind before spotting: *No, really: Am I dead?*

Marcus had a point, Tracy decided. She didn't bother reading more.

There was a light ahead, orange, promising, and weird, like a sunset at the start of the day. Tracy crouched down in the tunnel and switched off the flashlight, putting it back into her pack. She withdrew from the pack a few other items, counting some, assembling others. When she had everything sorted out, Tracy stood to luxuriate in one final bit of hesitation that she couldn't afford.

"Who am I?" she asked to psych herself up. "*Who* am I? I'm Zeus's motherfuckin' daughter, that's who!"

It actually helped. There was something to be said for a good, inspiring game of What Would Samuel L. Jackson Do? after all.

Long, long ago in the before-time, a young, lovestruck, and still-living mortal named Orpheus made his way into Hades, coming face-to-face (to-face-to-face) with Cerberus. Orpheus played a tune on his lyre so beautiful that it pacified the dog into letting him pass freely. Another mortal by the name of Aeneas made his way past with the help of some drugged cakes that he fed to the beast. According to Apollo, neither option was open to Tracy: Soon after the cake-drugging, Hades had fortified Cerberus's stomach lining against such weaknesses and assigned a dead musician to come by each day at noon to play for the creature until he grew accustomed to music. Indeed, as she crept slowly toward the beast that stood ahead, Tracy noticed that the middle head wore a set of headphones connected to an MP3 player on its collar and looked no less alert for it.

The legendary guardian blocked the path to the golden gates of Hades. Cerberus was the size of a grizzly, but shaped like a horrid wolf. Claws on enormous paws scraped the rocks as he watched her, midnight fur bristling along his massive bulk, ears up, tail whipping the air behind him. Again, Tracy hesitated. She forced herself closer. One of the heads lowered, red eyes flaring as it sensed the thread of life still within her.

Apollo's words came back to her. *"For all his fearsomeness, Cerberus will not harm you unless you attack him or try to pass alive into the land of the dead. Move slowly, take no offensive action, and you'll be just fine."* Comforting words, were it not for Marcus's, *"The 'gods' and all of their little friends are manipulative pricks!"* springing to mind moments later.

Tracy did as Apollo had advised, edging closer. All three heads watched her approach. The right one growled at her, the left one growled at her, and the middle one, bopping slightly to whatever tune played on the headphones, nevertheless also growled at her. She got as close as she dared, easily within striking distance of the creature's paws, and held out the three jumbo-sized doggie biscuits she'd brought. The center head perked up at that, alert to this new development.

The sudden motion spooked her and she tossed all three biscuits at Cerberus's feet in a startled offering. In a flash the creature jumped back a step. Two heads lowered instantly, their teeth bared, as the middle head rose high to bark out a terrifying thunderclap. Tracy froze where she stood, horrified that it had misconstrued her startled toss as an attack.

Time slowed to a trickle. The standoff continued. She had no idea how long she was standing there before she thought to hunch down just a bit, lower her head and her eyes, and make herself smaller and less threatening. (Because if there's one thing a massive three-headed dog is afraid of, it's a thin, five-foot-eight television producer with a backpack.) A trickle of sweat ran down the back of her neck. Slowly, the growling abated. Tracy suddenly realized she could have gotten a fortune for catching this all on camera.

Then the left head again noticed the biscuits on the ground. After a few tentative sniffs, it snapped one up, crunching. This caught the attention of the right head, which soon moved down to snap up a biscuit of its own just as the left, still chewing on the first, went back for seconds. The two got into a growling match, snapping competitively over the remaining biscuits for a moment until the center head let out another paralyzing bark. Tracy stumbled back in reflex. All three heads paused to regard her for a moment with what might very well have been amusement before they focused back on the biscuits. The center head snapped up both and then deftly tossed one to the right head. As his three heads munched happily on the Doctor Barkwell's Extra-Chewie Biscuit Jerky Yum-Yums™, Cerberus took a few steps back until his body fully blocked the gateway while he enjoyed his treats.

That was fine with Tracy. She didn't need to get past Cerberus at all; she just needed the creature pacified for a while. Yet only a fool would think that dog biscuits would buy her longer than a few seconds. What they did do was distract the creature while she grabbed from her back the tranquilizer rifle she'd assembled in the tunnel moments ago, aimed, and fired enough Corfentanyl into the base of the creature's necks to take down an elephant. The shot was on target, penetrated the hide, and—as it was nowhere near any pesky hardened stomach lining—dropped the creature near immediately.

It wasn't really a solution that Jason would have approved of, she mused, but this was *her* assign-mission-o-quest. She wondered if it might ever make its way into future tales, her own little story of confronting Cerberus, listed among those of Aeneas, Hercules, and Orpheus. Tracy Wallace, the daughter of Zeus, who sailed to Hades on a quest of the gods: to groom Cerberus like a French poodle.

She fished into her bag for shears and ribbons and wondered if she might not want to be known for this particular act at all.

CHAPTER THIRTY

"Likely owing to its secondary designation as the 'underworld,' Hades is often thought by modern mortals to be a place devoted entirely to damnation. The ancient Greeks, however, saw Hades as the domain of the afterlife in general, and indeed the Olympian gods appeared surprised when first confronted with the modern misconception. The realm of Hades, we are told, contains both paradise (such as the Elysian Fields, to name one of the good neighborhoods) and punishment (such as Tartarus, with its heavy push-boulders, lakes of fire, dark pits, and various specialized prisons both large and small).

"Obviously we cannot be certain just what the afterlife holds or how many facets something so vastly beyond human understanding may possess. Despite the Return, theologians, philosophers, and insurance salesmen continue to debate the question. As always, it is merely the intent of this bulletin to be sure the terms of that debate are properly defined."

—Biweekly Bulletin of Unrequested Pedantry

"YOU'D BETTER BE long gone when he wakes up," came Jason's voice from behind her. "I can't believe you're here alive and not filming this."

"You know, that's exactly what I—*Jason?*"

Nearly finished grooming, Tracy whipped around to find Jason leaning against the inside of the gates of Hades and wearing the same clothes as when he fell and . . . hit. He appeared surprisingly unwounded and cheerful, sporting the rugged grin he tended to have when there was no other expression needing more urgent display.

He was also semitransparent, which wasn't really much of a surprise either, considering.

"What are you—?" She stopped herself before asking the stupid question.

"Doing here?" he finished anyway. "That's kind of an odd question to ask, what with this being the land of the dead and me being, well . . ."

"Maybe that's why I didn't finish asking, you think?" With a glance at the still-sleeping Cerberus, she risked standing. "It's . . . good to see you. I mean, what I can see of you. You're sort of transparent."

"I am?" He glanced at himself. "Huh. Not to me. I'll have to ask someone about that when I get a chance. You didn't come looking for me, did you? I didn't know you cared." He grinned. "Though that doesn't explain why you're giving the dog the poodle treatment. You've gone mad with grief, huh?"

She frowned. "That's not really funny, you know. It hurt when you died." She supposed the event wasn't exactly painless for him either.

"Hurt, past tense, eh?" he teased. "I guess you got over me quick, or I've been down here longer than I thought."

"That Muse gave me a bit of a mood treatment," Tracy explained. "Long story."

"Just giving you a hard time. It's not like you and I were terribly close. I never even, you know, 'gave you a hard time.'" Jason grinned. Curiously, she didn't mind so much.

"I'm sorry you died," she said finally. "That you had to die saving us."

"It's one of the better ways to die, all things considered. Not nearly as fun as a few others I can think of, but this one got me a good place in the afterlife. At least that's what they tell me." He held up a stamped ticket. "Things are a little backed up in here, so I'm waiting until they call my number so they can—," he waved a hand, "—you know, do whatever they do. There's more paperwork and a drug test or something. Maybe they have to search my shoes."

"I'm—I'm glad to hear that." She blinked at him a moment, blanking on anything to say. "This is weird, isn't it?"

"First time for me too. So why, ah . . ." He pointed to Cerberus. "Changed the show?"

"This is more to do with the whole amulet-slash–Zeus's daughter thing, really."

He laughed. "And somehow I don't see the connection."

"Like I said, long story. Completing a quest is part of bringing back Zeus. Once I do this, then I'll have enough . . . whatever you want to call it. Heroic mojo or something."

Certain suspicious readers are likely now weighing the possibility that what Tracy has encountered at this point in the story might not actually be Jason, Jason's shade, Jason's spirit, Jason's soul, or anything related to Jason in any way whatsoever. These readers may have noted that Tracy stands just over the border in the kingdom of Hades, one of the conspirators arrayed against her, and they may have wondered if there might, just possibly, be some sort of trickery going on. This narrative has little to say to confirm or deny that possibility at this time, other than pointing it out to those who have not yet thought of it (not including the skimmers who skipped over this lengthy paragraph after detecting zero dialogue in it, and nuts to them). One might expect this whole question wouldn't be pointed out at all were it irrelevant, but this may vastly underestimate the desire of the narrative to mess with the reader.

Having said that, we shall continue, as lingering on the edge of Hades over the unconscious form of Cerberus isn't the wisest thing one can do.

"Then what?" Jason asked. "Find a hydra, give it earmuffs?"

"No, then we finish bringing Zeus back. We just have to find a—"

Cerberus growled softly in his slumber. Tracy glanced at the creature, considered something, then loaded another dart into the rifle, just in case.

"Find a what?"

She frowned and grabbed a few ribbons. "A place to resurrect him. I need to finish doing up the doggy, but don't go anywhere." She began to tie one ribbon in a tuft of fur. "Hey, he's knocked out, not guarding the gate. Does that mean you can come back with me?"

Jason considered the question. "I honestly don't know. I'd have to get the cranky guy on the river to let me back across, but how hard can that be?" She could feel him watching her as she brushed the fur on Cerberus's middle neck to fullness. "How much do you figure you need me?" he asked finally.

"I don't *need* you." The honesty came out before she could stop it. "But, you know, when this is all over the show's going to need a star. Plus, like I said, I hate that you died for us."

"Don't like owing me, eh?"

"Yeah, that too."

"I've had a glimpse of what the afterlife's got in store for me, Tracy. The show was great, like, really, really great, but I'm thinking I'm going to like it here. I'm tagged for a place called the Elysian Fields, and if it's anywhere near as fantastic as the brochures say . . ."

He crouched down near her. "Plus, you know me: I didn't really have anyone back there, anyway. That's why I could fight monsters each week and not care. Well, that and the adrenaline rush."

"And the babes," she smirked as she worked.

"You mean the fans."

"Don't forget that you're a little bit stupid too." Her smirk turned more than a little rueful as she flashed it up at him.

"The fans didn't seem to mind. I'll miss them." He blinked. "Which reminds me of something else I wanted to tell you: I think something kind of bad's about to happen."

Tracy's hand shot to the rifle. "Is he waking up?" Cerberus didn't seem to be stirring. Maybe the creature was playing at being asleep, trying to fool her into—into what? Being complacent so it could surprise her? Did a seven-hundred-pound, three-headed dog really need trickery to overpower someone her size? *Don't be stupid, Tracy.*

"No, not him. In general, back up there. When I died—right when I died—I caught a glimpse of something that was about to happen, or that just happened, or . . . I don't know."

"People sometimes get visions of the future as they're crossing over into death, according to classical myth."

"Yeah, that's what the pamphlet said."

"What'd you see?"

"I'm not entirely sure."

"How helpful."

"Something's going to get loose. Or be let loose. If it hasn't happened already, it will soon. Something was taken from a shop in a place called Swindon from a man named Sidgwick."

"I've never heard of Swindon, but Sidgwick sounds English. What sort of something?"

Jason chuckled nervously before answering. "Cans."

"Cans?"

"That's what I saw."

"What's in 'em? English cuisine?"

"I wasn't really paying attention, being busy *dying*. I just know that whatever it was, it was canned for a reason, not to be opened."

She nodded. "Definitely English cuisine."

"Not food—something destructive. And angry."

"You've clearly never had black pudding."

"I'm serious, Tracy."

"You're never serious, Jason."

"Well, that's fair." He shrugged. "But I'm serious now, so don't make jokes."

She finished tying the bow on Cerberus's third neck. "I don't mean to, but I'm grooming a creature likely to kill me when it wakes up, and I'm trying to resurrect a dead god, and there's only so much I can handle at once, right? I mean, what do you want me to do?"

"I didn't tell you to annoy you, though God knows that's something else I'll miss doing." He winked. "But hey, even if I'm dead I've still got to live up to that hero image, so I figure as long as we're chatting, I should warn you now while I've got the chance. They won't even let you e-mail the living from down here."

She chuckled, weary. "So I should just hear your message of impending doom and take or leave it as I see fit?"

"Pretty much, yeah. Oh, and one more thing: if you do manage to bring Zeus back, get him to do something about all those monsters. Fighting them was fun, but if there's a choice, the world's got to be better off without them."

"That'll kind of put a dent in the show, don't you think?"

"Ah, you can't replace me anyway." He grinned. "Call it a favor. Then I'll have died to rid the entire world of monsters, and how heroic is that?"

She chuckled again. "Okay. If I can, I'll ask."

Jason cast a glance behind him as if reacting to something beyond Tracy's ken. "Sounds like my number's up; gotta go off to my eternal reward and all that. Good luck with everything, Trace. I'd hug you but I don't think you'd feel it."

"Hey, before you go: if it's so crowded in there, why haven't I seen anyone but you and the ferryman since coming down here?"

"They're dead. Maybe you can't see them if you don't know 'em?"

"Didn't think of that." She stood, a bit frustrated that she couldn't hug the big heroic jackass. "Take care of yourself. I might even see you soon, depending."

"Ooh, cheery." He turned to go. "Is that Leif guy still following you around like a puppy?"

"Don't remind me. One of the good things about coming down here is that I had to do it alone."

He grinned. "Give the guy a break, Trace. He's sweet on you. At least have a little fun with him."

"Yeah, but he's so damned fixated without even knowing me! It's *weird*. And anyway, just because a person likes you is no reason to just 'have a little fun' with them."

Jason blinked. "We're very different people." He glanced behind him again. "Second call. Gotta go! Good luck! And be sure to think of some good last words for me when you air the retrospective!"

And with a wave, Jason Powers dashed into the haze beyond the gate.

Tracy watched him go before recalling the poodled-up Cerberus snoring behind her. She gathered up her gear and dashed down back the tunnel with the fervent hope that Cerberus couldn't track or swim. And that Marcus wasn't an outright liar. And that the headache wouldn't be so bad the second time she crossed the river. And that there'd be a good ice cream place on the way to Zeus's temple.

It was a less pressing need than the others, but after all the Olympian strangeness lately, she was really starting to crave a sundae.

Marcus picked her up a short while later and ferried her back as agreed. Along the way he told her how the gods themselves had created all the monsters running around up on the surface, as a means of entertainment. The revelation annoyed her at first, but she decided that getting too bothered about something from which she'd made a living was hypocritical, and so she let it go for the moment. Also, she had bigger problems to worry about.

And still no sundae.

Leif shot another perplexed look between the cards on the table and his hand. Tracy was overdue, he didn't understand the game Apollo was trying to teach him, and the motel they'd holed up in smelled like beets. His rapidly souring mood didn't help the learning process, and he was distracted with worry, but the card game passed the time at least. He frowned, threw down a pair of spades, and drew a card. It was a joker.

"Jokers are bad, right?" he asked.

Thalia glanced up from where she lay on the bed, flipping channels and slowly recovering from her dejection upon learning that Poseidon had locked up her sisters and deactivated her phone. "Jokers are *very* bad."

Leif frowned again, glanced at Apollo, and sighed. "Well, that's not what I drew, then, you can be sure about that."

Apollo threw down two more cards: two tens that he set in separate piles at his right hand. He then turned one sideways for a reason Leif couldn't quite remember. (Either it had to do with the trump suit or the times of moonrise in winter in Paraguay, and Leif was actually somewhat sure it was the latter.)

"So that means I have to come up with . . ."

"Three face cards, or two that begin with the letter *F*," Apollo answered.

"In English, right? Fours and fives?"

"Of course. Boston rules."

Leif rolled his eyes. "Well I knew *that*." His hand wasn't promising in that regard. He decided to stall. "Speaking of Boston, are you absolutely sure it was the Eiffel Tower in Paris and not the one back in Vegas?"

Apollo sighed, eyebrow raised. "Absolutely sure, yes, but that's nothing to do with Boston."

"Yeah, that part was a joke."

Thalia tossed him a sympathetic smile from the bed. "Not a very funny one."

"Gimme a break. I'm learning a weird game here." He put down an ace this time, drew the two cards allowed him by the rules (if he understood them properly) and got a two and a seven of diamonds.

This meant, so far as he could tell, absolutely nothing.

Apollo laid down his hand to show a collection of twos, threes, fives, and sevens. "All prime numbers," he declared. "With your ace on the table, that means I'm up a hundred points for this hand, unless you have . . ." The ex-"god" pulled Leif's own hand down. "Nope, you have nothing. Sorry."

"Nothing? Oh, come on. Look at that!" Leif fibbed. "It's clearly a royal fizzbin!"

Apollo just smiled and shook his head.

Thalia giggled. "Too bad it's not Tuesday."

Leif couldn't help but grin. "At least you got that. It flew right past him."

"He's not much into the classics." She winked, apparently cheering up a bit. Beautiful and geeky enough to get an obscure *Trek* reference— Leif decided he could really fall for her, if Tracy didn't already have his heart. Normally he didn't go for older women, but maybe millennia-old was the new thirty.

A knock at the door gave Leif instant hope that it was Tracy.

"It's Tracy!" announced Tracy from the other side.

He figured it was Tracy. "How'd you do?" he asked when she came in. "Are you okay?"

Tracy tossed her pack onto the bedspread and sat down with a relieved sigh. "It's done and I'm fine. And I'd thought my year spent grooming dogs was only good for paying for college."

She imparted her journey to them in what sounded to Leif like a rushed recap—save for details about the Battery Bunker and tense moments with dog biscuits. "Glad to be back. It's depressing down there, all that rusty light."

"Ugh," Thalia agreed. "Makes things all noisome and icky, doesn't it?"

"It's not like that when you get past the gates," Apollo told them. "Well, in the good areas. Just so you know."

"Yes, but I didn't get to see those areas, did I? I just got all the dread-filled spaces with monster-dogs and creepy rivers of pain. The Acheron gave me a headache, just from being near it." She tossed her hat to an empty chair across the room. "I'm glad it's over, glad to be back up here, glad it's done with."

"Well, congratulations!" Leif handed her a soft drink in the mug he'd chilled for her.

Apollo stood. "Yes, indeed. And now that you've groomed the fur of the most fearsome dog in all the world, we can be off."

"Off to where?"

"Ah, back down to the Acheron."

"Oh, ha-ha. Seriously, where to?" Tracy's features gradually darkened as she apparently realized he *was* being serious.

Thalia smirked and put a hand on her shoulder. "Don't tell me you didn't see that one coming."

"Really?"

Apollo nodded. "Sorry."

"We'll bring aspirin," Thalia assured her.

"But . . . why?"

"It's a painkiller, silly! "

"No, I mean—"

"Quite simply, it's the simplest and fastest way to get to where we need to go," Apollo explained. "The Acheron flows into the Styx, and the Styx surfaces in numerous hidden places throughout the globe. Since Zeus himself banned the construction of new Olympian temples thousands of years ago, the only existing temples to him are in our old stomping grounds around the Mediterranean. Transporting you halfway around the world myself would attract too much attention, so it's either try to catch a plane incognito, or sail the Styx. It's actually faster than flying anyway, given how the river works, and it's got enough mystical energy to mask our movements if we're not unlucky."

Thalia clucked her tongue. "Don't say 'not un-something,' Apollo. It sickens me."

"It's more apt."

"Sickening me is more apt?"

Tracy waved a hand. "Are we having the ferryman take us? 'Cause if that's the plan, we're going to need a lot more batteries."

Apollo shook his head. "I've made other arrangements. Now that you're back, we'd best get moving. Poseidon has all the gods looking for me now. The longer we stay in one place, the easier it will be to find us. And you. I fear you may have angered Hades with what you did to Cerberus."

"Oh, thanks. Now you tell me."

Leif sat beside her and hugged her with one arm. "Ah, we'll be fine. What's one more supernatural force arrayed against us when we've got our love?" That got him a light rib versus elbow, and he let go. "Sorry. That sounded corny as soon as it came out, I swear."

He stood to pack up what little things he had as Apollo offered Tracy a hand off the bed.

"Now you've completed your quest, does the amulet feel any different?"

"A little." Tracy lifted it appraisingly. "A little heavier, I think. Maybe warmer too, but I'm not sure. Maybe I'm just tired."

"That, at least, I can still fix." Apollo waved a hand over Tracy's face, and the fatigue in her eyes visibly decreased.

"Wow. That's almost better than coffee. I don't suppose you can conjure me up a sundae before we go?"

"Sorry. That's more Hestia's or Demeter's area."

"Or Hecate!" Thalia piped up. "Golly, she makes this thing with double-dark chocolate ice cream and almonds and the richest fudge you've ever—"

Tracy cut her off. "No torturing me."

"Oh, and the sprinkles! They're some sort of secret—" The Muse swooned against the wall. "Swell. Now I'm hungry. How *is* Hecate lately? I haven't talked to her in a while."

Hecate, if any are curious, was atop a cargo ship in the middle of the Atlantic, using the night sky to extrapolate Apollo's location via a complex mystical method involving star movements, ocean air currents, and ley lines. At least that was her official explanation. Really she was just staring at the Pleiades star cluster for a while because it was pretty.

She cared little for this frantic search for Apollo. He was up to something, and though she knew not what, frankly she applauded the effort. Things could use a bit of a shaking up, and anything that started with clocking Ares in the back of the head had her support. Plus the fact that the Muse Thalia was somehow involved—or at least hadn't turned up when the rest of the Muses were confined to quarters—increased her disinclination to get involved. Though not her favorite Muse—that title belonged to Terpsichore, who lately mused mysteries along with her older duties of choral song and business correspondence— Thalia was always nice to her, asked after her, and complimented her sundaes.

Hecate might possibly have been somewhat less easygoing were she aware that agents of the NCMA had recently broken into Sidgwick's Antique Shoppe in Swindon, England, and made off with the set of nine sealed cans that had appeared in the vision she gave to one Brittany Simons (a.k.a. Wynter Nightsorrow, a.k.a. the young woman from Chapters Four, Seven, and Twenty). It would not have affected her search for Apollo one bit, of course; the two topics were at the time no more connected to each other than nuclear physics and sock puppets (possibly less so). Yet she would have been far more worried on levels both personal and professional, and possibly even moved to take action that could have averted numerous catastrophes.

However, goddesses, even those who deal heavily in secrets, cannot know everything. Unaware of those aforementioned events, Hecate merely sipped her blackberry smoothie, snuggled into her deck chair, and contentedly watched the stars twinkle. As there is no currently accepted unit of measure for impending mortal suffering, it cannot be quantitatively expressed just how unfortunate this is.

This is not meant to impugn blackberry smoothies, which shared almost no blame in the matter (unless you listen to the loganberry lobbyists, but they're just a bunch of instigators).

CHAPTER THIRTY-ONE

"Though it pains me to say so, our Withdrawal must be absolute. I will tolerate no god to give hints or signs, or to accept sacrifices of any kind, lest they jeopardize this. Your mortal servants and priests must believe us to be gone completely. Toward that end, I command that no god shall go anywhere within a quarter-mile of any of our temples, for any reason, ever. Know that my law in this is resolute and inviolate; I do this to remove from you the temptation to risk my wrath. In time, we shall become used to existence without temples."
— Zeus's Withdrawal Edict, Article II, Section IV

AS APOLLO EXPLAINED EN ROUTE, they were bound for a temple of Zeus that was only a short hike away from the spot where they would leave the Styx. Zeus originally ordered its construction after a particularly spiteful feud with his brother, and he placed the temple on the edge of an exit from the underworld as something of a signpost: Hades's kingdom had limits, beyond which stood the dominion of Zeus. The wind long ago eroded the original lettering carved into the rock in ancient Olympian, displaying, *Zeus's domain. Suck it, Hades!* But according to Apollo, none of the Olympians had forgotten that the sign once existed, Hades especially. Meanwhile, the temple itself remained.

The river journey went quickly. Shut away in his shack, Marcus failed to notice the ex-god, Muse, and two living mortals who slipped down to the shoreline, inflated their river raft, and pushed off into the Acheron. (Or if he did notice them, they failed to notice his noticing, and for the purposes of this slipshod narrative, that's more or less the same.) Tracy thought she caught a glimpse of the shack's door opening when they fired up the raft's outboard motor, but by then, they were so far downriver that she couldn't be sure in the dim light.

Apollo also managed to shield them from the effects of both rivers as they traveled: Tracy's headache did not return on the Acheron. As no one began trying to beat anyone to death after the Acheron passed into the Styx—a.k.a., the River of Hate—she assumed Apollo's protection was working there as well. She did suggest that Leif try a swallow of Styx-water in hopes it would shake his fascination with her, but Apollo assured her that it was more likely to kill him. Despite everything, she decided she didn't want him dead, and so, after five or ten minutes of arguing, she dropped the matter.

Leif was starting to grow on her, she considered. Oh, he'd still end up with a broken heart, she was certain of that, but she would at least feel bad about it when it happened. Tracy guessed that would be of little comfort to Leif. She spent half the raft trip hating the position she was in, hating Leif for getting her into it, and hating that he just didn't get that "I'm not interested" wasn't a flimsy wall he could chip away at over time. She hated the smell of the water, hated the color of the raft, hated the stupid way bunnies would quiver their whiskers at you when they—

All right, so Apollo wasn't able to shield them from the river completely, she'd decided toward the end of the journey.

Thankfully her anger subsided when they pulled ashore above ground, along a thin shelf in a narrow canyon. The Styx only appeared on the surface for a brief stretch before disappearing again back down a rocky maw—much like the one from which it flowed up out of thirty yards upstream, defying gravity in a way that natural law seemed unwilling to debate. Above, the sky was clear beyond the edges of the canyon. Tracy couldn't help but recall the Erinyes chasing them down a similar stretch just a few days ago. A path led to a small tunnel (again with the tunnels!) through the rock. They left the raft and stood before the tunnel, through which further daylight beckoned.

"What are the chances the myriad of other 'gods' arrayed against us have guessed what we're doing and have the temple staked out already?" Leif asked.

"You really shouldn't do that air-quotes thing," Thalia advised.

Leif just shrugged with a grin.

"It's a good question, though," Tracy agreed. "Any prophetic visions along those lines?"

Apollo shook his head sadly. "No, nor is there likely to be. The cost of my exit from the Fates' realm was my skill with prophecy. I'm no better at it than the least of my peers, which is, I mourn to say, quite poor."

Apollo wiped the regret from his face before anyone could think to offer sympathy and tossed the matter aside with a smile and a wave of his hand. He turned to address them in a statesmanlike, Olympian fashion that Tracy deemed as impressive as it was unnecessarily flashy.

"Happily," he continued, "I may still answer Leif's question. Know this: in keeping with Zeus's edict of withdrawal millennia ago, the gods were physically barred from approaching within a quarter-mile of any temple. The Return cast down this law, yet its effects still remain in places to which Zeus was especially connected."

"Like his temples," Tracy finished.

"Correct. For now, this works to our advantage."

"So you're saying you can't get any closer?" Leif asked. "This is the part where the mentor has to die and/or go away so that the hero and his babe can soldier on alone, right?"

Tracy bristled. "'Babe'?"

Apollo shook his head. "Fortunately, no. My diminishment is ideal for slipping past this particular obstacle, so I will be with you the entire way. Of course, with Zeus gone these past nine months, the barriers he erected are fading with time. Eventually they will vanish entirely."

Leif cleared his throat. "And how long before that happens, out of curiosity?"

"About an hour, maybe less."

"You've got to be kidding," Tracy insisted.

Leif just sighed and shook his head.

"Yeah," consoled Thalia, a hand on both their shoulders. "Drama's a knock in the neck, huh?"

Apollo waved them on. "As such, we should probably hurry."

"As such, you should probably not have stopped to tell us that," Leif said. "Can you do that speedy-running thing again?"

"No."

Tracy missed hearing Apollo's explanation for that as she took a few steps down the tunnel and stumbled when her knees turned to noodles beneath her. She managed to catch herself before crumpling to the ground entirely. Thalia offered a helping hand before the others noticed.

"Still getting your land legs back, huh?"

"I know, right?" Tracy answered. "Thanks."

In truth, she'd felt a brief surge of weakness that didn't seem related to the transition from raft to solid ground. Her first instinct was to blame the Styx, yet somehow the amulet seemed the more likely culprit. Leif and Apollo continued on ahead, Leif continuing to yammer—so although her irritation remained at the "babe" comment, the chance to speak about it had passed quickly. They were almost there, anyway, right? A small hike to the temple, a little ritual, then Zeus would be resurrected, and all their problems would be solved.

"I smell the ocean," Leif was saying.

Apollo nodded. "The Mediterranean Sea is just on the other side of this ridge."

"I thought the Styx wasn't accessible from the surface? Or is this tunnel just so isolated that no one notices?"

"Both, in fact," the ex-god explained. "Watch."

They stepped out of the tunnel into the open air of a mountainside. Tracy watched. Nothing happened. She looked back at the tunnel behind them only to find it gone, replaced with solid rock. "Ooh," she whispered, rapping her knuckles on it. It looked solid, felt solid, sounded solid . . . and as she wasn't about to taste or smell it, she figured it must be solid.

Leif shrugged. "Big deal. Holograms and force fields."

Thalia shook her head. "There's no such thing as a hologram, sweetie."

Tracy wondered at the omission but let it pass, still feeling the rock. "I didn't even hear it close."

"It didn't. It's just one-way. I'd explain how it works," Apollo said, "but we've more pressing matters at the moment."

"Convenient!" Leif laughed, adding in Tracy's ear, "He just doesn't know."

Apollo turned and motioned for them to follow. "This way. Zeus's temple is not far."

"Not far!" Thalia added in a queer little voice. "Temple not far!"

They made their way up the mountainside. Apollo guided them along an animal trail at the edge of a ridge that overlooked the sparkling Mediterranean below. While not a sheer cliff, Tracy realized that if her legs grew weak again, she could very well stumble off the path; roll down a steep, rocky hillside of grass and wildflower tufts; and eventually pitch off a sheer edge into the water below.

More or less, anyway. She'd probably have to be pushed to get enough momentum to roll down the hill at least, and there'd likely be some chance to stop herself before she got to the drop-off into to the sea. There was also the fact that she was traveling with someone at least as powerful as a demigod who didn't want to see anything happen to her—not that she had any idea what demigodhood meant in terms of quantitative power, any more than she had an idea of what godhood meant, but she expected it at least included a parachute—so she relaxed a bit and enjoyed the view. Even so, she was growing out of breath.

"How high up are we?" she huffed finally. "Air feels thin."

"Not very. What's wrong?"

She pondered whether or not to tell them and decided there was no point in hiding it. "Weaker. Been feeling that way for a while. Did the Fates say anything about the amulet doing something to me? It wasn't in the vision I got."

"No," Apollo answered. "As it's my first immortal resurrection, I regret I have no theory to offer you."

"Maybe we should stop for a rest?" Leif suggested.

"Great." Tracy shook her head. "And no. Let's just get there and get this over with before it gets worse. We're almost there, right?"

"Not far now."

Thalia cast an encouraging smile back at Tracy and then appeared to focus on something farther behind. Frowning, she stopped walking and shielded her eyes from the sun as she peered.

"Apollo? I think something's coming."

Everyone stopped except Tracy, who continued on the path past Thalia toward Apollo. No sense stopping now, she kept telling herself. Get to the temple. Do the ritual. Worry about the rest later.

"Should we be worried that she said '-thing'?" Leif asked from the rear.

"What is it?"

"I'm not sure . . ."

Curiosity and fatigue got the better of her. Tracy sighed and turned around to see a line of stirred-up dust making its rapid way toward them on the trail below. The dust obscured whatever caused it. Unless, she realized, whatever caused it was invisible.

"You can't tell?" she asked with a step back. "Don't you have some sort of . . . god-vision or whatever?"

"Yeah, flip it on!" Leif insisted. "God mode!"

"Diminished-god mode," Thalia corrected.

"Still better than nothing. What do your diminished eyes see?"

Apollo made them wait only a moment for an answer. "Get behind me. Now!" All right, so that wasn't really an answer. Regardless, they did as they were told.

"What is it?"

Apollo drew a sword from somewhere down the back of his shirt, which is a neat trick if you can do it. "No time to explain!"

The dust drew closer up the path. Closer. Closer. Somewhere in the world, someone important checked a clock.

Thalia began to hover. Her hands patted anxiously at her hips. "Um, clearly there's explainy-time here, Apollo!"

Anyone who's been paying attention has by this point guessed that the Orthlaelapsian wraith had found them (and more to the point, they'd be correct). Incorporeal muscles pounding, it bounded across the final stretch of trail between them, flinging snarls from both snapping jaws. It flung itself at Apollo, left head catching the swing of his sword in its teeth to clamp down on the flat of the blade before it could do any damage. Wraith or not, the beast sent Apollo tumbling backward as Tracy and the others scrambled out of their way.

Now that it was upon them, Tracy could at least make out something of its form: like Cerberus but only two-headed, sleeker, and half the other's size without seeming any weaker for it. She could discern only part of its shape at any one time, as if it were partially concealed in an invisibility cloak that was low on batteries. The fierce wrestling match it waged with Apollo wasn't exactly helpful either.

Just after it pounced, the wraith gave a howl that was cut short by Apollo's grip locking around its right neck. It enraged the creature instantly. For a moment it seemed to be all Apollo could do to hold on as he tried to choke the beast and keep it from achieving the apparent goal of either giving Apollo a kiss or chewing his face off. The two combatants rolled to the edge of the path, kicking up even more dust and forcing the spectators back farther as they tried to avoid being caught up in the melee. For a moment no one could speak, mesmerized at the sight.Tracy picked up a rock, ready to hurl it at one of the wraith's heads, unsure if it would do any good; the wraith remained darned near transparent. Of course, it had knocked Apollo down and wrestled him just fine, but she would risk actually hitting Apollo with the rock during the scuffle. He probably wouldn't like that (really, few people did)—but she couldn't just *stand* there.

Tracy raised the rock and looked for an opening. With the creature atop him, Apollo struggled to sit up and strained to force it back with the sword and his own muscle. The wraith's back arched, its jaws clenched tighter on Apollo's blade, and for a moment, its hindquarters made a visible target amid the struggle and smoke. Tracy seized the opportunity and—

Leif caught hold of the rock before she could throw. "You'll hit him!"

"Karlson! Let go!"

"No throwing into melee! It's a basic rule!"

"Karlson, damn it—"

Then Apollo let go of his blade, trading it for a free hand to pummel the wraith's left head as he clenched its neck. The assault was enough to stun the creature, if only for a moment. Apollo wasted no time. Rolling the wraith to its back as he got to his feet, keeping his grip strong, Apollo flung the wraith bodily from the path. It tumbled down the steep, rocky hillside of grass and wildflower tufts, unable to stop itself before it reached the edge, scrambled madly, and spilled down the sheer drop to the sea below and out of sight, still clenching Apollo's sword in its teeth. For a moment they stood waiting, as if it might somehow fly back up again.

It failed to do so. The only sound was Apollo's labored breath.

"What the hell was *that?*" Tracy shouted finally.

Thalia flew down to the edge of the drop-off to peer after it while Apollo dusted himself off. "Any sign of it?" he asked her.

The Muse shook her head, flying back. "I can't see anything."

Apollo frowned. "It'll be back. We must hurry." He put up a hand to stop Tracy's repeated question. "And that was the Orthlaelapsian wraith."

Thalia blinked. "What? No, that can't be! They wouldn't! I mean, points for sending something that could track you so well, but shouldn't it be guarding—? Apollo, are you sure? I mean, I've never actually gone to see it so I don't know exactly what it looks like and I don't really like antiques anyway so I'll take your word, but—you're certain?"

Tracy, for her part, couldn't help but wonder how many other insubstantial, two-headed hounds were running around to the extent that Thalia could doubt Apollo's identification of this one.

Apollo nodded. "Quite certain."

Thalia gaped, then laughed. "Well shave my head and paint me blue! I didn't think—Wow! Speechless. You've really got them worried!" She collapsed into giggling.

"*We've* got them worried," Apollo corrected. "And this is not funny."

She nodded, still giggling. "Sorry. Sorry. I'm sorry but laugh or cry, ya know? Oh, gods, if they're pissed enough to send that thing after you, we're all going down in a burning blaze, aren't we?"

"We've only to bring back Zeus, Thalia, and things will be set right. I hope."

"He hopes!" she giggled again. "Just had to add the last part, didn't you? Oh, *katratzi*, we're so screwed."

"They're going to tell us what's going on eventually, you think?" Leif whispered to Tracy.

"I sure hope—You're going to tell us what's going on eventually, right? Like now?" Her adrenaline was fading and her fatigue was returning, bringing with it the desire to get on with things before she was out of strength entirely. Even so, Tracy didn't like being kept in the dark, not even on a sunny mountainside overlooking the Mediterranean Sea.

"Yes, but as we go." Apollo pointed up the path. "And hurry. It will be back."

Far below, the wraith paddled its way through the surf toward shore. A small setback, but it didn't mind. This is not to indicate any particular positive attitude on the wraith's part, of course. After all, it was a wraith; it had no mind. (Were someone to grab it by the tail and vivisect it with a meat grinder, it wouldn't mind that either. It might wonder, *Why a meat grinder, exactly?* But would it mind? Goodness, no.) So when it reported via telepathic link to its master, Hades, of finding and temporarily losing Apollo, only to be told, as it swam, to reacquire its target but not to attack again, it didn't mind that either.

Besides, it was a good boy, yes it was! Hades said so. Being a dog (wraith or no), that was enough.

As the wraith gained the shore and began its dash back up the mountainside, Hades ruminated but a moment on his options before telling Hermes.

"The wraith has found Apollo. Approaching Zeus's temple in the Ionians."

"Ah, brilliant! It's holding him there?"

"Tracking only." A more loquacious god would have expressed his hesitance to risk the wraith further in combat, perhaps even his regret of retasking the creature in the first place, but Hades had a reputation to consider, and left it at that. "We five will deal with Apollo ourselves and inform the Dodekatheon once he is caught. Tell the others."

Hades resolved that he himself would not be implicated in Zeus's murder. Let Ares take that cup if he wished; it would choke him eventually. They would learn Apollo's full intentions and secure his silence before they turned him over to Poseidon. Once Apollo knew what would befall him should he go before the Dodekatheon without the conspirators' support, the sun god would cut a deal. If he did not, there were other methods of persuasion.

"How close is he to the temple?" Hermes asked.

"Close. Why?"

"We're bound from going in there, if you recall. The last remnant of Zeus's edict hasn't faded yet. Soon but not yet. I'd ask how *he* got in, but since we're still trying to figure out how he's avoided Poseidon, I'm guessing we don't know that either. We'll need to flush him out first."

Black death, the limey bastard's right. "I'll take care of that. You inform the others. Be ready."

Leif walked backward up the trail ahead of Tracy, likely the better to voice his interjections to Apollo's story as the god brought up the rear. "So if I get what you're saying, this wraith thing: it can't be bargained with, it can't be reasoned with, and it absolutely will not *stop* . . . until we are dead. Right?"

"Or captured," answered Apollo. "Depending. It may be tasked with either, and the—"

"Whatever. My point is why didn't they think to send this against us before?"

"You're complaining?" asked Tracy.

"Well, yeah! Stuff like that bugs me." Leif shrugged. "It has to be pointed out."

"You are not possessed of all the facts," Apollo explained. "The Orthlaelapsian wraith normally guards something important to those of us on Olympus; it has done so for millennia. That the wraith would be given another task—"

"How important are we talking, here?" Leif interrupted.

Apollo frowned and shook his head.

"The key to the Titans' prison," Thalia answered for him. "In a manner of speaking. What? Who're they going to tell?"

At once Jason's warning launched itself back to the forefront of Tracy's mind. "Out of curiosity, does that have anything at all to do with a place called Swin—"

Tracy rammed into some sort of unseen force field that flung her into a fit of cursing. Already past the apparent force field, Leif turned immediately.

"Geez, what happened? You okay?"

The fact that Leif walked back through the invisible whatever-it-was didn't help Tracy's attitude. Muffled by a protective hand over her battered nose, Tracy's cursing continued another few seconds before she managed a basic, "What the hell?"

Amid the impact's lingering sting, Tracy noticed they'd nearly reached the end of the path. They stood in a flat, open area festooned with grasses, rocks, and a single oak tree that grew in the shadow of the small peak above them. A carved stone overhang supported by two columns formed the mouth of a tunnel into the peak, and leading up to the tunnel were a few weatherworn stone steps. The steps continued inside such that their elevation prevented her from seeing too far beyond the entrance. Though the rock face immediately in front of them was steep, around the sides more gradual, crumbling paths wove their way up some eight feet to the top of the mountain.

Thalia moved up beside Tracy, and ran an experimental hand over the barrier field. (That Thalia used the same experimental hand as Tracy—which is to say, Tracy's right hand—was a small annoyance Tracy was too fatigued to bother with.) Whatever the barrier was, it appeared (insomuch as an invisible anything can appear) to cover the entrance to a cave. Despite Leif's ability to step back and forth over the threshold with impunity, neither Tracy nor Thalia nor Apollo could breach it.

"Some sort of force field," Apollo surmised.

"Then why doesn't it affect me?" Leif asked.

"You couldn't warn me about it before I smashed my face?"

"Quite obviously I didn't know about it." Apollo uncovered Tracy's nose and ran his hand above it. "Stop complaining. There. Healed."

"Thanks."

Glancing upward, Tracy spotted signs of more carved stone columns that seemed embedded in the natural rock itself, as if the mountain had grown up around the temple in some geological attempt to consume it entirely.

"How high up do you suppose it goes? Or maybe it doesn't go all the way around the peak? We might be able to go around the field, climb up, and come back down from above."

Thalia blew a strand of hair out of her face and shrugged. "Maybe. I'll see what I can find. Watch for wraiths!" With that, she sprang into the air and vanished out of sight around the top of the stonework.

"I thought only gods couldn't go in?" Tracy asked, feeling around for gaps in the field.

"Not within a quarter mile," Apollo answered. "We're already far within that radius." After a worried glance back down the path, he ran a hand over the barrier himself to follow Tracy's lead in the other direction. "This is something different. This is something . . . else."

"Profound," quipped Leif.

"Quiet, Mr. Karlson." Apollo continued to study the barrier. "I would theorize it was designed to keep anything supernatural out, in order to reinforce the idea long ago that we gods did not exist. Thalia and I are obviously barred, and Tracy has an immortal parent. I seem to recall Zeus experimenting with force fields like this around all the temples, as a kind of failsafe built into the Withdrawal. It's individually erected, rather than being an automatic byproduct of Zeus's law, so it won't completely dissolve the way the quarter-mile prohibition is about to. But nor will it be strong enough to keep out a full god once the prohibition dissolves. Even so, if we can find a way inside, it may buy us some time against the wraith or any others sent after us in the meantime. A blessing in disguise."

Tracy didn't figure it was any kind of blessing at all, just another layer in the whole bothersome and complex task of hiking up a freaking hill and into a temple to get things over with. Just her luck they picked the temple with some overly secure force field prototype. Why did everything have to be so damn difficult?

Leif walked over to the oak tree. "Maybe there's a hole in the field up there where the branches can reach? It's a long shot, but we could climb the tree and check. Not that Thalia won't be able—"

"Guardian-tree am not for climbings!"

The voice that interrupted Leif was swift, deep, and came right out of the tree. Tracy briefly considered the likelihood that the voice had come from a talking, baritone chipmunk or other such creature, before spotting the vague outline of a face in the bark. The face itself was as tall as she; she doubted she'd have noticed it at all were the lips not moving. The fact that it was talking helped too, of course.

"You not needing climbings anyway," it continued. "Guardian of temple can be lettings you in! I am being guardian of temple! Hello, things with legs!" Leaves waved to them gently.

Overwhelmed by the urge to glance nervously behind them, the impatient impulse to continue, and the new stimulus of a talking tree, Tracy remained speechless. Leif was unencumbered by such a problem.

"What are you, like an ent?" he asked, studying it.

"No, am guardian-tree of temple!" answered the tree—or the guardian, Tracy supposed. Or both, even. "You not be hearings before when I say so? What is ent?"

"Er, it's from a book," Leif explained.

"What is book?"

"You don't get out much, do you?"

"No, I always just be standings here. Is book anythings like rock over there?" The guardian-tree pointed with a few branches.

"No, it's—"

Tracy put a hand on Leif's shoulder in hopes it would be enough stop him, just in case he was about to mention the material that books were generally made from. The unexpected physical contact distracted him enough for the tree to continue.

"What about other rock over there?" the tree asked, perplexed. "Is book like that? Or like sky? Or like—what else is being in world? Other tree? Used to be other trees, but that long time ago.

"Oh!" it suddenly boomed. "Is book like lizard? Lots of lizards being here all the times. Not now, but . . ." The tree's leaves drooped slightly. "Missing the lizards. They is good to talk to. Not being saying much, but good at listenings. Is good skill for lizard to haves. Lizard also be having legs, can be goings other places, seeing other rocks. And other trees. And sky. Lizard never mention book, but lizard never mention much at alls, really, so is hard to being sure."

"Ah, we don't mean to be rude," Tracy tried, "but you mentioned something about letting us in the temple, yes?"

Apollo, having resumed his watch down the path, nodded his approval.

The tree didn't nod so much as shimmy its trunk in an up-and-down motion, but the meaning remained apparent. "Did mention. You is being good listener too! *Can* let you in, is able! But is not being supposed to. I sorry."

"Says who?" Leif asked.

The effect of her touch apparently having worn off, Tracy removed her hand.

"Says Zeus! He is puttings me here many many many many many . . ." It trailed off in thought before nodding again with satisfaction. "*Many* years ago, giving or taking. Picks me up as acorn, holdings me in his palm, and then there is all this lightings and flashings and then I be having thoughts! . . . Not know why I am rememberings what happens before I be having thoughts. Is big mystery but is fun to thinking on too. You is *good* listeners!" it said. "Excepting for him. Why he is keeping looking down path? Is looking for more rocks? Plenty of rocks being here already. And grass. No lizards now, but we covers that before."

In fact, it wasn't so much that they were good listeners as it was that the they had failed in their numerous attempts at interrupting the tree's rapid yammering.

"Trees are supposed to talk slowly," Leif protested.

"I not be knowings other trees talk at all. I be thinkings I am special. I am being *oak* tree! Zeus is being likings oak trees, you knows."

"Zeus *liked* oak trees, actually," Tracy corrected, seeing a way to possibly get back on track. "Past tense."

"Ah, I is having troubles with tenses sometimes. Lizards is usually polite enough not to mind."

"No, she means Zeus is dead," Leif added.

The tree gasped and rocked back as incredulously as a tree can manage. "You is being speaking non-sense! Zeus is being a god, you knows! A god cannot die! Though that would being an explanation for why Zeus is not coming by to make visits in past thousand years or so. Guardian-tree just be thinkings he not liking me."

Tracy shook her head. "He was murdered nine months ago, which is actually why we—"

"The wraith is back!" Apollo announced, pointing to what looked to Tracy like an empty patch of path fifty yards away. He pulled both bow and quiver from somewhere down the back of his shirt, which is a doubly neat trick if, again, you can do it. An arrow was nocked and sighted down in a flash, though he did not release it. "It waits and watches only, but we must hurry!"

Save for a quick glance, the tree ignored this new development. "Zeus is only dying nine months ago? So I guessings that makes him jerk for avoidings me for so long before then. But I still have to be obeying what he is telling me to do: no one going into the temple until he say so otherwise. What is wraith? Is wraith anythings like rock over there?"

Tracy moved closer, putting the tree between her and the wraith just to be safe (easier said than done when she couldn't actually see the mostly-invisible creature at such a distance herself). "Tree," she began, immediately disliking the moniker, "er—do you have a name?"

"I am being called guardian-tree!" it declared. "I be thinking that is good enough."

Good, Tracy, nice waste of time there. "Guardian-tree, we're here to resurrect Zeus. We can't do that if we don't get inside. Don't you think he'd want you to do that for us?"

"Resurrectings? Not be knowing you can do that—but then not be knowings Zeus can be killed too. You is being sure you can do that? Maybe you just is confuseled?"

"We can!" Apollo called over his shoulder. "I am Apollo, god of healing, of music, of archery, poetry, and prophecy, and I swear that what she says is true." His attention turned back forward before he muttered, "At least I was."

Tracy nodded quickly. "I'm sure once Zeus is back, he can tell you that it's safe to let us in. In fact, I'm certain of it." She wasn't certain of it, but priorities are priorities.

"And he regretted not visiting you more often!" Leif added. "He told us! It's just that he was so busy with all the ruling and the lightning and—"

"Oooh, *lightenings!*" the tree shouted. "I can be doing lightenings. To be helping with the guardianing Zeus is teaching me how—or giving me the how. I knot really be knowings. Knot be knowings. (That tree joke!)"

Tracy balled her fists, fighting frustration. "We don't really have time—"

"You be watching now!"

At once the tree's leaves crackled and Tracy smelled ozone. Electricity flared across the tree's bark, and a bolt of lightning flashed out to a rocky outcropping a short distance down the path, blasting it to pieces. The shock alone (that lightning joke!) was enough to stand Tracy's hair on end. Or maybe that was the static.

"Seeings? Guardian-tree can shoot lightenings! Zeus is once telling me that quite the turnaround, though I not being knowing what he means. Just know lightenings good for guardianing."

Apollo backpedaled closer to the tree, bow still trained on the wraith in the distance. "Can you do that again?" he asked. "Can you see the wraith down there, hold it off with the lightning?"

"Yes, I can beings doing that. Though I have to wait for charge-up again. It not taking long. You wait half a day?"

"We don't have half a day!" Leif protested.

"Listen," tried Apollo, "the wraith isn't attacking. That means it's likely notified Zeus's enemies and been ordered to stand down. As soon as they figure out that they can't get near yet, something else is going to show up here. Tell us how to get inside!"

"I have to be turning off the shield for you to be gettings inside," it told them. "But as I be tellings you, Zeus said not to do that for anyone until he say so. Oh, hello agains, pretty flying woman!"

Thalia had returned just then, ceasing her quizzical look at the tree for only a moment to shake her head. Her search for holes in the force field had been fruitless.

Tracy barely kept her exasperation hidden. Her hands pressed against the barrier before she could stop herself. It was a compulsion akin to what she felt when she first picked up the amulet, but being aware of the attraction made it no easier to resist.

"Zeus created you," she tried. "You have to let us in; you have to let us save him! He only told you not to let anyone in because he wanted the gods and everyone to withdraw, but they're back now! They're out there, working publicly, building new temples and speaking on TV!"

"What is TV? Is TV anything like rock over—?"

"Please, just help us!" Tracy cried. Her heart pounding, her knees weak, she was growing crankier by the moment, taunted by the fact that their objective was so damned close and yet just out of reach. The urgency was building in her. The amulet itself felt like a beating heart on her chest. "I am Zeus's daughter, and I demand you let us in!"

"Oh! Why you is not being saying so? That allowed. Part of exception-clausings, I be thinking. Not know what 'exception' means, but is being o-kay."

Thalia's hands were on her hips. "You know, I was going to mention that, but I thought, 'No, Thalia, just this once, let them deal with it. Surely they already thought of that approach before you got back anyway, and it didn't work! Just keep quiet. Don't clutter the place with your beautiful voice!' First instincts, I should always trust them. It just goes to show."

No one responded. The tree, meanwhile, stretched a branch into a hollow between two boughs and pulled out a square marble block the size of an orange (not to mention that rock over there). Miniscule geometric carvings adorned one side, like a key. With little ceremony, the tree pushed the block into an indentation carved in a boulder standing outside the barrier field, turned it once, and pulled it away. A hum Tracy hadn't noticed before suddenly ceased. The feel of the barrier vanished beneath her hands.

"There we is going! You can be using your legs to walkings in now, Zeus's daughter!"

Tracy dashed into the entrance, gasping out a breath she hadn't realized she was holding. She paused long enough to make sure the others were coming and, after yelling a thank-you to the tree, made for the heart of the temple. There was a light ahead.

"Any others who may come are enemies of Zeus, no matter their relation," she could hear Apollo telling the tree behind her. "Do not reopen the barrier for anyone but us."

"I am knowings this. Why is tellings guardian-tree how to be doing its job? You is god of bossings around now that Zeus is killed or somethings?"

Tracy didn't hear Apollo's reply. On wavering legs, she continued toward the resurrection of a god, anxious for the final ritual, spurred forward by forces she didn't understand and noting with some dismay that she'd still not gotten that sundae.

CHAPTER THIRTY-TWO

"One constant in life is that nothing worth doing is ever easy. It would be trivial for the gods to change this; however, as the reverse of this adage must also be true (i.e., nothing easy is ever worth doing), they've decided it's not worth it."

—*Olympian Priesthood in Thirty Days!*
(*Day 1: Know Your Place, Mortal*)

DESPITE THE COMPLETE LACK of upkeep, it was an admirable temple. The wall carvings were eroded, the paint was long faded, and the place possessed a distinct emptiness, but its location within the mountaintop lent it an aura of mystical majesty. Though there were no torches to provide any sort of compelling firelight, sunlight shone down from the wide hole in the rock above with a power of its own. It highlighted the floating dust motes, illuminated the white marble altar in the center of the room, and deepened the shadows along the edges of the temple it could not reach.

The power of the place, faint but surely present, tingled on Tracy's skin as she made her way to the altar. Her feet moved of their own accord. This was less unsettling than it might have been, were she not of a mind to go where her feet led anyway. She said nothing, silenced by her own anticipation.

Leif was the first to break the silence. "The force field goes all the way up above, does it?"

"It doesn't cover the entire mountaintop, but it does wrap the portion that houses the temple, which of course means that skylight, yes," Thalia answered. "And thank you for doubting that I did a thorough job of checking."

"Not doubting, just doing a thorough job of asking."

Tracy continued her own thorough job of staying quiet as she climbed the couple of steps around the altar dais. *Well. This is it. Been a very odd week.* Her fingertips traced the altar's edge as she admired the lightning bolts and Greek lettering etched across it on all sides. The marble was cool, and though she supposed she ought to have expected that, it surprised her nonetheless. The amulet grew warmer, however, and soon bathed the marble in a soft purple glow.

"So what now?" she asked Apollo.

"Place the amulet upon the altar." Apollo, with millennia of experience in such matters, knew to make the distinction between placing an object *on* an altar, and placing it *upon* said altar. Though the practical result is the same either way, the latter sounds much more impressive.

Tracy did so. Even after her fingertips lay the amulet (up)on the marble and then let it go, the tingling sensation remained. She could sense an aura, felt more than seen, connecting her to the amulet regardless of physical contact. It swelled to envelop the altar as well.

"And then there was something I have to say, right?"

"You must speak some words of power." Apollo recited the preternatural phrasing of the required words and then repeated them more slowly for her to mimic. The words were in no language she recognized, though she was hardly a linguist. "It's Olympian," he explained in response to her unspoken question. "Try turning your tongue to one side. It helps." He repeated the words again.

"What's that mean in English?" Leif whispered.

"Literally translated?" answered Thalia. "It means 'some words of power.'" She sighed. "Yes, I know."

"Huh. '*Cthulhu fhtagn*' has more kick to it."

"Oh, you don't want to know what that really means either, I assure you."

"I thought that stuff wasn't real?"

"Yes, but—"

Tracy cleared her throat at the two kibitzers. They quieted, for the moment, and Apollo repeated the words for her once more. With a nod, she took a deep breath, closed her eyes, and took the plunge.

"Wijhr üairîe nah'c ûl'lá."

Nothing occurred. Or almost nothing: Leif's foot shifted against the ground, and a seagull gave a cry somewhere outside, but she figured those things had nothing to do with the ritual. Wait, did Zeus like seagulls? Tracy considered that maybe she just wasn't able to tell if the ritual had worked. Yet if she was going to resurrect a *god,* surely she ought to feel something, right?

"Is that it?" she asked.

Apollo frowned. "Nothing happened."

"Noticed that too, then."

"Maybe we have to wait for it to kick in?" Leif offered. "More dramatic that way?"

"No," Apollo told them. "It ought to have been immediate. Something's wrong."

"Maybe this isn't a temple of Zeus after all?" Leif tried. "You know, aside from the lightning imagery and the talking tree out front who said so."

"Don't forget the writing declaring this a temple to King Zeus," Thalia added with a sad pat on his shoulder. "You're grasping at straws, honey."

"It might be a trick!"

"It's not a trick," Apollo said. "Trust me. Though Zeus's death lessened the temple's power, I still sense it."

Tracy nodded. "He's right. I can feel—" A passing thought wandered out of Tracy's head and clocked her in the face. "Uh-oh. Oh, *damn it.*"

"Really shouldn't say that kind of thing in a temple," Thalia warned. "Especially while standing at the altar."

Tracy ignored her and turned to Apollo. "You're diminished."

Apollo winced like a man with a burgeoning compulsion to buy a ridiculously expensive car. "Of this I am aware."

"I got the quest through *your* oracle!" she explained. "She gains her power through you, isn't that how it works? So whatever quest she gave me, it wouldn't be enough! Is that it?"

"Oh, *damn it,*" Apollo agreed.

Thalia glared.

"Then there's no choice!" Leif said. "You have to seduce me."

"No!"

"Hey, I'm not exactly thrilled either, you know! There's hardly the time or comfort or privacy I'd have hoped for, but—Hey, can you two go outside?"

"There's another way!" Tracy shot.

"You mean spill your blood all over the altar? Are you freaking *nuts?*" He rushed to Apollo. "Tell me you can heal her after! You can do that, right?"

Apollo shook his head. "The amount of blood required would kill her. As with Jason, I cannot heal death."

"I'm sure Apollo could at least conjure up another tent," Thalia offered, not without hesitation.

"No!"

"And as I told you before, Leif isn't heroic enough for our purposes," Apollo reminded.

"I *beat* Dionysus in cards! Come *on!* She's already done her Cerberus thing, that's got to be enough to put her over the edge!"

"Leif—" Tracy tried.

"No! You keep acting like this is just about me getting to sleep with you, but for crying out loud, you're talking about killing yourself! Geez, if you're not worried about your *life* at least worry about giving me a hell of a complex!"

Tracy began to speak when Apollo cut her off with a raised hand. It was the sort of gesture that would have annoyed her had she any idea of something to say.

"Trust me, the both of you, when I say—"

Apollo himself was cut off by a bellowing rush of words from outside. *"No! Guardian-tree is not being letting flying uglies into temple!"*

"The guardian-tree!" Thalia announced so unnecessarily that it's a wonder the line itself wasn't edited out of this book before publication.

Leif shot Tracy a desperate look. "We're out of time!"

"It won't let them in."

The tree's voice lowered yet continued to filter in from outside. "Is chainsaw like rock over—?"

The rest was drowned out by the rev of a gasoline engine.

"Leif! Thalia!" Apollo pointed at them both. "Hold them off!" Joint protests erupted, but Apollo spoke over them. "Do as I say, or all of this is for nothing! Go now!"

Diminished or not, it seemed he could still be commanding when he wanted. Though it pleased neither, they nodded and made for the exit. Leif got as far as two steps away before he turned, rushed for

Tracy, and planted a kiss on her before she could stop him. Hurried and off target, he nevertheless stunned her to inaction until he broke the kiss and stepped back. A flustered, speechless look showed on his face before he turned and ran toward the sound of a chainsaw carving through a tree that could scream.

They'd vanished up the exit tunnel before Tracy regained her wits. Her heart pounded. Her mind raced for alternatives and found none. The option to run barely registered. Even were she not bound and determined to help her murdered father, the amulet had completely stolen the strength from her legs. Her arms, however, remained strong. She pointed to Apollo, fixing him with as firm a gaze as she could manage.

"I'm not going to sleep with you."

"I know. Though, would it be so bad?"

"Not the point."

"The sacrifice, then."

Thalia and Leif crouched midway up the tunnel from the temple, hidden from those outside. Though the voices were indistinct and spoke over each other like caffeinated six-year-olds, it was obvious to whom they belonged.

"Erinyes," Thalia whispered.

Leif groaned. They'd already killed Jason. What the heck could he do against them? The only thing he liked less than death was the thought of living the rest of his life without Tracy. The need to buy time for her so she could find a way to get through the ritual alive was all that kept him hiding behind the nearest rock. "Okay, so . . . here's the plan. We hold them here in this tunnel. It's narrow; it'll help us hold them off. Tactical advantage. We can do this, right?"

"Golly, let me think! Um, no! They're fury on wings; we're mice with toothpicks!"

"The tunnel's narrow! They can only come at us one at a time!" Leif's courage flared as he tried to rally the Muse. "This is our best shot!" His heart pounded. "This is our only shot!" His adrenaline spiked further as the realization that he was currently in Greece propelled him into a glorious culmination of, "This! Is! *Spart—*"

322 MICHAEL G. MUNZ

Thalia decked him right in the face before he could finish, grabbed him by the collar, and yanked him close to whisper. "First of all, we're nowhere *near* Sparta, and second of all, just *no!* And anyway I'm a Muse, not a fighter!"

"You just punched me in the face!"

"You're not a vicious, taloned vengeance-machine with blood gushing out your eyes, and anyway it had to be done! Maybe if *they* make some annoyingly clichéd reference I might be motivated to deck one of them too, but—"

The Erinyes' enraged shrieks cut through the air. Leif and Thalia reflexively pressed back against the wall as the voices carried in from outside.

"You see! The barrier's not fading, you spastic bitch! You killed it too soon!"

"Killing the guardian ought to have brought it down! That is how these things work!"

"Clearly not!"

"Then it should be! And you try being patient when wielding a chainsaw!"

The argument again turned chaotic and impossible to make out. Leif didn't bother to try. "They haven't found that key! Hurry!" He grabbed Thalia's hand and rushed for the exit. He was forming a plan, but he needed to get a look at things before he could be sure.

"This is foolish!" she cried, following him. "Foolish, foolish, foolish! Why did Apollo send *me?*"

"Stop whining! At least you're immortal!"

"That doesn't mean I don't feel pain and—"

They rushed out into the light and stopped short at the sight of all three Erinyes hovered above the guardian-tree's stump. The rest of the unfortunate being lay ten yards down the slope, its bark raked with talon marks, eyes shut, and mouth frozen in a silent yell.

Thalia removed the hand she'd clapped over her mouth, composing herself with a remarkable resilience to address the Erinyes. "Alecto, Megaera, Tisiphone. Whatever brings you here? Are you lost?"

"Musey!" cackled Megaera. "We've come for Apollo!"

"And anyone else in there!" Alecto added. She still held the idling chainsaw.

"Send him to us, and we'll spare you a world of torment!" Megaera continued.

"A cosmos of torment!" Tisiphone added.

"Torment-torment-torment!" Alecto cried.

Leif wondered if he was included in that offer, but the sight of Tisiphone skinning him alive with her eyes was not encouraging, and it wouldn't help Tracy anyway. In a flash he scanned the area. The barrier key was nowhere to be seen, so he hoped that meant it was still inside the tree itself. Trusting on the barrier to keep him safe, he turned his back on the Erinyes and tugged Thalia back into the tunnel mouth.

"We'll go get him!" he called over his shoulder.

"Hey!" called Megaera. "We were talking to her! Double-vengeance for rudeness!"

At this Alecto cackled maniacally, which is probably redundant, but there it is.

"Is this barrier a one-way thing like the one at the Styx exit?" he whispered. "Can you fly out while it's still up?"

Thalia gave a quick nod. "Yes. Or maybe. Just possibly maybe. I don't really know. I mean, I ought to know; you get a lot of barriers and force fields and the like in sci-fi, but there's really a broad variety and—"

"Is it likely?"

Thalia nodded again.

"So, new idea: you fly out and draw them away for a second or something. I'll grab the key when their backs are turned and run back behind the barrier. Problem solved!"

"Leaving me outside! What am I supposed to do then, did you think of that? I'm far too pretty to be rent and torn, and chainsaws are *very* bad for me. I have combination skin!"

The Erinyes continued their hovering, shrieking jeers at them and hurling rocks against the barrier (which—for some reason perhaps best left to philosophers—deflected the rocks despite their being utterly mundane). Tisiphone drifted back to break a branch off the felled tree, getting dangerously close to the key's hiding spot.

"Just—just do it, please?" Leif couldn't think of a better argument, adding somewhat lamely, "For Zeus? Before they find it! Just chuck a few insults at them, fly off faster than they can and escape!"

Thalia growled in frustration. "Calypso would call this all very heroic and I wish to the Fates she were here instead because this is the dumbest thing I've done since *Time Moronz!*"

She peeked around Leif at the Erinyes, who'd formed a midair huddle of their own. Their discussion was impossible to make out over Alecto's increasingly fanatical chainsaw-revving. Thalia ducked back with a tortured whine.

"Seven hundred years avoiding those virulent bitches and now I'm tangling with them twice in a few days? What has become of my life? I'm an *artist!*"

Leif punctuated his get-on-with-it gestures with a rapid nod. "There, angst! You're still an artist. Can we do this please before I lose *my* nerve?"

"Art doesn't have to be angsty!" she shot. "Oh gods, 'angsty'? That's not even a word! That's not even a *word!* Oh, stop looking at me like that, I'm going, I'm going! I'm older than you, you know!"

With that, Thalia stepped into view and grabbed a rock.

"Hey!" she yelled. "Alecto! A newborn puppy's more intimidating than you, you vacillating bunny-cuddler!"

Thalia hurled the rock in a direction that could only be generously described as "toward" the vacillating bunny-cuddler in question. Fortunately Erinyes take offense the way fish take to water. Before the rock could travel half a stone's throw, Alecto pointed her chainsaw and dived at the Muse with a shriek that became a wail upon her near-instant impact with the barrier. The chainsaw flew from her talons, careened through the air between her two sisters, and smashed apart on the side of a boulder.

"There, that's a little better," Thalia muttered. "Time to work blue." She launched herself straight up through the barrier, flipped off the Erinyes with both hands in an ascending pirouette, then made a beeline for that mythical place known as "the frog's balls away from there."

Even hidden as he was in a cleft of the rock, Leif knew the Erinyes took the bait from the way their shrieks faded into the distance. He gave Thalia a three-count to draw them away, gulped down a mouthful of fear, and bolted out of the tunnel. He passed through the barrier without trouble, and a dozen more hurried strides took him down the path to hunch over the poor guardian-tree and stick his hand in its knot.

"Please still have the key, please still have the key, please still have the—" It was then that he heard the voice behind him.

"So, Leifferson, we meet again."

"The sacrifice must be done with an appropriate dagger," Apollo told Tracy.

She swallowed, steadying herself against an onslaught of thoughts: a mix of self-preservation; self-sacrifice; and a last-minute, fruitless scramble for alternatives. And, of course, the unresolved sundae issue.

"Okay," she said finally. "Give it here."

Apollo looked uncomfortable. "I, ah, didn't bring one."

"You didn't bring—? Why not?"

"You performed your quest," he grumbled. "It followed that we wouldn't need it."

"Yeah, but—can't you pull one out of wherever you got the sword and the bow? And the tents? And—"

"It doesn't work that way. Such daggers are special, and—"

"It doesn't *work that way?*"

"They must be specially consecrated and can't be pulled out of thin air! And they've a lot of points and sharp edges that makes them a pain to carry concealed! If you are to repeat everything I say—" The god cut himself short, taking a breath. "This is a temple. There is likely to be something suitable lying about somewhere. We shall make a search. But hurry."

"Oh, gosh: hurry. Right. I didn't think of that."

She turned from the altar and rushed as much as she could on leaden legs. Why did everything have to be so damn *difficult?*

His arm still buried in the knot, Leif twisted around and nearly wrenched his shoulder off. Standing nearby, almost as an afterthought, was one Thad Freaking Winslow. Clever words failed to find their way to Leif's lips. All he managed to stall with was, "Er, hi. You're here too, then?"

"Shut up, geek, I don't want to talk to you. Just tell me how to get in the temple so I can get the hell back to civilization. What's this about a key?"

Leif didn't quit the search, but the knot seemed larger inside than out, and there was still no sign of the key. Smart-assed stalling tactics, however, began to flow more freely.

"How am I supposed to tell you anything if you want me to shut up?" Leif's fingertips brushed something squishy, something moving, something green (he had no idea how he knew that), and finally something very square, stony, and keylike. He grinned.

"Don't get cute. Just tell me or I call back the screechers. And give me the redhead's number." Thad loomed closer. If he wanted to, he could have stepped on Leif's back from that distance to hold him there. Fortunately he either didn't want to or hadn't thought of it yet. "The key's in there? Come on, out with it!"

Thad grabbed for his arm just as Leif stumbled back out of reach, key in hand. His heel struck the ground at a bad angle and momentum sent him flat on his ass.

"That's what we need, isn't it? Give it, now!" Thad demanded before yelling over his shoulder, "He's got a key!"

Leif raised an arm as if to hurl the key at the model's face. "You want it? Catch!" He threw as hard as he could without letting go.

It felt remarkably similar to baiting a dog with a falsely thrown tennis ball. As Thad threw his arms up to protect himself, Leif seized the opportunity to scramble back to his feet. Thad narrowly caught and then lost the back of Leif's shirt as he bolted past. A surge of elation carried Leif the final distance to the barrier.

"I love it when a plan comes togeth—"

The barrier field struck Leif like a swung trampoline, hurling him backward violently. Thad broke his fall in a collision that sent them both to the ground. In the few seconds before he could push off of Thad and regain his feet, two things crossed Leif's mind: the barrier wouldn't let the key past, and his perfectly excellent plan was now shot to bits.

Now his only instinct was to escape and get the key as far away from the lock as possible before Thad could grab him. On his feet again, Leif dodged around Thad again and made his way downhill. Before he managed even a thought about what to do next, Megaera exploded into bloody existence smack in the middle of his path.

Fright alone saved him. Leif's body twisted in pure shock. He spun onto an alternate course at a right angle to his previous one, around a bit of rock, and back up the slope as Thad again gave chase. Leif was rushing up one of the steep, narrow paths along the side of the mountaintop before he knew what he was doing. Nothing stopped him; no barrier field sent him flying back again. Deciding he was far enough away from the tunnel to skirt the field entirely, he redoubled his pace, kicking dust and pebbles back at Thad and the Erinys, who were surely only moments behind him.

"He's got the thing!" Thad yelled. "The thing that does the stuff with the thing!"

The speed with which Apollo searched for a dagger made Tracy feel like she was standing still. He rushed along the temple edges and found hidden compartments in the walls; he uncovered loose flagstones on the floor and searched their depths for anything useful; he moved with an urgent sense of purpose. Most of Tracy's effort involved putting one foot in front of the other, to the point where she figured it'd likely be just as useful for her to wait by the altar. But she couldn't bring herself to do that. After all, she'd already figured out the reason the quest didn't work, a reason Apollo himself missed. Who was to say she wouldn't again see something he didn't?

Tracy spotted a promisingly cracked wall Apollo hadn't yet noticed. One step at a time, she made her way toward it. As she continued to brainstorm alternatives to what she was about to do, her thoughts far outraced her stride. Neither got her anywhere fast.

"Is there any particular reason for the sacrifice?" she tried. "Or is it just 'cause the Fates said so?"

"A release of mystical energy is needed to finalize the ritual and allow the amulet to do its thing. To trigger that release, the offspring of Zeus must give a sacrifice of lifeblood, I was told. For what it's worth, I am sorry none of us thought of the oracle problem earlier. Father Zeus will elevate you highly when this is completed."

"He can bring me back to life?"

"No, but he will likely rearrange some stars to set your visage in the heavens."

MICHAEL G. MUNZ

Fat lot of good that did her. She'd seen the Perseus constellation; it looked like a freaking bent-over Y.

"Aha!" Apollo cried. He drew a box from a compartment in the base of a pillar, pulled away the crumbling top and withdrew a stylized, wicked-looking dagger. "A little worn, but still sharp."

Tracy broke through her own chosen compartment just for the heck of it. She startled the heck out of a mouse living within but found nothing else of value. She turned and took a few steps back to the altar before Apollo scooped her up and carried her the rest of the way. He set Tracy down on the top step, moved to the other side, and handed her the dagger.

"The blood must be spilled upon the altar."

"Yeah, I know. Every drop?"

He gave an apologetic smile. "Not every drop you have," he answered, "but enough that it would kill you."

"That'd be the 'lifeblood' thing." Not realizing the ritual required a specific quantity of blood, she'd actually been asking how much needed to hit the altar rather than how much she needed to spill.

"Right."

"Got it." She gripped the dagger tighter, struggling internally. At least her arms were still strong.

Leif neared the top of the rise, giddy and confused with amazement at Megaera's failure to seize him by his shoulders and hurl him down the mountainside. In fact, he seemed to have lost Megaera entirely and wished he knew just how he'd done that so he could be more impressed with himself. (In truth, Megaera remained below at the tunnel mouth, guarding it for a time until she was sure Leif wouldn't double back, unaware he could no longer pass through it himself. Erinyes are not brilliant, but they get plenty of practice chasing flightless quarry, so they know to cover their bases.) Thad, however, was still on his heels, and Leif was rapidly running out of mountaintop.

"Thalia!" It was a yell borne out of desperation. "Help!"

Only then did he seize upon another idea. Not only would it give his cowardly cry a purpose, but it might even prove helpful. A squarish, key-sized rock lay ahead. Leif spun around to kick dust into Thad's eyes below (even more satisfying when done intentionally), and then turned back to grab the rock. The blinded model cursed, tripped on the uneven ground, and conked himself to unconscious irrelevancy.

"Thalia!" Leif yelled again. He stuffed the real key into the inner pocket of his jacket, casting about for any sign of her.

"This is a *repugnant plan!*" Thalia screamed. She flew straight for him with Alecto and Tisiphone in her wake. Though faster, Thalia seemed unable to shake them. At the same time, Megaera exploded into being about twenty yards to his left.

Leif held the fake key aloft for everyone to see (or everyone still conscious without two eyefuls of dust, at least). "I got the key!" he yelled. "Catch!"

Thalia's eyes all but bugged out of her skull. "*What?* Don't give it to—*Monkey-cusser!*" The curse was barely from her lips when the false key sailed up toward her in a perfectly thrown arc (as far as Leif was concerned). The Muse caught it in mid-flight and redoubled her speed to streak out toward the Mediterranean. "This is a *worse plan!*"

"That's the key!" Leif managed to lie.

Though Tisiphone sped after the Muse, to Leif's horror Alecto halted in midair, her blood-gushing eyes fixed on him. "Meddling mortal! For this you shall pay!" she shrieked. "Pay! Pay! Pay! *Pay!*"

Megaera clocked her sister in the back of the head. "The Muse has the key! The key is important! After her!" Without waiting for a response, Megaera vanished in a bloody mess and reappeared right in Thalia's path. The latter swerved to the right and went invisible.

Even were Leif able to track an invisible Muse, Alecto gave him no time. She dived at Leif, talons slashing in an arc he narrowly ducked. "Pay!" she cackled. "Pay-pay-pay!"

"Listen to Megaera!" he tried, dashing across the mountaintop. "You're going to get in trouble!" And if that had any chance of working, thought Leif, he was a dragon-god.

Leif was, as it turned out, not a dragon-god. (Though that would have been wildly helpful, this book isn't going to pull that particular kind of crap.)

"Let the others chase after the Musey, mortal! You are mine! You will suffer! You will pay! Pay-pay-pay!" Alecto flung a stone across the back of Leif's thigh that cut him through his jeans. He stumbled, caught himself, and scrambled on against the pain.

"Anyone ever tell you you've got a real impulse-control problem?" he yelled.

In the temple, compulsion and duty rooted Tracy's legs to the altar dais. Her pulse pounded in her ears as the amulet glowed brighter (up)on the altar in what she could only assume was anticipation. The dagger shook in her grip, her muscles spasming with every moment she clutched it.

A part of her knew her rage at Zeus's murder was artificial, that the amulet itself compelled her. Even so, she couldn't bring herself to mind. Regardless of everything else, he was still her father, the father she'd been robbed of a chance to know. If her mother were murdered, would she not do everything in her power to bring her killers to justice?

Was this any different?

Above, Leif was trapped. To his left was the rim of the open roof of the temple, easily a fifty-foot drop to the stone below where Tracy stood; to his right lay another drop of much greater distance to ocean-battered rocks that no one could possibly survive. At his back stood a wall of rock, which, while scalable, would allow him only a sixty-foot drop to the temple floor or a greater-distance-plus-ten–foot plunge to certain death.

This, Leif judged, was unhelpful.

A small boulder shattered against the wall above him as if thrown by a giant wrestling personality-turned-actor. Biting shards of rock rained down on him. Alecto picked up another, cackling in a way that Leif thought might be infectious were he not about to die. "Pay!" she jeered again, clearly toying with him. "Pay-pay-pay-pay!"

Leif was running out of options the way Alecto was running out of vocabulary. He had no idea where Thalia was. Thad remained unconscious behind Alecto and gave zero indication of any impending change of allegiance, in any case. Leif could think of nothing clever to say, nor any semblance of a plan that could possibly save him. Below, Tracy stood with Apollo at the altar, dagger in hand. Leif felt a stab through his own heart at the sight of it. She was really going to do it!

"I am going to beat you senseless, mortal!" Alecto hissed. "Claw you until you pass out from the pain and skin you upside down like a hog when you wake! And then I'll do it all again somehow! This job allows for marvelous innovation!"

Leif took small comfort in knowing he still had the key. Yet they'd find it on his dead corpse sooner or later, and who knew how long the rest of the ritual would take to fulfill itself once Tracy made her sacrifice? What if the Erinyes got inside and stopped it before it all could take effect? Could they do that? Wasn't there some sort of common decency involved?

Leif cursed himself for not throwing the real key to Thalia. At least then he might be able to jump down through the barrier. If this were any sort of role-playing game, he'd likely survive the, what, five six-sided dice's worth of damage? Yet this wasn't a game, this was—

At once he knew what he had to do. The idea sucked, but it was all he had.

Alecto lost patience and threw another stone. It knocked off a chunk of wall that landed with a thud beside him. Leif's blood raced. There was no turning back. Before he took action, Leif risked a moment to add a flourish that he hoped might be impossibly cool.

"There's one thing you didn't think of, Alecto!" he yelled. "I am a leaf on the wind! Watch how I soar!"

Leif figured it would have been cooler if Alecto had responded before he said the last part, but the adrenaline hadn't let him wait. In what he desperately hoped was a fit of genre-savvy heroic sacrifice, Leif clutched the key through his coat and hurled himself off the cliff to the sea below.

The fall took long enough for him to think of at least three other outstanding choices for last words that he could have screamed before he jumped—and that he might have swapped "leaf" for "Leif"—but of course it was too late for that.

He doubted Alecto got the reference anyway.

Apollo glanced skyward toward Leif's voice and some sort of screeching.

"We have no time," he said.

She nodded. "I've never done this before. How far do I need to lean over?"

Apollo's crystal-blue eyes swelled with sympathy. "Slump over so the blood spills on the marble. Like this." He leaned across the altar and gripped the opposite edge in demonstration of the ideal posture.

"Okay, okay." She swallowed. Now was the time, she told herself. Now or never. It all came down to this. Here she stood at the crossroads. Time to pay the piper. It was a far better thing she did than she'd ever done.

Tracy ran out of clichés with which to stall. She raised the knife, leaned forward, and at that moment her plan changed. Suicide was senseless, especially with the other option staring her right in the face. Tracy hated to do it, but the only alternative was worse.

Tracy smiled across the altar to clasp Apollo's gaze with hers, steeling herself. "Does a woman get a kiss before she makes the ultimate sacrifice?"

Apollo blinked and leaned farther forward to oblige. Tracy followed suit. Her breath came rapid and short as she prepared to do a god right (up)on the altar. Apollo's eyes closed. His lips drew nearer.

His neck stretched vulnerably as he leaned over.

Tracy slashed the dagger across Apollo's jugular. She threw her arms over his head and lifted her feet off the dais to hold him over the altar with all her weight as blood gushed from the wound.

"I'm sorry!"

CHAPTER THIRTY-THREE

"Mortals are like matches: fun to play with but dangerous."
—Olympian saying, source unknown

IN HINDSIGHT, it surprised Tracy that it had taken so long for her to remember that Apollo was just as much a child of Zeus as she. From what he had stated, the Fates said nothing about the ritual requiring *her* blood specifically. It was a bit of a leap to guess that "lifeblood" referred to a set quantity that would kill an ordinary mortal, rather than the actual loss of life of the subject—but standing before an altar about to commit suicide does tend to open the mind to possibilities.

Tracy sincerely hoped she was right and that Zeus's resurrection would kick in before Apollo bled out. It hadn't even crossed her mind that she might be able to kill Apollo at all, even in his diminished state. That initially miniscule worry grew stronger and more gut wrenching with each passing second. He was still immortal, wasn't he? He said so, right?

Bitch move, Tracy.

"I'm sorry," she yelled again. "Please hold still!"

Apollo wasn't struggling; that much she had to be thankful for. Yet save for his blood rushing over the marble, nothing was happening. For a few terrible moments, she thought she'd been wrong, that she'd have to spill her own blood to finish things up, that she may have actually done permanent damage to Apollo, or that there wouldn't even be time to—

The altar exploded with light. It shone up through the blood and consumed the scarlet flood in a blaze of lightning that flashed in time with the amulet's gemstone. Its rhythm matched Tracy's heartbeat—

pounding, thundering, pouring through her. Something was being drawn out of her in heavy gasps, gathered up, stolen, and given all at once. Power surged from the amulet, the altar, the blood, all lancing skyward with a force that finally threw both her and Apollo from the dais.

Tracy landed on her back, unable to do anything but stare at what was now a column of electric light streaming up through the temple roof. The draining she felt inside subsided, and still the column blazed. The amulet crackled, shattered, and was consumed in the light, which only flared brighter. Tracy lay transfixed, awaiting the display's end, the return of Zeus, or simply the return of her strength so she could run the hell away before the whole place exploded.

In another instant it was over. The column ceased to exist, as did the cacophonous roar she hadn't even noticed. Tracy cast about for Zeus or even some sort of sign anything had changed.

As far as she could tell, nothing at all was different.

Across the temple, Apollo groaned. Tracy scrambled to her feet and stumbled over to where he lay clutching his neck with one ensanguined hand. A bit of golden light flared from his palm as she neared. When he removed it, the wound was healed. Apollo gave another gasp.

"Ow."

Tracy knelt, guilt replaced by a wave a relief. "You're all right?"

He nodded. "God of healing. Diminished or not, I can at least fix a knife wound. I ought to be furious with you, you know."

Tracy smacked him in the face, then punched his shoulder. "If you knew you could heal, why didn't you offer to make the sacrifice in the first place!"

"I didn't know it would work! When they told me 'child of Zeus,' it followed they meant you. Zeus sent no amulets to me, you know. Besides, have you ever had your jugular slashed? It really hurts!"

Tracy spent the next few moments agape and reining in the urge to strike him again. "You would have let me—? What the heck is wrong with you?" she screamed. "And where the hell is Zeus, anyway?"

Apollo stood. "I don't—I don't know."

Tracy wondered which question he was answering. "Something happened. Don't tell me all that light and stuff was nothing. Where is he?" she demanded, suddenly furious that she might have thrown away their chance entirely and screwed everything up.

Apollo paced the temple, eyes glowing as he looked about. "You may not like the answer. It's entirely possible that the Fates did actually mean for you to be the one to make the sacrifice. Using my blood may have had unintended consequences."

"Don't tell me we pulled up some *other* dead god or something."

"No, I don't think—" Apollo stopped in his tracks. "Uh-oh."

"No saying 'uh-oh' without immediate elaboration! What's going—?"

Three rifts appeared around them as reality parted like an opening gate to deposit three new figures into their midst. Tracy recognized two of them from pictures. The third she'd met personally a few days before. Ares, Hades, and Hermes now stood with them in the temple. Hermes held captive by the arm a decidedly unhappy Thalia.

"—on?" Tracy finished.

"The hour of time we had before full gods could get near the temple would seem to be up."

"Yeah," Tracy sighed, "I figured."

Hades raised both arms to send a pulse of godly power skyward. What remained of the force field crackled into sight and then burned off like a dissipating fog. The Erinyes swooped down into the temple with all of their usual shrieking charm.

"Hello, everyone," said Hermes. "Nice day for upsetting the balance of the cosmos, isn't it? You've been busy."

Precisely three moments prior (give or take a few)—in a rented flat just outside of London that served as the *ad hoc* English headquarters of the Neo-Christian Movement of America—Richard Kindgood, Gabriel Stout, and a small panel of experts sat around a humble wooden table. At the table's center waited the nine cans stolen from Sidgwick's Antique Shoppe in Swindon.

The theft had gone remarkably well. The shop's single alarm was no match for a highly trained group of Ninjas Templar (nor too much of a problem for the moderately trained group they'd actually sent), and no other security measures were to be found. In and out, the entire operation took eleven minutes and six seconds. Kindgood had no idea that all seven ninjas would have met their doom at the claws of the

Orthlaelapsian wraith had they shown up a day earlier, but as they didn't, it's hardly even worth mentioning.

The cans themselves were made of brass, each perfectly sized for soup containment, and covered in ornately carved pictures and distinctly un-American lettering. Phineas Rand, the NCMA's premiere mythological scholar, was busy translating the script while they all waited. He had assured them that the lettering was an obscure variant of ancient Greek. The confiscated parchment of Brittany Simons (a.k.a. Wynter Nightsorrow, a.k.a. the young woman from Chapters Four, Seven, Twenty, and briefly alluded to in Thirty) alluded that this lettering would detail the "great and powerful secret ritual" required to open the cans. Once known, the NCMA would have a weapon with which to destroy the Olympian false gods, and all would be right with the world.

Rand checked something in a notebook, made another few marks with his pencil, and actually laughed. "The translation is finished."

All around the table leaned forward, instantly energized.

"Well?" Kindgood asked. "What must we do?"

"How do we open the cans?" added Stout.

Rand chuckled. "In hindsight, it seems rather obvious. You, ah, have my fee?"

"We do this for the glory of God, Professor Rand!" Stout declared.

Kindgood restrained his subordinate's outburst with an upheld hand. "Certainly the money has been transferred. Rest assured."

"All right, then. The means of opening each can, as inscribed . . ."

"Yes?"

"I've checked this against each of them, you understand."

"All right?" Everyone leaned farther forward.

"Beyond being in another language, it was also in code, you realize. I had to use a cipher from the Simons parchment to decode it."

Kindgood acquiesced with a hurried nod. "You did say as much." They now leaned as far forward as the table would physically permit.

"I just want to be clear. Even after decoding, I verified it, cross-checked it, made sure each one said the same thing, and . . ."

"And?" Kindgood was on his feet by then without realizing it. Stout followed suit and banged his hip on the table's edge. "For God's sake, don't keep us waiting, man!"

"It reads . . ."

Rand paused for emphasis. Had he been writing a book, he probably would have tried ending the chapter at that moment. He swallowed.

Kindgood swallowed.

Stout held his breath.

The others around the table swallowed and held their breath, just to be safe.

Inquisitive minds may be curious as to why, if these cans somehow contained the imprisoned Titans—or at the very least the means to release them—they were lying around in an antique shop, guarded or no, instead of being shut away safely in the gods' halls on Olympus, where one would assume they ought to be. These inquisitive minds have answered their own question.

After all, why hide something where everyone expects it to be? The world is a large place. If one wishes to hide a needle in a haystack (no one ever does, but one thing at a time here), one does not lay the needle on top of the pile with a signpost pointing to it. (Nor does one, as some myths of the Titans tell, guard it with hundred-handed giants. Hundred-handed giants are as easy to spot as they are costly to feed, and in any case, the myth of such guardians alone is deterrent enough.)

That said, Zeus did keep the cans close to him for quite some time until, perhaps inevitably, he gifted them to a young woman in order to impress her into bed. The seduction was indiscreet, and the poor woman was trampled to death in a cattle stampede soon after. (Hera made sure to have an alibi, but no one could miss her retributive signature.) The woman's family then sold the cans, and they drifted throughout the world, their true nature unknown. The gods dispatched Hades's Orthlaelapsian wraith to shepherd them through their anonymous journey, and the cans were believed to be secure.

Though some Olympians initially complained about the situation, Zeus insisted it was the safest course. They need not worry about the cans being opened, he told them. Even in the event that someone found them (unlikely, he counseled), recognized that they could be opened (highly unlikely, he insisted), and somehow evaded the unerring guardianship of the wraith (practically unthinkable, Hades claimed)— the cans were constructed in such a way that none but the wisest, most patient, most intellectually capable people could comprehend the highly arcane method of doing so. All Olympians eventually agreed that anyone *that* wise would know how foolhardy it would be to open the cans at all, and they finally stopped bothering about it in order to observe the Renaissance.

Now that those inquisitive types are placated, we return you to the London flat.

Rand checked his notes one more time. Calmly, he read: "'Push down . . . and turn.'"

Silence took the room, broken finally by Kindgood. *"Push down and turn?"* he demanded. "That's it? We paid you how much?"

"We do this for the glory of *God!*" Stout declared again.

Rand shrugged. "As I said, I've double-checked it. I'm certain that's what it says on each one. There's nothing more."

Kindgood spared a few moments to take the temperature of the room. None of his subordinates appeared willing to take lead. "All right, then, if you're certain. If it is to be done, best that it be done quickly." With no further preamble, he snatched up the top can, pushed down the lid, and turned.

It didn't budge.

Kindgood shrugged, pushed down again, and turned the other way. Again, nothing. He strained, he twisted, he shook and forced the lid, he wrenched it, he gripped it until his hands were slick with sweat and slipped across the brass. He tried turning it again in both directions, to no avail.

Frowning at last, he tossed it to Stout. The man possessed the forearms of a professional baseball player, after all. "You try."

"For the glory of God," Stout answered. "But you loosened it for me, sir."

"Just shut up and try it."

Stout's superior strength proved no more helpful. Frustrating, thought Kindgood, but at least his pride was salvaged.

The group tried further methods. Each of the seven Ninjas Templar who'd captured the cans took a chance, with no success. Special can openers, lock-wrenches, vice grips—all failed to budge the lids in any fashion at all. It was after hours of trying—when frustrations were high and talk was bandied about that perhaps Rand didn't deserve his fee after all—that Rand offered another suggestion.

"It's entirely possible the cans may only be opened in the same land in which they were sealed," he said. "Bear in mind that my specialty is language, but from what I've learned of these sorts of things in the past year since the gods came back—"

"*False* gods!" Stout corrected.

"—it's a fair assumption. You may have more luck if you take the cans to Greece."

Kindgood pondered this a moment. "All right. We go to Greece."

He prayed to God they spoke English there.

PART FOUR:

THE STYX HITS THE FAN

CHAPTER THIRTY-FOUR

"Zeus was god of law, of justice, and of lightning. He was not merely the king of the gods but also the master of the sky and an unrepentant philanderer. As Zeus is now dead (a fact checked numerous times before we included that 'unrepentant philanderer' bit), mentioning him at all in the temples of other Olympians—Poseidon's and Hera's especially—is exceedingly unwise, and that's pretty much all the time we'll waste on him here."

—A Mortal's Guidebook to the Olympians' Return

THE NIGHT WAS HUMID.

That was his first thought. It was also his only thought for another ten minutes. Immortal or not, when one wakes up after being dead for the greater part of a year, a little disorientation is natural. Of course, being dead when one is supposedly immortal isn't natural at all, but neither is being immortal in the first place, so there's no point in getting priggish.

After a while Zeus became aware of lying on his back in a field of tall grass located—judging by the visible stars—somewhere in the northern hemisphere. He struggled to sit up and found he could not. Yet he could feel strength begin to stir in his limbs, as surely as memory trickled its way into his thoughts.

The last thing he remembered was . . . what? A present left unopened, Aphrodite, an amulet that both annoyed him and gave him hope; all of these images floated through his mind, trying to sort themselves out and not having much luck. Something was important, but Zeus couldn't put his mighty finger on it. (At least his fingers were still mighty. Somehow that comforted him.) He concentrated and willed it all back. He'd been watching someone on the big screen, hadn't he? Someone hiking . . .

MICHAEL G. MUNZ

Tracy!

Zeus lunged to his feet as the memories flooded in. The amulet, the god-killer, Tracy . . . and the two millennia-old prophecy he was now certain he'd misinterpreted. He cursed his mistakes even as he praised his foresight in preparing the amulet. And he was alive! Tracy—his child, his champion, his ace in the hole—must have completed the ritual to return him to life, and with incomplete instructions on top of it all!

Pride swelled him to bursting. If he'd known daughters were so useful, he'd have sired more than one in the past four thousand years.

And then there was the other side of that, the reason he'd needed Tracy at all: Someone had *dared* to murder him! Him! Their rightful king, perhaps even their father!

Fury exploded through him at the very thought. Wrath tore its way out in a bellow. Lightning erupted from his palms, his mouth, his eyes—scorching the entire field, blasting it apart in showers of soil, and streaking up to the sky in barely controlled arcs. In his rage Zeus unleashed an electrical storm of such power that it would have driven Nikola Tesla mad, were he able to somehow get close enough to witness the display and survive (a hypothetical situation perhaps rendered moot by the fact that Tesla was already dead, but there it is).

By the time Zeus regained control, he'd carved a crater out of the field. The god's hands remained clenched as he surveyed the destruction, his breath still ragged. Cathartic as such violence was, it might well attract attention. He could ill afford to be so foolish. The others might come to investigate and force a confrontation before he was ready.

"So now must I hide?" he grumbled to himself. The idea stung nearly as much as the blow of the god-killing weapon itself. Yet Zeus, no blustering fool like Ares, was smart enough to realize the truth of the situation.

"Murderers!" he screamed in an aftershock, unable to stop himself. He seized an unearthed boulder, poured his surplus rage into chucking it up to the stars, and then, somewhat more calm for it, took to the sky himself.

In hindsight Zeus hoped he'd given the boulder enough of a kick to get it out of the atmosphere; if it wound up landing on some innocent mortal somewhere, he'd feel rather bad about it. Was there time to track it and see? Should he even bother? Should he try to get his money back from those anger management classes he secretly took in the nineties?

Zeus pushed the questions aside. There were far more important things to deal with. He'd been dead for more than nine months; that much he could sense. What transpired in that time? Who stole the god-killer and used it on him? Who would stand with him now that he'd returned? And a more immediate concern: why in the dryads' armpits had he woken up in a field instead of one of his temples, (up) on an altar?

Come to think of it, Tracy ought to be around too. Or so he thought, anyway.

It was his first resurrection, after all.

On the plus side, while he did not wake in his own temple, neither did he wake surrounded by murderous fellows who might seek to instantly recommit their original crime. Their absence also indicated that they didn't know where he'd appeared. Or, he supposed, they were unaware how vulnerable he would be immediately following his resurrection. Whatever the reason, now safely away from the immediate area, he had time to get his bearings.

He knew the other gods couldn't locate him by the usual means. A god could be sensed by only those of an elder generation, and after the Titan War, none of Zeus's elders were a factor. For the moment, Zeus was both back and hidden. Things had actually worked out for the best. All the same, Zeus hoped his resurrection was at least *felt* by the others.

He had no experience in such things, of course. No Olympian god before him had been murdered and reborn, but it stood to reason that the other Olympians should sense such a rebirth. Besides, he was the almighty Zeus! That they could be ignorant of his return offended his ego. They'd darned well better know! Let them tremble!

When he first learned someone had stolen the UnMaking Nexus, that cursed god-killer, he'd planned to find the culprit, learn his or her intentions, and inflict punishment accordingly. Creating the amulet had served only as a contingency plan should his suspicions prove true and the worst happened. Now that it had, any punishment he might have given before his death paled in comparison to what the murder (murderers?) would suffer. He would inflict such terrible justice upon them that the Titans themselves, imprisoned in their dark nothingness, would hear of the murderers' fate and thank their defeated hides that they'd been spared his full fury!

All right, calm down, you godly stud. Intelligence-gathering first, wrath later.

His first order of business was to do some searching of his own. In his flight from the field, he'd passed into mountains. Recognizing the slate mines, the lakes, and the single rack-and-pinion railway that identified the highest peak as Mt. Snowdon in Wales, Zeus landed on the windy mountaintop to choose his next move. Eyes closed, he stretched out his senses and took stock of the locations of every greater Olympian within his power to feel. Aphrodite, his favorite: the Great Hall on Olympus. Ares: also in the Great Hall on Olympus. No surprises yet. Artemis, Athena, Hephaestus: all also on Olympus. No doubt there was some sort of meeting going on about his rebirth, but he kept going.

Dionysus: top floor of the Dionysian *Hotel and Casino?*

What the Styx? He made a mental note to look into that later. Continuing, he found Hermes also on Olympus. As for Apollo . . .

Zeus opened his eyes, frowned, and tried again. Once more he came up empty. Where was Apollo? Two possibilities came to mind immediately: either the rest of the Dodekatheon found Apollo guilty of Zeus's murder and banished him to Tartarus (or simply turned the god-killer on him); or Apollo stood up for justice on Zeus's side and was struck down himself by Zeus's enemies. Zeus forced himself to not jump to conclusions. In any case he wasn't going to learn much sitting alone on a mountaintop.

Again he took to the sky.

For the most part, catching up with the mortal perspective on the past nine months proved elementary. A combination of mortal interrogation, Internet searches, and perusal of a book called *A Mortal's Guidebook to the Olympians' Return* brought him up to date. He snooped around the White House, 10 Downing Street, the Kremlin, and (for old times' sake) the office of the Prime Minister of Greece to see how governments had reacted (predictably, as it turned out).

The most difficult part of it all was keeping his anger in check at everything he learned: Ares had taken credit for the murder. The claim was suspect, knowing Ares, yet deserving of wrath for its sheer boldness. Poseidon had seized his throne in a traitorous instant—Zeus blasted another couple of craters after reading *that*—and Hera had the nerve to marry him after all of two hours of mourning! (Two *hours?* Was he not Zeus the Unforgettable? That the faithless harpy was Poseidon's problem now was scant succor to his ego.)

Perhaps worst of all, the other Olympians seemed to have cast down his decree of withdrawal before his corpse had grown cold; the disloyal curs had all but tripped over his dead body to get back to public life and mortal worship! If that was true, lightning was too good for any of them, murderers or not!

Yet aside from such obvious and public facts, his search bore few details of what had actually transpired among the gods themselves. Zeus soon decided that learning more along those lines would require stepping back onto Olympus itself or finding an ally to do so for him — yet rage clouded his mind too much for him to decide just how to pursue either option. He needed somewhere comfortable where he could cool down enough to think.

Zeus did his best thinking in the middle of a lightning storm. A couple of nights after his return, there was a fantastic one over Paris that led him to perch invisibly on the antenna atop the Eiffel Tower and brood over exactly how to proceed. For more than an hour, he stood watching the storm strike the tower's lightning rod and letting the tension ebb from his being. He was beginning to calm when he spotted the blond mortal crawling his way up the ironwork above the top observation deck.

Here is a brave fool.

It was an engaging distraction. The mortal would surely be arrested by the Parisian authorities if he failed to fall to his death, but regardless of the numerous laws he was breaking, he impressed Zeus. (Most of the gods have a soft spot for brave fools, as brave fools are so very often courageous enough to perform the tasks demanded of them and lack the sense to realize how likely such tasks ware to kill them. Entire legions of brave fools who *failed* to kill hydras, sail through the Cyanean Rocks, or frolic upon the shores of Axe-Murderer Lake at night go unsung and forgotten, but the gods still appreciate the fools' willingness to try. Such diversions provide them something to watch during dinner.)

And so the deposed king of the gods observed in amusement as the mortal made his ascent. Lightning flashed again, heralding a rush of rain.

The mortal cast his gaze upward into the sudden deluge with a desperate scowl. "Zeus!" he yelled, staring directly at him.

It startled the god so much, he nearly lost his perch. Zeus was invisible—he double-checked to make sure—yet the mortal could see him? Unable to leave the matter unexplored, he released his invisibility completely and finally asked, "How did you find me, mortal?"

"Wow, déjà vu," the climber answered. The two stared at each other as rain fell from the darkness above, plinking off the tower and drenching them both before the mortal spoke again. "Um, it's good to see you and all that, but do you think we could possibly go somewhere else to talk? Somewhere, you know . . ." The mortal glanced down just long enough to appear to regret it. ". . . else?"

This one most definitely has nerve, Zeus thought. Yet nerve had its place. "You will first answer my question, mortal, then we shall see."

The mortal had the temerity to roll his eyes. "I know your daughter! I know Tracy! The rest is a long story I'd rather not tell straddling a giant lightning rod! No offense."

Zeus scanned for any sign he was an Olympian in disguise. (It would be a foolish ploy doomed to failure were that the case, but it didn't pay to be careless.) Once satisfied, he snatched the man up by the arm and brought both of them up the Seine River to the shelter of the southern bell tower of Notre Dame Cathedral. It was perhaps an ironic choice to retreat to a church, but Zeus didn't figure He'd mind.

"I would have your name, mortal, and your answer as to how you knew where and when to find me."

"Leif Karlson. And I really only knew where. Apollo had a vision of me finding you on the Eiffel Tower, so I figured if I went there, I'd find you. Kind of illogical and circular, but I tried not to think too much about that. I'd have been up earlier, but the line into the tower took me an hour and a freaking half to get through."

"The stairs would have been faster. Shorter line."

"Yeah, well, I fell off a cliff a couple days ago when I was helping to bring you back, and my legs hurt."

"You helped? How? When did you last see Tracy?"

Leif launched into a rambling tale of Apollo finding him in a Bellingham café, of Leif's immediate willingness to help, and all that proceeded from that point: the amulet, Thalia, the Erinyes, Thad, Dionysus, and the final struggle at the mountaintop temple. Cheered by the new information and the prospect of potential allies, Zeus listened to the entire story before commenting.

"Mr. Karlson, in your time with Apollo, did he never tell you of my ability to discern when a mortal speaks falsely to me?"

"Um, he neglected to mention that, no."

"Care to revise your story a little bit?"

Leif squirmed, but not to the extent that Zeus lost too much respect for him. "You couldn't have called me on that earlier?" The mortal shot an annoyed glance at the wall. "Fine, so I wasn't immediately all for helping Apollo. Can you blame me? But I came around just fine after a while!"

"I opted to give you just enough rope to hang yourself. I shall not fault you much for wishing to appear more heroic, but lie to me at your peril."

"Er, well, I did come around, like I said."

Zeus smiled, just a bit. "Indeed. For which you have the gratitude of a god." The smile turned to a smirk. "You failed to mention just how you know my daughter."

"Oh. Yeah. That." Again, he squirmed. "I, ah, love your daughter, sir."

The declaration only brought Zeus further amusement as he took stock of the mortal in a new light: wanting of any true muscle definition, skinny legs, light hair, and skin more feminine than masculine—yet he was tall, at least, and obviously not without amply demonstrated courage. "Before my murder, she was seeing someone named Kevin."

"Never heard of him."

"A teetotaler. I never much liked him, myself. How long have you been dating my daughter?"

Leif swallowed uncomfortably. "We're not exactly dating."

More traditional fatherly values battered through Zeus's amusement like a giant through tinfoil. He drilled scrutiny into the mortal, who was apparently just diddling his precious child on the side. For a long time, Zeus silently let him stew in his own discomfort. To his credit, Leif did not break.

"Excuse me?" Zeus asked finally.

"Er, well—I mean, she doesn't really . . . feel the same. She's made that clear. I keep hoping, but I can't seem to change her mind. So far. I don't get it; I'm not the sort of guy who can't get a little action when he wants to—Er, not, not that your daughter is—" Zeus deepened his scowl, and Leif gave a desperate chuckle. "I'd do anything for her. Sir.

Which is why I came along on Operation Resurrect Zeus in the first place. Not that I didn't think bringing you back was a good thing either, of course, but . . ." He trailed off.

Zeus let the half-truth of the final statement slide past without a direct challenge. "So you mean to say that you're stalking my daughter."

"No! . . . At least I don't see it that way."

"Few stalkers do."

"I can't help it! I don't even really get why. She annoyed the heck out of me when I first met her, but—"

"So my daughter is annoying? She is unworthy of your adoration?" Now he was just messing with the kid. Counterproductive, yes, but a welcome diversion. Zeus did his best to mask his returning amusement.

"Don't I get any points for keeping her safe? So she could bring you back? Or for climbing up the freaking Eiffel Tower? That's not easy, you know! I hate wrought iron!"

"Come closer," Zeus ordered. "I command it."

The mortal's compliance was not immediate, nor even existent. "Why?"

Zeus answered with only a stern gaze. Having ordered around gods for millennia, he was quite good at it, and Leif, finally, complied. Zeus took the mortal's head in both hands to study his features in clinical fashion. He peered into Leif's ears, scrutinized his eyeballs, and checked his pulse before letting him go with a nod.

"Please don't say, 'turn your head and cough.'"

"The love you feel is Aphrodite's work," Zeus said.

"Isn't all love supposed to be Aphrodite's work?" Leif smirked. "She claims to be the 'goddess' of love, no?"

"Can the air-quotes, boy. And yes, all love is her domain. Your particular case, however, is more directly induced. I expect she's indulged herself by flinging around quite a number of love-barbs in the general population after the Return. Or perhaps she did it with purpose; a clandestine way of providing Tracy an ally on her quest."

Yet, Zeus realized, would Aphrodite not have picked a more classically heroic figure than this mortal? The question brought up another possibility. "It may also be the work of Eros. Difficult to tell, as he derives his power from hers, of course."

"Oh, of course. Who's Eros?"

"Better known as Cupid, her Olympian son. Minor god. Did you receive any word or aid from either during your quest?"

"Not that anyone told me about, anyway. I thought Apollo might have done it somehow," Leif answered, annoyed. "So this is fake? I didn't care so much when I wasn't sure, but now I know I've been drugged or whatever . . . Can you fix it?"

Zeus couldn't hide a smirk. "And now my daughter is unworthy of your love. Is that it?"

"I—Are you just screwing with me or what?"

"Perhaps. To answer your question, your love is no more a faked emotion than the lightning bolts I hurl are fake electricity. Nor can I fix it. Divine gifts, once bestowed, cannot be revoked. It must run its course like any love."

"Great. Swell. I can't get enough of unrequited love; it's a real hoot. What good is being king of the gods if you can't fix things like this?"

"Even if I could, this love makes you an ally of mine. Why should I wish to fix it?" Zeus frowned, turning away. "And I am no longer king of the gods. My power is not what it used to be."

Leif snorted, earning a glare from Zeus demanding an explanation. "It's just that there's a lot of that going around," Leif told him. "Apollo diminished himself to stay off the radar after he was forced to attack Ares."

"Truly? I shall greatly reward the sun god's devotion when this is over," he vowed. "But make no mistake, I am not diminished in the way Apollo has chosen. I remain a full god."

"Then I don't understand. And, 'make no mistake'? Who talks like that?"

"You're dangerously insolent, mortal." Zeus couldn't help but admire the quality but kept that to himself. Insolence had a time and place, neither of which involved addressing the rightful king of the gods, as far as Zeus was concerned.

"Yeah, surviving four-hundred-foot falls tends to do that to a person. Though I guess I was like that before too. So what's with the less-powerful thing if you're not diminished?"

"Though I am still a full god, *make no mistake,* I am simply less than I used to be, as I am not holding the throne and my place as the king of the gods. My rightful place, I might add."

"You're talking about being able to delegate?"

"Certainly not. I speak of my own personal power, which while still mightier than most, is less than it was when I was on the throne. One of the first things I did upon returning to life was to seek a prophecy of the future. I learned nothing."

"I thought prophecies were Apollo's thing?"

"Again, you interrupt," Zeus warned.

"I do that. It's a valid question."

"Apollo has the most aptitude, but all gods have at least some ability. Most are so poor at it that whatever they learn only leads to confusion, so they have long abandoned the art—but I used to have some skill, when I was king. I shall not have it again until I am king once more. Being king shines power upon a god, like standing in the focus of many spotlights."

"Spotlights of power."

"So to speak."

"So Poseidon could do it now? The prophetic vision thing, I mean."

Zeus shrugged. He disliked shrugging, but it was appropriate. "Possible. But the power gained through ruling is cumulative, and nine months is not enough time to accumulate much. This will work in my favor."

"Got it. Glad we got that established."

"Thus do I wish to find Apollo. What became of him after the ritual?"

"You mean what'd I see from my lofty perch in the waves far below?" Leif asked. "No idea. You don't happen to know where Tracy is either, do you?"

"No. Under normal circumstances, the location of any mortal child of mine should be known to me at any instant I wish to find them, but I cannot see her. She must be somewhere hidden from my sight, intentionally or otherwise."

Leif faltered a moment. "Does that mean she might be dead?"

Zeus considered his response. The day before, Zeus had tried making that determination himself, though he couldn't be sure without asking Hades directly. Instead he had disguised himself as Hermes and risked a quick side trip to the Acheron crossing, with the intent of asking Charon if he'd seen her spirit board the ferry. The discovery that some guy named Marcus was running things forced him to shelve the matter until he knew more about what was going on. While it was possible that Tracy died resurrecting him, his gut told him otherwise. In any case, Zeus wasn't about to tell that to a mortal whose loyalty was tied more to Tracy than to him.

"I have no evidence to think so," Zeus answered. "It might be helpful to describe what happened when you did see her last."

"Like I said, I was outside the temple with Thalia trying to buy Tracy some time and keep the Erinyes from getting inside. Oh, they killed that guardian-tree you made, by the way."

"Fiends!" Zeus declared. "I liked that tree."

"Sorry. They didn't find the key to that barrier thing, though, so I ran out and grabbed it. Then they cornered me in a place I could see her down below in the temple, still doing the ritual. I figured the only way I'd get out of there and keep the key out of their hands was by hurling myself off the cliff, and that's pretty much all I know."

Zeus gave the mortal a shoulder slap. "You truly meant to sacrifice yourself to buy Tracy the time she needed, yet your valor and mettle still fail to move her heart? Unbelievable." *Women!*

"I don't think she saw that part, and I haven't seen her since, obviously." Leif frowned. "And, ah, I didn't really think I was sacrificing myself. It looked like a fall no one could possibly survive, so . . . I went for it."

"You speak of an unsurvivable fall, yet deny intending sacrifice? Your meaning is muddled, mortal." Zeus frowned. "Perhaps you struck the waves harder than you are aware."

The mortal, again, had the temerity to roll his eyes. "You don't see many movies, do you? If it's a fall 'no one can possibly survive,' it's pretty much guaranteed that a person'll survive it. That's just how it works."

"That is ludicrous."

"No, it's called being genre-savvy."

"It sounds like hubris to me. However, we will pretend for a moment that you have such a power. What would you do were you in my position, Mr. Karlson of the Genre-Savvy?" While dubious, Zeus could ill-afford to dismiss possible assets at this stage.

"Hard to say without knowing a few things."

"For instance?"

"Why'd you order that whole god-withdrawal in the first place? Apollo said you never explained it."

Zeus laughed at the mortal's audacity. "And you believe I shall tell you, a mere mortal, simply for the asking?"

"A mere mortal who risked his life to help you," Leif corrected. "Who still wants to help your daughter, and who seems to be one of your few allies at the moment. Hey, you asked."

Again, Zeus could not hide his amusement, though Leif mistook it for refusal.

"Worth a shot," Leif muttered after a time.

"Hiding the reason no longer matters," Zeus answered finally. "There was a prophecy."

"Great. More prophecies."

Zeus blasted Leif with a tiny manifest of power that knocked the wind out of the mortal with a gasp. After allowing him a moment to recover, Zeus continued.

"My own prophecy, that there would come a time when Olympian lust for mortal worship would swell to disastrous levels. According to the prophecy, such a thing would come hand in hand with an end to my reign. At the time, I took this to mean that the others would somehow devise a way to gain enough power from mortal worship to overthrow me. This led to the natural conclusion that by hiding ourselves from mortals, the others would never reach such a state.

"I now believe that it was denying them access to any mortal worship at all that drove them to murder me."

"Probably would've worked the way you thought it would, if you hadn't made them withdraw. One of those 'damned if you do, damned if you don't' sort of things."

"Yes, exactly!" declared Zeus. This mortal understood. There were no such things as self-fulfilling prophecies; sometimes the cosmos was simply out to get you no matter what you did. The mighty Zeus was not at fault! "And my daughter doesn't like you at all, you say? Unbelievable."

"Yeah, you know, I think you ought to maybe mention that to her when we see her."

If she still lives, Zeus thought. "You've yet to give your 'genre-savvy' suggestion."

Leif nodded and leaned against the wall with his arms crossed. "Well, you can't confront everyone immediately. Do that and you'll just wind up locked in a hole somewhere or killed again. You need to gather allies first. Unless . . ." He trailed off, drumming his fingertips. "Unless you show up at some dramatic point, surprise the crap out of everyone, and immediately take out one of the conspirators in one shot. Say, Ares or something. The sheer awesomeness of that moment ought to help you do what you need to do. But for that you'd need to find somewhere in the shadows to hide and wait for the opportune moment. Or some sort of costume to disguise yourself."

"So your advice is either to gather allies and go in force, or to not gather allies and go it alone."

"And wait for a dramatic moment."

Zeus frowned. "You could have simply said you have no idea."

"I have an idea! I have lots of ideas!" The mortal shifted uncomfortably under Zeus's expectant watch. "I just don't know which one's right. I'll tell you this for sure, though: there's got to be some sort of twist coming. Or some final last-minute betrayal."

"Really."

"Definitely. Like, I don't know, someone's actually someone's father, or Hades is really Apollo, or maybe Ares is actually on your side. Stuff like that always happens. Just watch for it, even if it's some minor point from earlier that turns out to play a major part in everything. Or maybe Buddha shows up in a super-powered divine attack helicopter with a clone army in tow. That would *kick ass.*"

There were so many things wrong with that last statement that Zeus chose to ignore it completely. As for the rest . . .

"Vague warnings and lists of things that may or may not happen are what put me here in the first place," Zeus grumbled. Perhaps it was too much to hope that this mortal could be so grand an asset. Though he was right about needing allies, even a blinded man could see that.

The problem was that all the major Olympians deserved his wrath, even those not actively involved in his death. Every single one swore an oath of loyalty to Zeus, an oath broken when they ignored the crime of his murder and raced over his still-cooling corpse to throw down his decree of withdrawal. If there was one thing Zeus could not abide, it was an oath-breaker. (As it happens, there were many things Zeus could not abide, those things numbering among them chastity belts, nosy wives, and those weird hairless cats. Yet oath-breakers topped the list, so the statement stood.) Every single Olympian knew this. Who, then, would join him, knowing their eventual reward would be punishment?

Apollo would; through his previous efforts, Apollo already numbered among Zeus's allies and would, therefore, be spared for his loyalty. Yet Apollo alone was not enough, especially diminished. Furthermore, the other Olympians had betrayed him once. What guaranteed that they would not betray him again, perhaps—just as Leif theorized—even before this business was finished? Though Zeus loathed admitting it, he was fallible. He might inadvertently recruit one of those who'd

MICHAEL G. MUNZ

killed him, only to be betrayed anew at a key moment and cast into Tartarus while he was weak, so the usurper could raise themselves up as the new ruler. In the time since his resurrection, Zeus had considered the possibility that only one option may remain, given the stakes.

He might have to flush the whole blasted pantheon.

Apollo could stay, of course. And perhaps Aphrodite, about whom Zeus was still uncertain. The others would have to go.

Zeus returned his attention to Leif. "While your advice lacks a kernel of usefulness, mortal, you may continue to earn my gratitude—and a good word with my daughter—via other means."

"What other means?"

"I require a loyal liaison between myself and another group of mortals who are working on something that may help me. We were in contact prior to my death—something of a long-shot contingency, you might say. As the grant funding ought to still be valid, I can only assume they continue their efforts. Swear an oath to serve me, and I shall make you my priest so that you may contact me telepathically."

"I'm not arm-wrestling immortals or slaying dragons or anything like that, am I?"

"For the time being, I simply require someone who won't attract attention, unlike myself." Zeus also figured that Poseidon may have remembered Zeus's passing mention of this particular project and could be keeping an eye on it. Were that the case, Poseidon would either not notice Leif at all or spring a trap on Leif in Zeus's stead. Zeus obviously preferred the former, but the latter would at least give him valuable information.

The mortal considered Zeus's offer. "Meals are covered in this deal, right? I'm a little low on funds and that climb took a lot out of me."

Zeus nodded and fabricated a steak gyro.

"All right, fine, I'll do it." Leif took a bite and asked before he'd even swallowed, "Where am I going?"

"Switzerland. Have you heard of the Large Hadron Collider at CERN, mortal?"

"You know, I'm getting a little tired of all you guys calling me 'mortal.'"

"Yes, mortal, I can see how that could get annoying." Zeus smirked. "Should you succeed, I shall call you that no more."

CHAPTER THIRTY-FIVE

"Wheat is one of my favorites—so versatile, so abundant! How rewarding it is to toil in the fields; reap the benefits of a good, honest harvest; and then use a modest portion to make flour for cake! Everybody enjoys cake!"
—Demeter, 2010 Farming Almanac

AS ZEUS EXPECTED, the other Olympians indeed sensed his resurrection, and on Olympus the effect was akin to kicking over a hill of egotistical, self-serving ants. Some argued over strategy; others hunkered down and tried to look busy. Many did both at the same time or switched between the two courses depending on the moment and the look of the sky. Poseidon's initial attempts at organizing everyone—or anyone—against Zeus failed like a man trying to build a house of cards in a stampede of burning cattle. The question of what to do with Apollo, now captured, was lost amid the chaos. He was chained in the Olympian cellars next to some abandoned exercise machines and forgotten.

Or at least mostly forgotten. When Zeus failed to return to Olympus immediately, the chaos gradually turned to hushed waiting. Some of the gods moved among the rest and sowed further plots, alliances, and contingencies. Others hunkered down to scan the horizons for lightning storms. Yet someone did, finally, think to pay Apollo a visit.

Apollo lifted his head at the scrape of the opening door.

"Wakey-wakey!" rejoiced Demeter, entering. "And how are we feeling today?"

Apollo tugged demonstratively at the god-forged chains that held him fast to the wall. "I've had better days. And you?"

"Just peachy, and thank you for asking, dear. Oh, but I'm sorry you have to stand. Your tootsies must be tired! Soon I'll knit you some nice, warm slippers!"

"I'd like that," Apollo said. Humoring Demeter was usually the best option. He nevertheless added, "Though letting me out would be even more helpful."

She clucked her tongue. "Oh, now that's not really my decision, is it? But you're a good nephew; I'll have another chat with that Poseidon and see what he says. I just don't understand why he's all up in a snit about everything, striding about Olympus with a big puss on his face like everyone else now that Zeus is back. You'd think he'd be excited to see his brother again, but everyone's just got bees in their bonnets about how he's going to come back angry and start fighting, the poor darlings."

"You don't think so?"

"Oh, Zeus does have a temper, now doesn't he? But worry is wasted energy, I always say. So I got to thinking, what makes anything better? A big, scrumptious apology cake made from fresh soft wheat! Which reminds me! Artemis, bring it in, dear!"

At that, Apollo's sister came through the door, smiling sadly in greeting. She pushed a gold and ivory dessert tray topped with a wide doily, atop which sat a sheet cake decorated with broad cursive strokes of white icing on chocolate that read: "Sorry we had to lock you up, Apollo!" Traces of smeared white along the cake's outer edges seemed to indicate previous lettering that had been scraped off.

Apollo beamed at his sister. "I didn't think they'd let you see me. I heard about the oath."

"I'm forbidden from coming here in order to speak with you," Artemis explained with a wan smile. "So officially I'm only helping Demeter with the cake. Any talking to you now is purely incidental, then, is it not?"

"Thank the Fates for loopholes," Apollo said.

Demeter clapped her agreement, adding, "Over and under, around and about, that's what shoe-tying's all about!"

Neither twin corrected her.

"Would you care for some cake?" Demeter asked. "It used to say, *Welcome back, Zeus, and sorry you got murdered!* But now, of course, it says this. Zeus still hasn't shown up yet, so I redecorated before it got stale. I thought it might cheer you up a bit."

"I expect he'd love some," Artemis answered for him, "but he'll need to be freed if he's to eat it."

"Don't worry, dear. We'll feed it to him. You're not too grown up for that, are you, Apollo? Let me take that knife; I don't want you kids hurting yourselves!" She snatched the cake knife from Artemis and went to cut.

Artemis moved closer to whisper. "Did any of your visions include this, Brother?"

He ignored the rebuke. "No sign of Zeus at all yet?"

"No, and the longer he takes to show up, the weaker he looks in everyone's eyes and the less they fear him. I've heard some gods wonder if he'll try any wrath at all."

"Trust me. He will."

"I can tell when you're lying, Apollo."

"It's not a lie!" He gritted his teeth and had to make an effort to keep his voice down. "Fine, so I'm uncertain. But about some things I was right: Ares killed Zeus and now I know he had help. Dionysus, Hermes, possibly Hades, and one of the goddesses I'm not sure about."

"I know. I'd not heard anything about Hades and a goddess, but the others admitted their involvement. That's secondhand, though."

Demeter remained busy with the cake, dividing the entire thing into far more pieces than necessary.

"Now they admit it?" Apollo whispered. "Why?"

Artemis shook her head. "I can't. Some things I've been specifically ordered not to tell you."

"Then let me tell you what I know, and maybe you can—"

She put her fingers to his lips. "No. If you tell me anything new, I'll have to report it. I'm bound from helping."

"So you're just making a social call?"

"Don't sound so annoyed!" she whispered. "If you'd trusted me enough to involve me fully, things might've worked out different!"

"I was trying to protect you!"

"Well done! I've only had to swear myself to Poseidon to save my own skin! Things could hardly be worse!"

Demeter broke in before Apollo could answer. "Artemis dear, where are the forks?"

"Lower shelf under the tray," she answered without looking.

"Oh, yes!"

"How are we going to get out of this?" Artemis whispered.

"I don't know, but I'm not entirely without hope. Help me with Demeter."

"I don't know that I can."

"Do your best?"

"Here we are!" Demeter hurried over with two pieces and presented them proudly. "Cocoa-fudge with raspberry filling! It's not quite as fresh as it could be, I fear, but I'm sure you don't mind, do you?"

"I'm just grateful you thought of me," Apollo answered, at least thankful for the first visit he'd had in a few days. Now he simply needed to figure out how to use it to his advantage. "What about Zeus, Demeter?" he tried.

Demeter offered him a forkful. "Don't worry. I'll bake him another after this."

"That's not what I—"

Demeter pushed the cake into his mouth. He'd have said more, but talking with one's mouth full in front of Demeter tended to aggravate the goddess.

"I just love cakes," she went on. "They're really one of the best uses for wheat and sugar. Aren't crops marvelous?" She got another forkful of cake for him just as he swallowed the first, asking, "So, Apollo, you do intend to apologize to poor Ares, don't you? Apologies make everyone feel better."

"I really think there's more to it than that. Do you realize—?"

Demeter shoved another bite into his mouth. "Oh, tish-tosh! Don't be so stubborn. It's just a little apology. You should play nice."

"Let him talk a little, Demeter," Artemis tried.

"He needs cheering!"

Apollo swallowed and decided to switch tactics. "Speaking of playing nice, Demeter, do you know what's become of Thalia?"

"Oh, she's fine, the poor darling. Back in with her sisters, though Poseidon still has them under house arrest. No chains, though."

"And Tracy?" he managed before the next bite invaded his mouth.

"I'm sorry, dear, who?"

Artemis only shook her head, perplexed.

"Tracy Wallace? The mortal who was with me at the temple. You didn't hear about that?"

"No, I didn't hear about any mortals. One of your little crushes?"

Apollo frowned and tried to decide what it signified that Demeter knew nothing of Tracy. Either Hades, Hermes, and Ares had kept her a secret after she and Apollo were captured, or they'd killed her. There was also the possibility that she had escaped somehow, but that was about as likely as Ares writing decent poetry. If she was truly dead, would Zeus hold that against him? In any case, Apollo would be sorry to learn she'd come to such an end after displaying so much heroism.

Artemis cleared her throat. "I expect I should go before you say anything further, Brother." The unspoken words "that I'd have to report" hung plainly in the silence. Artemis said good-bye and, after a frustrated hug that the chains kept him from returning, turned to go.

"Watch yourself," he told her.

"Likewise," she whispered. "I'm sorry I can't do more."

Apollo watched her go and wondered if Zeus would regard her oath to Poseidon as betrayal.

"Demeter, about this mortal," he began once she'd left, "I don't suppose you could find out for me? Ask around? I'd like to know."

"Oh, so she is a crush!" Demeter beamed. "It's so nice to see you're dating again, a handsome, young god like you. If I hear anything, I'll let you know."

"I'd be glad for that. Might I also trouble you to carry a message to the Muses for me?"

"Poseidon said not to, dear. I'm sorry. But I can ask him if he'd change his mind for you if you like. Oh, you've got a bit of frosting on your chin. Hold still!" She licked her thumb and wiped it off.

He grimaced. "I doubt he'll change his mind."

"Oh, he may, dear. You know what he's like, 'as swiftly changing as the sea,' as they say. Though there was that whole Odysseus thing, I suppose, wasn't there? But that only lasted, what, two decades? Two decades goes by like that!"

"I fear Zeus will be back before then, Demeter. Why not just let me out now? Join me? Like you said, Zeus is going to be angry, and—with no dishonor to your baking—I don't think a simple cake is going to appease him."

"Of course not! I've knitted a nice, thick sweater to go with it."

Apollo forced a smile. "Nevertheless. Some of the other gods murdered him, and I doubt he'll be thrilled with how we all violated the Withdrawal the moment he was gone. I helped to bring him back; the only wise course is to side with me. Free me, and you help Zeus. You'll be spared his wrath!"

Demeter tugged away the next bite of cake she was about to offer. "It's poor manners to threaten your Aunt Demeter, Apollo. Now say you're sorry, or no more cake."

"Demeter, please. I'm warning, not threatening. For your own sake. And mine." He shouldn't have added that last part, but he couldn't help himself.

She sighed. "Oh, you boys and your silly theories! You're all just being mean."

"Aunt, please! Some of the others are directly responsible for killing Zeus! For *killing* him! Are you comfortable knowing some of us can actually kill the others?"

"Oh, I know. Ares, Dionysus and Hermes," Demeter answered. "They told everyone yesterday."

"Not Hades or . . . anyone else?"

"No, no. Hermes simply came to me with Ares and Dionysus to ask if I'd side with them and the rest of the gods when Zeus gets here. He said some foolishness about how we all need to stand united under Poseidon because Zeus will be angry and want to toss us all in Tartarus."

It was a good strategy, Apollo considered. Though dethroned, Zeus would still be a force to be reckoned with. The remaining Olympians stood their best chance if they united, but fear and political maneuvering might very well keep them from doing so unless they were assured of victory. A god-killing weapon on their side might be just enough to provide that assurance. The timing of the conspirators' confession gave them a way to turn their culpability into an asset and gain power without the others wishing to lynch them on principle.

"But you told them no, right?" Apollo asked.

"What I told him was that Poseidon is king now and I'd of course do whatever he says we ought to do."

"I suspect Poseidon will tell you to do whatever lets him keep his throne."

"Hush! All you worry-warts! Everything will work out; you'll see. It's just like that thing with the Titans. It worked out for the best for everyone."

"I daresay the Titans would disagree."

"Nonsense! The Titans went to live on a farm where they can run through the fields and chase rabbits all day!"

Apollo sighed against the urge to correct her, choosing his battles. "And the fact that Ares, and the others, committed deicide doesn't bother you at all?"

"Oh, tsk, Apollo, of course it bothers me. It's terrible manners, but Zeus got better, so there's no harm done. If worst comes to worst, we might have to put Zeus down here with you just to give him a 'time-out' until he calms down, I suppose, but after that we'll all be one happy family again."

"Or the others may try to kill him again! And after that, what's to stop them from killing anyone else who stands in their way?"

"Manners, Apollo!" Demeter whacked him on the forehead with the curve of the fork. "And stand in their way of doing what? Olympus's doorways are quite wide enough."

Before Apollo could think of a response, the horn that summoned the Dodekatheon into assembly sounded throughout Olympus. A trio of extra notes declared that all gods and beings upon Olympus were required to attend.

"A universal summons," Apollo tried. "I'd best go too. If you'd please help me get free, Demeter?"

"Oh, I'm sorry, Apollo. Poseidon told me specifically that you must stay here until he sends for you by name. You just rest up and remember: turn on the love, even when you don't get what you want!"

"You'll remember to ask if I can see the Muses?" Apollo called after her. She was out the door so quickly that he couldn't be sure if she'd even heard.

He tugged at his chains again; they still refused to budge. Once more he wondered at the meaning of his vision of Zeus talking to Karlson on the Eiffel Tower. That Karlson had fallen into the sea was the one detail Thalia had managed to whisper to Apollo when they'd been captured at the temple. Could Leif have survived somehow, or was the vision merely a figurative one?

In any case, if Apollo was to get to Paris himself and meet Zeus, he was rapidly running out of time, if he had any left at all. Perhaps the call to assembly heralded Zeus's return. What could Zeus possibly do on his own against a united force of Olympians? What would Apollo's own fate be when they triumphed?

It is uncertain just how Apollo might have reacted to the knowledge that around the same time, Tracy herself was alive on Olympus. As she occupied a prison of her own, however, it likely would not have given him much hope.

It was at least comfortable, for a prison. Tracy had to admit she'd never actually been in a prison before, so her basis for comparison consisted of only what she'd seen in films and that one hotel in Kansas with the three thousand crickets in the bathroom.

This place was at least better than Kansas.

In fact, given the brightly shining skylight above, the glorious view from the balcony (which dropped off much too far to consider it a means of escape), the plush furnishings, and numerous flowers adorning the place, she didn't realize it even was a prison until she discovered the door was locked. And that no one responded to her yelling. And the helpful "So Now You're in Prison" pamphlet on the bedside table.

In hindsight that should've been her first clue.

Decidedly tired, Tracy had languished for an indeterminate amount of time before the door opened at last. She waited on the edge of the bed to find out if someone was coming to rescue her or if her jailors were coming with a meal, and given the growl in her stomach, she couldn't decide which option she'd prefer.

Hermes entered, bringing neither food (on account of being empty-handed) nor rescue (on account of being Hermes). She gave no greeting, barely even making eye contact as she estimated her chances of running past him and out the open door in the split second before he closed it: surely impossible.

She bolted for it anyway. Hermes grabbed her by the back of her shirt and lifted her off her feet in an instant. Her estimate's accuracy at least made her feel a little better about the failure. Plus, she figured, points for trying, right?

Hermes closed the door and set her back down. "Tracy Daphne Wallace," he said with a smile. "Mortal daughter of Zeus. How did that escape us for so long?"

Despite the numerous snarky comebacks queuing in her mind, Tracy said nothing.

"Zeus rarely sires mortal daughters," Hermes went on. "He prefers strong, heroic young lads. Perseus. Hercules. Davy Crockett. I suppose that's part of why you slid right under the radar. Crafty ol' Zeus, switching to his least-favorite gender just to trick us all." He sat down on the other end of the bed. "Not a very smart move, trying to bring him back to life."

"Better than killing him, isn't it?" she tried.

"It's not as if we didn't try other options first. He was a tyrant, you know. A world-class, manipulative git. Power mad. Made us all retreat from the public eye without even a word about why. 'I command it!' he would shout. Nearly his favorite phrase, after 'Can I read your T-shirt in Braille, miss?' I daresay. Quite frankly we did the world a favor, putting him out."

"What do you want?"

"Oh, this and that. World peace. Fat-free doughnuts. Winged sandals with better arch support." Hermes shrugged. "And for you to see things from our point of view. Despite everything, I meant you no personal harm. I *like* mortals; I'd prefer to call you a friend. You might better understand if you could see what a manipulative bastard Zeus really is. Or was, rather. That ritual he demanded of you would have killed you if it had worked."

But the ritual *had* worked, Tracy insisted to herself. Hadn't it? After all, blasts of electric light like that didn't just happen, right? . . . Anyone? The nagging doubt she'd kept locked up since her capture sprang forth, empowered by her continued imprisonment and Hermes's insinuation. She tried to quash the worry and keep a brave face as a trickle of sweat slid down her spine.

"Aren't you the god of tricksters?" she asked finally.

Hermes rolled his eyes. "Hardly a question anyone answers 'yes' to, is it? Shall I try to deny, knowing you'll doubt me even if I tell the truth?"

"Call it rhetorical if you want."

"Unfair would be more like it." Hermes shook his head with a sigh. "Put a couple of whoopee cushions on the wrong chairs, and suddenly you're the 'trickster god' for the rest of existence. A misrepresentation, I assure you. More chiefly I am god of merchants, travelers, and boundary crossings. I *love* a good gate." He shrugged. "But every ounce of trickery in me I inherited from Zeus, and he has it in spades! Take that amulet of brainwashing you wound up with. The loyalty to Zeus you felt when you had it, that irresistible drive to bring him back—did you feel nearly so loyal and zealous once the amulet was gone?"

He did at least have a point, she thought. When she had the amulet, she'd hardly cared about herself, willing to do anything to find justice for a father she'd never known. Yet now the worry about her own fate loomed much larger.

"Let me go," she said.

"We will, soon enough. For the moment I am required to show you something." Hermes stood and opened the door for her. "Do follow me. And don't try to run again because . . . well, Hermes." He smiled apologetically.

"Where?"

"To see something the others have made," he answered. A long horn sounded, followed by three short blasts. "I only ask you to remember this was not my idea."

CHAPTER THIRTY-SIX

"The angry swearing of oaths by the Styx is seldom a wise idea and should be avoided."

—*sign, Styx riverbank*

"No wading. Keep dogs on leash. Under no circumstances feed anything purporting to be a duck."

—*sign, adjacent to first*

BROADCAST FROM THE HIGHEST PEAKS of Olympus and delivered around the world via satellite on a frequency discernable to only the highest tier of Olympians (and, for some reason, rhinoceros beetles), the message comprised an effective means of both reaching Zeus and irritating the stuffing out of him. That particular method of communication necessitated a dreadfully high-pitched shriek, which both preceded the message and continued to fill his ears for the entire duration. Knowing that there was no other guaranteed means for his former subjects to reach him did nothing to reduce Zeus's irritation, nor did the knowledge that his siblings must also endure the shrieking; it was disrespectful to the point of making him curse each and every one of them under his breath before the actual message had even begun.

To say that the content of the message itself failed to appease his irritation would be an understatement worthy of government inquiry:

"The remaining United Gods of Olympus, one unified force under Poseidon, Earthshaker and Lord of the Sea, send this message to Zeus the Deposed, Zeus the Throneless, Zeus the King of Nothing: Your hiding serves only to underscore your cowardice. If your sense of vengeance proves so weak as to leave you cowering in some cave, perhaps love for your own mortal offspring shall prove sufficient to move you toward a measure of bravery! We have captured your mortal daughter, one Tracy Daphne Wallace, and now hold her in the Tyrrhenian Sea one hundred fifty nautical miles due south of the city of Rome. You refused us our rightful presence in the mortal world for millennia, yet broke your own law by fathering her with a mortal woman. We therefore deem her an illegal child who, with her execution, shall pay the price for your hypocrisy. Present yourself there and surrender within the hour, and she will be spared. Fail to do so, and she will die.

P.S. Please bring your appetite. There will be cake."

"Mr. Karlson," spoke Zeus through gritted teeth. Speaking itself was actually unnecessary. The telepathic link between the two functioned just fine, but actually speaking aloud felt far more satisfying and kept him from accidentally sending stray thoughts. "How soon?"

The mortal's response sounded immediately in his mind's ear: *"Soon. Those meteorites they recovered this morning are actually torn from Saturn's rings. Looks like you were right."*

His teeth ground harder. "Of course I was right! All is ready, then?"

"More or less. They ought to be set to integrate the final components once you bring them in, but the lead guy here says they'll need some time to adjust the supercollider, and that could take anywhere from six hours to a full day. Something about leptons and the Uncertainty Principle and some labor standards thing with the European Science Foundation or whatever. Unless you can do something to speed that up?"

Spawns of Cronus, that wouldn't be enough time! "This cannot be sped up."

"Guess you should get here soon with those mystery components and start the process then, huh?"

"No," Zeus ordered. "Order Dr. Kowalski to do what they can to adjust the collider now. They will have the final components soon, but first I must confront the Olympians."

"Er, didn't you say you needed allies? Zeus, do you see a little golden ball anywhere nearby?"

"I can wait no longer. The others grow bold enough to challenge me directly!" Zeus growled. "They dare insult my commitment to my own laws! They mock my courage! Such insults to my honor cannot be ignored!"

"Insults to your honor?" the mortal had the impudence to ask. *"So what? I mean, you want to go get yourself killed again, that's fine, but it occurs to me that if something happens to you when I'm all linked up to you like this, it won't go so well for me either. I don't want—"*

"They have captured Tracy!" he roared. "And they have the temerity to threaten the execution of my own daughter if I do not appear to them within the hour!"

"What? No!"

"Yes!" His rage grew the more he thought about it. *"My* daughter! As a united front, they have taken that which is mine and threatened its destruction! Throughout history there was one rule, *one* rule highest above them all that none dared break: Thou shalt not *fuck* with Zeus's children!"

"Wait, are—?"

"Such audacity cannot go unanswered!" Zeus could not help but shout. "I shall storm down among them, burn Poseidon's skull with a single bolt of lightning, and deliver unto them such wrath as they have never seen! I swear by the river Styx that no Olympian there shall go unpunished for this affront to my authority!"

"Er, saving Tracy is in there somewhere too, right?"

"Oh, they will expect that, won't they? Her fate may be sealed, but her sacrifice will be remembered! She will be set among the stars as the one who—"

"You're just going to sacrifice her?" The mortal's indignation howled across their link. Zeus made a mental note to alter their telepathic bond so that in the future, yelling was allowed only *down* the chain of command. *"After all she did for you? Don't you care about her at all?"*

"Silence, I command it! She will be honored in death, highest among—"

"But she'll still be dead! You care more about an insult to your authority than your own daughter! She's not just a thing to—"

"Will you stop interrupting!" Zeus roared. Mortals had such limited perspective in their short, finite lives! Obviously he would prefer for

Tracy to prosper during her brief time alive; he was no monster! Yet her death, especially compared to that of a god such as he, was not such a large thing in the grand scheme. Her legacy was far more important!

"You have to try to rescue her!"

"I will do what is necessary! You are not one to be giving *me* orders!"

The mortal may have wished to express himself further after that. Zeus knew not. He muted the link, lunged to his feet, and stormed straight out of the New York Public Library, greatly relieving the group of flustered librarians drawing straws to determine who would ask him to please be quiet.

By the time Zeus reached the spot where the traitorous heretics held his daughter, whispers of rational thought had begun to penetrate his anger. As satisfying as it might be to simply show up and knock heads together, the sheer degree to which Zeus was outnumbered would doom such a strategy to failure. On the other hand, not all of the gods would be as committed to their course as Poseidon and the others who had murdered Zeus. He would give them a chance to come over to his side before the lightning struck. The delay would also give him time to discover the dangers of this trap, for a trap it certainly would be.

In the exact spot described in the message, his enemies had raised in the sea a circular shelf of stone, its uneven surface dotted by sea spray blowing up over the raised edges around the shelf's outer rim. The center was open to the water below, giving the entire shelf the look of a flattened doughnut some fifty yards across. From the northern side of the hole rose a stone tower with a broad spar that itself extended over the seawater in the hole below. Dangling from the spar like a hanged man on a noose was a transparent box containing his daughter. Tracy pounded on the box like a crazed mime—alive, for the moment.

There was no sign of anyone else.

At least not at first. Invisible himself, Zeus circled the area, peering down among the rocks and waves for the telltale shimmer of other invisible gods, spotting one, two, then three. Others surely lurked nearby, perhaps waiting in the ocean itself or, like he, flying invisible in the sky where light and movement would better conceal them. Rather than call them out immediately, he continued to observe.

Though divinely summoned, the shelf appeared to be no more than regular rock—somewhat slippery when wet, but little to be worried about otherwise. Yet something was off about the stone pedestal holding Tracy's prison. An energy shimmer, barely visible, seemed to pulse in and out of existence. Zeus continued to circle, focused on the pedestal, unable to determine its nature.

Was it designed to explode if touched? No, that wouldn't account for the pulsing.

Was it stone at all, or simply some creature crafted to look like it until he got close? While transmogrification was not Zeus's specialty, it didn't quite look right for that sort of thing either.

Zeus stopped and hovered in place so he might focus further. Only then did he realize the thing wasn't pulsing; the shimmer was not around the pedestal at all, but beside it, rising up from the water under the spar to surround Tracy's prison in a pillar of barely discernable energy. His orbit caused the illusion; only with the pedestal as a backdrop was the energy field visible at all. At all other times, the field was either impossible to discern or blocked entirely by the pedestal.

A phlegmatic field!

Formed of the emanations of the thousands who had died of boredom while on hold with customer service, phlegmatic fields represented the most powerful of the few joint creations of Hades and Hephaestus. Though such fields normally crackled with ennui, Zeus's treacherous subjects had hidden this one well. A more foolish god might have swooped in and tore the chain that hung his daughter's prison box from the rock above, only to be caught in the field—divine essence shackled in a swaddling of lethargy that would slow his movements, dampen his powers, and render him as effective as a snapping turtle without the "s". The field's effects would not last long—perhaps a god of Zeus's stature might shrug it off in less than a minute—but it would be long enough for his enemies to pounce and render him further helpless in myriad other ways.

Even without the field, the chain itself might very well be durable enough to cause a problem. Hephaestus could make some strong stuff. Though Zeus could break it, such a feat would take time and effort that would leave him vulnerable, phlegmatized or not. The chain would surely be resistant to lightning. Though fools, the other gods were not idiots.

Most of them, anyway.

Again, the betrayal and audacity—from his siblings, his children!—stung like a whip. They'd worked together to create this trap; they were here, waiting for him to make a mistake. Zeus summoned two fistfuls of lightning, stretched out his arms, and burst into sight amid a web of electricity. Thunder rolled across the sea in a slap of power that shook the air and rocks alike.

It was a good entrance. Not his best, but it would do.

"Brothers!" Zeus bellowed, beginning to circle the shelf anew. "Sisters!" he continued. "Children and subjects of mine!" (No sense leaving anyone out.) "Hiding becomes you not!"

When none came forth, he went on. "So. Shall you prove to be keepers of the cowardice of which you dare accuse me? Do you hide in your cloaks like vulgar assassins, waiting for me to fall into your trap, too frightened to face me on your own? Where are these mighty 'United Gods of Olympus, one unified force under the mighty Poseidon, Earthshaker and Lord of the Sea,' eh? You call me deposed, my Olympians. You outnumber me yet still you fear me! What does this tell you of my power? What does this speak of my rightful place among you? I know you to be here! Show yourselves now or be branded cowards and betrayers in the tales for all time!"

A distortion caught the corner of his eye as a still-invisible someone descended from the sky to land near the base of the pedestal. He glared at the unknown figure directly and repeated his demand with a matching roll of thunder. *"Show yourselves!"*

That did it. One by one, they appeared. Ares came first, revealed to be the figure near the pedestal base, clad in his finest battle gear. Hades, Demeter, and Hera comprised those three already spotted on the stone. More appeared in the sky. Some, such as Athena, circled warily, watching for trouble. Others simply hovered in wait. All were tense, with the exception of Dionysus, who relaxed in his sky-hammock. Zeus kept silent as they appeared, marking their positions and taking a mental roll call that—perhaps unsurprisingly—failed to include both Apollo and Hermes. Apollo remained missing in action, and showing himself in such a situation was simply not Hermes's style.

Poseidon revealed himself last. On the other side of the shelf, a stationary crest of frothing surf lifted him from the waves up to a position exactly one head higher than Zeus's own altitude. His brother had the nerve to form the top of the crest into a throne.

"Brave words, little brother!" Poseidon declared. "Brave and foolish! Present yourself for surrender, or face—"

Zeus shook the sky with lightning. "I will not hear the words of a usurper!" he shouted over his brother. "Nor any who delivered the blow to my backside you *thought* would kill me! Yet I say to the rest of you: you can still be redeemed! I know Poseidon and his pack of murderers bullied you into supporting them! Yet have I not returned, undaunted by their treachery? Join me! Join the side of your rightful king, the side of victory, or be forever cast down as the Titans were before you!" Zeus rose higher than his brother by a full ten yards. The gesture bought him just a moment of time to size up the gods' reactions.

Scornful laughter sliced through the air, as mocking as it was familiar. He might have known Hera would open her mouth to that.

"You act as if you defeated the Titans singlehandedly, Brother Zeus!" she sniped. "Was it not all of us, working together, who did so? All of whom and more who are now aligned against you! You would claim that victory for yourself, taking the lion's share, pushing us to the side, just as you did as king for so many millennia! I played no part in the plot to slay you, yet once widowed, I found little cause to grieve! There was a reason why no one cared to find those responsible for your death! The world was a better place without you in it!"

"I expected such bile from you, dear *wife*. For all your bluster about the sanctity of marriage, you cast your spousal duties aside at the earliest convenient moment!"

"I was widowed!" she shrieked. "You speak to me of marital duty when this mortal's very existence gives evidence of your infidelity!"

"I always stood by you when it mattered, Hera! Am I to be blamed for thinking sex is fun?"

"If sex is fun, you're not doing it right!" she spit back.

Hera, as expected, was a lost cause. It was time to go for the soft targets. "I will not be drawn into such ancient disputes, Hera!" Zeus returned. "You may hold no love for me, but I know there are those who still do! I say again that I understand the quandary in which you found yourselves when I was slain! No matter what others would have you believe, I bear you no ill will! When there existed a device that could seemingly kill the mightiest among you, what choice did you have? Fall into line with Poseidon's new order, or be struck down yourselves?"

"A lie!" boomed Hades's echoing whisper.

"A lie most definitely!" Poseidon echoed. "I wielded no such heinous weapon! I am king by legal Dodekatheon vote!"

"So you say, Poseidon! Votes coerced in back rooms under threat, perhaps!" The truth of it did not matter, Zeus knew, only the appearance that he believed it. The others would not rejoin him without an excuse for their previous behavior, so Zeus offered that excuse on a silver platter, along with assurances it would be accepted. "I knew of the god-killer, the UnMaking Nexus crafted by the Fates at the end of the Titan War! I myself commissioned it for the good of us all! And when it was done, when it was no longer needed, I did not use it to curry favor! I did not use it to threaten you with a final death! And why?"

"'Cause you're a skirt-wearin' coward!" Ares shouted, turning to the others. "Who in the name of my musty armpits wants to follow a coward, eh? *Eh?*"

Zeus roared and hurled a lightning bolt at the stone between Ares's feet. It knocked the war god on his back as intended, with little damage to anything but his pride.

"And *why?*" Zeus repeated, speaking before any could take the lightning for a herald of a greater attack. "For your own good! Knowledge of such a weapon would surely have set us to civil war!" He stretched out a demonstrative hand toward Ares as the god scrambled to his feet. "Would you now take up with those who would wield such power for their own selfish uses? I work only for the good of us all! I am a uniter, not a divider, and I know that despite how it may appear, you did not truly rejoice in my death!" Another political lie, but after millennia of marriage to Hera and ruling an entire pantheon, Zeus was practiced at faking sincerity.

"Ha!" was Ares's witty rejoinder.

"Hephaestus!" Zeus called, facing the god he entreated. "Peace-loving as you are strong! I know you do not wish this strife! Athena, bearer of my shield, my trusted bodyguard! Your failure to protect me from their cowardly assassination shall be forgotten if you only stand beside me now!"

Both seemed to consider his words. The others were, so far, letting him speak more than expected. Suspicious of his good fortune, he nonetheless went on.

"Aphrodite! Beautiful Aphrodite! You are goddess of love, not of strife! Surely you cannot stand to be estranged from the father who so doted upon you! Artemis, daughter of mine and sister of Apollo, who alone among you has aided me, at risk to his own immortal life! Would you not stand by your brother?"

"Artemis is sworn to me, Zeus!" Poseidon declared. "In all things, by the river Styx! You cannot turn her allegiance now!"

Artemis, sadly, nodded to this and faded, shamed into invisibility.

"In *all* things?" Zeus asked, incredulous. "Is this how you rule, Poseidon? Are you so unworthy of allegiance that you need oaths of blind faith to compensate for your lack of merit?"

Poseidon sneered at the implication. "She is the only one! It was the choice she made after Apollo betrayed us, lest his crimes drag her down with him!"

Zeus laughed, squeezing as much mockery into the act as he could manage without resorting to hand gestures. "So having enough conscience to act for justice is a crime under Poseidon's rule, is it?"

"Ah, I do so fancy political speeches, Father! They're always so rousing, so exuberant, so teeming with half-truths and prettied-up lies!"

It was Hermes at last, revealing himself atop the stone pedestal and wearing the grin that always roused Zeus's suspicions. Zeus had long ago realized that half the time the grin itself was the only mischief, simply designed to worry him. Yet to suspect that was the case in such a vital confrontation was to suspect that slugs could play the tuba without lessons. "Apollo was as happy as the rest of us that you were gone! His 'aid' to you did not even begin until he saw a vision and decided he had no other choice."

"And yet he gave that aid nevertheless!" answered Zeus. "It was not too late for him, just as it is not too late for the rest of you!"

Hermes laughed. "And they call me the trickster god!"

"This is no trick, boy," Zeus growled.

Hermes's grin grew only more infuriating. "Oh, no? Would you instead blame weak-minded forgetfulness for your ignorance of the oath you spoke within the hour? Listen well, all of you!"

Hermes held aloft his caduceus and touched a button at the center. Immediately a recording of Zeus's own voice boomed with rage for all to hear: *"I shall storm down among them, burn Poseidon's skull with a single bolt of lightning, and deliver unto them such wrath as they have never seen! I swear by the river Styx that no Olympian there shall go unpunished for this affront to my authority!"*

The effect among the others was immediate. Some fled to invisibility again; still more simply recoiled in their own defense, drawing weapons or rattling those already drawn.

"An abominable trick, from the king of tricks himself!" Zeus roared.

"You swore it, Zeus! The only trick I have done is place a wiretap on the Styx itself! Quite the clever idea, if I do say so myself." Hermes taunted.

"No oath sworn by the river Styx may be broken!" Poseidon reminded all. "Even should you aid Zeus—"

"In his weakened state!" Hermes added.

"—and somehow gain victory, you escape not his anger!"

"See how he comes here and lies to you!" Hera joined in. "Forgiveness in one hand, wrath in the other!"

Even the briefest glance at the others gave Zeus ample evidence that opinion was against him. To think they trusted Hermes more than him! It was reprehensible, regardless of the fact that Hermes was in the right. Yet Zeus had not become king by rolling over and taking abuse.

"Very well!" he boomed, no longer masking his contempt for their combined betrayals. "And why should I not be angry? Hermes is right! You do have cause to fear me! I have said this before; I shall say so again: I am the mightiest of all. Make trial that you may know. Fasten a rope of gold to heaven and lay hold, every god and goddess; you could not drag down Zeus! I have stated that if I wished to drag you down, I would! And now—"

Hermes made a yakking hand motion, rolled his eyes, and cut off Zeus with mocking recitation: "'The rope I would bind to a pinnacle of Olympus and all would hang in the air, yes, the very earth and sea too.'" Hermes finished his quote of Zeus's words from the Trojan War with all the reverence of a schoolyard taunt. "I always gave you points for a good bluff on that one, Father, but you're hardly in a position to pull it off now, are you?"

Poseidon took up the pulpit. "You're weaker now, Brother. You've lost your throne, and we all stand against you!"

Zeus glared at his brother. "And yet you only stand! You do not attack! If you are so confident, then make your moves and see how you fare against the mighty Zeus!"

Aside from Hades's restraining grip at Ares's shoulder, no one but Poseidon reacted. He sprang down from his wave crest to land on the opposing side of the hole from Zeus, so that the phlegmatic field lay between them. "Neither does the 'mighty Zeus' attack!" Poseidon spit. "If you have any strength left in you, combat me now!"

Lightning flared as Zeus growled and circled to one side. Poseidon matched every movement he made, keeping the field between them. "I see your trap, Brother! You cower behind it like—"

Aphrodite, bless her heart, thankfully interrupted Zeus before he had to come up with a suitably biting comparison. "Stop it!" she cried. "Stop it, all of you!"

She moved in radiant light that beguiled the growing darkness as she flew in front of Zeus to interpose herself between him and Poseidon. "You're being stubborn like you always are," she insisted. "This isn't going to fix anything, either of you."

"Exactly, dear!" came Demeter's voice from somewhere above. "I still have the cake ready to cut. Hestia, did you think to bring napkins? Has anyone seen Hestia?"

"Not now, Auntie Demeter." Aphrodite didn't look up, remaining fixed on Zeus, her eyes shining in that loving, doting smile that always melted his heart. Was she coming over to his side publically now, revealing herself as Apollo's helper? She would be little help in a direct confrontation, but perhaps her beauty might soften some of the other gods' stances.

Zeus kept watch for attempts by the others to take advantage of the distraction. "Aphrodite," he said quietly so none other could hear, "thank you. I have always favored you above all."

Her smile grew greater. Joyous, loving. It gladdened his heart. "Thank you, Daddy." She turned to the others, hands held out. "Stay your anger, if only for a moment! Please let me talk to my daddy!"

Poseidon seemed to relax. Hermes pulled back a bit. Even Ares lowered his weapon.

Aphrodite moved a little closer, creating a pocket of stopped time for them to speak. "I've missed you, Daddy. Did you really mean what you said when you swore that oath?" Her eyes were as large as seashells.

"I was angry, Daughter. But you were swept away in all of this, I'm sure. Your punishment will be light and postponed. You must help me now. Was it you who gave Tracy an ally in the blond mortal?"

She moved closer, arms open to him. "It was, Daddy. He helped your cause, didn't he?"

"He did, Daughter. Thank you."

"I love you, Daddy." She embraced him.

He returned the embrace, thankful for the chance while the others waited frozen outside the pocket of stopped time.

"I want you to be happy."

"As I love you, Aphrodite. I want you to be happy as well."

She squeezed him tighter, whispering in his ear. "I knew you'd understand, Daddy. And you should know: the box with the god-killer inside *was* from me."

Immediately the pocket of stopped time collapsed under the violence of a blade piercing Zeus's back. He gasped in pain and betrayal as Aphrodite drew back, one of Ares's wicked daggers in her hand.

Though the blow was far from mortal, it was sufficient to stun him long enough for the others to swarm him. Ares drove his fist into the side of Zeus's head as Poseidon and Hades both tackled him to the stone shelf. Zeus roared, lightning flaring around him enough to throw off Poseidon, but Hades remained, his grip monstrous enough to hold him still so Ares could take Poseidon's place. Down swooped Athena; she smashed into Zeus's chest with his own shield as Hermes seized Zeus's lightning bolts with gloves of divine rubber. Dionysus clobbered him with a hammer that sent his entire body reeling with a hangover. Others stood by, looking for an opening. Sad Artemis with her arrows trained on him; Hephaestus, Hestia and Hera holding the same golden rope he'd dared them with; even Demeter stood dejectedly by a cake, knife in hand, looking disappointed but ready to serve up some aid to the others if needed.

"Aphrodite!" Zeus screamed amid his struggles. It was a waste of breath when he needed every effort for fighting, but he couldn't help himself.

Hades cut off the rest, seizing him by the neck. Zeus brought up a foot to his brother's groin and kicked, sending the death god flying backward toward Aphrodite.

She sidestepped her uncle's path and continued to speak to Zeus as he struggled and Hades rammed against the wall around the shelf.

"It's really quite logical, if you think about it!" she explained. "I wanted the mortals to worship me again, and I know you're happy when I get what I want. I'm happy when I can make you happy, so because I love you, I had to help kill you. And now that you're all back and angry, it makes me happy to get away with it. I really hate to do this to you, Daddy, but it comes from love! So really this hurts me more than it hurts you!"

Festooned with the other gods, Zeus rolled across the shelf, wrestling them all toward the phlegmatic field in the hope of using it against them if he could. "You are *no* daughter of mine, Aphrodite!"

The goddess crossed her arms and glared. "Appreciate my sacrifice, Daddy!"

"Shut yer yammerin' and help us, ya bleedin' goddess!" Ares shouted. Hades rushed in beside him to lend his strength to the others, slowing their approach to the field. "And where's that ruttin' rope!"

It is difficult to say just what might have happened then, had things continued. As the others flew in with the rope . . . as Athena calculated the odds of everyone letting go at once to let Zeus roll himself alone into the field with his own momentum . . . as Aphrodite drew her dagger once again to demonstrate the force of her love on her father's exposed kidneys . . . and as Tracy watched it all in a daze from her swinging prison with its rapidly diminishing oxygen supply—the world sneezed.

It was a sneeze as violent as if it were issued from an enraged elephant, and it trumpeted throughout the world. From the barista who woke from his nap in the stock room of the Sacred Grounds Café to the investigating officer at Sidgwick's Antique Shoppe in Swindon, no one who felt the sneeze knew what it was—no one save for the Olympians. So extreme was their horror that all struggling on the shelf ceased. Zeus and the others lay together, staring into the sky at the waves of blossoming energy that glowed far beyond the mortal spectrum and recoiling from the immediate realization of far greater problems.

For, hundreds of miles away in downtown Athens, Richard Kindgood and six other members of the NCMA had done something terrible, something unthinkable, something transcendently shortsighted: they had stopped at an American burger chain for lunch instead of trying some authentic Greek gyros.

Also, they released the Titans after dessert.

"Oh!" Demeter cooed. "They're back from the farm!"

CHAPTER THIRTY-SEVEN

"A powerful ritual, once completed, will manifest results almost instantly. It's the really powerful ones that make you wait. No one knows when annoying suspense got tangled up with quality, but it's exactly the sort of jerk-ass thing most would blame on Hermes if it hadn't started before his birth. Some suspect him regardless."

—Olympian Priesthood in Thirty Days!
(Day 24: Rituals Best Avoided)

AT THE BASE OF MOUNT PARNITHA, Stout regarded Kindgood across a rock where the nine brass cans lay open. "That can't be it, can it?"

Kindgood cast about for any change in the world. Beyond the deafening quiver of air that had whooshed out of nowhere when the last can was opened, all was silent. There were neither bright flashes of light from the heavens sent to purge the false gods from the Almighty's creation, nor archangels wielding swords of blazing white. There was not even a single bush that might be considered mildly smoldering. He had the terrible suspicion that he'd fallen victim to the spiritual equivalent of the joy buzzer—that the cans were some great bit of mischief on the part of the false gods or their followers, intended to mock the efforts of the faithful, and that the NCMA would certainly refuse to reimburse him the cost of plane tickets and lunch for all seven of them.

Stout awaited his answer with the look of a man similarly troubled. As the one in charge, Kindgood knew it remained up to him to respond appropriately to his fellow's crisis of faith.

"I think you did something wrong," Kindgood told him. "God grant me strength to forgive you. I will do my best to make sure our superiors understand you didn't mean to . . ."

A swirling bit of blue light appeared between them.

Stout stepped back, pointing. "A sign! By the glory of God, a sign!"

Kindgood stepped back a bit himself, fighting his own amazement. It was indeed a sign! He'd done it! Holy crap, he'd done it!

"God has chosen me to be filled with the power of His forgiveness!" Kindgood declared to the group. "I opened myself up to Him that I might forgive you, Gabriel Stout, and through me His glory is made manifest! I am the vessel through which He creates —" Kindgood pointed at the growing light, grasping for words. "—This!"

All seven of them staggered back as the light crackled and swelled. Ribbons of energy rippled across it and stretched the light taller and wider until it was a broad, blue vortex an arm's span across. Power gusted forth like a burst of wind to knock the group on their backs. The vortex swirled faster, continuing to grow and rising into the air above them as the brass cans trembled and rattled in place.

Pure power whipped Kindgood's hair and tugged at his clothes. "Now the false gods' time is at an end!" he yelled, exhilarated. "Now they shall reap the fruits of their blasphemy! Now we shall—"

The pull grew stronger, grasping at loose stones.

"Now we shall—"

A seagull shot backward over his head and into the vortex with a shrill cry.

"Now we shall . . . withdraw to safety and rejoice in—um . . ."

The vortex's lower edge sliced into the stone beneath it, cracking it in half and sucking the brass cans and their lids into blue oblivion. Stout scrambled to his feet on the other side, lost his balance against the pull, and tumbled screaming into the vortex after them.

"Run!" Kindgood yelled it more to his own body than to the others, who hardly needed him to tell them that at all. As the frightfully blue maw grew, both looming above and spinning like a saw blade into the Earth itself, someone grabbed his hand and tugged him to his feet. Desperate, he yanked on the helping hand and flung its owner backward to gain ground for himself. The helper disappeared into martyrdom; Kindgood didn't look back.

"For the greater good!" he called in apology. "I must escape to spread word of your sacrifice!"

It bought him no more than a few seconds. The pull raged stronger around him. It yanked the soil out from under his feet and set him scrambling. He fell forward, then up, legs flailing, arms grasping helplessly as he toppled head over heels into the vortex with the final thought that God sure as heck better be grateful.

Though there were none left to witness it, the vortex continued to grow, sucking in everything nearby until it was as tall as ten men. There it halted at its full dilation, blanketing the surrounding landscape in sudden, vortex-ie silence. The pull subsided. The blue light faded to gray mist. For a moment, nothing moved.

And at last a hand appeared from within, then another, and nine long-trapped entities began to crawl forth from their prison, gasping with the effort of their escape. It goes without saying that they were incensed.

Having said it anyway, it's still an understatement.

CHAPTER THIRTY-EIGHT

"The enemy of my enemy is my friend."

—*proverb, originator unknown*

"Some dolts'll believe anything if ya make it a proverb."

—*Ares*

"I AM GONE," Zeus seethed, "for nine small months . . . and you let the Titans get *released?*"

He'd recovered before the rest of them and seized the opportunity to yank himself from their shocked grips and spring to his feet. They followed suit, without renewing their assault.

"Really they didn't get released until you came back, strictly speaking," Hermes pointed out.

The lame joke sustained the silence for just a moment before all began shouting at once. Accusations flew like ice in a blizzard: some yelled at Hades; some yelled at Poseidon; some just yelled in no particular direction. Zeus couldn't even make out most of it, and he didn't care. He drew a mighty breath to silence them all.

His brother beat him to it.

"Silence!" Poseidon bellowed, slamming his trident into the stone and stealing Zeus's thunder. (Zeus quickly checked to make sure it was merely figurative. It was.)

"Our business with Zeus shall wait," Poseidon went on, glaring at Zeus, "and his with us! The Titans will be weak from their release, but it shall not last!"

"We take care o' Zeus first!" Ares yelled. "I ain't fightin' with him! 'Longside, anyways!"

"And have the Titans fall upon our backsides as we battle Zeus? No!" Poseidon slammed the trident down once more in emphasis. (He'd gotten better at it since becoming king, Zeus had to admit.) "We strike now, all of us together, beat them back into their prison again before it's too late, and *then* we shall deal with these matters! The Titans must be fought at once!"

"Oh!" Demeter gasped in revelation. "What if we simply—?"

"This problem cannot be solved with baked goods!"

"Well! Certainly not with that attitude."

"But Ares is right!" Aphrodite flung a petulant arm at Zeus. "Zeus vowed to punish the lot of us! You can't possibly suggest we trust him now! He disowned me! I'm his *favorite!*"

"Silence!" Poseidon ordered. "You will do as I say! I am your king!"

"For now," Zeus grumbled.

"Ya *see?*" Ares summoned a spear to his hands in an instant. He roared a battle cry and rushed before anyone could stop him.

Zeus was ready. He seized the spear in his bare hands and stepped to one side to yank Ares off his feet with the god's own furious momentum. It carried Ares around in a full circle, once, twice, three times as Zeus whirled the hapless war god like a hammer until finally the spear itself broke. Zeus timed it perfectly; Ares flew straight into the phlegmatic field and Tracy's dangling (and nearly forgotten) prison. The impact snapped the chain clean through and sent both phlegmatized war god and prison sailing clear out over the edge of the rocky shelf to splash into the waves.

Zeus hoped that thing was airtight.

"Who's next?" he demanded, bristling with cathartic release. Impending Titan threat or no, he almost hoped Ares would rise up again immediately just so he could smack him around again. How could one of his few children born in wedlock still turn out to be such a bastard?

"No one!" Poseidon demanded, putting an end to his fun. He pointed to Aphrodite and Hermes. "You, two, fetch Ares! The rest of you, gird yourselves! We battle the Titans!"

Hermes laughed. "Ah, yes, Titan-fighting requires completely different girding than Zeus-fighting. There's a whole color scheme, lots more lace!" Nevertheless, he did as Poseidon ordered.

"And you!" Poseidon pointed his trident at Zeus. "You had best help us, Zeus. If we lose to the Titans, they will seek you out to complete their vengeance just as you do now for those who struck you down!"

Zeus ground his teeth, barely restraining himself. If Poseidon thought to persuade with a reminder of the Olympians' crimes against him, he was a fool. "Of that I am certain," he growled.

"Assemble on Olympus!" Poseidon ordered them all. "We strike from there!" He rose upward and cast a final glare on Zeus. "Remember what I say!"

"Every word, *Brother*."

The others joined Poseidon. A beleaguered Ares, supported between Aphrodite and Hermes, lamented something about how people kept breaking his favorite spears. A brilliant flash of light later, Zeus was alone on the shelf.

Out amid the waves, Tracy's prison floated and bobbed. Zeus launched himself after it, scooped it up by the chain, and headed for shore.

Tracy was half-conscious already due to her suspension within the phlegmatic field—but Ares's impact into her prison had knocked her unconscious before she even hit the water, so one really has to wonder why the narrative now switches to her point of view. After all, she didn't see Zeus picking her out of the water or witness the singular experience of flying at lightning speed across the water in an airtight box. She did not even know that he carried her to the Cinque Terre on the Italian Riviera—a beautifully rugged stretch of five villages built upon sea cliffs, where she quite coincidentally had always wanted to vacation when she had the time. Yet through the magic of books, we can learn of such things regardless of Tracy's state of awareness.

Just promise not to tell her.

Or do tell her; it doesn't really matter. If you've not figured out by now that these people can't hear you, you've larger problems to worry about. Even if she could somehow hear you, she'd only be disappointed. She won't be staying in the Cinque Terre long. (More important, if you do tell her and she actually appears to hear you, seek help. Seriously. That's not a good sign. And shame on you for telling her anyway.)

It was the crack of Zeus ripping the top off the prison glass that finally jarred her to consciousness. Tracy opened her eyes, her body thick with residual fatigue, as Zeus lifted her from the box and stood her up without a word.

"It should be illegal to feel this bad without the fun of being drunk first," she grumbled.

"Easy, Daughter. You've been phlegmatized."

"Oog. I'm pretty sure that's not a word."

"It is now. Divine license."

"Uh-huh, sure." She groaned again and tested her legs. Though her body felt as if it were wrapped in thick rubber, her head was at least beginning to clear a little.

"How do you feel?" Zeus asked.

Zeus asked? For the first time, it registered as highly relevant that Zeus stood here helping her rather than being too busy in oblivion. She'd watched the entire scene on the shelf unfold from within her prison, yet this was the first time it didn't seem like a dream or a poorly written piece of fiction.

"Zeus?" she marveled . . . and then decked him in the arm. "Why did you *do* that to me? Do you know the kind of crap I've gone through in the past few days? What my friends have gone through? One of them died because of all this, for crying out loud!" Okay, she admitted to herself, Jason was really more pain-in-the-ass coworker than friend, but she was suddenly too pissed to let that soften her. Jason hadn't deserved what he'd gotten.

"And you just sprang it on me!" she went on. "No details, no nothing, just a vision and vague impulses to help you! And you messed with my *mind!*" She punched him again. "All this loyalty and burning need to bring your killers to justice!"

"You claim you would feel no anger at any murder?" Zeus demanded. "That you would not do what was in your power to find justice? I did not raise you, but you are my daughter, and I know you better than that! The amulet told you the truth of your heritage and amplified your natural tendencies. There was no brainwashing."

Even if it was true—and she couldn't be entirely sure it wasn't just further manipulation—the fact that it made sense only infuriated her more.

"But—you didn't even ask me!" Tracy pounded out her accumulated anger on his shoulder, punctuating every other word with a blow of her fists. "I find this damned thing in a cave and then there's Erinyes and pissed-off gods and idiot models coming out of the freaking woodwork!"

Zeus caught her forearm in mid pound and held it still with a warning glare. She stopped, out of breath and more than a little flustered, yet managed to match his glare with one of her own. To her surprise, he laughed.

"You have your father's temper."

She swallowed, cooling just a bit. "I always thought I got that from Mom."

"Jointly gifted, then. But I warn you, Tracy, as much gratitude as I have for what you've done, I will not allow you to raise a hand against me. I've suffered the treachery of one daughter today; I will brook no more from another." He released his grip. "I am sorry about your friend. What was her name?"

"His name," she corrected, still cranky. "Jason Powers. I actually ran into him on the way to his afterlife. He seemed happy with it, at least. No family."

"Suitable memorial will be given when this is over, I promise you."

"Yeah, well . . . good."

She would later wonder what it meant about her feelings for Jason that the potential ratings from Zeus's tribute for *Monster Slayer*'s fallen star didn't enter her mind until a good while afterward.

Tracy gave a long sigh, collecting herself. "So it all worked at least, right? You're not just half back and need me to do the Three Labors of Hercules or something, do you?"

"Hercules did twelve labors, not three." (Or thirteen, depending on who you ask.)

"I know. I lowballed it." She disliked bringing up the possibility of even three labors. No freaking way was she going to mention twelve.

"I see. You needn't worry; you completed the ritual."

She couldn't help but smile at that, as tentative and tinged with residual annoyance as it was. "Then we did it?" After everything, it didn't seem so easy to believe there wasn't more.

He grinned. "You did. Without full instructions, I might add. Were I any more filled with pride, I would surely rupture."

"Don't you dare. I'm not going through all that questing stuff again. Is Apollo okay?" she asked, not without a pang or seven of guilt. The question of Thalia's and, unfortunately, Leif's fates also sprang to mind, but one thing at a time.

"Captured, I suspect. Further questions must wait for the moment. We're far from out of the woods yet."

"Oh, of course. Because safety at this point would be too much to ask, right? And what's this 'we' stuff?"

"You—"

Tracy put up a hand. "*Oh*, no! I did what I was supposed to! I brought the king of the gods back to life! Don't I get a little vacation? A little rest? A little chance to get my life back in order?" At the very least she needed to call *Monster Slayer*'s production company to let them know what happened to Jason. And, she realized, to check on Dave and the doctor. Geez, she'd completely forgotten about them.

They're still fine, by the way.

"You brought me back, Tracy. Should I fail to regain my throne, the others will seek vengeance again. Our best hope lies in Switzerland. We must fly."

She balked. More endless traveling. "You're not diminished or anything, right? Wouldn't teleporting be faster? I've seen you guys do that."

"We are traveling somewhere secret, and teleports can be traced. Even with the others distracted by the Titans' release, I will take no chances. And no child of mine has a fear of heights. Come with me."

Zeus offered his hand, and she took it without thinking. (Zeus had a knack for that sort of thing.) "I'm not afraid of heights, but . . . I can't just come with you. I've got a life to get back to and responsibilities and—and it feels like I haven't eaten in days!"

They flew into the sky—or at least Zeus flew. Tracy mostly just hung on and dangled.

"Food I can fix quite easily."

"Good! Maybe if I get a little food, I can think about this better. And a sundae because I've been craving—"

Sudden recognition of the rapidly disappearing coastline beneath them cut her off.

"Hey!" she finally managed. "We're in the Cinque Terre? And we're *leaving?*"

"Yes."

Tracy groaned, still staring behind them in horrified disappointment. She waved good-bye to the ruggedly beautiful isolation and vowed to make Zeus take her back there at some point.

They soared toward the Alps, faster than Tracy would have thought possible until she recalled she was flying with a god. The speed placated the impatience that had been growing inside her since she'd escaped the prison. Wind rushed past her, whipping through her hair and continuing to clear her mind. Something else clicked.

"Hey!" she shouted through the wind. "Did you say something about the Titans?"

It was at that point, perhaps without coincidence, that the sky turned the exact shade of violet to best indicate that something was very, very wrong.

It was sort of a magenta-lavender with a twist of azure and nausea.

CHAPTER THIRTY-NINE

"It is difficult to confirm the names of the nine Titans imprisoned in Tartarus. The Olympians avoid speaking of the ancestors they insist are securely locked away. The only information given comes from an interview with Hermes who once listed their names before changing the subject. According to him, the trapped nine are as follows: along with Cronus (the Titans' leader and father of the first generation of Olympians) there is Astraeus, Coeus, Hyperion, Iapetus, Kreios, Menoetius, Phoebe, and Steve."
—A Mortal's Guidebook to the Olympians' Return

ON THE ROOF OF the CERN facility, Leif finally halted the pacing he'd begun when Zeus had effectively called Tracy a lost cause and hung up on their telepathy. He hadn't cooled; his worry had only increased, but his feet ached in worn-out shoes, and he was getting tired.

Also the sky was now suddenly the color of neon barf, so stopping to gape in wondering fear seemed more than appropriate.

"Zeus?" he tried. *"Zeus, answer me! What's going on!"*

Yet again, Zeus gave no response. Why the heck did the guy give telepathy if he didn't answer? Par for the course, really; Zeus was an idiot, just like all the other gods, or extra-dimensional beings, or whatever they actually were. Zeus didn't listen. Apollo didn't listen. Oh, sure — sometimes they had the same ideas as Leif did, but otherwise they were too stupid and stubborn to realize they were wrong.

And now Tracy was probably dead and the sky was barf.

There wasn't a thing he could do about it either. Not a single frelling thing. Except . . . maybe one.

He began hurling the potted plants off the roof patio into the parking lot below. It wouldn't help a damned thing, but at least it gave him something to do.

"Stupid!" he yelled. A potted maple shattered on concrete three stories down.

"Frelling!" he screamed. Edelweiss and soil burst across the hood of someone's Lexus.

"So-called *gods!*" he shouted, chucking some other kind of plant onto the lawn. (He had no idea what that one was. He wasn't a botanist, after all.)

"Okay, Leif," he tried telling himself while struggling with a larger maple. "Calm down. Get a hold of yourself. None of it matters. It's just real life . . ."

It didn't help as much as it usually did.

"Mortal!" Zeus shouted from behind him and through the telepathic link, startling Leif all but over the edge himself. He dropped the maple to the deck and barely avoided crushing his own feet. "Stop playing with gravity! Things are dire!"

Leif rushed at Zeus and stopped short of tackling him. (He was angry, not stupid.) "Where's Tracy?" Leif demanded. He also flung an arm demonstratively at the sky for some reason. Tracy ostensibly was not in the sky; Leif could only guess his right arm wished to make an inquiry about that whole barf matter on its own behalf. For the moment, he let it.

Zeus rose up to his full height, one eyebrow cocked, as if giving Leif a moment to change his tone. Leif met him halfway with a meek inability to repeat his question, merely swallowing and waiting. He tried to force additional furious expectancy into the set of his jaw and succeeded only in making his chin quiver.

"Tracy is inside," Zeus said at last. "She is fine."

Leif dashed past him and through the doors to beat a path down the roof stairs.

"Where?" he thought to Zeus.

"Apologize for your earlier lack of reverence. You are a priest of Zeus; I command you treat your god with respect".

Leif exited the stairwell and looked in both directions down an empty hallway. "Tracy!" he tried, fruitlessly. *"Fine,"* he sent to Zeus.

"I'm sorry I got angry when you sounded like you left your own daughter to the wolves. Now, please, where is she?" His arm again flung outward, pointing to the sky this time through a window at the end of the corridor. He yanked it down.

"That wasn't so hard, was it, Mr. Karlson? Now: status report. Is the collider prepared?"

Leif continued his search, rolling his eyes at the question. Zeus just didn't listen. *"No, the collider isn't prepared! I told you they couldn't do anything about it until you got here with the final bits! What did you expect?"* He stopped short of telling Zeus that "they cannae change the laws of physics."

He missed Thalia.

"Respect!" Zeus thundered.

"Okay, okay. What did you expect, sir! Sheesh!" Wait, did he just think the "sheesh" or actually send it? This telepathy stuff was a pain in the butt.

"I will see them immediately, as you are clearly too distracted. Tracy is at dinner in the commissary. I will join you swiftly."

"Thank you," sent Leif with genuine relief.

"Your gratitude is noted. And, Mr. Karlson? Do not get grabby with my daughter."

Leif sincerely hoped the mental image that had thrust itself into his mind didn't go across the link. As no lightning struck him immediately thereafter, he guessed it hadn't.

He dashed down the hall, shot down another flight of stairs, and burst through the commissary doors to find a beautifully haggard-looking Tracy munching on a burger with a substantial banana split sundae waiting nearby. She glanced toward him, stopped chewing, and—perhaps surprisingly—smiled.

What truly did surprise him was the standing hug she gave him when he got to her table. He stood there in shock and only belatedly thought to return the embrace. Through his elation he couldn't help but wonder what sort of tampering might have occurred in her brain since he'd seen her last.

"Zeus told me what you did," she said. "Thanks."

"Well, you know, just . . . trying to help."

"I appreciate it." She let go and sat back down. Burger in hand once more, she pointed it at him sternly. "But to be clear, that was just a gratitude hug, understand? I'm not running off with you to some chapel or anything."

Leif took a seat. "Well, duh. We'll start slow. Dating. You like bar trivia?"

"No. No dating." Tracy chomped a bite. "Jusht friendsh."

Leif cursed inwardly. At least he'd made progress. He grinned. "You hugged me."

"Right. Don't make me regret it." She smiled wearily. "And anyway there's worse things to worry about. Did you see the sky?"

"The sky?" He'd nearly forgotten. His arm shot outward, pointing for a third time. "I mean, yeah. I assumed something else horrible happened but was just so glad to see you."

"Something else horrible did happen. The Titans got loose."

"Oh," said Leif. "Is that all?"

She gaped. "Is that all?"

"Well aside from the fact that every 'sky blue' color swatch in the world is now misnamed, it's not really our problem, is it? They're not some ultimate evil; they're just the previous administration of—whatever the 'gods' are."

"And they're pissed!"

"I don't blame them, but I didn't shut them up in tartar sauce!"

"Tartarus."

"I was being funny."

She bristled at him. "You don't think a bunch of god-level types duking it out is going to cause some problems for the rest of us?"

"Well, maybe, but—"

"And you know who they're mad at the most? Zeus! I—we—just risked our lives to bring the guy back, to say nothing of how he's my father—and now they're going to come try to do I-don't-know-what to him!"

"Are you mad because he's in danger or 'cause you might've gone through all that for nothing?"

She chomped another bite, chewed all the way, and swallowed before she answered. "Both! And besides, Apollo, Thalia—you like them, right? They're in danger too!"

"Okay, but there's not really much we can do about it, is there?"

"You should at least be upset! Or worried. Or something!"

He grinned. "I'm still high on seeing you alive again."

She sighed. "I think I envy you. Right now all I really want to do is just eat and rest. Ignore all of this, but . . . Geez, I don't know. Maybe you're right."

"Sure I am. It'll all work out somehow. We've done enough." Another thought hit him before Tracy could respond. The grin fell. "Hey, you don't think they'd do something to you for being Zeus's daughter, do you?"

"Thanks, I was trying not to think about that one," she answered. "But the other gods went off to fight them, so I figure I'll be safe enough for at least a little while with Zeus around."

"Don't be so sure," Leif grumbled.

"You're not exactly being helpful here. What's that supposed to mean?"

The commissary doors swung open again. Zeus made straight for their table, looking pensive in a way that clearly didn't suit him. *"Do not answer that,"* he thought to Leif.

Leif hesitated to answer long enough to let Tracy notice before he turned to Zeus. "The Titans are out? Is that true?"

"It is."

"And . . . ?"

"And what, Mr. Karlson?"

"More information would be nice. Ancient enemies, out of prison, probably pissed I'm sure. This is bad, right? Or is it some part of your plan? You let them loose?"

"Only a fool would let the Titans loose. Yet now that they are free, it may work to my advantage. The enemy of my enemy is my friend."

"Are you talking about the Titans or the other Olympians?" asked Tracy.

"Both. Either. Whichever. It depends on how things go. The struggle will weaken both sides."

"Rather Machiavellian of you," Leif observed, not without relish. He didn't often get a chance to use that word. "You really didn't let them loose yourself?"

Zeus scowled and pointed a stolen French fry at him. "What did I just say? The last I knew, they were safely hidden away in an antique shop in Swindon."

"When I was in Hades, I saw Jason's ghost. He said something destructive and angry was going to be released. Something to do with

Swindon." Tracy pointed her burger at Leif. "And that's another reason I'm upset about this."

"Well, you should've mentioned that."

"Bite me."

"The Titans were dealt with before," Zeus assured them. "They will be dealt with again. But not yet."

"Not yet?" Leif balked just a little. The threat the Titans posed to Tracy had begun to worry him, especially given how willing Zeus was to declare her an acceptable loss. And the whole "destructive and angry" bit bothered him more than he liked. "Shouldn't you be out there now before they can do much damage?"

Zeus shook his head. "The others fight them now. They will keep them busy, for a time."

"Yeah, but—suppose they can't do the job fast enough without your help? What then?"

"I will make no move until I am ready," Zeus declared. "In this my will is immutable."

"But—" Leif tried.

"I command you to speak no more of this, Mr. Karlson," Zeus warned. "Even now Dr. Kowalski's team makes the final adjustments to the collider. Only once it is complete shall I enter this battle, on my own terms, and no sooner. Eat, then rest, both of you." He pointed at Leif. "You especially."

"Destructive and angry!" Leif repeated. "And anyway weren't you going to put in a good word for me with . . ." He indicated Tracy with a nod that she didn't appear to notice.

"Patience," growled Zeus. "I command it."

As Leif and Tracy slept, the Second Titan War raged. Out of the vortex had come the nine imprisoned Titans, and though their forms were weak from the transition to our world and millennia of atrophy, their power was nonetheless a force to be reckoned with.

(Go on, reckon with it a bit. There you go.)

While the Titans still lay in gasping wonder in the light of the Tartarus vortex, recovering their strength, Poseidon led the Olympian assault against them. They would hit the Titans when they were weakest, he'd declared; not a moment would be wasted.

There was barely time to get organized, almost zero time to form any sort of battle strategy, certainly no time to release Apollo and secure his loyalty, and not even time—Demeter and Hestia both lamented—for a good, hearty bowl of oatmeal. The Olympians had one objective only: force the Titans back into their prison through any means necessary.

Understand: the concept of god-level beings fighting is a tricky one. They bring cosmic energies to bear for both attack and defense, in manners both overt and involuntary. Battling gods trade supernatural attacks, parries, and counterattacks of increasing complexity and reality-rending power, building them atop each other at a frenetic pace. A mortal witnessing such events can neither discern every nuance nor truly comprehend the nature of what is occurring—so far is it beyond their understanding, their grasp of the universe, and very possibly their vocabulary.

The very same goes for trying to depict such battles in a text such as this. Even describing every intricacy of a brief cosmic arm-wrestling match would take pages—the reading of which would require hours beyond the fraction of a minute the match would take to complete. To describe every instant of an entire Olympian-Titan battle would require several carloads of text with at least thirty-seven supplemental appendixes. Simply reading such a depiction would likely take months. To comprehend even half of it would require a dozen doctoral degrees in the hard sciences, psychology, and—for some reason—fishery sciences. Such texts are a very hard sell for publishers (despite Ayn Rand's success), and for this reason even the shortest god battles in this narrative, as alert readers have surely noted, are described in abstract terms that capture the general appearances and magnitude of the struggle. (A true description of every element relating to Apollo's earlier clocking of Ares would truly make Einstein weep.)

Yet even in abstract terms, the opening moments of the second Titanomachy were violently impressive.

The Olympians descended upon the Titans while cloaked in a field of darkness projected by Hecate. (Guilt-ridden over her part in the affair, she had volunteered her powers immediately when the time came, hoping desperately no one would discover the true reason behind her uncharacteristic cooperation.) They assailed the Titans, launching at them arrows, energies, and other baneful projectiles from the goddess's flying mass of obscurity.

For a brief time, it worked. The Titans scrambled to their feet and sought to shield themselves from the Olympian's strikes. Some struggled to cover; others hurled rocks, trees, and energies of their own into the blackness, unable to find a target. Yet, even though the Olympians succeeded in restarting the suction of the Tartarus vortex, they could not drive the Titans back into their prison. Instead the Titans fled *en masse* up Mount Parnitha with the Olympians at their heels until the Titans turned and sprang down into the darkness from the mountaintop. Flailing their arms blindly, one of them struck Hecate in the face by sheer luck. Stunned, she flew into the Aegean and sank for a time under the waves, her darkness dispersed.

The Olympians, suddenly vulnerable, scattered.

Then the battle began in earnest. The younger generation reformed into smaller groups, ganging up on individual Titans in an effort to weaken them one at a time so that they might be recaptured.

Athena, still holding Zeus's mighty Aegis shield, gave cover to both Ares and Artemis, who flung death at the Titans. Artemis launched volley after volley of silver arrows, while Ares yelled in defiance behind his bucking cosmic-repeating-depleted-uranium gauss rifle.

Less organized were Aphrodite, Dionysus, Hephaestus, and Hermes. Unused to full combat, they eventually worked out a chaotic mix of flying about trying to get the Titans drunk, seduce them, and hit them in the face with a forge hammer. Though Hermes kept the four of them moving too fast to catch, the rest of that plan didn't work particularly well.

With the exception of Demeter and Hestia—who worked together to weave and wield a huge hemp net that Hestia continually insisted would be better constructed if she could just work on it from home— the elder generation fought alone. Veterans of the first Titan War, they were no longer children, and long ago mastered the weapons they'd only begun to use in that original struggle. Hera wielded blades formed of sheer strength of will. Hades dived bodily upon the Titans with pure inexorable strength and pummeled them with fists of heavy metals. Poseidon, strongest of all, shook the Titans from their feet with earthquakes, assailed them with tidal waves, and punctuated both methods with signature trident thrusts.

Yet without Zeus's strength, his lightning, his power, the battle was nothing but a furious stalemate. For every Titan stunned, another surged forward to beat off the attackers and regain lost ground. Devastating forces hurled Titanic bodies across the landscape, mighty blows pummeled the Olympians in retaliation, and collateral damage obliterated the city of Athens within minutes. The Olympians could not keep the Titans from straying from the vortex, and soon the war raged out of control across the globe.

As far as the planet's mortals could tell, the very forces of nature were at war under a hideously colored sky. Only by the flash of Poseidon's visage in a hurricane, or Hades's booming whisper ordering the Titans back to their prison, could they infer a fraction of the battle that was underway.

This did not stop every single news media outlet, blogger, or pundit from reporting on it, of course.

CHAPTER FORTY

"Titans released! Can we fling enough blame to fix the problem?"
—*Cable news ticker*

TRACY WAS STARING IN RAPT ATTENTION at the news reports, absentmindedly munching a bowl of cereal in the room at CERN that Zeus had converted into her bedroom, when Leif arrived. Though she missed the details of his morning greeting, she managed to tear herself away from the screen long enough to nod at him and point at the TV with her spoon.

"This is insane," she said.

He grabbed a bowl of his own and sat down. "How long have you been watching?"

"Got up half an hour ago."

A blaring fanfare drowned out Leif's response. With it, a news logo exploded across the screen in fire and lightning that read, *WAR! Between the GODS!*

"Not technically correct," Tracy said.

"On a number of levels."

It was better than some she'd seen so far, though. Every single channel was reporting on the struggle with the Titans, with each channel using its own unique catch phrase, title logo, and theme music. Differentiation was important, but there were only so many good titles to go around. (ENT!'s reports chose to call it Titan War 2: Olympic Boogaloo! It *was* rather catchy, she had to admit, but the accompanying disco-lyre music had forced her to find a different station.)

Leif snorted. "Nice logo, though. *Their* reporting must be top notch."

"People always mock the logos," Tracy mumbled. "Research shows they work."

"What research?"

"Do you mind?" She pointed at the screen and tuned out Leif to focus on a live report from outside the White House. Nothing was occurring behind the reporter, and as it was evening in Washington, D.C., the altered color of the sky was barely discernable. Still, it made for a nice backdrop.

"*. . . United States is among the many nations from which Ares is calling in favors. As armed forces mobilize to assist the Olympians, the question remains as to how effective they can possibly be. The Titanic struggle moves quickly, says the Pentagon, leaving military forces insufficient time to maneuver into striking position before their targets move on. When asked what this means for the defense of American cities, officials would only state that they are working with the Olympians and will not discuss further details with the media at this time. Yet with the destruction of Athens, Maui, and large swaths of land across the European mainland and Canada . . .*"

"Athens and Maui are *gone?*" Leif burst.

"Yeah." Tracy fixed him with a grim look. "They came out of this big blue vortex thing near Athens—no one's sure why—and the fighting started there before it spread. One of the Titans tried to shove an Olympian down one of the Maui volcanoes; they're not sure who, but I think it was Dionysus, judging from the footage. I think he escaped, but it set the volcano off and they had to evacuate the island. They're throwing mountains around in Canada; *some*one had a wrestling match in Eastern Europe. It's out of control!"

"Zeus still hasn't done anything to help stop it either," he said. "He says he's got a plan, but if he doesn't get his ass in the fight soon and help them stop this . . ."

Leif trailed off as the news report showed a map of the globe. Areas in red marked locations where numerous divine struggles had taken place. Most were in less-populated areas, but the sheer number of them horrified Tracy. Professionally critiquing the media coverage of it all was almost her only coping mechanism at the moment.

"Reality sucks!" Leif cursed. "Mythology was a lot better when it was fake."

"Even with the crap and danger I've had to deal with since finding out Zeus was my dad, the whole gods-being-real thing still fascinates me. But this is too much."

"No kidding. This stuff needs to go back to being fantasy so I can enjoy it again." Leif straightened a bit. "Yeah, sure, we'll be there in a sec." He rolled his eyes, adding, "Sir."

"Excuse me?"

"Zeus wants us to come down to the collider. It's a telepathy thing," he explained in response to Tracy's incredulous stare. "Sounded like a good idea at the time."

Tracy switched off the TV at the sight of an unidentified Titan appropriating Jefferson's head from Mt. Rushmore and throwing it. Only then did she spot the cranberry orange nut muffin Leif had apparently brought for her. With an appraising look to make sure his back was turned on his way to the door, she snatched it up and followed.

The two soon entered an elevator that took them hundreds of feet beneath the surface to the reactor level. From there, a small electric car carried them the rest of the way along the subtle curve of the collider, to what Leif described as a secretly built auxiliary chamber adjacent to one of the collider's detector caverns. Leif still had no idea just what the device that Zeus ordered to be built in the auxiliary chamber did, but he explained that in the detector caverns, proton streams would cross at velocities close to the speed of light and could be made to collide using magnets.

"Magnets are important," he explained as they entered the chamber. "I remember being told that much."

"Apollo!" Tracy shouted.

The diminished sun god stood atop the stairs leading up to what seemed to be some sort of reaction chamber, his hands clasped behind him as he examined it. He turned and waved.

"How'd you get out?" Leif asked. "Why aren't you out fighting? Still diminished?"

Apollo's smile faltered. "Yes, still. Please stop bringing that up."

"I shall fix that posthaste," spoke Zeus. He descended a different staircase, this one leading down from what looked to be the control room, judging by the wide windows and numerous, smartly pensive lab-coated individuals milling about. "The others left him more or less unguarded in the chaos. His rescue was hardly a challenge."

"Good to know you're doing *something*," Leif muttered. Zeus appeared not to catch it. "Is Thalia with you?"

"On Olympus with her sisters, but safe for the moment," Apollo told them.

"Despite Calliope's skill with slow-motion kickboxing," Zeus explained, "the Muses are little help in a fight of this nature."

"We've noticed," Tracy said.

"Thalia did help keep the Erinyes out of the temple for you, you know," Leif said.

Tracy's eyebrows raised. "Fighting?"

"No, but she made for a helpful distraction. She did good."

"Remind me to thank her."

"Be sure to thank Thalia." Leif turned to Zeus. "So we're all here to see this master plan of yours that's kept you from helping out with the Titans, right?"

"Most assuredly," Zeus announced. "You are all to be witness to evidence of my glory and foresight; Apollo's own skill at prophecy notwithstanding, of course."

Apollo nodded in polite acknowledgment.

"Here, in this specially built room, through the miracle of science held aloft by my own power and knowledge as rightful king of the Olympians, I shall return stability to the world and to the pantheon upon Olympus. I shall create the means to justly punish those responsible for my untimely, heinous, and astoundingly uncouth demise!" Zeus, beaming more proudly than Tracy had ever seen (which is to say, since meeting him late the previous afternoon), called up to the control room. "Dr. Kowalski! Begin proton acceleration!"

This sparked a rustle of activity in the control room as scientists dashed about in their obedience and white coats.

"That," Zeus declared, "is the first step! Hydrogen protons are now being ripped from their electrons and accelerated via oscillating magnetic fields"—("See? Magnets," Leif whispered.)—"faster and faster through successive circular tracks until they carry masses and energies not seen since the dawn of *time!*" Zeus paused. "Or so they tell me. It's not precisely important beyond the fact that, eventually, they'll be rapid enough and massive enough to unleash the energies we need." He pointed through the wall to the detector cavern. "Protons will collide—right there!—over and over. That energy will be drawn into this chamber here, whereupon it shall be manipulated through processes far too complicated to explain. Suffice it to say it incorporates a combination of my own divine power, rocks of ancient power culled from the rings of the planet Saturn"—("Named after your grandpa's Roman name, which has something to do with . . . something," Leif whispered to Tracy again.)—"and one last thing, which I picked up myself just this morning."

Zeus showed them a small silver platter, upon which sat six large pieces of what looked to Tracy like—

"*Fudge?*" Leif asked.

"Really *good* fudge," Zeus corrected.

"I mentioned that to you once," Apollo told Leif with a chuckle. "You doubted it then too, as I recall."

"Chocolate," Zeus continued, "is the key to numerous divine machinations, and this particular process needs top-quality stuff. Why do you think I made them build this place in Switzerland?"

Tracy held back about half a dozen questions on that topic. Zeus was building to a fervor:

"Make no mistake!" (Leif snorted for some reason.) "Were I still in my rightful place as king of the gods, I could do this—I *have* done this—without the collider at all. Yet in this time of strife, this time of betrayal, this time when I can trust few but those assembled here, I must take drastic action! Desperate times call for desperate measures! When the going gets tough, the tough get going! And . . . so forth."

Tracy cleared her throat. "But what does it do?"

Zeus laughed. "Ah, my dear daughter, so sharp, so inquisitive. Never lose that; I command it. What does it do? It makes *gods.*"

"From scratch?" Tracy asked.

"No, not from scratch!" Zeus laughed. He indicated the three of them in turn. "But from a diminished god, and from the daughter of a god, and from the high priest—more or less—of a god! And from . . . other things."

Tracy's eyes went wide. "Hold on. I never agreed to this!"

"And that has what to do with the price of ambrosia?" Zeus asked. "I am your father, your king. I—"

"Command it, yes," Tracy finished for him. "At least give me a few moments to think about it, right?"

Zeus gave her the same look her mother did whenever Tracy tried explaining her objection to getting breast implants. "Think about what?"

"Geez, *Dad,* don't you know anything about me? All my life I've tried to work for everything because I want to be able to look back on my achievements and know that I earned them: my college degrees, creating and producing *Monster Slayer,* even bringing you back! If something falls in my lap because I'm pretty or privileged or I seduced my way into it, what good is it? Now you want to hand me freaking godhood because of what, nepotism?"

"Um, Titans destroying the world here . . ." Leif muttered.

Zeus silenced him. "On the contrary, Tracy. Most of my relatives either stand against me or have actively tried to kill me. Just yesterday Aphrodite literally stabbed me in the back. I am handing you 'freaking godhood' for the sole reason that you've proved your loyalty."

"And because I'm your daughter. What about the scientists who've helped you with all this? Do they get godhood?"

Apollo frowned. "Your stubbornness is becoming quite the character flaw, dear half-sister."

"The scientists fear that becoming gods will shed doubt on the accuracy of their experiments here," Zeus answered. "Something about invalidated calculations, scientific method, and the difficulty of publishing papers with proper peer review. In any case I do not wish to risk them in combat with the Titans, in case I have need of their skills a second time."

"That's another thing!" Tracy declared. "You're bringing me into a war, here! Don't I get to be nervous about that after all I've been through already? All right, so that's a bit cowardly, I know something needs to be done, it's just . . ."

"You want to get this on the merits of your talent," Zeus finished with a smile. "I could point out that your skills and talents were also inherited by virtue of your simply being an Olympian's daughter. Even were you to 'earn' this, you would owe it to your genes."

The assertion slapped her in the face almost palpably as she realized she'd never thought of it that way before. "I just want to be normal," she groaned.

Leif's groan echoed hers, with an extra tinge of annoyance. "Oh, yeah, poor you, Tracy, you're cursed with awesome. Must be rough. Just suck it up and deal with it, all right? You're like someone who wins the lottery and then whines about all the taxes they'll have to pay." His scowl vanished the moment Tracy turned to see it. "Still love yooouu!" he cooed.

She squared her jaw, envious of all Leif had accomplished recently without the help of any supernatural genes. Why couldn't she be like that? Why couldn't she get something done that people couldn't credit to her genes? Or at the very least, what was wrong with her that she couldn't just shut up and accept it, as everyone was saying?

"Enough hesitation!" Zeus declared. "I command it! Your father needs you, your people need you, and that's all there is to it. I must retake my throne. The carnage of the Titanomachy must be extirpated!"

Tracy sighed to draw out the moment as long as possible. "All right, fine. If it'll extirpate carnage." It wasn't a gift, she told herself; it was a favor to Zeus. "I can renounce it all right after we deal with the Titans, though, right?"

"Oh, I expect you'll pretty much have to." Zeus nodded. "But there will be a chance for you to reconsider."

She took a deep breath and reconciled herself to the decision.

"Watch your necks," Apollo warned. At least he said it with a grin.

"I said I was sorry about that. Let's do this before I change my mind."

"Yes, let's!" Leif agreed. "And before Ares starts flinging nukes around too! Hey, speaking of that, who gets to be god of what?"

"Details to be worked out later," Zeus commanded. "Apollo first."

As it turned out, recharging Apollo wasn't nearly as flashy as Tracy would have expected—at least not from her vantage point outside the windowless chamber. Zeus sealed him inside with a bit of fudge, called a few orders up to the control booth, then pressed his hands against the door in concentration. A powerful hum swelled and set everything vibrating ever so slightly, until those in the control booth announced the opening of safety locks and the countdown to proton stream collision. Tracy had only five seconds to decide she didn't care why Leif found "Safety lock open!" so funny, before she jumped at a rapid series of bangs that sounded like an MRI machine firing. The vibrating subsided, and then it was over.

The chamber door opened to reveal Apollo, frankly looking just as he had before save for a beaming smile and a brighter twinkle in his eye.

"How do we tell if it worked?" she asked.

"Trust me," Apollo said. "It worked."

Well, there it was, then.

Leif paused halfway into the chamber. "It won't kill me, right?"

"Oh, heavens, no!" Zeus answered. "Nothing like that, I'm sure."

"Okay, but if I wind up flying through time putting right what once went wrong, I'm not going to be happy." He nabbed the fudge and stepped farther into the chamber. "Hey, it won't kill me, but is it going to hurt very mu—?"

Zeus sealed the chamber. The process began anew. Humming swelled, safety locks opened, countdowns began in dramatic fashion, and another series of MRI-ish bangs later, the procedure was finished.

Zeus opened the door once again. "How do you fee—? Oh. Well, then. Apollo, check to see if he's dead, will you?"

Apollo rushed in beside Leif, who lay slumped against the side of the chamber with a slight nosebleed and his mouth open wide enough to swallow a Studebaker.

"He's all right," Apollo reported. "Just a bit stunned, I expect. There is new power within him, though."

"Excellent. Bring him out. Give him a bit of time to adjust. Daughter?" Zeus motioned her inside.

Though her stomach knotted, she followed suit. Leif would not outdo her. The door closed.

Only then did she notice the sign on the inside of the door: "Warning: Do not eat the fudge."

There was nothing to do but wait, smell the fudge in her hands, and try to breathe. Again the humming began, rising until she could feel the fabric of her clothes buzzing across her skin. A metallic iris opened behind her to reveal a long tube lined with strange-looking rocks that immediately began to spin rapidly. Her heart pounding, she clutched the fudge into a gooey mess, frozen in place until at once there was a blinding flash from all around her. Energy fired from the tube into her body with a rapid series of bangs, and the fudge burst into white, engulfing flames that carried her into eternity. In an instant that was perfectly ordered in its intricacy, reality presented itself for her inspection, gave itself over to her and—amid a flowering cascade of glorious beauty and unwinding mystery the likes of which few mortals ever encounter—willingly became her plaything to control.

And then it blew up.

Tracy woke after Leif did, finding herself on a couch in one of the facility's aboveground offices. The heinous, purple sky casting its light through the windows swiftly brought her back to reality. She jumped up with a start, careened off the ceiling, and then somehow landed on her feet.

Well, she thought, that was unique.

"Aha, she wakes!" Zeus declared.

Apollo added his smile to Zeus's. Leif, who'd rushed to catch her before she landed fine on her own, gave a little wave.

"How long have I—?" *Thirty-eight minutes.* The answer jumped to mind before she could even get the question out. She was sure of it, just as sure as she was that her boots were black. Highly accurate internal clock? If she kept this godhood thing, she could get rid of her watch. Then again, she liked her watch.

"Been out?" Zeus finished for her. "Thirty-eight minutes. It took you a little longer to adjust than the others."

"How do you feel?" Leif asked.

"Good. Powerful. Why is there an oak tree in the corner?" Tracy asked upon turning around for the first time. She felt power radiating from it with enhanced senses she'd only begun to realize.

Also, the tree moved.

"Is that . . . ?"

The tree waved a branch. "Hellos to you, Tracy Zeus's Daughter! Did you be havings a good nap? This is being strange place, isn't it? All the rocks are looking funny. And . . . squishy." It picked up a couch cushion and squeezed demonstrably.

Tracy couldn't help but grin. "You elevated the guardian-tree?"

"Call me not 'guardian-tree'!" burst the guardian-tree. "Am guardian-tree no more! Am being *god*-tree, and now you call me by new true name I be having! I am . . ." Here the tree paused for some sort of dramatic arboreal breath-taking. "Jerry!"

"Jerry used to be dead," Leif explained. "I don't think you saw that part."

"Skinny man is being right! Big, ugly womans with buzzing rock-stick cut Jerry in half! In *half!* But is O-kay! Cry not for Jerry! Zeus is making me better, which almost is making up for many, many, many years ignoring Jerry."

"He wasn't, strictly speaking, dead," Zeus explained. "Not in the sense that mortal humans can be. There was no spirit to retrieve from the underworld. Jerry is best described as an elevated force of nature given divinity by the same process you experienced. Clearly it was the prudent thing to do until I can determine which, if any, other mortals are trustworthy. Jerry is one of three created in this way. I suppose you could call them brothers."

"Only three?"

"I must save my strength, Tracy. Even with the help of the collider device, granting you such power drains me for a time, and there is battle to be done!"

"Yeah, speaking of which . . ." Leif checked his watch out of what Tracy could only assume was habit. Then again, maybe he didn't get the same sort of power she did.

"Aetoc is returnings!" Jerry declared, pointing toward the open door to the deck outside. A sizable golden eagle soared in from beyond to alight on the deck railing with the grip of a single talon. In the other, the eagle held a large fish of some sort. Tracy guessed a trout, but fish were outside of her area of expertise and, apparently, additional knowledge of them was not within whatever powers she'd been granted.

(Don't feel sorry for Tracy. As valuable abilities go, instantaneous fish identification—while not without its uses—is not among the top ten.)

The eagle—named Aetoc if "Jerry" could be trusted—leaped from the railing, sailed the short distance through the open door, and deposited the fish onto the seat of a broad chair before perching on its back (the chair's, not the fish's). After a greeting nod of his proud head to Tracy, he reported, "The area remains clear, Lord Zeus. No Titans nor Olympians for at least a hundred kilometers."

His voice startled Tracy, not because he had a voice at all (previously encountered talking trees tend to blunt such surprises), but for its sound: soft as feathers, yet sharp as talons. She supposed it was appropriate and moments later hoped he would speak again.

"One of Jerry's brothers," Zeus explained quite needlessly.

"Pleased am I that you have woken, Tracy Wallace," Aetoc whispered, nodding again.

"I love the eagle as I love the oak tree," continued Zeus. "It was a simple choice. His eyes are better than any other of Olympus. Were Hermes lurking invisible in the shadows a mile off, Aetoc could spot him easily. He is noble, he is proud—"

"He is *quiet*," Apollo muttered with a sidelong glance at Jerry.

"Aetoc is not being quiet!" Jerry boomed. "I be knowing him for twenty minutes, and he is being more talkative than all birds and lizards I be knowing putted together!"

"What's with the fish?" Tracy asked.

"Um, he likes fish?"

Aetoc nodded and then tore into the fish without getting an ounce of mess on the chair.

"I think we should introduce her to Baskin now," Leif said. "And then, ya know, do the save-the-world thing, 'cause that usually winds up taking longer than you'd expect, and I still think there's got to be some big twist to get out of the way."

"Rush me not, Mr. Karlson," Zeus answered. "Nevertheless, you are right on the first count at least. Baskin! My daughter has awoken! Return and meet she who inspired your existence!"

From the parking lot came a cry of, "At last!"

Zeus grinned proudly. "He's been guarding the entrance since I elevated him. He is *fearsome*."

On cue, a fat, milky white hand speckled with flecks of color grabbed the balcony railing from below. Another followed, heralding a grunt of exertion as the new divine being apparently known as Baskin hauled itself up to the deck. Tracy stared. Dumbfounded amazement barely held her brewing laughter in check.

"I believed it fitting that I create the third brother out of an element that my only loyal daughter loves," Zeus said.

"He came out a little . . . odd," Leif whispered.

"One might say he's a little nuts," Apollo added. "But, not I."

The seven-foot-tall Baskin regarded her from the deck. Seconds later he swept into the room in a cascade of movement while she continued to stare.

"You're . . . an elevated sundae?" she asked. Amusement was winning out over amazement.

"Believe it!"

She grinned, unable to help herself. "Sweet."

Baskin recoiled in a swirl of offended richness. *"Sweet?"* he boomed. "I am not sweet! I am a being of fearsome violence and power! I am frigid *might* lurking between the carcass of a banana that bladed *violence* has cleft asunder! My strength is undeniable, born in ice and cravings irresistible! My will is glacial, forged by cream brutally whipped beneath a cherry the color of crimson *blood!* None—I say none!—shall stand against me! I am an ice cream headache incarnate! I am frozen terror! I am *power overwhelming!"* Baskin surged forward. His wide mouth blasted her with cold breath, demanding, "Do you declare yourself loyal to Zeus?"

"That's a—"

"Do you declare yourself loyal to Zeus!"

Tracy held her ground in the face of violent absurdity. "I'm the one who brought him back to life!" Good cripes, she thought, she was yelling at ice cream.

Apparently satisfied, Baskin backed down. "Then we shall have no problems! *My* loyalty is to Zeus the creator, to whom we owe our allegiance! Let it be known that any who claim otherwise—that any who raise even a finger against him—shall know the terror of my sprinkles!"

Zeus held out a calming hand. "Thank you, Baskin. You are indeed a mighty force for my glory, but please, save your passion for the battlefield."

"Yeah," Leif muttered, "chill out."

"Eat me!" Baskin roared back.

Tracy, for the moment, was speechless.

"Do we now go to fight against those who would claim false dominance over you, Lord Zeus?" asked Baskin. "I am ready!"

"I regret that we must wait."

"Still?" Leif shot. "Oh come on!"

"Do not question our Lord Zeus!"

Zeus restrained Baskin with a single hand. "Seizing victory from the crisis we face requires strategy. The time to strike grows close, but we must allow the two sides to weaken each other with their struggle. Then we take full advantage."

"I hate to say it, but I have to side with Leif on this one," Tracy said. "The longer we wait, the more people get hurt. I know the Olympians seem to be trying to keep the fight out of populated areas, but they can't do that forever. Haven't you seen the news?"

"We cannot move too soon," Zeus insisted.

"We cannot move too late either, Father," spoke Apollo. "Tracy is correct: further delay risks the very lives of the mortals who worship us."

Zeus dismissed this. "They will find their deserved rewards in the afterlife. Were you not overwhelmed by the sheer number of worshippers flocking to you, Apollo? Consider it a blessing to lose a few."

"Um, putting aside the morality of *that* for a second, doesn't being worshipped give you power?" Leif tried. "What about that?"

"We have never learned to gain any but the most negligible amounts of power from worship. Recall that I was not part of the Return. I have no worshippers. If it worked that way, I would be doomed indeed. Worshippers give us pleasure and status only."

"Their lives still matter," Apollo insisted.

"Please," Tracy pleaded.

Zeus frowned and seemed to consider this. Tracy awaited his answer with Leif and Apollo. Their newer companions waited beyond. Baskin trembled with barely restrained anticipation as Jerry happily continued the study of the room that he'd begun before Baskin's arrival. Aetoc maintained a dignified attentiveness while chewing thoughtfully on his fish.

"Very well," Zeus said finally. "The sooner we join the battle, the sooner we may mark the opportunity to strike. But you must all obey my orders! We strike as one coordinated force, as I command, when I command. Is that understood?"

"My sprinkles shall fly at your word, Lord Zeus!" Baskin declared. "After almost half an hour of waiting, our time is at last at hand!"

As the others merely nodded, Jerry raised a branch. "So we is waiting here until they be showing up? Jerry is wondering, how this be working? Is awfully small room for battle."

"You can move now, Jerry," Zeus reminded him. "We go to them."

"Go . . . to them?" Jerry blinked, screwing up his mouth in a vexed attempt to sort that one out before he finally burst out in delighted laughter. "Go to them, yes! Is being just crazys enough to work!"

Zeus led them toward battle.

CHAPTER FORTY-ONE

"No, gods can be temporarily fatigued by epic tasks. Otherwise we couldn't brag to each other about who's stronger. Yet your listeners may rest assured that from the mortal perspective, we remain all-powerful."

"Oh, quite. We've far more stamina than a mortal can match. Would you like me to show you, Rebecca?"

—*Apollo and Dionysus* (Rebecca, Live! *interview, August 22, 2009*)

THE OLYMPIANS' PROTRACTED STRUGGLE was becoming desperate. For all their efforts, Poseidon's Olympians simply could not force even one of the Titans back through the vortex. Though weakened and wounded with battle, every hour the Titans spent outside their prison saw them grow closer to their former strength. Every moment risked greater collateral damage to the Olympians' worshippers, and more than once an Olympian escaped grievous and crippling injury by no more than the skin of his or her teeth.

What military assistance the mortals could provide proved near futile. Even when mortal weapons were within range, the Titans were too fast for all but the most state-of-the-art targeting systems, and those shots that did reach their targets made barely a dent. Even so, the mortals refused to shirk the duty of defending their people from the Titan threat. Air strikes, cruise missiles, armored divisions, even small arms—they brought all weapons to bear.

All weapons, that is, save for nuclear strikes. Ares suggested it, of course, even outright demanded it; he would have emptied every launch tube around the world were it not for Athena. While the two Olympians long ago had devised a way to initiate a global combined launch—for the sheer heck of it—Athena refused to turn her key.

It was in the late hours of the European morning that Poseidon's patience reached its limit. Seizing the battered Dionysus and Aphrodite by the hair, he demanded the use of the UnMaking Nexus. The weapon would serve its original purpose.

The spilled Titan blood pooled on numerous battlegrounds proved ideal for priming the weapon. Poseidon's first strategy was simple: throw the Nexus at the Titans. As the Titans rarely held position unless fighting, it required perfect timing—an Olympian strike against the intended Titan target would have to withdraw right before the weapon was deployed, in order to ensure the target remained in place.

The plan proved disastrous. Hecate, withdrawing last from the melee while shrouding the others' escape, fell to friendly fire as the Nexus struck out at the first immortal it could find. She collapsed in her own darkness, first horrified, then mortal, then dead.

Chagrinned, Poseidon reversed his strategy: throw the Titans at the Nexus. While this worked far better—Poseidon and Hera annihilated the Titan Menoetius by flinging him into a pit containing the recharged Nexus in a fragile wooden crate—surviving Titan witnesses spread word of the threat immediately. Upon its next use, they were ready. They trapped the weapon before it could strike, sealing it inside a lump of molten metal and swiftly cooling it with a blast of frigid breath. Then the Titans hurled it into space before the Olympians could recapture it.

The Olympians were not having a good day.

Aetoc spied every moment from his vantage point in the stratosphere before returning to Zeus beyond the battle's outskirts.

"They have lost the Nexus," Aetoc reported. "Olympian morale plummets as Titan confidence soars. I offer that it is time."

"Indeed," Zeus agreed. "They grow weak. Apollo, send word to the Muses. They are commanded to deliver the message."

"Do you really think this'll work?" Leif asked no one in particular.

414   MICHAEL G. MUNZ

"It worked on Dionysus," Tracy said.

Apollo nodded. "The Muses know their business."

At Apollo's signal, the Muses leaped from their perches near the last sighted location of the Titan leader, Cronus. Nine gloriously groomed birds of varying types and colors sped on the wind, each grasping a golden string tied to the same small box. They winged their way through the chaos of battle and dodged bursts of violent energies to reach a mountaintop where Cronus surveyed the fight, planned his next move, and looked in vain for any evidence of Zeus. Calliope pulled up short and shifted to womanly form high in the sky as the other Muses continued on course with the box.

"Cronus! We are servants of Zeus, come in peace to deliver a message!"

At that, the remaining Muses released their strings to send the box straight on target to Cronus's chest. The string-wrapped box plunked off his collarbone and tumbled down the front of his makeshift armor before coming to a stop somewhere along his navel. The nine Muses scattered, disappearing into the sky as quickly as a fleeting thought.

Suspecting another device like the Nexus, Cronus seized the box through his shirt and yanked, tearing both shirt and box from his body. Instinct told him to hurl it away. Anyone not an idiot would surely stab a spork in his eye before trusting a box delivered mid-battle by his mortal enemy (figuratively speaking), and Cronus was not an idiot.

Well, not usually.

Foolish curiosity assailed him in that moment. He'd seen no sign of Zeus at all since their escape. Poseidon seemed to lead the Olympians. Was there not a chance Zeus might serve to be an ally against the others, however temporarily? Might the message contain some proposal of an alliance or vital intelligence? And so it was that Cronus, king of the Titans, father of Zeus, and generally despicable jerk-ass devourer of his own children, opened the box and dumped the contents into his palm.

Within the box was a little golden ball, and taped to the little golden ball was a message on that remarkable substance known as paper: *If you have the courage to face me, if you wish your revenge, you will bring your Titan fellows to the slopes of Mount Parnitha. There, treacherous Father, we shall do unceasing battle until one of us is vanquished.*

The message was signed by Zeus with a small postscript that read only: *Bring the ball.*

Enlisting the Muses was the first step the group had taken upon leaving Switzerland. For them, relocating the Idiot Ball from the drawer in Poseidon's throne was a simple matter, and their experience made them the best equipped to handle it safely. Having delivered the ball to its target, they returned to Zeus.

"He took the bait," announced Calliope.

"Well, you know, we figure he did," insisted Thalia.

"Hope and pray he took the bait," warned Terpsichore.

"We shall soon see, in any case," said Clio.

"If he did not, we are all doomed! Doomed! *Doomed!*" cried Melpomene, trailing off. "Just sayin'."

Calliope cleared her throat with a glare at her sisters and repeated more firmly, "He took. The bait."

Zeus shot an expectant glance to Aetoc, who peered into the distance.

"The Titans gather," he confirmed. "They return to Greece."

A smug smile spread across Zeus's lips. "To the vortex."

"To battle!" Baskin screamed.

"Is too much talkings goings on at once!" Jerry threw his branches over where his ears ought to have been.

"You have done well!" Zeus told the Muses. "Now make yourselves safe, but stray not too far. There may still be opportunities for you to help."

Calliope bowed, pleased. "Of course. Clio and I will be recording it for posterity in any case."

Off to one side, Thalia caught both Leif's and Tracy's eyes and winked. "Looking good, you two. Immortality suits you. Aren't you glad I lightened you up and bossed you around all those times? Wasn't it all worth it? Isn't flying fun?" She patted Tracy's arm with another wink.

"This is temporary," Tracy insisted.

"For you, maybe," Leif grinned. "I'm really starting to get the hang of this."

"Of course you are; I told you it suits you and I'm hardly one to lie! Unless it's funny, I mean, or unless I feel like it, or unless I'm talking to a 'creative' executive or the Erinyes, or I suppose it could happen in any number of situations, really, so no guarantees, but I'm not lying about this, you can trust me on that. Oh, my sisters are leaving! Time for us to go find a shady spot to watch and catch up on paperwork! Have fun being gods," she called as she floated up after the others with a wave, "but I'm not going to say anything about storming the castle! Oh—don't forget to spout lots of one-liners! And *smile*, Tracy, you're getting that look again!"

As the Muses sailed off, one turned to call back, "Good luck, Zeus! Be sure to add some sort of twist! Every story needs a good twist!"

"This isn't a story, Terpsichore!"

"Nonsense!" she shot back, looking quite anxious about the matter. "Everything's a story! There must be a twist!"

"Sorry," Apollo apologized as the Muses vanished into the distance. "Terpsichore muses thrillers, you know. I fear her demand for twists lately has begun to border on cliché. It's the stress of the Return, I think. Overworked."

"But she's right," Leif pitched. "By definition, this is an epic struggle. There *will* be a twist. There has to be. Just you watch for it."

Cronus gathered the Titans swiftly. Each withdrew from individual entanglements and followed him to Greece, to the base of Mount Parnitha, to the vortex. The battle-weary Olympians, grateful for respite, let them go, only to notice their destination with mystified curiosity. Surely it must be a trap, they thought, yet they could not afford to dismiss the opportunity. They followed, cautiously at first. Then, seeing the Titans amassed near the Tartarus vortex—now grown into a raging swirl of suction—and unable to discard their luck, Poseidon dived down with his fellows, desperate to wrestle the enemy back into their nearby prison.

When the Titans turned to defend themselves, Zeus struck. He gave no glorious speech, no witty, pre-battle banter. Springing from concealment, Zeus drove his new allies like a lance into the Titan flanks. The battle was well and truly joined.

Iapetus, uncle to Zeus, fell in the first moments to the combined might of his nephews, first stunned by Zeus's lightning and then kicked end over end and screaming into the vortex by both Hades and Poseidon. Yet even only seven strong, the Titans fought back like death itself.

Titans, Olympians, and neo-Olympians smashed into the landscape around the vortex in a storm of cosmic violence. Were Athens not already destroyed, it would not have survived the ordeal.

Spared from the previous day's fighting, Zeus's group held a dangerous advantage. Wielding the lightning and arrows that had served them for millennia, neither Zeus nor Apollo were strangers to battle. As elevated forces of nature, Aetoc, Jerry, and Baskin fought in the ways that came natural to eagles, trees, and frozen dairy treats. Tracy swiftly opted to manifest her power in the form of the "producer's whip" that Jason so often had joked about. Then she decided to use two for good measure. Leif was more distracted, switching at random between various types of weapons (or none at all) in a wild effort to eschew predictability.

Yet even with the old Olympians lending their strength in an unofficial truce, the Titans were no pushovers. Coeus and his consort-sister Phoebe caught Aetoc in midair as he tried to distract them. They ripped him apart by the wings and hurled the still-screaming pieces into the vortex. His sacrifice allowed Leif and Tracy to get hold of the distracted Coeus and wrestle him closer to the vortex with whips and muscle. Even so, the Titan fought back and might have escaped entirely were it not for a sudden onslaught of sugary, multicolored death. With a bellow of, "Suck sprinkles, treacherous hooligan!" Baskin lunged from the sky to blast Coeus full in the face. Leif and Tracy renewed their attack and soon hurled the blinded Titan back through the vortex to Tartarus.

At the same time, Apollo and Artemis struck at Aetoc's other killer. Bowstrings singing, they peppered arrows into Phoebe to drive her back alongside her brother. Stumbling backward in a mad effort to shield herself, she might still have escaped were it not for Jerry. The god-tree's preference for ground fighting served him well as he thrust his gnarled roots up under Phoebe's heels and tripped the Titan backward toward the vortex. In one final combined slam from the archery-twins, Phoebe's fate matched that of Coeus.

"You know, technically she was our grandmother on mom's side," Apollo said.

Artemis shrugged. "Given our family, that's not exactly a character reference."

"Is not matterings!" Jerry screamed. "Titan-grandmother was being bad! Aetoc was friend!"

"Mourn later!" Baskin yelled. "Fight now!" With a yodeling battle cry, he flung himself toward the mountainside where Zeus battled Cronus.

Yet even with their dual victory, the battle did not go as well for every Olympian. Not for nothing was Cronus king of the Titans. He beat back both Zeus and Baskin with two uprooted trees and then turned on Dionysus and Hermes to knock them toward the vortex with one massive swing. While Hermes managed to zip sideways enough to avoid oblivion, Dionysus fared less well. Screaming for a beer, he toppled through the vortex and out of the narrative entirely.

All around, the struggle continued. Weapons clashed and fists pounded. All combatants tried their best to throw their enemies into Tartarus or at the very least beat, slash, or shoot them senseless. Amid the chaos Hermes, weakened and still dizzy from Cronus's walloping, found Tracy hunkering down against an onslaught from Hyperion. Though her defenses held, the blazing balls of energized quarks the Titan hurled at her kept her on the defensive. Hermes, posing as a rabbit, scampered up her leg to perch on her shoulder.

"Hello, Tracy! Still fighting for Zeus after all the manipulation and lies, then?"

To her credit, Tracy gave Hermes no more than a second glance after recognizing his voice. Also, Hyperion shattered the rock in front of her so she had other things to worry about. Slinging her whip out to cover her escape, she leaped to another section of cover and hunkered down again, strengthening the rock itself against the next volley.

Even in his weakened state, Hermes kept up with her.

"Hardly the time!" she shot.

"Nonsense! I realize you're new to this whole ball of kippers, but when we god-sorts get close, we can do sort of a—"

The whole mountainside shuddered as Hyperion launched himself in an arc over Tracy's cover, blasting destruction down on her that she barely managed to divert with Hermes's help.

"Stop-time thing, I know!" she finished for him. "Except I don't want to talk to you!"

She darted for a new spot before Hyperion could make another attempt.

"Hardly being friendly, are you?" Hermes asked as Tracy slipped into a game of cat and mouse with the Titan. "Why not hear what I have to say?"

Tracy raised a finger to her lips to shut Hermes up, popped from hiding around one side of a boulder, and slung her whips at the Titan's ankles. He jumped and blasted more destruction her way, forcing her back to cover.

"Because I don't trust you, maybe?" she hissed. "Now either help me or get lost!"

Hermes clung tightly, creating the first ever moment in any battle involving a combatant with a rabbit in her hair (with the obvious exception of the Franco-Prussian War). "I beg your pardon?"

Tracy fled from Hyperion's next assault, taking to the sky in a shield of her own leptons. "You said the ritual failed! Well, hey, did you notice Zeus is back? You lied!"

"A misunderstanding, I assure you. Zeus is a tricky one—we were still trying to get a bead on him at the time. I thought it *had* failed!"

"So why did you tell me that right before using me as bait to trap Zeus?"

"Rather worth a shot, at least, wouldn't you say? Incidentally, incoming."

Intent on her flight path, Tracy entirely missed spotting two green storms of energy headed straight for her. They blasted into her shields, jolted her from body to essence, and knocked her straight down into a narrow chasm. She barely stopped her fall before hitting bottom. Her entire body stung from the blow, energy temporarily sapped, or muted, or—whatever the heck a god should call getting wounded, she didn't know. Hyperion hadn't followed. Yet. Recovering her strength, she waited, preparing to whip the ever-loving crap out of whoever stuck a face into the chasm and hoping it was someone who deserved it.

Hermes scampered down from her hair to cling to her chest and stare up at her, whiskers twitching. "Very well, I'll help you. After all, we're both against the Titans, all big, bad, and destructive as they are. I have to hand it to Zeus; it was the perfect diversion, unleashing them. I doubt that'll be of much comfort to everyone who's died, but—"

"He didn't release them," she whispered, doing her best to shield herself from Hyperion's senses. "He's got no idea how they got out."

"Ah, yes, no idea. Just like when he told Hera he had 'no idea' how those seventeen models got into their bathtub. He'll say whatever it takes, Tracy. That's thousands of years of experience talking. That's why we had to put him off. We didn't want to. It was quite simply our last resort."

A victorious laugh from above heralded Hyperion's rediscovery of her. Two whiplashes later he bellowed in pain and darted back out of sight, clutching the eye Tracy had just put out. Tracy widened a crack in the chasm and dashed through it, forcing Hermes to shift to his normal form just to keep up.

"You're trying to get me to switch sides," she whispered.

"Rather obviously, yes."

"Yesterday you tried to kill me. Or was that whole locking me in an airtight box over the ocean just, what, a friendly hazing?"

"Surely someone as smart as you can recognize a bluff when she sees one. Why kill you? We simply needed Zeus to show himself. He arrives, distracts us with releasing the Titans, and then plays the gallant rescuer and claims coincidence! You all but admitted he manipulated you with that amulet. Did you ever ask him about that, or did he feign innocence in that too?"

She stopped short of insisting that the amulet had only amplified her own natural tendencies, which really just parroted what Zeus told her earlier. Though the circumstances continued to nag at her, any opinion Hermes offered on the matter would be suspect.

"It wasn't like that," she answered.

"Oh, 'it wasn't like that.' I see." Hermes chuckled. "It's as plain as the stupid on Ares's face that you're not so sure. Zeus tricked you into thinking he hasn't tricked you, hasn't he? The cad! You see what I mean. He's had millennia of practice."

"So have you. You're trying to trick me into thinking he tricked me into thinking he hasn't tricked me."

"Oh, that was good. Are you dizzy?"

"I'm getting a little tired of it all, no matter who's doing it!"

"I'm only trying to give you more information."

Tracy wheeled on Hermes. "No! You're trying to do your own—"

Hyperion tore off a piece of rock above them before she could tell off Hermes. Both of them flew skyward on instinct.

With a pat on her shoulder and a cry of, "Think about it!" Hermes shot past the Titan, poking him in his remaining eye as he went. Hyperion roared anew and blindly hurled the gigantic rock at Tracy.

Yet it was just rock, and poorly thrown at that. She caught it in her bare hands. Harnessing the power of every ounce of the frustration she felt over the constant manipulation assailing her on all sides, she phased the rock to pure energy and hurled it back at Hyperion with a furious yell. It exploded in the Titan's face with a blast that would have been much more satisfying were she farther away. She regained consciousness halfway across the battlefield a few moments later.

There was no sign of Hyperion.

The rage of battle around her gave her no time to think. Amid the bitter aftertaste of Hermes's words, Tracy resumed the struggle, teaming with Leif and Jerry to combat the remaining Titans.

One by one, their dwindling numbers and battle-weariness in the face of Zeus's fresher forces pushed the Titans back through the vortex until only Cronus himself remained. Now enraged by both his former imprisonment and his utter failure to skewer Zeus on a pike, he stood at the very peak of Mount Parnitha clutching a spear stolen from Ares in one hand and the (divinely reinforced) roof of the Parthenon in the other, and there he screamed for his children to try to throw him off.

Zeus turned to Apollo and the Neo-Olympians. "Wait here," he ordered. "I must do this myself."

Without waiting for acknowledgment, Zeus moved to answer Cronus's challenge.

His brothers did the same. Each charged their father alone only to have their attacks rebuffed. The inexorable Hades ran inexorably into Cronus's shield before his father kicked him straight down the mountain. Poseidon turned aside Cronus's spear with his trident only to be knocked senseless by a fist to the face. Zeus tackled Cronus straight on. Lesser gods scrambled for cover as the two tumbled halfway down the mountainside in a rolling melee that sent their weapons flying, until Cronus finally picked up Zeus and threw him straight at the vortex.

He might have gone through were it not for Baskin. Unable to stand idle, he dived for Zeus and batted him to safety with his giant pink spoon at the last moment.

Yet Zeus and his brothers were only a distraction. Hera, Demeter, and Hestia, having taken the mountaintop during the struggle, plunged down on Cronus. Once Demeter's and Hestia's net wrapped the ambushed

Titan in temporary helplessness, Hera slashed into Cronus's backside. He pitched farther down the mountain, struggling to tear the net from his body when Hades was suddenly upon him, seizing up the net's loose ends. Even then Cronus forced his way to his feet. Poseidon knocked him off his feet with an earthquake, and still Cronus resisted, finally blasting the net apart in a flash of power. He fought his way free again, roaring in rage as five of his children grappled him about the legs, arms, and neck. Yet the five were weary. They only slowed Cronus, able to neither drag him down nor lift him off his feet.

Zeus brought the stalemate to an end. Rushing back to the fight, he hurled lightning repeatedly into Cronus's chest. Focused on Zeus's siblings, Cronus took the full brunt of the attack. Zeus wasted no time. He grabbed his stunned father from the frazzled grips of the others, yanked a fragment of extra power from Cronus's essence, and then hurled him single-handedly into the vortex.

Cronus didn't have time to even curse.

Zeus shot a triumphant grin at Tracy. Leif and Jerry cheered as Baskin, bubbling with battle lust, regarded the Olympians. Apollo only heaved a sigh of relief from where he watched over Artemis, who lay weak and wounded from the fighting. Zeus indicated for them to wait and be ready, and then he turned to deal with his brothers.

CHAPTER FORTY-TWO

"Zeus joined the battle, Terpsichore. What about that?"

"He said he would, Urania. That's hardly a twist! I need more, something unexpected! You know what I mean, don't you, Melpomene?"

"Well, I didn't expect Hermes to turn into a bunny."

"Please, stop musing children's books until you do more tragedy. A bunny? You're getting soft!"

"Puns are lazy wri-ting . . ."

"Clam up, Thalia."

"You clam up, Terpsi. Why get so worked up about it?"

"I muse thrillers, you tosspot! I demand surprising developments! If there isn't some sort of twist soon, I swear I'll—"

"Um, everyone? This conversation is showing up in one of the chapter openings. How'd that happen?"

"We're Muses, Sister. It happens."

"Hee hee! Look at it go! Ooh, is that enough of a twist for you?"

"Do you really think I can settle for that? No, what I need is—"

"Sisters, please! Clio's trying to transcribe the battle!"

"Yes, Calliope."

> —Muses Urania, Terpsichore, Melpomene, Thalia, and Calliope
> (final moments of the Second Titan War)

ZEUS SIMMERED WITH smug triumph. "Once more I turn the Titans aside!" he declared to the Olympians. "The vortex must now be sealed, my subjects, but you may rest yourselves. Be not ashamed of your weakness! Mighty Zeus shall do the sealing himself!"

Poseidon could not abide this. "Weakened or no, it is we who shall accomplish the feat! We need you not, Zeus. You are hardly stronger than all of us; you shall not claim this victory for yourself!"

"I hardly think you up to the task, Poseidon," answered Zeus with a laugh. "You aren't fit to lead a parade in your current state. I shall do the sealing single-handedly, and then you shall witness the glory of Zeus and why he is the most fitting to rule you all!"

"You shall do nothing but stand aside!" Poseidon insisted, continuing the classic shall-off. "Olympians, lend your strength! We seal the portal ourselves!"

"Are we to argue the matter until Cronus escapes again? As you wish, Brother. I stand aside."

Zeus returned to stand by Apollo and Tracy. "He would block my efforts just to ensure I do not get the credit," he whispered. "I expect I would do the same in his position, were I foolish enough to get myself into it. Poseidon is prideful."

Next to Tracy, Leif laughed. "Pot calling the kettle . . ."

"Silence! I command it!" Zeus commanded, and did not notice Leif's responding gesture. "The effort of sealing will weaken them further. Observe."

"Did Poseidon pick up the Idiot Ball in battle or something?" Tracy asked.

"No, this is simply politics."

"Where *is* the Idiot Ball?" Apollo wondered.

Once the Olympians gathered together, it happened rapidly. Energies poured from their hands and minds. They rewove the dimensional fabric, first tugging the vortex closed and then locking away the seams within the re-gathered cans. Their task complete, they collapsed, exhausted.

Zeus clapped. Slowly. "Well done! You show the strength of your will, unconcerned that it leaves you weak as kittens!" ("Don't knock the strength of kittens," Leif muttered.) "Bravo! You now will surrender to me, unconditionally."

Poseidon and Ares were the first to their feet at this. "Never!"

"The time for discussion has passed!" Zeus thundered in murderous contempt. "Surrender now!"

Ares stepped in front of Poseidon to glare at Zeus. "Ares don't surrender!"

"Surrender now, apostate!" Baskin cried. Standing before Zeus, he mirrored Ares and brandished his spoon in frigid readiness.

Ares sneered. "And he definitely don't take no damned orders from ruttin' sweets!"

"I am not sweet! I am shock and awe with a cherry on top! I am your frigorific *doom!*"

("Frigorific?" Tracy whispered. "It is a word," Apollo answered sadly, "though I believe it should be otherwise.")

"Upstart!" Ares yelled.

"Traitor!" Baskin screamed.

"Second banana!"

Perhaps had Baskin known him longer, the semi-cleverness of Ares's retort might have momentarily stunned him. As it was, Baskin could take no more. He launched himself at the war god, screaming all the way.

The two clashed in an explosion of rage and cream and touched off a brawl that spread instantly among the ranks on both sides. Pandemonium again took the mountainside as the cacophony of battle drowned out Poseidon's and Zeus's shouted orders. No matter how reluctantly some of the combatants fought (Hephaestus, a dutiful husband battling only to protect Aphrodite, loathed every blow he gave; Artemis and Apollo avoided each other entirely), none escaped involvement in the struggle for supremacy.

Even the Erinyes—whom Poseidon had kept in reserve as fresh troops for this very circumstance—exploded into existence and tore into the maelstrom with unrestrained glee. While no direct match for a god, they were not without their strengths. They harried Zeus's forces, serving as a violent, screaming nuisance that distracted them at key moments and keep them from full effectiveness.

Yet, ultimately, it backfired. Jerry spotted the Erinyes mere moments after they appeared. Fury alone propelled him across the battlefield until with a vindictive cry he leaped, seized all three by the ankles with his branches, and hauled them out of the air. More branches grew instantly to trap them further in a divine wooden grip stronger than iron. The Erinyes screamed vitriol and tried fruitlessly to teleport away, held fast by the god-tree's newfound power.

"Bad ugly-womans!" he shouted. "You kill Jerry and be makings Jerry mad! You not be being nice!"

"We don't do nice! We do vengeance!"

"We were only following orders!"

"Vengeance! Orders-vengeance-orders!"

"Zeus is tellings me you is supposed to be being avenging king-killings and father-killings! Zeus is king *and* father! Why you not avenging hims? Why!" He shook them violently and constricted further. "You will be answerings Jerry!"

"Because we—"

As one, the Erinyes stopped to consider this. That they couldn't move an inch in Jerry's grip possibly had something to do with that.

"Rather right, isn't he?"

"Right, wrong, I care not!" Tisiphone screamed. "We get to fight either way! Make him release us!"

"Splinters!" Alecto wailed, to little point.

"Very well!" Megaera yelled. "We fight to avenge Zeus! Let us go!"

"Yes, truce!"

"You being saying you be sorry! And fight beside Jerry!" He squeezed tighter while the Erinyes screamed in pain.

"Yes! We're sorry!"

"We swear!"

"Splinters! Splinters-splinters-splinters!"

Jerry released the Erinyes. Together they sprang into the fray.

Ares swiftly proved lactose intolerant. He fell to Baskin's superior might, temporarily frozen and out of commission. Yet when the sundae-god stood to catch his breath, Hades avenged his blustering nephew, drawing molten metal up from the earth and showering it over Baskin in a desperate use of his remaining strength. Tracy watched in horror as it reduced Baskin to a useless, melted mess.

Even with Baskin sidelined, so weakened were Poseidon's forces that the fighting ended soon after. Tracy herself whipped Hades's legs out from under him and hauled him to the growing pile of defeated Olympians while Zeus fought on, apparently unmoved by Baskin's fate. In his eyes shone gleeful vengeance that surpassed even that of the Erinyes as he gathered up his enemies. Apollo, Leif, and Jerry fought by his side, yet none so well as Zeus. Soon every offending Olympian was wrapped in a double-lasso of golden rope just as he once promised, bound together in a hapless, weakened cluster, and held fast in his grip.

Once Tracy shoved Hades into the center of the group, Zeus passed the twin lasso tails to Apollo and Jerry. Each gave a wrenching tug in opposing directions to lash the captives to the ground.

"We surrender!" Hera spit.

"No we do *not!*"

"Stuff it, Ares!"

"Isn't it fun to get together as a family?" Demeter spouted. "Does anyone have a deck of cards?"

Not surprisingly, no one answered her.

"The time for surrender is past!" Zeus declared, grinning wickedly. "You had your chance! I make no empty threats, and now you shall have your punishment! I tolerate your presence no longer!"

With that, he blasted lightning into the ground beneath them and then poured energy into the crater until light burst forth like a fountain, streaming up beneath the captured Olympians. It launched them into the air and would have blasted them into orbit and beyond, had it not been for the efforts of Apollo and Jerry. The two strained and pulled, struggling to hold on to the ropes as Zeus had ordered.

"I declare you all banished!" Zeus boomed, clearly relishing the moment. "Into the vast emptiness of the stars you shall go, to rot in darkness away from mortal worship and the joys of this world!"

The entirety of the captured Olympians might have been banished right then were it not for the Muse Terpsichore. Having grown increasingly obsessed with the lack of a decent twist, she finally took matters into her own hands. The Idiot Ball had fallen from Cronus's grip not long before his final struggle, and she'd snapped it up into its protective case before anyone else had seen it. When Zeus lassoed the others and began his speech, she slipped in behind Leif, whom Thalia had mentioned often during her retelling of their journeys. With nothing more than a wicked giggle, Terpsichore spilled the Idiot Ball from the case and shoved it—quickly—down the back of his pants.

"We need a twist," she whispered in his ear.

He nodded vacantly. "Everything needs a twist."

"Good boy. Zeus gave you power; now use it! The fight and creation of that exile-fountain has made him weak. He's kind of a jerk, isn't he? Now's your chance to overthrow him and win!"

"He *is* kind of a jerk. Nearly all the gods are, I've noticed. And he still hasn't put in a good word for me with Tracy!"

"Exactly! Er, except Apollo."

"Except Apollo." Leif nodded. "But—if I exile Zeus, Tracy'll hate me!"

Terpsichore giggled. "Oh, no she won't."

"Why not?"

"Um, because?"

"Ah." Leif grinned. "It all makes sense now!"

Zeus poured his energies into the fountain, working it into a geyser that would blast the captured Olympians off the planet forever. They struggled in vain to break free of their bonds. Some yelled protests; others hurled insults, but neither seemed to do any good.

Leif moved up behind Zeus and elbowed him in the back of the head.

Far too distracted and weakened from creating the exile-fountain, Zeus failed to react fast enough. In a flash Leif spun him around, grabbed his wrists, and kicked the elder god's feet out from under him toward the fountain. It yanked Zeus's ankles skyward and pitched him nearly upside down. Only Leif's grip kept the violent currents from propelling the furious Zeus into an exile of his own.

Ares let out a weary whoop as everyone else tried to figure out what was going on.

"Are you mad?" Zeus cried, clearly unsure whether to laugh or rage. "You will put me down at once!"

"Oh, yeah, 'cause you're the nice, forgiving type, right?" Leif asked. "Sorry, I'm taking over! Leif, king of the gods! I'm pretty sure that means I win!"

Tracy entangled a whip around Zeus's ankle, holding fast should Leif release her father's hands. "Uh, Leif?" she asked.

"What? You've seen what he's like! What they're all like! He let the Titans wreck half the world before he joined the fight, just to make sure he had an advantage! This is our chance to get rid of him and take over for ourselves! Do you know that when you were captured, he cared more about the insult to his authority than he did your own safety?"

"It's true!" Hermes chimed in. "You remember what I said! You're on the wrong side! Let him fly into exile, save the rest of us! Clean slate!"

"Shut up, Hermes!" Tracy shot.

"He didn't need you anymore then," Leif went on. "I'm surprised you made it out alive! Besides, god-mode's fun, but I want to call the shots!"

Unable to free himself from the force of the fountain, Zeus could only blast impotent wrath at his captor, amusement fading fast. "You traitorous, pea-brained little geek! Do you know what happens to the power I gave you when I'm gone?"

"Um . . . it . . . gets better?"

"It's *temporary,* you ungrateful lout! Kick me out now and you're powerless! Instantly!"

"You said I'd be immortal! Immortal isn't temporary!"

"I can make it permanent in time. Let me go now and you get nothing, not even Tracy! Or do you think she'll want you after you betray her father?"

"Er, well, it made sense at—Okay!" Leif tried. "Here's the deal! I pull you back down, and . . . you make it permanent and—and *then* go away!"

"Must I forever endure shortsighted fools?" Zeus demanded. "I returned from *death,* Mr. Karlson!"

"Yeah, but you're weaker now, aren't you?" He shook Zeus a bit, grinning. "You fought! You poured your energy into this fountain! Lightning god needs food, badly!"

Tracy renewed her grip on the whip, a gesture Zeus did not fail to notice.

"Weaker," Zeus answered, "but never a fool. I built your divinity with safeguards, mortal. Now that you, too, have betrayed me, it ought to be slipping from your fingers right about . . . now."

Zeus yanked his wrists from Leif's grip and let the fountain's current propel him briefly higher before the anchor of Tracy's whip jerked him to a stop again. His hands free, he hurled lightning into Leif, blasting him backward. Leif smashed into a boulder that popped the Idiot Ball from his pants like a wet balloon. He rolled off and slumped, stunned, to his knees.

"Ow."

"Once more you make me proud, Daughter," Zeus said aside to Tracy. He regarded Leif with the same lethal contempt he'd shown Ares. "Perhaps I see now why this liar failed to interest you. Haul me down and we shall finish this."

Yet Tracy was busy with thoughts of her own. Her response was neither immediate nor helpful.

"You never meant for them to surrender, did you?" she asked after a bit of pondering. "You just wanted an excuse to kick their asses no matter how much it risked the rest of us, huh?"

"I am sure I don't know what you mean. Now pull me in."

"As a matter of fact," she continued more pointedly, "you probably knew Baskin would attack Ares like that."

It must be said for those who have not experienced it that floating in an exile-fountain is no picnic. Aside from the already uncomfortable upward pressure that was rapidly giving Zeus an enema, the sheer sensation of being poised on the edge of the possible end to one's power is rather akin to that of being stretched on the rack while surrounded by howling cats.

"Do it *now*, Daughter."

"I don't think I want to yet. In fact, I'm starting to think maybe Leif had the right idea."

Zeus's face settled into an eerie calm, much like the air before a tornado. "Excuse me?"

"Oh, I'm not trying to be queen of the gods or anything. It's just that I've been manipulated one way or the other since the start of all this, by you especially, despite what you've claimed, and frankly I'd like to do a little manipulating of my own now. The thing is, Leif does have a point, right? He's just going about it in his usual obtuse way. (Also I think he might've had the Idiot Ball, but that's not really the point right—)"

"Daughter! You will stop this immediately and—!"

Tracy let go of the whip and grabbed it again at the last second. The fountain's current shoved Zeus higher before he jerked to a stop once more above the bound mass of Olympians. It shut him up for the moment.

"My own power's fading as we speak, I'm sure, so you'd better let me talk 'cause there's no one left to catch you, is there?"

Zeus glanced to Apollo and Jerry. Even if ordered to help, it was all both could do to hold on to the Olympians beneath him. The second either let go, the whole mass would knock Zeus free of Tracy, and they'd all launch into exile together.

"Here's what I want: you and all the other Olympians withdraw again. It was fun while it lasted, but I'm thinking things got out of hand.

And like Leif said, some of you can be jerks. I found the monsters as interesting as anyone, but that was before I knew you all created them intentionally! So clear those out, especially the damned razorwings."

"They were not my—"

"Quiet! I command it!" She shook the whip again; it set Zeus dancing amid the current. "Sorry, power trip. Also, don't exile everyone, right? Artemis helped us out; she just got a raw deal, and I don't think Demeter and some of the others ever meant to do anything bad. And lastly, I want immunity for all of this, for me and Leif. No one comes after us for any of this stuff, not you, not someone you tell to go after us, no one. Agree to all of that, swear by the Styx since that hate-water seems to have some power over you types, and I'll pull you down."

"You cannot expect—"

"Grip's getting weak, Dad. Better swear!"

"Fine! I swear by the Styx to hold to your conditions! Pull me down!"

She did so. Her divinity failed a moment later. Isn't it remarkable how often the timing of such things works out like that? In fact, it happened just in time to end the chapter.

EPILOGUE

"Please note: the temple is currently experiencing technical difficulties in contacting the gods. We are doing our best to fix the problem. For your convenience, please leave any valuables you wish to sacrifice with the high priest. Sacrifices will be completed in the order received once the problem is resolved, and a receipt will be mailed to you. We (and the gods) appreciate your patience."

—sign outside an Olympian temple following the Second Withdrawal

ZEUS KEPT HIS WORD in the end, rethinking his banishment of the entire pantheon and settling instead for reducing the Olympians to mere vanilla immortals with no powers beyond living indefinitely and having spectacular skin. (Their egos, of course, they could keep as well.) The punishment wasn't irrevocable, but as he told them, they'd have to kiss his bum profoundly for a while before he'd consider reversing it. After all, Zeus reminded them, even those who didn't kill him had accepted his death without protest. Anyone swearing to his terms was free to escape banishment.

Anyone, that is, except the remaining conspirators. Offering them no such deal, he launched them into exile once the others were freed. The world would simply have to do without Aphrodite, Ares, Hades, and Hermes. The fountain flung them into the void between the stars, never to return without Zeus's explicit permission—or at the very least some other contrivance of plot should it become necessary.

Apollo retained full godhood, joined by Jerry and Baskin once Zeus, who resumed his place as king, gathered the power to make their elevation permanent. Though the gods withdrew once more, as Zeus had agreed, there were still tasks to be tended to and fewer Olympians to tend to them. Apollo didn't mind; he no longer needed to respond to e-mail and evaluate the talent of bands such as Twig (or Stick, one of Twig's many tribute bands that sprang up after their first recording went double-platinum). He still found time to go shooting with Artemis on weekends and did his best to nudge Zeus toward forgiving her enough to return her godhood.

The Muses were similarly pleased, even if Thalia did have to put up with the occasional severed head left on her doorstep, which she attributed to vindictive Erinyes. The Idiot Ball, swiftly recovered after the whole exiling debacle, was safely returned to the Hall of Creative Abstract Concepts. In time, the pace of sitcom production recovered.

Roaming monsters, both old and new, began to disappear nearly instantly. Regarding this, too, Zeus kept his word. A cloud of razorwings over Albuquerque vanished without a trace just as the Albuquerquean Civil Defense was loading the world's largest ball of yarn onto the world's third-largest catapult. (They fired it anyway because, frankly, who could possibly resist?) Sightings of unnatural creatures within urban areas dropped to nearly zero within the span of a single week.

Nevertheless there would be numerous reports in the weeks and months that followed of monsters still lurking out on the fringe, deep in the wilderness. None could be verified. (A vigilant hiker in the Canadian Rockies did record a twenty-second video of what appeared to be a giant ice cream sundae screaming at a walking oak tree, but general Internet consensus was that anything so ludicrous had to be faked. Curiously, all copies of the video vanished a week later.)

Thaddeus Archibald Winslow, who did manage to recover from the blow to the head he received at Zeus's temple, wasn't sorry at all to find the Olympians gone. (It was some time before he realized the Second Withdrawal had happened at all, of course. Keeping up with current events was for losers.) Fellow models who'd claimed Olympian heritage fell out of vogue, and his "pure mortal" blood became more popular than ever. In fact, he received absolutely zero comeuppance in the end, which is disappointing, but life is like that sometimes.

By strange coincidence, "life is like that sometimes" is also how one Brittany Simons (formerly Wynter Nightsorrow, formerly the young woman from Chapters Four, Seven, Twenty, and briefly alluded to in Chapters Thirty and Thirty-three) explained to her furious parents why they were still paying tuition after she'd flunked out. Her goth urges sated and her goddess gone, Brittany got herself readmitted the following year using a few secrets she'd picked up about the Dean of Admissions.

She refused to tell anyone her major.

As for humanity itself, the gods' sudden disappearance after the Titan debacle was interpreted in as many ways as mankind could imagine (which is to say, four). Some insisted the gods were lying low for the moment, recovering strength, soon to return. Some assumed the Titans and Olympians had destroyed each other, never to be seen again. Others declared the entire nine-month Olympian ordeal to be a mass hallucination perpetrated by the Illuminati, the Liberal Media, and the Li'l Camper-Scouts of America in order to draw attention away from the fact that alien mind control had at last broken the tinfoil-hat barrier. ("Humanity is doomed! Evidence culled from the Mayan calendar supports this! We have a website!")

The final theory was that God himself had had enough of the entire lot of Olympians and had booted them from His creation. (He Himself seemed silent on the matter, save for a single postcard of a burning bush received at the Vatican that simply read, *No comment.*) The NCMA assumed that the group sent to Greece had something to do with the gods' disappearance, despite—or perhaps because of—the fact that they'd never been heard from again. They erected a statue in Richard Kindgood's honor, flanked by Ninjas Templar. The statue bore more of a resemblance to Gabriel Stout due to a photo mixup, but the name spelling on the statue's plaque was more than 90 percent accurate.

"I just couldn't take it anymore, you know?" Tracy told Leif over lunch a few weeks after it was all over. "A lot of the things you said when you had him in the fountain made sense, and there were other things too."

Leif shuddered. "I still can't believe I did that."

"It's fine. You had the Idiot Ball. I saw it."

"That just makes it more embarrassing," he answered. "What other things?"

"Being fed up with manipulation on all sides, for one. Zeus, Hermes, even Thalia and Apollo, though I don't really blame them as much. That anti-betrayal safeguard Zeus threw in, like he couldn't even trust us—"

"Well, he couldn't," Leif pointed out. "Frankly it wasn't a bad idea."

"Doesn't mean it didn't get on my nerves. Plus, Jason's last request was that I try to get rid of the monsters."

"I'd have figured it'd be, 'Bury me at Make-Out Creek' or something. So that part was just for him?"

"No, not just for him. Did I ever tell you what I learned on the way to Hades? That the gods themselves sent the monsters into the world just for the fun of it?"

"Um, no, I think I missed you mentioning that one. You know you made a living off of that, right?" he asked meekly. "Er, not to judge or anything."

She smirked at the addition. "I always thought it was a side effect. You get gods, you get monsters. Tornado-chasers aren't happy about the tornado's damage, but they're a force of nature; no one's responsible for them."

Leif considered pointing out that it depended on who you asked lately but, to his credit, actually kept his mouth shut.

"I didn't think I cared that much when I first heard they created the monsters—too much on my plate, maybe. But I think it bothered me more than I realized at first. Dionysus tossing minotaurs at people, hydras loosed to wander around probably just to see how long it takes us to deal with them . . ." She shrugged. "I just saw the opportunity to really do something good for the world, and it seemed like that demanding that things go back to the way they were was the way to do it. The new Olympian world order was interesting, but I'd had enough. Oh, plus I think Zeus killed my grandparents."

Leif nearly choked. *"What?"*

Tracy blinked thoughtfully back at him. "It tracks. I never knew them, but they disowned my mom after she got pregnant from a one-night stand. Up and booted her out of the house. A few weeks later, they died in a lightning storm."

"Dick move on Zeus's part."

"On everyone's part, I figure, but yeah. If he did it. I should probably call my mom and tell her about everything. Ten-to-one she'll complain about me giving up his genes before she gets mad at him, though."

"I still can't believe you did that — or figure out how 'giving up genes' even works. And anyway, no one says basketball players are any less talented for being naturally tall."

"I thought you didn't watch basketball?"

Leif shrugged.

"Billions of people get by with regular human genes. I can too."

"Not going to try to take even an ounce of advantage of it." Leif shook his head. "You at least ought to use your career connections, star in your own reality series. 'Zeus's Daughter Does . . . Stuff.'"

"Nope. I stay behind the camera. Why don't you do it?"

"A *reality* show?" Leif laughed. "No way. Though we should at least sell the story."

"How about this: you sell yours; I'll manage you."

Leif grinned. "A partnership?"

"Of a sort. We'll have to figure out a strategy."

"Deal." Leif grinned wider. "We'll go out tonight to celebrate."

She chuckled. "I told you: no dating."

Leif pouted. In his defense, he was only half-serious. "Oh, come on, you're supposed to finally fall for my charms at the end."

"The end of what?"

"The end of the thing! You know, the whole . . ." Leif waved his glass about, searching for the word. "Adventure!"

"But this isn't the end. We're going to do this project together, right? Heck, we haven't even finished lunch." Tracy smirked. "Or do you mean the end of our association? I fall for these charms of yours and never see you again? Want me to leave right now?" she teased.

"You need to watch more movies."

"Don't try to change me, Karlson."

"Hey, that's another thing people do at the end of things," Leif added. "They change somehow so . . ."

"I told you this wasn't an end," she said.

"Yeah, well."

"Ooh, good comeback."

Searching for a better one, Leif glanced out the window at someone busily painting over a mural of the Olympians with an ad for the latest smartphone. Poseidon's face, half covered already, stared blankly out at them with his single remaining eye.

"Hey, whatever happened to Dave and the doctor, anyway?" Leif asked suddenly.

"Geez!" Tracy smacked her forehead. "I have to call them back!"

They're still fine, by the way.

The End

"MYTHOLOGICAL" WHO'S WHO

For the uninitiated, the forgetful, or those who just like to read stuff

Alecto—One of the three Erinyes. Also known as "Alecto the Unceasing."

Aphrodite—Daughter of Zeus. Goddess of beauty, love, lust, and much of the entertainment industry.

Apollo—Son of Zeus and the minor goddess Leto. God of the sun as well as medicine and healing. Also music, poetry, prophecy, and light. Plus archery, gelatin desserts, and a few other things. Nicknamed "the multipurpose god" by his twin sister Artemis.

Ares—Son of Zeus and Hera. God of war and strife. Involved in a millennia-long affair with Aphrodite. Shoots first, asks questions only if drunk.

Artemis—Daughter of Zeus and Leto, twin sister to Apollo. Goddess of the moon, hunting, and nature. One of the last chaste goddesses.

Athena—Daughter and former bodyguard of Zeus. Goddess of wisdom, defense, and tactics.

Atropos—One of the three Fates. Responsible for cutting the threads of mortal lives.

Calliope—Leader of the nine Muses. Responsible for inspiring epic poetry and fantasy novels.

Cerberus—Fearsome, three-headed dog-beast who guards the entrance to the Underworld. Music aficionado.

Charon—Lesser immortal in charge of the ferry across the river Acheron to the Underworld.

Clio—One of the nine Muses. Responsible for inspiring histories, historical fiction, and travel writing.

Clotho—One of the three Fates. Responsible for spinning the threads of mortal lives.

Demeter—Oldest sister of Zeus. Goddess of agriculture, grain, and textiles. Also enjoys baking and knitting.

Dionysus—Debaucherous god of wine and revelry. Son of Zeus and a mortal woman, but elevated to full godhood by Zeus via "a bit of star-stuff and some really good fudge."

Elvis—Not actually a god. Sorry.

Erato—One of the nine Muses. Responsible for inspiring romance, erotica, love songs, and crossword puzzles.

Erinyes, The—A trio of lesser immortals (consisting of Alecto, Megaera, and Tisiphone) responsible for wreaking vengeance and protecting the natural order. Not usually welcome at parties.

Euterpe—One of the nine Muses. Responsible for inspiring music, lyric poetry, television theme songs, and movie scores.

Fates, The—A mysterious trio of figures (Clotho, Lachesis, and Atropos) who spin, measure, and cut the threads of mortal lives. Also known as The Moirae.

Hades—Older brother of Zeus. God of the Underworld a.k.a. Hades (he named it after himself), death, and precious metals. Not evil, just strict.

Hecate—Goddess of the night, magic, and the supernatural. Also known as "Queen of Secrets" and "Queen of All Witches." Adopted member of the pantheon. Reported to make a fantastic dark chocolate sundae.

Hephaestus—Son of Zeus and Hera. Gentle god of the forge, building, volcanoes, and technology. Married to Aphrodite. Also known by his Roman name of Vulcan. Star Trek fan.

Hera—Queen of the gods, sister and former wife of Zeus, and married to her brother Poseidon following Zeus' murder. (It's okay, they're gods.) Goddess of marriage, women, and childbirth. Loves pomegranates.

Hermes—Mischievous son of Zeus and an immortal mountain nymph. God of merchants, thieves, travelers, messengers, and spies. Has a British accent due to extensive time spent in Britain during his formative years.

Hestia—Sister of Zeus. Goddess of the home and hearth. Doesn't get out much. Doesn't want to, either.

Lachesis—One of the three Fates. Responsible for measuring the threads of mortal lives.

Leto—A minor goddess. So minor she's not even mentioned in this book by name. Except here, but that doesn't count. Also mother of Apollo and Artemis, so at least she's got that going for her.

Megaera—One of the three Erinyes. Handles most of their paperwork and hotel reservations.

Melpomene—One of the nine Muses. Responsible for inspiring tragedy, horror, and children's books.

Muses, The—A group of nine lesser immortals, led by Calliope, who collectively inspire the creative and scientific arts. Assistants to Apollo.

Polymnia—One of the nine Muses. Responsible for inspiring sacred songs, speeches, and lyrics. Also rhetoric and advertising copy.

Poseidon—Brother of Zeus, elected king of the gods and married to Hera following Zeus' murder. Also god of the sea, earthquakes, and horses. Inventor of the motorcycle.

Terpsichore—One of the nine Muses. Responsible for inspiring choral song and dance, business correspondence, mysteries, and thrillers.

Thalia—One of the nine Muses. Responsible for inspiring comedy, science fiction, and poems about farming.

Tisiphone—One of the three Erinyes. Not a good speller.

Titans, The—Ancestors of the Olympian gods, deposed by Zeus after the Titan War. Nine of the most dangerous Titans became trapped in the Underworld prison of Tartarus. Their leader is Cronus, father of Zeus and his siblings.

Urania—One of the nine Muses. Responsible for inspiring astronomy writings, calendar photos, and sayings on coffee cups.

Zeus—Son of the Titan leader Cronus. Youngest and strongest brother of Demeter, Hades, Hera, Hestia, and Poseidon. King of the gods as well as god of the sky, lightning, and law until his assassination at the end of Chapter One.

ABOUT THE AUTHOR:

An award-winning writer of speculative fiction, Michael G. Munz was born in Pennsylvania but moved to Washington State in 1977 at the age of three. Unable to escape the state's gravity, he has spent most of his life there and studied writing at the University of Washington.

Michael developed his creative bug in college, writing and filming four exceedingly amateur films before setting his sights on becoming a novelist. Driving this goal is the desire to tell entertaining stories that give to others the same pleasure as other writers have given to him. He enjoys writing tales that combine the modern world with the futuristic or fantastic.

Michael has traveled to three continents and has an interest in Celtic and Classical mythology. He also possesses what most "normal" people would likely deem far too much familiarity with a wide range of geek culture, though Michael prefers the term geek-bard: a jack of all geek-trades, but master of none—except possibly Farscape and Twin Peaks.

Michael dwells in Seattle where he continues his quest to write the most entertaining novel known to humankind and find a really fantastic clam linguini.

Connect with Michael online:
Website: www.michaelgmunz.com
Twitter: @TheWriteMunz
Facebook: www.facebook.com/MichaelGMunz

Want to read a trio of "prequel" short stories for *Zeus Is Dead*? Sign up for the email list on Michael's website and get a free e-copy of *Mythed Connections: A Short Story of Classical Myth in the Modern World!*

~   ~   ~

If this book made laugh, crack a smile, or even briefly took your mind off of being trapped up an evergreen tree by a rabid badger, please consider leaving a review online.
Thank you!

Maybe next time you'll learn not to antagonize a badger, huh?
Good luck with that.

Made in United States
Orlando, FL
15 January 2023

28697516R00264